CHASING THE BLACK EAGLE

CHASING THE BLACK EAGLE

A NOVEL

BRUCE GEDDES

DUNDURN
PRESS

This is a work of fiction. While some references to historical figures, events, and locales are based on historical records, they have been used fictitiously. All other names, characters, places, and incidents are the products of the author's imagination, and any resemblance to persons living or dead is entirely coincidental.

Publisher and acquiring editor: Kwame Scott Fraser | Editor: Robyn So
Cover designer: Laura Boyle
Cover image: vectorstock/GeraKTV (plane)

Library and Archives Canada Cataloguing in Publication

Title: Chasing the Black Eagle : a novel / Bruce Geddes.
Names: Geddes, Bruce, 1969- author.
Identifiers: Canadiana (print) 2022025513X | Canadiana (ebook) 20220255148 | ISBN 9781459750593 (softcover) | ISBN 9781459750609 (PDF) | ISBN 9781459750616 (EPUB)
Classification: LCC PS8613.E33 C53 2023 | DDC C813/.6—dc23

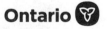

We acknowledge the support of the Canada Council for the Arts and the Ontario Arts Council for our publishing program. We also acknowledge the financial support of the Government of Ontario, through the Ontario Book Publishing Tax Credit and Ontario Creates, and the Government of Canada.

Care has been taken to trace the ownership of copyright material used in this book. The author and the publisher welcome any information enabling them to rectify any references or credits in subsequent editions.

The publisher is not responsible for websites or their content unless they are owned by the publisher.

Printed and bound in Canada.

Dundurn Press
1382 Queen Street East
Toronto, Ontario, Canada M4L 1C9
dundurn.com, @dundurnpress 𝕏 f ⊚

For Gena

This novel is a work of fiction. While Hubert Julian was a real person (and other real people make appearances), some of the events described are fabrications. Others are based on historical sources, many of them dubious.

PART ONE

Friend, there are different sizes of fruit, just as there are different sizes of men. I choose the biggest and the best, and I'm going to have them.

— COL. HUBERT F. JULIAN, *Autobiography*

1

THE FLEDGLING MENACE

ALL OF WHAT FOLLOWS IS TRUE.

Except for maybe this first part. Here, I've had to imagine a little. Because on the day I'm about to describe, August 2nd, 1922, I wasn't in New York City, much less anywhere near Seventh Avenue and 135th Street. I'd never heard of Marcus Garvey, nor the Universal Negro Improvement Association he founded and ruled over. Hubert Julian was still a stranger to me. As for Agent Riley Triggs of the Bureau of Investigation? We were still eight months and thousands of miles away from our first meeting.

So what I'm saying is that I don't actually know — for sure — if Agent Triggs was up in Harlem that day. But over the last thirty or so years I have wasted countless, often involuntary, hours thinking about Triggs and struggling to understand how it all started between him and Hubert Julian, a.k.a. the Black Eagle of Harlem.

I keep returning to the same conclusions. Triggs had to be in Harlem on that August day in 1922 because that was the day Marcus Garvey and his Universal Negro Improvement Association shut down several blocks of city streets for the opening parade of their annual worldwide convention.

It only makes sense. Yes, Triggs could have been on an apartment rooftop, perhaps concealed behind a brick parapet. Or maybe he was sweating it out in the front seat of his own car. He might've taken a window side table at a nearby diner, munching doughnuts, drinking coffee to stay alert. Those details don't really matter. What matters — not only because of what happened that day but also *because of everything that happened to me over the next fourteen years* — is that Agent Triggs needed to be in Harlem for the UNIA parade.

Triggs was not a Negro, nor was he all that concerned with race improvement. At the Bureau of Investigation, he worked for the General Intelligence Division, also called the Radical Division. His chief there was John Edgar Hoover, then a young lawyer and just starting his rapid rise to the Bureau's top job. It was no secret that Hoover had it in for Garvey, one of a few foreign-born, radical elements he'd been chasing since the riot-plagued summer of 1919.

Hoover put together a special squad to build his case. Triggs must have been part of it, probably among the first to volunteer, hungry to prove to Hoover that he shared the same concerns about Garvey's growing militancy, the surging power of the UNIA, and the columns of restless Negro partisans all over the world.

Three years of false leads and frustration followed, until finally, they got lucky. Garvey slipped up. In an advertisement promoting shares in the UNIA's Black Star Line, he printed a photo of the S.S. *Phyllis Wheatley*, a cargo ship they'd recently purchased and were eager to show off. Except the photo he used in the advert was not of the *Wheatley* but of the *Orion*, another cargo ship, but crucially, one that the UNIA did not yet own.

The Bureau boys rubbed their hands together and issued an indictment. Mail fraud, they called it. A bullshit charge and everyone knew it, but they managed to make it stick. Now, pending an appeal he was sure to lose, Marcus Garvey was going to jail.

The team would have celebrated the victory. Manhattan's best chophouse. Shrimp cocktails and inch-thick steaks. Potatoes fried in butter, apple pie, and wedges of cheddar. But even with the backslapping and handshaking for a job well done, I can't see Triggs enjoying himself with the others. Instead, I see him pulling on his unlit pipe, staring through the bubbles rising in his glass of club soda, worried. Yes, they'd taken care of the Marcus Garvey problem. In a few months, he'd be mouldering in a square cell, cut off from Negro America and no longer a threat to the nation's security.

But did that mean they'd stomped out the danger? No matter what Hoover or the others said, I have to believe that Triggs felt it was a matter of time before the threat — until now confined to that round Jamaican's body — would, like an evolving virus, find a new host, another black vessel to stir up Negro America with talk of the revolution and mother Africa and doing to white America what the Republican Brotherhood had done to England in Ireland. The rolls of the UNIA teemed with names of ambitious agitators eager to fill the void. Unionists. Churchmen. Bolsheviks. Plus other unaffiliated troublemakers.

But here's where Triggs had a problem. He knew enough to know that someone would take Garvey's place. But who? Without knowing the particulars, Triggs had to allow for some disturbing possibilities. What if this new man turned out to be more dangerous than even Marcus Garvey?

Any man aspiring to take Garvey's spot atop the UNIA would definitely have showed up at that parade. To demonstrate solidarity. To raise his profile and win support among the delegates. So you see? Triggs *had* to have been there, too — observing, noting, trying to identify the next fledgling menace. And having been there on that remarkable day, he would been alert to the first gurgles of the airplane's engine.

I have since spoken to witnesses who were on the street that morning. While the particulars differ, they all agree that a strange rumble from above silenced all conversation, demanding every delegate's attention. As the noise grew louder, it bounced off the streets, the sidewalks, the brick walls of apartment buildings. Soon, everyone was looking up, searching for the source until finally, the biplane appeared from the south, following the path set by Seventh Avenue.

There was excitement, but perhaps a little fear, too. Some inched away from the viewing stand. Bodyguards moved their hands toward hidden holsters. But Marcus Garvey held his ground, his eyes following the plane from under the shade of his admiral's hat. I imagine Triggs would have found something curious about Garvey's reaction, how calm he remained amid all the confusion.

One witness described the way the plane flew, its tail swinging left and right, like a tadpole swimming through the sky. The plane was a single-seater, painted military green, its narrow wheels dangling on thin struts below the cockpit. A slogan in large block letters ran along the length of the fuselage: *The New Negro Is Not Afraid*. It was something Triggs would have seen before in UNIA papers or at their rallies. But words on a placard among hundreds of placards are one thing; the same words scrawled across an airplane streaking over the streets of Harlem announced something else, a new level of commitment.

This was only the beginning. A different kind of excitement began to buzz through the crowd. Murmurs turned to cheers and then a hot, steady, jubilant roar of approval. Many had never seen an airplane so close. Fewer still had ever seen one piloted by a Black man. As the cheering continued, I can see Triggs glaring at the viewing stand, a grinding voice in his head asking, *"What the hell is Garvey up to now?"*

2

A CREDIT TO THE RACE

TRIGGS WOULD GET HIS ANSWER THE NEXT DAY WHEN, together with thirty-five hundred flag-waving, banner-bearing delegates, he went down to the Seventy-First Regiment Armory to hear Garvey speak.

Official UNIA photographs show Garvey draped in a long, black velvet robe. With its green and red stripes, he looked like a college dean, decked out for graduation. According to the official minutes, the speech touched on familiar themes. Freedom for the Negro race. Freedom for Africa. This was nothing new for Triggs; he'd read it all before. At the Bureau's office they had a file full of Garvey's speeches, including early drafts snatched by inside informants.

But this time, Garvey took the opportunity to air personal grievances. It wasn't hard to read between the lines. With Garvey facing mail fraud charges plus jail time, mutinous elements were emerging to challenge his position. Wary of the threat, he reminded the assembled delegates of his years of sacrifice and service, not only to the UNIA but also to African people around the world and right here in Harlem, where just yesterday, he'd arranged for a spectacular display of Black aviation.

With that, Garvey finally invited yesterday's hero to join him on stage. The pilot had dressed the part: starched white shirt, crisp plus-fours, the unfastened straps of his leather pilot's helmet hanging loose. He was a solidly built young man, broad in the shoulders, trim in the waist, not quite six feet tall. He shook Garvey's hand, saluted the assembly, then stepped to one side, standing at strict attention. His back arched like a bow ready to fire.

Back at the mic, Garvey had to raise his voice over the cheering to be heard. "My dear friends, I give you the first Black man to qualify as a pilot in the Western Hemisphere, a true credit to the island of Trinidad and to the race. Lieutenant Hubert Julian."

Garvey waited for the crowd to settle then brought them to their feet again by giving Julian a title: First Air Officer of the UNIA.

Hubert Julian. Had Triggs heard the name before? Sometimes, when I find my sympathies inexplicably bending toward Triggs, I try to understand it all from his perspective as he tied himself into tight knots of fear and rage. I think about the fact he and his buddies had just worked for thirty-six months trying to get Marcus Garvey. And, if you ignore their tactics and their loose interpretation of mail fraud laws, they had succeeded. The charges had been laid, the trial date set, the steaks grilled and eaten.

But what did it matter if, in all that time, those long hours spent digging into every detail about the UNIA and the people at the top, the name Hubert Julian had never once come up? Tomorrow or the next day, delegates would scatter back to their towns, their cities, and states, and soon the name Hubert Julian — this new Messiah of the Skies who, with an eight-minute flight, had become the talk of the convention — would resonate in every Black home in America. What a colossal waste of time and manpower it would all amount to if this Lieutenant Julian were able to continue Garvey's work.

Triggs must have gone to Hoover. He was too much of a rule-follower back then. He must have summarized his findings and outlined the new threat. He may have brought up the riot in Tulsa, where white pilots dropped grenades and firebombs into the streets of Black neighbourhoods. If Negroes started training pilots, next time it might be white businesses to get torched. How hard did Triggs plead the case? I don't know. What did Hoover say? I don't know. But I know this: Whatever Hoover said was not to Triggs' liking.

And yet, Triggs didn't let go. Several months later — April of 1923, it would have been — Triggs saw the name again. It appeared above him in giant letters, on one of several billboards Julian had rented around town. *Watch the Skies!* it demanded. *Julian Will Land Here!*

No doubt, seeing that poster set off a thousand alarms in Triggs' head. Now this Negro pilot, this possible, *probable*, heir to Garvey's crown, was proposing a parachute jump from an airplane to a vacant lot on 135th Street. In those days of skyscraper climbing, pole sitting, and other daredevilry, a successful jump would guarantee untold levels of popularity. To the country's millions of Negroes, he'd be as powerful as the pope is in Catholic circles. And probably just as infallible, too. I can see Triggs staring fiercely at the two seven-letter words that comprised the name Hubert Julian, asking himself over and over again: And then what? What would the man do with all that power?

I don't know exactly how long Triggs meditated on his problem. I never will. Nor will I ever know if he consulted Hoover again or if he spoke with other Bureau agents. Or if he sought opinions or considered options before arriving at his plan to bring an end to America's newest problem. Here's what I do know: At some point in all this undocumented plan-making, Agent Riley Triggs decided that I would play a major part of it.

3

GO ON, TAKE IT

WHILE TRIGGS STARED AT BILLBOARDS AND MULLED HIS next moves in New York, I was stewing in a holding cell in Oswego County, some five hundred miles north of Harlem, alone, frightened, and clueless. I'd been arrested aboard the *Barbara Lynne*, a forty-foot pleasure yacht that had been gutted and stripped of every pleasure and comfort in order to smuggle whisky across Lake Ontario.

I had joined the crew three nights before, one of five men who gathered before the *Barbara Lynne*'s captain on a weathered pier on the Canadian side of the lake. The captain was a large man with cracked lips who hid his grey-black hair under a fraying wool cap. Lighting a thin cigar, he looked over the crew, pausing to give me a skeptical look. I was still an inch or two shy of my full five foot eight, my frame still boyish and slender, and while I doubt I presented a picture of innocence, he could probably guess that this was my virgin voyage into the criminal world.

He ordered us to form a line and unload whisky from a trio of waiting trucks. When all three were empty, he handed me a rifle.

"You know how to use that?"

I nodded.

"You speak English?

"Yes."

"God's mercy," he said. "What's your name?"

"Arthur Tormes."

"What are you, Mexican?"

"I was born in Trinidad," I said.

"Here's what you do," he said, pointing to the foredeck. "Stand there. Watch out for anything."

"Like what?"

"Anything. Poachers. Ice. Cops. Ice, especially."

"And if I see something?"

"Sound the alarm, what else?"

"Is there a rope? A button?"

I wasn't trying to be difficult, but my questions tested his patience. "Look, if you see something, shout a lot. It's not such a big boat, is it?"

I stood where I was told, next to a strapped-down stack of whisky that rose to my chest. There were forty or fifty cases at least, with ten times as much stowed elsewhere on the boat. Thirsty Americans were willing to pay seven or even nine bucks for a bottle that cost less than a dollar in Canada. No wonder the captain gave us guns.

Another armed man was posted on the opposite foredeck. He was different from the others, a little older maybe, just as poorly dressed but better groomed. Also, while every nerve in my body had been twitching since I arrived at the dock, he seemed awfully relaxed by comparison. Now on deck, he leaned as casually against the whisky, as he would against the bar of his favourite watering hole.

We launched soon after dusk. I watched the shrinking lights on shore: a hobo's bonfire on the beach, kerosene lanterns glowing orange in cottage windows, the day's last train streaking behind a screen of cedars. A quarter-hour later the shore lights fell below the horizon and the new blackness swallowed everything. I could barely see my shoes and for a while it was as though I were floating above the water. It must have been around then that I felt my first shiver.

"Good that it's dark, eh?" the other man said.

"How do you figure?"

"Harder for them to see us."

"Harder for us to see them, too."

"True. I never thought of that part. My name's Carl Fischer."

He waited for me to return the introduction but I hesitated. It seemed unwise, given the nature of this business, to be too candid with personal information.

"That's okay," he said. "You don't have to tell me. I get it. But I reckon we're going to be working together for the next bunch of months. Might as well be friendly about it."

I saw his point. "Arthur Tormes."

"Good to know you, Arthur Tormes. Smoke?" He reached across the top of the whisky.

In such darkness, I had to lean over to see the top of the open pack.

"Thanks," I said, accepting the match's flame from his cupped hand. I took a few shallow puffs to get it burning. I'd never really taken to smoking — my mother had banned it in our house — but I welcomed the heat on my hand. I switched from right to left and let it burn down to a nub before flicking the butt into the lake.

Over the next hour or so, I learned a bit about Carl Fischer. He came from a small town called Pulaski. He attended a Lutheran church there, but not so regularly. He'd been to France in '18, but didn't see much action. For the last few years he'd been working as a roofer before a friend of a cousin used a connection to Harry Hatch to land this job.

"You ever meet Harry?"

"No."

"What do you know about him?"

"Nothing, really. Just the name."

"He's a big man in Canada. Controls the booze trade up there. You must have heard of him."

"I'm from Trinidad."

"Oh," he said. "Well, that's interesting, too."

"Is it?"

"Maybe not," he said. "You a married man, Arthur?"

"No?"

"Course not. Too young. Got a girl?"

"No."

"Atta boy. Gotta love the freedom. My wife's all right, though. She makes damn good sausage." Carl began rummaging in a pack strapped to his shoulder. "Want to try?"

"I'm okay, thanks."

He pulled out a package, unwrapped the wax paper, and sliced off a hunk of meat with a big knife.

"Come on. Have some. It's good."

Nobody had bothered to tell me to bring anything to eat and the night was young yet, so I accepted.

"Well?"

"Damn good," I said. "Like you said."

"Greta — that's the wife's name — she was born in Bavaria, like me. We're both immigrants like you. Here, have another piece. Go on, take it. You cold?"

"Nah," I said, chewing into the fresh slice, though the temperature was down since we left, and the dampness now bit at the back of my neck. My ratty cotton jersey and pea coat provided paltry protection against the whipping chill.

"I got four layers going," Carl said. "Top and bottom. Scarf, gloves, a wool cap for the bean. I mean, this ain't the tropics. Nights like this, you probably wonder why you ever left Trinidad, am I right?"

"I guess."

We stayed silent for a few minutes, doing our jobs by staring into the blank bobbing darkness. To the west, a few bluish stars showed in cloud breaks. It wasn't getting any warmer, though. I leaned the rifle against the whisky and stuffed my hands down the front of my pants, but when we hit a wave the rifle fell to the deck and would have slid off under the rails if I hadn't caught it with my foot.

Back into my sentry's position, hands clutching the weapon, I felt a poke at my shoulder. Carl's rifle butt.

"Hold this," he said. After handing over his rifle, he quickly unbuttoned his outer layer, a dark plaid mackinaw, which he then swapped back for the rifle. "I'll hold your rifle while you put that on."

"Are you sure?"

"Of course. Give me the gun now. That's it. No point freezing to death before we get paid, right?"

4

SOMETIMES YOU CAN'T TRUST PEOPLE. BUT OTHER TIMES, YOU CAN

I FELT CARL'S WARMTH IN THE COAT'S WOOL LINING. IT WAS big on me but I didn't mind the extra length, especially where the sleeves covered my gloveless hands.

"How's that feel?" he asked.

"Good. Real good. Thanks."

"Guess you did most of your sailing down in warmer waters. What was it? Fishing? Maybe cargo?"

Carl was being more direct with his questions, but in the coziness of his mackinaw it didn't feel right to let them go unanswered.

"Cargo," I said. "Three years on a tramp steamer called the *Diego Hurtado*."

"A tramp steamer? My hat's off to a man who can survive a turn on one of those. You must've been plenty hard up."

"It's a long story," I said.

And one I wasn't yet willing to share, at least not with someone I barely knew. But he had the basic idea. I was desperate and had no other choice. What happened was, not long before I turned thirteen, my mother, Antona, took ill. Doctors came, prescribed pills, tinctures, and syrups, but nothing eased her suffering. They told her she had to stop working. With no money coming in, it wasn't long before we ran dry of both cash and credit. Nothing for food, nothing for rent, nothing for the ever-higher doses of morphine Antona needed to beat back the pain.

It was after the grocer cut us off, but before she took to her bed for good, that Antona contacted Blind Sal Patero, owner and captain of the *Diego Hurtado*. Later that same night, as I prepared her needle, she explained the arrangement.

"Blind Sal has agreed to pay off our debts and provide a small allowance."

"All of them? Fantastic!"

"It's not a gift, unfortunately."

"What do you mean?"

"It means that when the time comes you will join the crew of the *Diego Hurtado*. Blind Sal will deduct each month from your wages until you've paid off what we owe him. I wish it could be different, but we're in no position to negotiate. And anyway, it may be better for you to leave Port of Spain. Stay here and our debtors will make things very hard. Is that needle ready yet?"

"Almost."

"It won't be so bad. Captain Patero will take care of you. I made him promise that much."

"How do you know we can trust him?"

"It's a low character who breaks a promise to a dying woman. I need your help with this sleeve."

Two weeks later, I moved my mattress into Antona's room and slept on the floor, next to her bed. We both knew the end was near and on the final night, we both cried. In her weakened voice, she gave me her blessing. "Try and be good and may God guide you. I raised you well and now I've left you with a good master."

❖

While I remained half-lost in memories, Carl spoke up. "Well? Give me the short version, then."

"Why did I sign on to the *Diego Hurtado*?" I said. "Same old story. I needed the money."

"Welcome to the club," he said, in a way that actually made me feel welcomed.

"Even for a tramp steamer, the boat was garbage. Leaks everywhere. Barely able to keep afloat in calm waters, she was a death trap in storms. Once we lost all power and had to wait it out below decks. Three days of twenty-foot waves tossing us around like dried beans in a maraca."

"Why not bolt?"

"Good question." In fact, I'd wondered the same many times. I once thought it had to do with my obligation to my mother, the debt, and her promise to Blind Sal. I didn't want to disappoint her — even in death. Plus, the *Diego Hurtado* gave me a bunk and a blanket, and while the food was paltry and unappetizing, at the very least I knew I'd have something to eat each day. But those reasons were hardly enough to explain why I put up with four years on that boat. I could have taken off at any time we tied up in port. So why not, then? Even today I'm not sure, and after so many years asking, I'm not even sure I want to know.

Instead of answering Carl, I skipped over the question.

"Last September we landed in Montreal with a load of Cuban sugar cane. We had our first day off in months. I wandered around, found some new clothes to replace what I'd outgrown, ate a good meal for once and after that full day, I went back to the port. But the *Diego Hurtado* had disappeared."

"To where?"

"I thought Blind Sal must have taken off without us. To get out of docking fees or wages or some other money he owed. That was definitely the kind of thing he'd do. But no."

"No?"

"She'd sunk right at the pier. Still tied up."

Carl laughed. "At the pier? After everything? Come on. You putting me on, Arthur? After I shared my wife's sausage?"

"I swear I'm not. I knew when I saw the cane stalks. They just floated up to the surface and got tangled and woven up with each other, like a big green sheet covering the boat. Like when they pull a sheet over the face of a dead person."

"You want another cigarette? How about some more sausage? Come on, I can't eat it all."

I thanked him and bit into a generous slice. "I'll bring something tomorrow night," I said.

"Don't worry about tomorrow night," he said. "What'd you do next?"

"Not much."

"You must've done something."

"I stuck around Montreal. I ended up driving a cab for a while, hacking for a few guys, you know, and that's how I met Breech. Mr. Samuel Breech, Esquire. He needed a chauffeur."

"Rich guy, then?"

"A businessman."

"What kind of business?"

I shrugged. "He wore a suit every day and lived in a big house. Had a lot of appointments. Whatever business that is. The car was a Duesenberg. It was a pretty good job all in all. But something happened to his business. Misunderstandings in the accounts, he told me. It turned out that Mr. Breech owed a lot of money. He had to sell everything, the Duesenberg included."

"Unlucky for you."

"Yeah, well. Breech always treated me square, so no hard feelings on my part. Last day working for him, he set me up with this job. Told me to call a friend of his and everything'd be taken care of."

"What was the friend's name?"

"Called himself Barry. Or maybe Gary."

"Last name?"

"No last name. Anyway, through all that, you know what I learned, Carl?"

"What?"

"I learned that sometimes you can't trust people. But other times, you can."

"Boy, ain't that the truth!"

5

CHANGE OF PLANS

WE SEEMED TO BE MAKING GOOD PROGRESS SLICING through the mid-lake chop. Now pleasantly warmed into a contemplative state by the big coat, I began to think about the money. We'd been promised twenty sweet dollars a night, plus a fat bonus for holding out until the ice firmed up. By then I'd have a couple of thousand banked, a real fortune to me. I'd already dreamed up a few plans, including going back to finish high school. That had been Mr. Breech's advice. One Sunday evening he called me into his den and invited me to sit in one of the stuffed leather chairs.

"You're a smart kid. I can tell that just from talking to you," he said. "But what you're missing is confidence. A man needs confidence if he wants to make it in this world. Some of it you learn just living your life, but some of it you get through knowing things. The numbers especially, but also a little history doesn't hurt. I myself studied the greats. A lot of my success in the business world comes from knowing how the Borgias and the Fuggers operated in their day."

"Yeah? What business were those Fuggers in?"

"You see, Arthur? This is what I mean. You need a little maturity, too. You can't make jokes about the Fugger family and expect to make anything of yourself. Tell you what. You enrol in classes for the fall. We can work something out work-wise."

I was actually touched by the offer. Antona had always put great weight on education. We shook hands and he poured me a glass of whisky. Obviously, this was before Mr. Breech had his business troubles. But he'd planted a powerful seed in my head and now, with the money I'd earn, I could stick to the plan. I'd finish high school in a year, two at the most, and after, I'd find a respectable position somewhere. I was neither greedy nor ambitious; I didn't mind not being rich, but I would work hard. I never again wanted to know the kind of poverty that had forced me onto the *Diego Hurtado*.

It was strangely exhilarating to be thinking so positively about the future. I felt like celebrating.

"How about another smoke?" I said to Carl.

"No problem, friend."

For too long now I'd been bobbing along, thoughtlessly content to ride currents directed by other men. Now, thanks to millions of liquor-loving Americans, big changes were on the way. In just a few months I'd be the one deciding on the whats and wheres and whys of my life.

I took a deep drag, enjoying the heat in my lungs and the swirling lightness in my head. That was when I saw the light. At first, I thought the cigarette was making me see things. I squinted at the low horizon. A pale dot, green maybe, or light blue, floated above the water. Tiny, but growing larger. I hesitated. Half a minute later, the light's greenness no longer in doubt, I concluded we were headed straight for it. Or it for us.

"Hey, Carl, do you see it?"

He did. "Stay here," he said, and disappeared in the dark toward the wheelhouse.

I braced the rifle across my chest, barrel pointed at the sky. The green light grew larger, brighter. Definitely another boat. Then I heard a second engine buzzing on top of our own. I slid the rifle from my shoulder. Safety off. Bolt pulled back and rotated. I raised the stock to my shoulder, aiming at the light.

Carl returned and spoke in a normal voice across the tower of whisky sacks. "Lower your weapon," he said. "The light's from the boat that's meeting us."

"Captain said we'd be unloading at a dock."

"Change of plans."

"Are you sure?"

"Hell yes, I'm sure. Is your gun down?"

I could hear the other engine more clearly. It sounded smaller than ours. I released a sigh. "I almost shit myself there," I said.

"And you with only the one pair of pants."

Then a new sound seized my attention. An electric thunk, followed by a crackle and sizzle. I had an instant and terrible premonition of disaster. White light blasted through the dark. A voice from a loudspeaker commanded the captain to cut the engines by order of the New York State Police.

The voice bounded over the empty lake and for a moment, nothing moved. The wind calmed, the water stilled. The searchlight silently panned our deck's length, illuminating the mute crew. I lifted my rifle, aiming at the light, though with my shaking hands, I couldn't fix the sight.

"Carl? What should we do? Carl?"

He'd disappeared. I wanted to chase after him but before I took the first step, I glanced up at the wheelhouse and saw the captain, bleach faced and frozen at the helm. We weren't running. Did that mean we were giving up? And where was Carl? I didn't know what to do. I wanted someone to tell me. I moved my index finger across the curving steel of the trigger, stopping when I reached the halfway point between the first and second knuckle. I looked once more for Carl but he hadn't returned. Moving slowly, careful not to make any noise, I returned the bolt to its safety position, bent my knees and torso into a crouch, and laid the rifle at my feet.

I was still crouched down when the first shot rang out. It came from the police boat, I think. Maybe someone on the *Barbara Lynne* fired back because right then, the cops unloaded on us, a brief but concentrated volley. Bullets pinged off our riggings, cracked into the wooden hull, and smashed into the crates and bottles of whisky. I turned away and twisted my hands and arms around my head, inhaling fumes as the liquor poured out and pooled around my shoes.

Then the shooting stopped. The spotlight found two men on deck with their hands in the air. Two others emerged from below and assumed the surrendering stance. The other boat drew near, its deck lights shining white against the black, showing a dozen uniformed cops ready to board and put us in cuffs. I raised my hands. While we waited, some inner voice I chose to trust told me to get rid of the rifle. When the spotlight moved off me, I gave the thing a kick. It planed along the whisky-soaked deck, tumbled over, and broke the lake's black surface with a light splash.

6

SOMETHING MOVING
BEHIND THE WALLS

THE STATE POLICE HAULED US INTO A WAGON AND THEN TO the Oswego County Jail. We were all accounted for, all except for Carl. I asked around, but in all the shooting and confusion nobody had seen what happened to him. Maybe he had dived in, swum to shore, and escaped, they suggested. I nodded at this possibility but had private doubts. Those frigid waters. Even minus the mackinaw, the heavy layers he had going would drag him down. You'd have to be a superhuman swimmer to have any hope of making it.

The two other Americans in the crew posted bail the next day. On the third morning the police let two more go, men with charges waiting for them in Ontario. On the third night, they freed the captain, and in my isolation, the fear came on. I asked, of course, many times I pleaded for information, but no one in uniform would tell me why I'd been held back. The night guard knew nothing. Same for the cop who let me out to use the toilet. I asked again when another guard tossed me a bag lunch. He replied with an indifferent shrug. I couldn't imagine a more frightening response. It was one thing to realize I'd lost my freedoms, that I could not leave this cell, talk when I wanted, choose the foods I ate. But worse was the fact that the guards didn't care what happened to me. Even on the *Diego Hurtado*, where I had been almost as much a prisoner as I was in Oswego, at least I could count on my fate being entwined with Blind Sal's — if the boat went down, we all went with it. It wasn't like that here.

Early on the morning of the fifth day, a guard pulled me from the holding cell. My hopes lifted as I imagined release. But no. Instead, he led me to a door, then paused to fix a bandana across his mouth and nose. When the door opened, I turned my face from a mixture of rancid odours rising up a stone-lined stairwell. He ordered me forward, and as I stepped, my beltless pants began to slide. With my hands still cuffed, I had only my awkwardly wide gait to keep them hoisted. At the bottom of the stairs was a dark corridor. Water pooled in the dips of the stone floor. There were cells on one side of the corridor, each occupied by a prisoner, each furnished with a simple cot and a steel bucket. I wanted to cover my nose but was still locked in the cuffs. Fighting the urge to puke, I wondered if Carl might be down here. But these guys couldn't be other rum-runners. In one cell a man pulled at what remained of the hair on his patchy head, while in the next, the inmate licked the wall. None of these prisoners seemed quite right in the head. At the echoes of our footfalls, some scuttled back to their bunks or to the most distant corner of the tiny cells, turning their faces to the bricks, and bending their heads into the collars of striped shirts. The stony quiet was broken only by nervous spitting and babbling.

The guard stopped me near the passage's dead end, where the steel door to the only unoccupied cell sat open. He shoved me inside, hard enough that I tumbled and skidded on the gritty stone floor. When I turned back, the guard was pointing to the cell's electric bulb, which hung from the ceiling inside a cage. "See that? In Oswego, we even lock up the light."

I climbed onto the bed and looked around. Previous occupants had carved dates, initials, attempts at something lewd into the soft limestone wall. Black mould thrived in the oldest grooves, some that dated back half a century.

With the guard back upstairs, the other prisoners grew lively again. Shouting matches restarted, some apparently without an opponent. There were hysterical vows of violence and retribution. I heard the sound of streaming liquid against the stone floor followed by a furious voice promising to cut that thing off if the pisser ever tried it again. Ass-fucking was repeatedly brought up, sometimes as threat, sometimes as accusation.

I turned my body to the wall, buried my nose between my knees, and tried to send my mind elsewhere.

That night, sleep was once again impossible; the lights battered us all night. The cacophony abated only when guards came down with a breakfast of stale bread and water. My shoulders were sore from hours of constant tension in the dank coldness. I tried to surrender to the fatigue but couldn't sleep. Mind and body seemed to separate. I began to believe something was moving behind the walls, looking for the weak spot in order to bust into my cell.

Eventually, I joined with the others in their useless shouting. "Shut the fuck up!" "Shut your fucking hole!" More meals of bread and water followed, but with the lights always on and no view of the outside, I lost track of time. I felt my senses dulling; I didn't think I could trust them anymore. Sometimes I wasn't even sure of the difference between up and down. At some point, breathing dust and cobwebs, I passed out under the cot.

I woke to the barks of a guard at my cell door. Cracking open my eyes, I saw black leather boots. "I said get up, Tormes! Someone's here to see you."

7

YOU COULD BE A BIT NEGRO

UPSTAIRS, I SUCKED IN CLEAN AIR AND FELT REVIVED. THE guard ordered me to strip and shoved me into the shower room. A bar of soap bounced off my head and landed at my feet. For the next ten minutes, I scoured and scrubbed at filth so thick the soap refused to lather.

After, a guard gave me new clothes and took me to a room with a heavy stained table and four ordinary wooden desk chairs. There were framed pictures on the walls, unsmiling uniformed cops in formal rows, a black Ford Wagon with the words *Police Patrol* painted on the panel, other shots showing cops mounted on horseback.

Left alone, I went to the window, holding the bars for support. The sky glowed, lighting up the leafless trees and the dull, dormant grass. The view relaxed my shoulders and my breathing but I remained generally spun up in confusion and fear.

The door swung open. I turned to find a heavy man in a three-piece suit. He did not look at me as he took a seat at the table and opened a cream-coloured folder. Without raising his face, he said, "You'll want to step away from that window and go ahead and sit down now."

He was about forty-five, maybe older. Dark, short-cropped hair, martial but not quite military. Clean-shaven. He wore wire-framed glasses that seemed to annoy him; throughout our meeting he took them on and off many times. His ears looked like they'd suffered repeated cycles of insult and healing, perhaps on the wrestling mat. In fact, overall, he had the build and manners of an ex-athlete, the kind who might have won trophies but never liked to practise.

"Are you my lawyer?"

"Unfortunately, no," he said and placed a pipe and tobacco pouch on the table. He unscrewed a pen, posted the cap, and returned his glasses to his face to read, pausing here and there to examine me across the three-foot span. Finally, he spoke.

"You're not a Negro," he said. I sensed disappointment. "I keep looking for it but ..." He pointed lazily at my face and let his stare hang, in case he'd missed something.

"Nope," he said. "I keep looking, but I just don't see it. But you are from Trinidad?"

"Yes."

"Huh. Isn't everyone in Trinidad coloured?"

"Not everyone," I said. "Is it a problem?"

"Could be," he said. "What are you, then? Arab? Moorish?"

"I'm not sure," I said.

"Italian, maybe? The south? Sicilians tend to be a darker sort."

"It's possible."

"You don't know?"

"I never knew my father, and my mother died before I knew enough to wonder about it."

"I imagine that happens a lot down your way," he said. "Probably got a bunch of half-brothers or -sisters you don't even know about." Something curious about Triggs: when he spoke, his teeth remained invisible.

"Boy, I keep looking, but ... I suppose you could be a bit Negro. That little curl in your hair. Brown eyes, just like a dirty diaper. The nose, though. Too pointy. Maybe you're an octoroon? Or a hexadecaroon?"

"I don't know what that is."

"That's half an octoroon," he said. "But you say you don't know?"

"No, sir." I said. "Sorry." It felt like a strange reason for me to apologize.

He closed the file and leaned back. "Well, maybe it doesn't matter," he said. "For now, at least. I'm short on time and I've come too far to leave empty handed. How are you doing, anyway? These fellows here treating you okay? I heard about what they keep downstairs. Sounds like a whole lot of hell."

His concern made me believe this man was here to help me. "It's pretty awful."

"And you. Just a kid, too. Says here seventeen, but looking at you now, I'd've said younger. Fourteen, fifteen. How old are you for real?"

"Seventeen."

"Doesn't seem right. You probably want to get the hell out of here, eh?"

"Yes, sir."

"Let me ask you this: Can you read? Can you write?"

"Yes."

"Well, that's good. That's actually very good. It makes things a whole lot easier."

I had no idea what he meant, but this brought a close to the prologue part of the interview. A gear shifted in his head. He set the tips of his stiff fingers lightly on the table, as though checking for heat.

"My name is Special Agent Riley Triggs. I'm from the Bureau of Investigation," he said. "That's T-r-i-g-g-s. You'll want to remember how to spell it." He opened the pouch, pinched at the damp tobacco, and stuffed the empty bowl.

"I don't think they've charged me yet," I said.

"That's true," he said. "But a case like yours is complicated. It takes time. The D.A. here likes to be diligent. Diligence, like any other thing you want done right, takes time." He removed his glasses. "To a crook like you it probably looks easy, but it's no small thing to send a man to prison for twenty to thirty years."

8

HE COULD SEE I HAD
SOME DOUBTS

"TWENTY TO THIRTY YEARS?" I SAID, MY VOICE SQUEEZED,
the pitch rising with every word.

"It's a pretty typical sentence. Though of course, with some bad
luck, you could get more."

"That seems like a lot of years. Twenty to thirty. Isn't it a lot of
years?"

"Oh, it certainly is a lot of years. Half a lifetime. More than half,
since that kind of time inside tends to lower a man's life expectancy.
But you know what? There's an old saying among jailbirds: you only
serve two days. The day you go in and the day you get out."

"But for smuggling liquor? Isn't it more like a fine, normally?"

"The Volstead violation is just one charge you're facing," Triggs
said. His hands searched his pockets for matches, patting away
until he felt a box in his trousers.

"I don't understand," I said. "What other charges could there
be?"

"How about shooting on a police boat? With state police officers on deck? Yeah, that's called Attempting to Murder an Officer
of the Law."

Attempted murder? With his words, all the symptoms of my sleepless nights flooded in. My eyes felt thick, like they'd been plucked out and replaced with seashells. My head drooped, and for a moment I forgot where I was. I felt my pulse pounding in my neck and in my ears and all through my chest. It was difficult to speak. I had to force the words from my mouth.

"But, sir. I never even fired the gun."

"I'd like to believe you, Mr. Tormes. Because unlike many men in this business, I genuinely prefer to see the good in people. But I've consulted the evidence, and in your case I just can't do it. Believe you, that is. The evidence says you tried to murder a cop. You need a hanky? Here, take mine."

"But that's not true! I didn't even fire the gun."

"A witness claims you had a rifle —"

"Yes, but — that wasn't — I never fired it."

"So you keep saying."

"So why don't you believe me?"

"Well, for one, you're a crook and crooks like to lie. For two, my eyewitness says you used it. We have shell casings. Plus slugs pulled from the police boat. It's really — when you think about it — some very strong evidence. A very strong case against you. I'd be surprised if the trial lasts more than a day."

"Look, I admit that I had a rifle, the one the captain gave me. Where is he? He can tell you? Or Carl? I never fired it. I kicked it into the lake."

"That's just not what our witness says." Triggs lit the match and held it up, twisting his hand to inspect the flame from all sides. Whatever he saw wasn't right. He shook the match out.

"What witness?" I asked.

Triggs rose from the table. At the door, he mumbled something to the guard.

"I swear to you, sir. I never pulled the trigger. I don't know what you're talking about. Where's everybody else? Why am I the only one being blamed?"

"Calm yourself, Tormes. Your face is turning red. Best to save that for the jury."

Footsteps sounded from the hall. A man in a suit entered. When he removed his hat, I recognized him.

"Carl! Am I glad to see you!"

"May I introduce Officer Molles. Though I guess you already met."

"Molles? No. That's Carl. Carl Fischer."

"Nope. His real name is Molles. Molles is an old friend of mine. Now he's with the state police. Knows how to work a case. He's the one who busted your friends. Big bust. Probably get you another promotion, will it, Larry?"

"There's been some talk that way."

"Only bad thing about Officer Molles is he doesn't know the difference between a white man and a coloured man."

"What's going on, Carl? What's happening here? Tell him what happened, would you?"

Molles ignored me. "What you said, Riley, was to call if anyone from Trinidad came through. This one's from Trinidad. Pretty good bullshitter, too. Told me some stories out there. That's good for what you need. And no record, either."

"And I'm grateful and in your debt."

"You sure as hell are."

Before leaving, Molles looked at me. "No point crying, Arthur. Those are the breaks. This guy here's a real prick, but if I was you, I'd do what he says. Catch you later."

Triggs swung back to me. He clasped his big hands on the table. "What did he tell you?"

"That you tried to kill a police officer."

"He's lying! I didn't even pull the trigger. I was a lookout. I'm no murderer."

"*Attempted* murderer," corrected Triggs. "One good thing for you? You're not such a good shot. Or maybe Molles managed to switch rifles so that yours wasn't loaded."

"He did?" I asked, remembering the exchange for the warm coat.

"Maybe."

Outside, clouds slid into the window frame, and the sky turned the colour of tea with too much milk. I craved tea, milk, water — anything to relieve my parched mouth.

"His wife's name is Greta."

"Yeah, I know. Makes sausage. You have any idea how many guys like you've worn that mackinaw?"

"No."

"Molles can be very convincing. You should see him in court when they put him on the stand. Hey, maybe you will!"

I would learn later how Triggs relished this part, the quiet accumulation of power and the sweet moment that follows, when the man in the other chair cottons on to the true depth of his troubles. At the poker table, I bet Triggs gathers his chips real slow. Not so much to savour a victory as to prolong the pain of the other's defeat.

"What now?" I asked.

Triggs retracted his thick arms. His cuff buttons scraped across the table. "As it happens, I'm prepared to offer you a unique deal. If you agree, you work for me. If you don't, you go to trial for attempted murder. And you'll want to know you're probably going to land yourself in Sing Sing."

He allowed this idea to settle in. The unlit pipe went into his mouth. I noticed the stem, ragged with bite marks.

"Look, I can see you have some doubts. If you want to go back downstairs, if you want time to think it over, I can wait and we can talk another day." He extracted a leather-bound calendar from an inside pocket and whipped through the pages. "I can come back in ... no, not there ... looks like I don't have another opening until ... June."

He was making the decision easy for me.

"What would I have to do?"

"Good boy," Triggs said. "Good, good boy. Smart. That's good, too. It's simple, really. I need you to keep an eye on someone."

"Here?"

"In New York City. Plus wherever else he ends up. Right now, he's in New York City. Up in Harlem. You see, I thought you'd be a Negro, a transplant like him. You're not, which is too bad, when you think about it. You'll do, though. It'd be harder if it was the other way around.

"I don't live in New York."

"You will."

"For how long?"

"Until you're finished the assignment," he said. "Is that a problem?"

I felt a strange and urgent need to win his approval. "It won't be a problem," I said. "Believe me, sir, it won't be a problem."

"Good. One other thing. This arrangement stays strictly between you and me. That's not an option. Nobody else knows about it, understand?"

"Yes."

"If you tell anyone — your barber, your dentist, your girlfriend, if you ever get one — the deal is off, get it?"

"Yes."

"You go straight to Sing Sing and it's 1950 before you see the outside again. Got it?"

"I understand."

"Say it again."

"I understand."

"Again!"

"I understand. I swear I understand completely! I won't say a word — not to anyone! I've never understood anything so well in my life!"

"Of course you do. I had a good feeling about you."

I didn't know how to take this evaluation. Was he praising my common sense? Or my cowardice?

"Now wipe the snot from your face. Have some pride, Tormes."

"Do I need to sign something?"

"That won't be necessary."

"Who's the man?"

"His name is Hubert Julian."

"What did he do?"

"That, I do not yet know." He shook a match free of the box and swiped it on the side to get it lit.

"Is he a Red?" I asked. "An anarchist?" In those years, all the authorities were worried about Reds and anarchists.

"Unclear," Triggs said, finally touching the flame to the pipe's mouth. He circled the bowl with the match head, sucking in smoke with shallow puffs until he had it burning. The smoke smelled fruity and acrid at the same time. "But I know he's up to something. It's on you to find out what."

9

IN THAT JUMBLE OF VOICES
I HEARD SOME THINGS

A COUPLE SUNDAYS LATER, I STOOD AMONG A THOUSAND Harlemites on an otherwise ordinary block of 140th Street, waiting for Hubert Julian to drop from the sky. I had arrived early and claimed a square of sidewalk with a clear view of the lot where Julian proposed to land. The day was mostly sunny, a little cool for late April, though what did I know from typical NYC weather? I'd been in the city less than a week.

A couple of kids in sharp black suits with plain black ties asked me for my dollar admission, offering a pink receipt in exchange. I tucked it safely into my pocket, just in case Triggs demanded proof of attendance.

I stood alone for a while, feeling sort of lost and wondering how to begin my mission. As a spy, I was a novice, and Agent Triggs had been stingy with instructions. The crowd began to swell, spilling from the lot to the street and halting traffic. Some had arrived straight from church, men in dark suits, women in bright spring dresses with matching hats and veils like fine nets over their faces. Newsmen clustered together near the lot's edge, checking their watches. A stout woman hawked hot dogs from a basket fringed with tea towels, while two kids circulated with a cooler full of ice and Coca-Cola. I bought one, paying six cents, even though everywhere else a Coke cost a nickel.

I'd just taken the first sip when I overheard a comment about the wind speed. "Uh-huh, definitely picking up," a man near me said. His friend agreed, and the authority in his voice prompted me to inch closer as they predicted trouble for Julian. The first man pinched his cigarette and pointed to the tracks of the Third Avenue L.

"He'll fry, that's what," he declared. "That electricity will cook him through and through."

"If the train don't flatten him first, that is."

They spoke in paternal tones, like fed-up fathers who no longer understood the mad spirits that drove their sons. They pointed to telephone wires and radio antennas. And what about the East River? Yet another mortal hazard. Was Hubert Julian a swimmer? What's it matter? With that 'chute on his back, the current'll pull him under before he takes the first stroke.

A more bullish voice reminded everyone of Julian's parachuting experience, that he'd jumped successfully before, including at a recent show out on Long Island. "I'm telling you the truth: the man knows what he's doing up there."

But the cynic wasn't moved. "Into an open field!" he said. "That's a whole different thing."

"Did you all hear about Howell's mortuary? Paid Julian a hundred dollars for the right to put his corpse on display."

"A hundred dollars!"

"What happens if he lives? He get to keep the money?"

I leaned into the discussions and debates, absorbing what I could. But I caught only fragments and half-heard phrases, which was a little like trying to build a house with only scraps of wood and chunks of broken brick.

"… but then you said he from Canada."

"I said no such thing. I said he *lived* up there. You gotta listen to …"

"… because his daddy is rich, rich, rich. Owns a quarter of Barbados *and* a gold mine. Or maybe it's the Bahamas his daddy owns? I don't remember."

"Doesn't matter where he's from," said the friend. "When a man has that much money, he can …"

"… might have been Tuesday that I saw him at Hart's."

"Plenty of folks shop up at Hart's."

"Not shopping. Working."

"I don't like Hart's. Prices are too damn high and them salesgirls …"

"… flew in the war and took down something like, what was it, twenty Germans …"

"… in New Orleans when they murdered the Reverend Eason, may he rest in eternal peace."

"You know there's no truth to that. You'd better take that back or …"

"… I heard he came from Cleveland …"

"… a doctor in a hospital by the …"

I made pages of notes in my head. *Canada. Reverend Eason. Rich father. Cleveland?* Everyone seemed to know something about Hubert Julian, but no one was certain of everything. Women agreed: he was handsome and, from what they'd heard, still a bachelor.

And then, finally, I heard something I knew I could put to use.

"I don't know about Cleveland," said a man holding a cigarette in the corner of his mouth. "But someone high up in the Garvey organization said this Julian went to the finest school in Trinidad."

I lurched forward, surprised at my boldness. "Which school was that?"

"It was … I don't remember what it was called," he said.

"Can't you try?"

"A good school. What's the name matter for?" he said. He tried to return to his private conversation.

I grabbed an arm just above the elbow. "Was it the Eastern? Could it have been the Eastern Boys' School?"

He removed the cigarette. "The Eastern?" he said. "Maybe. It doesn't sound wrong."

"He said the Eastern Boys' School? You're sure?"

The man looked at the hand gripping his arm. I unclamped my fingers, apologized, and backed away. The news, if true, was a real gift. Because the Eastern *was* considered the best in Trinidad. So what? So nothing. Except this: up until a few months before my mother died, I happened to have been a student at the *very same school*.

The information tripped a pressure valve and I felt terrifically relieved. I hadn't done a thing toward completing my work for Triggs, but I gave in to the sense of accomplishment. And it was that easy!

I let my imagination wander, even as I scanned the sky, searching all the compass points for the now overdue Julian. In no time, I figured I'd find something to use against him. Evidence of some crime or plans to commit one. I'd deliver it all to Triggs, accept my congratulations, and once again be on my way.

I was so wrapped up in these visions of pending success that I failed to notice the girl in the fancy dress who had slipped into the empty space beside me.

10

SOME KIND OF DEATH WISH

FIRST CONTACT WAS A BUMPING OF ARMS. HERS AGAINST mine. An accident, I figured. Normal in any gathering this size. I shifted half a foot before flipping my eyes back to the sky.

But she'd been trying to get my attention. "Hey, you," she said. "Hey! You think this'll be worth something some day?"

In an ungloved hand she held up her little pink receipt, identical to the one I'd stowed in my pocket. She blinked twice, waiting for an answer. Her eyes were the colour of sugar for caramel, the edges smudged with sooty powder. Not really makeup; more like a poorly applied disguise.

"What do you mean, 'worth something'?" I said. I was cautious, feeling like she might have an angle.

"This ticket. The receipt. You think maybe someone'll want it? Like for their collection."

"A stub of paper?"

Her unbuttoned coat showed a field of bare skin and the fringes of something plunging. Her shoes, glittery black, were not the kind a girl normally wears on a Sunday morning.

"For your information, a ticket for the return voyage on the *Titanic* just sold for twenty-five bucks. And it was a third-class ticket, too. What does that tell you?"

I looked quickly to the sky and back to the girl. "Is this really the same as the *Titanic*?"

She covered a yawn with plum-coloured fingernails. Even with that mussed makeup, her skin was pale, her round cheeks deflated. It was as though she was missing something in her bloodstream, an essential vitamin or mineral.

"You don't think so?" she said. "Are you a betting man?"

"I don't know," I said, now certain she was trying to con me. "Depends on the bet."

"How about on the future price of this ticket?"

"What future?" I said.

"I see your point," she said and bent her mouth to blow a twist of hair from her eyes. "How about instead we bet on something more in the moment? Or is it *of* the moment?"

"Like what?"

A shout prompted me to look across the sky again, but it remained empty.

"Like how about this Julian? I say the clown doesn't make it. I say he splatters on the sidewalk. I have a quarter that says so."

She touched the ribbon in her hair and tucked in a few curly strands, but they refused to be tamed. Her face turned stern, her eyes stilled with concentration as she tried again. Watching this minor struggle felt oddly intimate, as though this were the most recent episode in a long battle for control over her own hair. After a fourth attempt she managed to wrangle it and the victory appeared to give her a lift.

"Do you know about Franz Reichelt?" she asked. "Did you see the newsreel?"

I shook my head. "I don't think so."

"Oh, you'd remember. He was this poor slob over in France who had an idea for a parachute. A simple tailor with big dreams of money and glory. But he had to prove the thing could work, right? So he — are you sure you didn't see the newsreel?"

"Like you said, I'd have remembered."

"Trust me, a good memory's not always such a blessing," she said. "Anyway, this Franz fellow climbs up the Eiffel Tower. As high as you can go. And all his friends are down on the ground saying, 'No! Franz, no!' But Franz doesn't want to listen. His ears were plugged to their appeals. Plugged with dream wax. He went ahead and gave that parachute thing a test flight, and guess what happened? He damn well died. You see it all happen in the newsreel. This little speck of black, Franz's body, streaking straight down. And fast. I mean, like a damn rock. It's a hell of a dramatic scene. You just don't expect … I'm sorry. I don't mean to be emotional."

"It's okay." Now she had me thinking that Julian might be in for something similar. What would Triggs do with me if Julian ended up dead?

"I haven't had much sleep," the girl said. "I was out all night. You don't need to know the details, but I was heading home when the billboard for this Julian fellow just sort of appeared before my eyes, and I knew I just had to stay awake a few more hours to see him jump. So what do you say? How about that bet?"

"Is this really the same as the Frenchman?"

"He was Austrian, actually. He died in Paris. But his country was Austria."

"It seems wrong to bet on a man's life."

She rolled her eyes. "What is this guy, a friend of yours or something?"

"No," I said, and then added, "Not really. We're both from Trinidad."

"If it makes you feel better, I heard he took a thousand dollars from an undertaker for the right to put his dead corpse on display. So he's betting on his own life in a way. Maybe he's got a death wish."

I had never before heard of such a thing. "Why would a man *want* to die?"

"I can think of plenty of reasons. Maybe he lost all his money. Maybe his wife cheated on him."

"He's not married."

"So he *is* your friend! Why would you lie to me? We barely know each other."

"I'm not lying. I've heard some things, that's all."

"Have some confidence, then. Prove me wrong and win big. My name's Jean Fox. What's yours?"

"Arthur Tormes."

"Well, Arthur Tormes?" She challenged me with raised brows, though I think she was also just trying to keep her eyes open.

"I'm sorry. I can't take that bet."

Jean Fox gave me a hard look, like she wanted a shot at changing my mind with other arguments. But before she spoke, two cannon shots cracked in the air above us, silencing the crowd. Out of the ensuing quiet I heard the low hum of an approaching engine. I looked to the sky, squinting and shading my eyes.

There! An Avro biplane. Flying steady and smooth over the Harlem River. Airplanes were still a rare sight. I'd seen a couple in Trinidad, a few in Montreal, but they were not so demystified that I wasn't fascinated all over again every time I saw one.

A few seconds later I was able to distinguish the Avro's features: the tan-coloured fuselage, the crescent-shaped cutaways for the cockpits, the block numbers stamped in white on the rounded tail. Most visible of all was the figure standing on the lower wing, feet spread, knees bent for balance, holding tight to a strut.

"That must be Julian," I said.

"Who else would it be?" Jean said.

As the plane drew closer and the details presented themselves more clearly, I saw that Julian was dressed strangely in coveralls, or a suit of some sort, maybe a costume. It was coloured crimson, an outrageous red that ran all the way down his legs and arms. He stood out against the sky like a drop of blood on a blue window screen, and while there were no horns or pointed tail, I couldn't help thinking how much Hubert Julian looked like a devil, hitching a ride on a passing biplane.

11

HE LAID CLAIM TO THE SKY

THE PILOT TOOK JULIAN DIRECTLY OVER THE LOT, TURNING every face upward. But nothing happened. Then he circled back. On this approach I could see him under the fuselage, trying to get the harness attached. That's how it worked in those early days when cockpits were too tiny to fit both a jumper and the bulky parachute. Instead, they stowed the chute underneath, which made strapping-in a tricky and dangerous manoeuvre. At any moment, an air pocket could buck the plane and if the jumper wasn't holding tight, he'd be knocked off with nothing but his arms to flap until he collided with the ground. I thought about the story the girl had just told me, about the unlucky French tailor. Not French, Austrian.

By the time the plane banked and flew back toward us, Julian had the parachute properly fixed to his back. The brown canvas sack hung loose below his crotch. He waved to the horde below, producing a loud cheer he couldn't likely hear. And then he jumped.

At first he seemed to be floating, as though still attached to the plane by a thread unravelling from his crimson suit. Then, as he fell and gathered speed, I thought of that streak of blood, except now it was dribbling down the screen. After a couple of seconds he ripped open a sack of flour and for the next hundred feet, a streak of fine white powder blazed his path.

With the sack emptied, he pulled the rip cord. The parachute spat from his back, fluttering above like a wet sheet, shapeless until it caught the air and bloomed creamy white. I joined in the cheering as his swinging subsided and he continued the descent in a straight, steady, perfect line. I looked for the girl. Lucky for her I hadn't taken the bet. But she was no longer beside me. Maybe this Jean Fox wasn't the type of girl who could admit when she's wrong.

Julian was on target to stick his landing in the lot but not before he unfurled a sponsor's banner. *Hoenig Optical Is Open Today!* The mob cheered that, too. How could you not admire the courage and poise required to remember a sponsor while falling into city streets. I thought about his other sponsor, the undertaker Howell, and how he'd be deprived of a corpse for his window today.

But then the mood in the lot shifted. A gust of wind had taken Julian off course and now he was drifting west, rocking wildly, his feet scrambling in the empty air. He tried to correct by yanking the guy lines, but this only aggravated the swinging and gave the wind more of the open chute to push him further away.

The mob surged onto Seventh Avenue. I ran along with them, weaving between cars, dodging buses, lampposts, and carts. I spotted Julian next over Eighth, dropping quickly. I lost him again behind an apartment building and had to rely on the crowd to guide me to a tenement a block away. There, all arms pointed upward, and I feared that Julian had smashed through a window.

Different spotters found him on the edge of the same tenement's roof, now trailing parachute silk and tangled white lines. Incredibly, he'd landed safely and appeared uninjured. He stood tall before the throng, wearing a stern and serious expression, and I thought, that is the look of a man who has proven himself to the world.

All Harlem celebrated the triumph, instantly forgiving the botched landing. They chanted his name and cried and pumped their fists. On the rooftop, Julian soaked in the love. With a swagger to his step, he went from one corner to the other, staking his claim, the building more pedestal than apartment. Other men owned the jazz clubs and the dance halls, the boxing rings, church pulpits, restaurants, drug stores, and newspapers. But until that Sunday in April, no one had ever owned the sky above Harlem. Now it belonged to Hubert Julian. Like an old-world explorer, he'd planted his flag in clouds hovering above Lenox Avenue.

I was beginning to understand why Agent Triggs was so concerned.

12

I HAD THE WATERS FLOWING
IN THE RIGHT DIRECTION

TWO AFTERNOONS LATER, I LEFT MY PLACE AND HEADED
straight up to Harlem, hoping to find Julian. My plan was vague
and based entirely on a comment I'd heard at the lot about Julian
being employed at A.I. Hart's.

I turned north on Lenox, where tall buildings blocked so much
afternoon sun it was like walking through a trench. By 110th Street
the traffic had turned heavy and angry, slowed by construction sites
along the way. Jackhammers competed with blasting car horns and
the air sharpened with acrid smells of hot tar and burning oil where
crews filled winter potholes with macadam.

People in heavy coats and hats poured from trams and buses,
joining others streaming from shops and offices. Shoe soles and
hard heels shuffled and clicked and crunched the grit, everyone
walking with terrific purpose. Home. Work. Urgent appointments.
A train to catch and then another. Again and again, I yielded
and stepped aside and by 125th, simply moving forward was a
chore.

On 141st, I scanned the signs and storefronts for A.I. Hart.
With the little I knew about Julian, I imagined big, brass revolving

doors and twenty-foot display windows filled with toy trains, appliances, and mannequins in business suits or evening wear. In the end, there was nothing special about the place. If I hadn't been looking for it, I probably would have missed it.

With fifteen minutes before the store closed, I bought a copy of the *Daily News* and placed myself on the other side of the street, between a lamppost and a post box, where I started reading the front-page story about the pilots Kelly and Macready. That same afternoon, they'd taken off from Roosevelt Field in a Fokker T-2 Liberty, aiming to fly to distant San Diego and break the current endurance record. By now, four hours after takeoff, they'd be flying over Pennsylvania. The whole trip would cover twenty-six hundred miles in only twenty-eight hours. They wouldn't stop, not even once.

Fascinated as a schoolboy, I read on, wondering how Kelly and Macready would fly at night. How would they go to the bathroom? And what happened if something went wrong? In the flat plains they might easily find a place to set down. But once they were over the peaks of the Rockies, landing would be a trickier task.

Engrossed in their bravery, I missed the actual moment when Hubert Julian exited the store and noticed him only because he paused to check his reflection in the window. I watched him button his coat, fix his bow tie, straighten his hat, brush one lapel, then the other. He turned east, walking with such vertical energy that his suit flaps bounced with each step.

Two street corners on, I managed to catch up.

"Hubert Julian!" I began. "I knew it. Well, well. I read that story in the *Times* newspaper, and I said to myself, I wonder if that's the same Hubert Julian I once knew back in Port of Spain? I just had to find out. Sure enough, here you are."

"Here I am," he said with an automatic smile. His hands shot to the knot of his tie for an unneeded adjustment.

"I don't believe it. You don't meet many old boys in New York from the Eastern."

"You were at the Eastern?" There was something unusual in his accent. It leaned British. *East-ahrn.*

"Sure! You don't remember? Was it really so long ago? Of course, I was just a kid then."

He studied my face. The more he looked, the more I feared that I'd failed to convince him. My plan was fine except for one flaw, and a biggie: it expired after a single use.

Then, remarkably, he smiled, flicked his shoulder forward, and pointed an index finger. "I remember you."

"Of course you do."

"I have a perfect memory for faces." He spoke with effortless volume, as though to reach the upper balconies. "We were in a class together. McPhee, for science."

"McPhee! That's right. That old crank. You do have a great memory."

But he didn't. My days at the Eastern had ended before I made it to McPhee's upper-year science class. It didn't matter. I had the waters moving in the right direction and needed to encourage the flow. And so, "That's right! Of course! That old bastard! I remember the way he used to call me out: Ar-thuuuuur! Tooooorrmes. Ar-thurr Tooorm-es. Arthur Tormes."

"Arthur Tormes. Yes. That's exactly how he used to say your name. Man!"

He laughed at the false memory. Relieved that he'd bought my story, I joined him. We laughed together in a restrained way. Strangers trying to act like old friends.

My confidence fortified, I continued. "I read all about that parachuting exhibit you had on the weekend."

"You do something like that, people tend to notice," he said.

"Notice? I think every paper in town covered it."

"The *Evening Mail* missed it. So did the *Telegram*. Which is too bad for them. From what I hear, they could use the boost in circulation."

"But all the others. The *Daily News* ran a terrific piece," I said. "A whole column."

"And every word of it bigoted. The *Daily News* doesn't appreciate a coloured man accomplishing something newsworthy. Did you see what Smith called me in the *Herald*?"

"I didn't have a chance to look at the *Herald*."

"He called me the 'Black Eagle of Harlem.'"

I shook my head, disgusted. "It's like they don't even know slavery ended over —"

"I like it," Julian said. "The Black Eagle of Harlem. Don't you?"

"Actually? Yes, I do. Very catchy."

"I'd been thinking about a nickname. Like a boxer, you know?"

"Like 'The Toy Bulldog.' Or 'Sailor Tom.' Or 'The Stinging Ant.'"

"The Black Eagle of Harlem will do fine. I had been considering 'Lucky Julian,' or 'Julian the Lucky.' Something along those lines. You see, a few years back I met an interesting woman who told me I'd be lucky."

"Smart lady."

"A special kind of woman. She promised I'd be luckier than a thousand four-leaf clovers."

"That's a considerable amount of luck."

"Some are saying I'm bigger than Bojangles."

"Bojangles is certainly a good dancer. But he's no parachutist."

Julian adjusted his hat, leaving it a little higher on his head. "That's precisely the point. He's good at what he does, but he's no parachutist."

Julian suggested tea. We ducked into the first café.

"You and I think a lot alike," he said after ordering. "I don't often find someone whose thinking is so well aligned to my own."

"You know what, Hubert? I take that as a compliment."

After two pots, a slice of sponge cake each, and a long conversation he happily dominated, I rode the subway back south, feeling like someone who'd actually completed a full day's work, the way people who sweat at machines or drive rivets into girders must feel when the whistle blows. I had made contact. I had confirmed a few rumours I'd heard on Sunday, cast doubt on some others. Maybe none of it proved sedition or a threat to America, but at least now I had some gristle to feed Triggs.

13

TRUST ME, IT'S A REAL CHORE

OUT OF THE SUBWAY, I STOPPED AT A GROCER'S FOR DIN-
ner, a can of Van Camp's Baked Beans I'd heat up at home. Home
(which isn't the right word) was a beaten-up, six-buck-a-week,
shared room in an 89th Street pile run by an old Finn named Mrs.
Lipoma. House rules prohibited cooking in the rooms but the old
woman was too lazy to climb the stairs, which meant the rule was
generally ignored.

The hot plate and saucepan I used belonged to Sergio Pratti,
my anarchist roommate, but he didn't mind me using it so long
as I shared the food. I had met Sergio less than two weeks before, but in that time we made an easy friendship. We had one big
thing in common: both of us had migrated to America against our
will.

Sergio was born in Italy, where he had been enjoying a happy
childhood — the only son of a successful pig farmer and his
wife — until a dispute erupted between his father and a neighbour.
It escalated to the courts where the local magistrate ruled in his
father's favour. Vowing revenge, the neighbour used connections in
the occult to arrange for a curse. Two months later, swine flu swept
through the herd, wiping it out. Rather than seeking justice at the

risk of more curses, Sergio's father threw in the towel and moved the family to America.

They'd done well here. They owned a house in East Harlem and ran Macelleria Pratti, a butcher shop known in the neighbourhood for its porchetta. "Nobody else gets the skin so crisp," Sergio boasted. "It breaks apart like glass." After high school, Sergio won a scholarship to Columbia College, class of 1918. He studied literature and philosophy, but by graduation time he'd committed himself to anarchism and refused to accept his degree.

By the time we met, he'd been at Mrs. Lipoma's for two years.

"Not my idea, not by a long shot," he explained. "After the bombs on Wall Street, the cops put the screws to us anarchists. Mitch Palmer's boys found my name on a few mailing lists and decided they wanted a chat."

Sergio told his stories with an acrobatic energy that circulated through his body, up and down his rubbery limbs, even reaching his long, black hair. He seemed endlessly flexible, every joint doubled. His shirts fit large, adding baggy volume to his churning arms as he mimicked both friends and enemies.

He lifted one foot to the seat of the wobbly desk chair we shared.

"Me? I don't like trouble for the sake of trouble, so I cooperated. I'm a good American. Like Mark Twain and Christy Mathewson. In the end? No charges, no summons. But my innocence didn't matter to my father. He didn't like seeing a couple of big Irish cops lurking in his living room, wiping their muddy boots on his rug. It spooked him. He'd already lost it all once and had no appetite for starting over again. He decided that if I wasn't found guilty this time, I would be the next. The next day, he sent me to the street. That's how I ended up in this place."

Despite his first-rate education, Sergio Pratti remained jobless. Sometimes his mother brought him food from the shop, which he was kind enough to share with me. Otherwise, money meant nothing to him. Less than nothing since Sergio actually put considerable value on nothingness. "In a pinch, you can use a sawbuck to wipe your ass, but otherwise, what?"

Unlike most anarchists in those days, Sergio rejected the so-called propaganda of the deed, meaning he didn't go in for bombings or assassinating financiers. Instead, he found his politics in print. The shelves next to his cot sagged from the weight of so many books. I don't know if he'd read them all, but whenever we disagreed on something and our discussions turned into debates, I would glance over at that bookshelf and feel my disadvantage. He had too much backup for a fair fight.

Many of the books arrived as gifts from admirers, with select pages carrying faint traces of their perfumes. Other books concealed a bonus: a nude snap slipped between pages. These he shared freely. I won't say I didn't look. I gave many of those photos very careful study. But even when the women had cautiously turned from the camera or covered their faces, I felt embarrassment, like I'd barged in on a private moment. But no, Sergio assured me, these girls were different. "They won't mind."

Some were definitely more different than others. In one of the more explicit shots, a woman pushed her breasts together. In another, the girl gripped a lit candle in a suggestive way.

"I should have been an anarchist," I said, passing one of the photos back.

"It's not too late! There's no test to pass or anything. Pretty much all you have to do is say 'I am an anarchist,' and you're in. But then comes the hard part. You have to make a lot of changes to live like a true anarchist. I know I make it look easy, but trust me, it's a chore. And I have the advantage of my working-class roots. Born with dirt under my fingernails, you know? For you it would be harder still, with your blue blood."

"What blue blood?"

He brought his palm to his heart. "Don't be offended. I can certainly see how capitalism has chopped you down. At first, by the look of you, I thought gypsy. But then I heard the way you talk. There's money in your voice. Land, I'll bet. Stolen from Indians?

Worked by slaves? Mama and Papa must have served on all the committees. I bet your family tree includes a few titled bastards with blood on their hands. Again, I say this as a friend and with no offence intended."

"You couldn't be more wrong."

"No?"

The way I talked was Antona's doing. "We never had money. I never knew my father. But my mother wanted me to be educated, like her, and she managed to send me to a good school."

"Smart woman," Sergio conceded, his forefinger tapping at his temple. "Though you can see how it sets you apart in some ways. What was she like?"

Cautiously, I told him about Antona. How she wore her hair balled in a bun and sewed her own dresses from patterns she ordered from England. How she brewed ginger beer and baked black cake with rum-soaked raisins. How I couldn't remember a night from childhood that didn't end with her reading to me.

I listed my favourites. "*Treasure Island* and *Captain Courageous* and *The Swindler.*"

"I don't know the last one."

"It's a terrific old story. I'd read it again if I ever see a copy."

It felt good to remember those near-forgotten things: the books, the food, Antona's hair, her dresses. Once I got going I didn't want to stop. "She was afraid of howler monkeys. She knew all the church hymns by heart."

Of course, I reserved some details. Specifically, I did not tell Sergio that my mother had been among Trinidad's most exclusive prostitutes. Her creamy skin gave her stature on an island with few white women and she charged a premium. Clients included bishops and judges, governors and sugar barons, even the headmaster of the Eastern Boys' School.

Also, when it came to telling Sergio how she died, I did not mention the syphilis. Instead, I blamed tuberculosis.

"The white plague," he said, bowing his head solemnly.

"I'm pretty sure anyone can get it."

I'm not ashamed. Not anymore. I will say that it took many years. But I didn't have it so rough. I never wanted for food or proper clothing, and thanks to Antona, I received as good an education as the son of the colonial governor. What's more, I was well loved and I knew it. Whenever Antona spoke to me about the future — ours, and then, toward the end, only mine — she made me believe that life held out some kind of unbreakable promise for me.

It's funny. As a child, I never wavered from this belief, perhaps because Antona reinforced it so often. Then, still a child I guess, I sailed off into the world with Blind Sal on the *Diego Hurtado*. Over the weeks and months, that promise began to show its fragility. Now, four years later, it astonished me to think I could ever have been so gullible and stupid.

DEBRIEF WITH SPECIAL AGENT RILEY TRIGGS
■ MAY 6, 1923

—Sorry I'm late. I got lost.

—What's five minutes on a fine spring day like today?

—Thank you for understanding.

—Then again, what's twenty years in prison?

—…

—Of course, they say you only serve two days. The day you go in and the day you get out.

—Yes. I remember you saying that.

—While I was waiting, you know what I was doing? I was watching those dogs over there. The shepherd and the what-do-you-call-it.

—I don't really know dog breeds.

—You know what a mutt is, I bet.

—…

—Sure you do. So like I was saying. The shepherd dog was sniffing the other one's asshole. Pretty common among canines. They do it to get a feel for the other dogs. Which ones to trust. Which to leave alone. Friend or foe.

—Yes, sir. Makes sense.

—Made me think: wouldn't it be something if they could do the same for people? Sniff a fellow's asshole and know if he's guilty or innocent. No need for trials, judges, juries. Just cops to catch them, dogs to sniff their bungers, and someone to throw the switch.

—That makes sense, too.

—Sure. Wishful thinking.

—…

—You made contact with our friend. How'd you manage it?

—It turns out we went to the same school in Port of Spain.

—They have schools down there? Thought it was all sitting around and listening to toothless elders bang out lessons on bongos.

—I have some things to tell you. And these newspaper clips are for you, too. All of them mention Hubert Julian.

—I see he's a popular man with the press.

—And with the police. After his jump, they fined him five bucks for disturbing the peace. All the details are in the clips.

—How did he take being fined?

—He said he thought he should be knighted, not fined.

—Knighted?

—For proving the worth of parachutes.

—Knighted by who?

—He didn't specify, actually.

—Was he serious or joking?

—Hard to say.

—It's your job to know that.

—Yes, sir.

—What did he say about Garvey and the UNIA?

—Nothing.

—Did you ask?

—I thought it would be less suspicious to let him bring it up.

—Could be he doesn't trust you. Not good. Tell me that's not all you have.

—No. Of course not.

—...

—Did I mention the car he drives?

—No.

—A McFarlan.

—Jack Dempsey drives a McFarlan.

—Fatty Arbuckle, too.

—What does one of those cars cost? Six, seven grand? Where did he get the money for a car like that?

—I'm not exactly clear on that.

—Did you ask?

—Not yet. But I absolutely plan to.

—A *lot* of money. Had to come from somewhere, right?

—I know he bought the car in Canada. In Quebec.

—You said he was from Cleveland.

—That's what I heard. But Julian's never mentioned the city, so ...

—And the number?

—The number, sir?

—The number on the licence plate from Quebec.

—I didn't …

—Jesus, Tormes. If you can't do this job —

—I'll get it, sir. I'll get the plate number. I'm seeing him on Friday. I'll get it, no problem. I promise.

—Anything else?

—No.

—Good. Now, I have something else for you. Fellow named Cleaves will be getting in touch soon.

—Who's Cleaves?

—He's someone I know. You do what he says. If you don't, you know I'll hear about it.

—Can I ask what it's about?

—You can ask and then you can thank me. I got you a job.

14

HE LIKED TO STOKE MY ANXIETIES

NAPPING IN MY ROOM THE NEXT DAY, I DREAMED OF A fanged German shepherd chasing me through a maze of back alleys. Dark corridors leading to darker passages. Over and over again the dog lunged at my back, not to bite me but to sniff at my ass. I kept shoving the huge snout, with its wet nose, aside. The dream looped on like that until Sergio came into the room and flicked an envelope in my face.

"A letter for you," he said.

From Clive Cleaves. Who Triggs had warned me about. Handwritten in black ink on unmarked stationery, the note instructed me to present myself at the corner of Broadway and 75th that same night. Eleven o'clock sharp. The whole thing gave me an uneasy feeling. What kind of a man, what kind of a job needs you to be at a street corner so late at night?

And yet, as I would learn many times over the years, this was typical of Riley Triggs and the ways he worked me. Most of the time, especially in those early years, I didn't know what was coming next. With every interaction, he liked to nourish my ignorance, unsettle my mind, stoke my worst fears, feed my highest anxieties. And you know what? He did a pretty good job of it, too.

❖

At the appointed intersection and hour, I crossed from corner to corner to corner, looking for someone who might be looking for someone like me. After four rounds, I switched directions, completing the circuit twice before Cleaves found me.

"Hoping to turn a trick, Tormes? You're about thirty blocks too far north."

The two large men posted next to him laughed in a familiar way I didn't appreciate. Cleaves introduced them as the brothers Dwight and Ronnie Bisinhed, though he did not say who was who. They were young enough that their wide foreheads were dotted with reddened bumplets of freshly popped pimples, but their compact, powerful bodies suggested two fully grown men. (In fact, as I would learn later, both Bisinheds attended NYU, where they studied dentistry and wrestled for the varsity Violets.)

"We're waiting on Valentino and the newsman," Cleaves said. He had a narrow face broken by bloodless lips and sunken eyes, like buttons on a cushion. Even with the fedora, I could tell he didn't have much hair left. He didn't look as frightening as I'd imagined, but when he held out two twig-like fingers, one of the boys immediately produced a cigarette while the other rushed in to light it. Cleaves took three shallow puffs, blew the smoke in my direction, and said, "You know about the job?"

"Agent Triggs didn't tell me anything."

"Well, that man's mind don't work like most people's. You probably figured that out. Don't tell me how he found you, I don't want to know. What are you, anyway? Turk? Don't worry about it, here's Valentino and the newsman," he said, nodding to two approaching men. The one with the camera bag over his shoulder began to excuse their lateness.

But Cleaves didn't care. "Forget about it. Let's go."

The Bisinhed boys led the way, trailed by Valentino and the newsman, then Cleaves and me. We turned onto a street of quiet, mostly darkened apartment buildings, places that housed people whose lives held to normal hours.

Cleaves explained the business.

"I do missing persons, union busting, surveillance, divorce raiding. I used to do insurance fraud, but those corporation types make it hard on you. Mountains of paperwork, which is something they don't pay extra for. You can spend a couple of hours on a job getting what you need — some guy pretending to be crippled who isn't, say — and then it's another four hours in front of a typewriter. But they only pay you for the two. No fucking thanks. I don't type. That's part of the problem. So no more insurance fraud.

"Missing persons? A gold mine. It takes so much damn time, the hours really pile up. I'd do it exclusive if I could. But fewer people go missing than you probably think. And most of them that do don't want to be found. I might get one case a year. Two if the stars align for me, which they basically never do.

"Mostly what I do these days is divorce raiding. It's steady because you can always count on people to screw up their lives." He released a little laugh. "Here's the client. Be polite. We don't need him any more loco than he's already gonna be."

The client watched us approach with a sad, unmoving gaze. His feet seemed fixed to the sidewalk, as though to move would pull a plug and siphon all his courage. He may have been tight, too, trying hard to hide it.

Without a word, the man passed a pair of keys to Cleaves and joined our party. His name was Mr. Grayson Cross. He was thirty-six years old, sold business machines to government agencies and lived on 68th Street. (All these details I would learn later from the newsman's story.) He led us to a three-storey building with tall front doors.

Everyone seemed to know to stay quiet and step lightly. On the stairs, Cleaves lowered his voice to explain the operation to me. "We go in. Valentino takes pictures. I get the names and addresses. That's important for the trial. The Bisinhed boys are here for muscle. In case the man wants to fight. Believe it or not, it happens. Sometimes we go in, these guys are like hot pistons. You figure seeing these two hulks would make them stop and think about it, but sometimes the fella's just not in his right mind. Few weeks back, Ronnie gave a chump a concussion. We had to keep the guy awake because if you let them sleep maybe they don't wake up ever, and that kind of trouble is bad for business."

We u-turned to go up the next set of stairs. "And my role?" I whispered.

"It's on you to keep the woman in check. Hardly ever happens. Which is why you get paid less. But you never know, right? These broads can get hysterical." Cleaves paused, as though remembering something sweet. "Something else you should know: from time to time, the other woman's a man, and from time to time, the other man is a woman, if you know what I mean. In those cases, mostly what those poofs want is to hide. But every once in a while we get a proud one, so you have to be ready. Any questions? Ask fast. We're almost there."

We'd arrived on the top floor and a door indicated by Mr. Cross. Cleaves ordered us into position, which meant he and the Bisinheds cozied up to the door, the key poised at the lock. My heart thumped. Cleaves inserted the key and turned his wrist. The latch clicked, and I felt the sudden need to go to the bathroom.

Cleaves took a step forward and shouted: "Clive Cleaves! Cleaves' National Detective Agency!"

It seemed a careless way to enter an already tense situation. But I figured out later that the provocation was deliberate. Cleaves actually wanted violence, bloodshed, broken bones, anything to get the story (and his name) moved up a few pages in the next day's paper.

Inside the apartment, Valentino started snapping pictures, blinding the two bed-bound figures with magnesium flashes. The woman screamed. Her name was Evelyn Cross. The man demanded to know what was going on. His name was Travis Kitchak.

Evelyn, with one breast peeking from behind her sheet, blurted, "Gray! My God!"

Which gave Kitchak the answer to his question. And that was when Mr. Cross shot past me and launched at Kitchak, who just managed to rise from the bed before Cross swung. Kitchak dropped the bedcover to defend himself. Evelyn screamed again. The two men grappled, and Valentino aimed his camera at the fight, illuminating the violence in brief bursts. Fighting a man when he's so naked and vulnerable didn't seem fair, though at these moments why should anyone be expected to follow rules?

"Gray!" Evelyn cried. "How could you!" Caught in the act, she chose to defend her lover. Or maybe it wasn't a choice and more of her natural inclination.

Cross glared at his wife, his face suspended between competing expressions of rage and heartbreak. I felt for his double humiliation. The distraction allowed Kitchak to wriggle free. He boxed Cross' head, but landed only the one blow before the Bisinheds wrestled him to the ground. On the way down, they knocked a table and a lamp and a full ashtray crashed to the floor with them. Cleaves ordered Valentino to shoot all the damage.

"I'll smash that damn camera!" shouted Kitchak, but the Bisinheds had him trapped. In his useless struggle he looked like a baby on the changing table, resisting a clean diaper.

Meanwhile, Evelyn refused to relent. Propelled by unimaginable hatred, she screamed and slapped her husband about the head and face.

"Get in there, Tormes!" Cleaves ordered.

I flew over and wrapped my arms around Evelyn, trying to catch her wrists as she swung. She back-kicked, landing her heel on my shin. Her husband took the opportunity to back away. "Please," I said. "Can't you see it's over?" Heat rose from her back. Her naked shoulder blades poked at my chest. She kicked again, hitting the same spot. "Okay," I said. "It's done." Her arms relaxed. Her whole body, in fact, sort of half collapsed in my grip.

Near the door, Mr. Cross felt his face for blood or other damage. With Kitchak's surrender, an uneasy calm settled over the room, and nobody knew what to say or do next. Valentino lowered his camera. Dwight and Ronnie allowed Kitchak to stand but stayed close. The newsman recorded notes in a little black book. Cleaves lit a cigarette and kicked a pair of white shorts to Kitchak, and with that, we were more or less done.

After every job, Cleaves took the team out for drinks. He knew and was known at every speak in town. Even if I'd earned the drink, I couldn't enjoy myself with the others. If I wasn't so paranoid about Triggs finding out I wasn't being a team player, I'd have skipped the drinks and gone back to my room. Because even then, I knew it was wrong to make money in such a base, contemptible way. I tell you, it was never my choice, it was my job. But all I had to do to justify it to myself was to think about Riley Triggs and being locked away for thirty years in Sing Sing.

15

GOD BLESS THE BLACK EEL

NEXT TIME I SAW HUBERT JULIAN, HE INVITED ME TO A party. "Pretty exclusive," he said. "But I can get you in."

I met him on 139th Street. His suit looked like it had been made that day. Cut to fit, lightly checked, the full trousers tapered regally at the cuffs. He paid close attention to the details, too. His tie clip gleamed with recent buffing. His bootlaces were wax stiff. When he shook my hand, I heard the quality of the suit, the crisp *shush* the fabric whispered on bending.

"I didn't realize this was such a fancy affair," I said.

But it wasn't fancy or exclusive at all. The hosts had pasted flyers to lampposts and telephone poles, inviting everybody to their rent party.

At the right building, we followed the noise up the stairs and halfway down a hallway. When the door opened, a stream of hot air swooshed past my ears. Inside, a hundred or more people jammed into the space of a small classroom. Rugs were rolled up and hidden, the furniture removed. Guests sat on windowsills and spilled onto the fire escape. The band's five pieces were so crammed, the trombone player was forced to stand on a stool, playing his instrument above the drummer's head. Even still, they managed to play, and the music looped around the mostly Black and mostly West Indian guests. A man came around with paper cups and a bottle, offering his gin for a dime a shot. Julian responded by raising a stiff hand and when he announced "I do not drink," I made a note to tell Triggs.

The band ended the number with a hard stop, and a sweaty, roundish woman in a midnight-blue tuxedo peeled away from the dancing core and tapped over to us. She greeted Julian with a straight jab to the upper arm.

"Ain't you the one who jumped from that airplane?" Then she turned to me. "Am I right? It's him, ain't it?" The booze on her breath smelled hot and fruity. She swayed a little as she spoke.

Julian perked up. He attempted a little bow, but no one could bend a body in that cramped space. A second and then a third woman shouldered through other guests to join the first. They confirmed with each other that this man standing before them was the parachute jumper.

"Weren't you scared?" one asked. "I'd have just died!"

Julian tugged his lapels. "Ladies, I will tell you. The trick is to keep the fear on the outside." He formed his hands into claws as if to choke a man. "Keep it out and there's no way it can hurt you."

Two men inserted themselves into the conversation. One waved for his girl. She slid over with a friend. Struggling to hold my place, I didn't see who spoke next, "When you gonna do it again?" the voice said.

Hubert glanced over their heads at me before answering, "When am I *going to* do it again," he corrected. "As a matter of fact, I have another jump planned. This time, with a twist. As I float down from the heavens, I shall play the saxophone."

"Play the what?"

"Man, that's crazy."

"It can't be done."

"It certainly can. It just takes skill. Maybe a little luck where the wind is concerned. I'm considering playing 'Running Wild.' Not an easy tune but neither is jumping from an airplane!"

The group nodded, and Julian leered at a woman whose shoulders glowed under a beaded ivory dress. "How about you?" he asked her. "Do you like 'Running Wild'?"

She shrugged, unimpressed. "You know what, sheik? You talk funny," she said, and shuffled away from the group.

"Well, I think it's nice," another said. "Really marvellous."

"And it's just the beginning," Julian said. "In an era where art and science are converging in remarkable ways, I'm the rare man who can draw on expertise in both."

"You don't look like no Einstein to me," a man said.

"Dr. Einstein and I are similar in numerous ways. I happen to have a more accomplished barber is all."

"What are you? The Black Wright brother?"

"I don't need a brother to help me make my mark. Whose apartment is this, anyway? I'd like to offer my thanks to the host for the invitation."

"I seen a flyer on a lamppost," the tuxedo'd woman said, fanning her face with her hand. "I go to these shindies every weekend. Every weekend, I get good and tanked. I love my liquor. I'm just starting up now. Hey, who wants to dance?" She corralled a man on her left and together they bounced into the middle of the room.

The bassist launched a thumping solo punctuated with single notes from the trombone, and then the drummer took over, tapping out a wordy telegram on his cymbal, making the lone brass disk sound like three. Then the trombone returned with a scorching line of notes, and the whole band circled back to pick him up. With everyone blasting hot, using all their breath and bones, the walls began to shake.

A man named Lou introduced himself. In return, Julian offered a card. Lou read aloud, "'Lieutenant Hubert Julian, M.D., World's Champion Parachutist.' Thank you, sir! I admire a nice card."

I leaned to Julian. "I didn't know you were a doctor."

"M.D. stands for Mechanical Draftsman," he said. "Up in Montreal I invented the parachuttagravepreresista."

"The what?"

"Parachuttagravepreresista. It's an airplane safety device. I designed it and —"

"Look at that!" yelled Lou, who hadn't ventured far.

At the room's vortex, three women had climbed atop a dining table, where they danced with sweaty incaution, encouraged by the accelerating music. Legs whirled, arms reached for the ceiling, straps slipped down silky shoulders. Splayed, groping fingers reached up to touch. The music beat faster. The air vibrated and burned.

Lou pointed to the tall one. "I heard she danced the ballet in Russia. Trained by the Soviets. Tell you what, those Reds taught her good."

The hoofer's hips spun in tiny circles. Loop after suggestive loop.

"And that one? For shots of real corn whisky, she'll take it down to nothing. What I hear? She can't tell the real from the phony."

Lou turned again to Julian. "You got a good thing going. Jumping from planes must get you plenty of nicky nack."

Julian laughed, neither confirming nor denying.

"Unless you're already hitched or something."

"I was married once. But she died."

Lou said nothing, which meant it was up to me. A wild bash like that, with the music and everyone having such a fine time, was no place to delve into the subject of a dead wife.

And yet: "I'm sorry for your loss. What happened?"

"It was up in Montreal during the war," he said. "Not long after I arrived from England. Her name was Edna. I miss her every day. But you have to move on. Like with everything else."

"Like with everything else," I repeated. And then, "May Edna rest in peace, your Edna." So as not to forget the name.

A demanding woman pushed through to our corner, rattling a jar of coins in our faces. Glittery makeup on her eyelids glowed in the dimness. This was the hostess.

"Thank you for having me," Julian said.

"Pleasure's mine," she said. "How about a dime?"

"A dime?" Hubert asked.

"For rent! This is the party, isn't it? How about a quarter, then?"

"I didn't realize."

"Now you do. All this?" She flicked her head. "I'm trying to keep the bear off my back."

"I see," Julian said. He went into his pockets. Both hands came up empty.

"You got that dime?"

"I have something better than a dime," he said, reaching for another of his cards. "If you have a pen, I'd happily sign it."

Another woman joined the hostess. Her sister, perhaps. She stood with a skeptical bend in her hip.

"That's real sweet. But the landlord's upping my rent by five a month, so I'm going to need that dime now." She shook the jar for emphasis.

"Perhaps you don't understand. Collectors will pay for a signed card. Fifty cents, maybe a dollar. Wait a few years and who knows?"

"I don't want your damn calling card," she said. "Give me a dime or get the hell out."

"Everyone else paid, mister," the sister said. "*Every*one."

"Look, maybe you don't read the papers, but my name is Hubert Julian."

"And?"

"I'm the Black Eagle of Harlem."

"I don't care if you're the Lord Jesus resurrected. You still gotta pay your dime."

"Man, just give her the coin, would you?" the sister said.

A difficult silence followed and threatened to spread around the room, and I was struck with the same gut feeling I'd got in the seconds before Cleaves busted in on a love nest. I went into my pocket, emerging with a quarter, my subway fare.

"For the both of us," I said, dropping the coin into the jar and thinking about the fifty blocks I'd be walking to get home.

The hostess nodded. The band returned to their stools. The
piano tried a few scales. Dancers reclaimed the floor. The hostess
turned to join them.

"Wait," Julian demanded. He opened a long leather wallet, and
as the drummer tapped out the beat for the next tune and all the
horns filled the room again, he extracted a twenty and held it above
his head.

"Let it be known that the Black —"

"What?"

"Let it be known —"

"I can't hear you, doctor."

Julian stuffed the bill into the jar and shouted, "I said, let it be
known that Lieutenant Hubert Julian, the Black Eagle of Harlem,
is always generous with his neighbours."

The woman watched the bill drop though the jar's mouth. It
landed on its side, erect atop a bed of pennies, nickels, dimes, and
my quarter. She showed her sister. They embraced and together
held the jar aloft.

"God bless this man!" she shouted into the packed room. "God
bless his soul! God bless the Black Eel of Harlem!"

16

I WORRIED I'D EXPOSED MYSELF

AFTER THAT PARTY, I CAUGHT UP WITH JULIAN ABOUT ONCE a week. My visits were always unannounced, but Julian didn't complain and never seemed surprised when I showed up. Sometimes he acted like I'd never left, starting conversations somewhere in the middle, without preliminaries or explanations, and leaving me to fill in the blanks.

In those days, he rented a room in a brothel, a thriving business hidden in a tall brownstone. A special arrangement with the madam gave him the whole top floor. As a visitor, I had to give my name to a doorman and cool my heels outside. I imagine anyone passing took me for an indecisive customer.

We would go to lunch sometimes or sit down to sweet cakes and tea. Sometimes we stepped in at Lafayette Billiards for a game of pool or wandered over to the 9th Coast Armoury to catch the boxing. I remember many of the names. Panama Al Brown, a future champ, who dipped and feinted like he could see the future. And Midget Irla, the bantamweight who surprised Izzy Schwartz with a knockout and made a winner of Julian, who'd bet against the odds. "See, Tormes?" he said. "Lucky."

Julian liked to talk and through him, I learned more than I
thought possible about aviation. Every day, it seemed, he had news
of technological advances or records being set. He was especially
interested in feats of endurance and told me about John Richter
and Lowell Smith, who flew an Airco DH.4 and smashed a dozen
records.

"Thirty-seven straight hours in the air," he informed me.
"Thirty-two hundred miles."

"Didn't they run out of fuel?"

"Refuelled in the air. A hose that ran from one plane to the
other."

"Incredible."

"Yes, well," he said, considering. "Though it's a far easier thing
when you've got the U.S. Army behind you."

He told me more about the parachuttagravepreresista, how he'd
sold the patent to a company in Canada and had been querying
aviation companies here in the States, confident he would soon
find a buyer.

One day I took a train out to Curtiss Field to watch an air show
organized by Bill Powell as a benefit for Hellfighter vets. Julian
landed on target after jumping from a plane piloted by Edison
McVey. Bessie Coleman, the day's headliner, showed off tricks she
had learned in Europe. With so many Negro aviators displaying
their talents, I figured Triggs would appear. In fact, I spent so much
time searching for him in the bleachers and on the fringes of the
field that I missed most of the show.

I tried to confide in Julian about divorce raiding, hoping for
a sympathetic hearing. I ranted about the lousy money and the
hours and how being party to so much raw misery was eating at
my spirits. I was having trouble sleeping, I told him, and a rash had
developed in a hard-to-reach place. Even the phony jobs, where the
man and wife were merely looking to expedite an otherwise uncon-
tested divorce; even those easy ones brought me down for days. Yes,
these people got what they wanted, but given what they had to go
through to get it, they never seemed at all happy.

"There are always plenty of jobs out there for a man willing to work. My father taught me that. He's a wealthy man now. Why not quit?"

He'd posed a fair question, for which I had no honest answer. So I bluffed with a shrug and told him I would stick it out a little longer, and after that we never talked about the job again.

For the record, Julian never once mentioned Marcus Garvey. Nor did he say anything about his position in the UNIA. In June, when a court sentenced Garvey to five years for wire fraud, I took the opportunity to ask him directly.

"What do you think will happen with the UNIA?"

For a moment, he looked at me like I'd offended him, enough that I suddenly worried I'd exposed myself. Then he shrugged and before I could do it myself, he changed the subject. "Did you once tell me you used to be a chauffeur?"

DEBRIEF WITH SPECIAL AGENT RILEY TRIGGS
■ SEPTEMBER 13, 1923

—You're late. Again.

—Sorry, sir.

—I'm beginning to wonder.

—It's just that there are three different alleys near this intersection. And you didn't say which.

—Where would you prefer? A cell on Blackwell's Island?

—...

—That's what I thought. How's the job?

—Fine.

—You're welcome.

—Thank you. Again.

—Divorce raiding is no job for a respectable man. But for you, it'll do. Who knows? Work hard and you could move up. There's easy money in finding dirt, especially on celebrities and politicians. This is the world we live in. What about Julian?

—He was in an air show.

—Flying?

—Parachuting. There were other pilots. I wrote down their names. Edison McVey, Bill Powell, Bessie Coleman.

—A girl pilot?

—That's right.

—Your concern is Julian. Did he land the jump?

—Yes, sir. Right on target.

—Could be he's training. Getting up some sort of parachute troop unit.

—...

—What else?

—He wants me to be his chauffeur.

—His driver?

—He prefers the word "chauffeur."

—Why you?

—I told him I used to drive for a businessman up in Canada.

—Is that true?

—Yes, sir.

—You should have told me that sooner. Why does he need a driver?

—To drive his car, obviously. … Hey! What was that for?

—For thinking you can be smart with me. Put your hand down. Do not even think about it.

—You're wearing a ring!

—Don't be a baby.

—I don't like being hit.

—Who the hell does? Why does Julian need a driver?

—…

—Stop rubbing. Answer the question.

—He needs me to drive because he's got this invention he's trying to sell. It's an airplane safety device. It's called a parachuttagrave-preresista. It's patented. Here. I have a diagram for you.

—I don't get it. What does it do?

—From what I understand, it helps disabled planes land safely.

—How the hell did Julian learn about airplane safety appliances?

—I believe in Montreal. That's where he sold the patent.

—For how much?

—I don't know exactly. Enough to buy the McFarlan. Now he's trying to sell the invention to Glenn Hoskin Aviation. Over on Long Island.

—You just told me he sold it in Montreal.

—Yes.

—You can't sell the same thing twice. Once you sell something, it's no longer yours to sell.

—No, sir. Of course not.

—Well?

—I don't know what to say. He's got a meeting with Glenn Hoskin, of Hoskin Aviation. I'm driving him.

—Interesting.

—He got me a uniform and everything.

—Is he paying?

—He promised a bonus when he sells the invention.

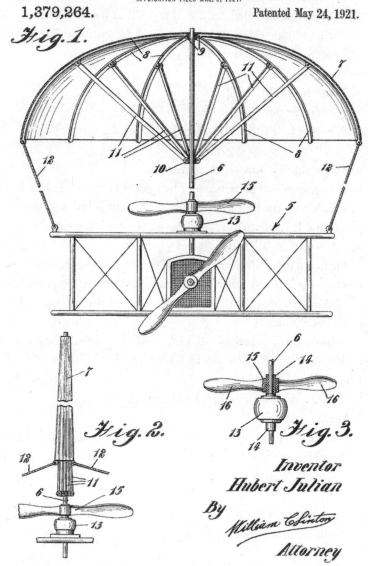

H. JULIAN.
AIRPLANE SAFETY APPLIANCE.
APPLICATION FILED MAR. 9, 1921.

1,379,264.

Patented May 24, 1921.

Fig.1.

Fig.2.

Fig.3.

Inventor
Hubert Julian

By
William C. Linton
Attorney

—Sounds like a shitty deal. Then again, your life's basically one shitty deal after another, isn't it.

—…

—Anything else?

—Yes, sir. He brawled last week with a man named Simon Bernard, who claims Julian owes him money.

—He fight a lot?

—I'm not sure, actually.

—How many times have you seen him fight?

—Just that once. But I didn't personally see it.

—Why not?

—I wasn't there.

—You should have been.

—I'll be there next time for sure.

—Is he a violent type?

—He has a short temper.

—A man who can't control his temper is his own worst enemy. But there's no helping it. I've been known to go off myself. But I can generally trace the problem back to a medical complaint. What else?

—That's all, sir.

—Nothing about the UNIA?

—Nothing.

—…

—…

—You know what bothers me about the UNIA? It's the "Universal."

—I guess it's meant to say that they represent Negroes all over the world.

—That's just it. Why worldwide? It's like they're saying the U.S.A. isn't good enough for them. Why not *American* Negro Improvement Association? What I don't get is why they have to bring foreigners into it.

—…

—…

—Would you like me to ask, sir?

17

ACCELERANTS OF AN INEVITABLE
CONFLAGRATION (THE FIRST)

AMONG THE THINGS I HATED MOST ABOUT DIVORCE RAID-
ing was the role the press played in our operations. Cleaves insisted we read all the stories, not only those written about our own
jobs but also the competition's, too. Pitts and Lowe, in Brooklyn.
Hubert Boulin, in Harlem. "Boulin's got a good thing going with
the coloureds," Cleaves admitted. "His name's in their papers every
week. We need to be where he is. But in the white papers."

Every story was an unwelcome reminder of my shameful liveli-
hood. Breathless accounts of loose women, Negro lovers, unnatural
sex acts, ménages dripping in illegal liquor and narcotics. The press
named names, even the phony ones given to hotel clerks or land-
lords. They printed addresses and alimony demands. And all of it
in that finger-wagging prose. As if those writers had never sinned.
As if they had never been caught up in something they'd been
powerless to prevent.

Because by the end, I understood that the guilty were innocent,
too. Sure, we walked in on plenty of guys flattering themselves with
someone young and pretty. But we also caught women who'd married the wrong man for the wrong reasons. People who were lonely,

desperate, curious. I saw nothing criminal or corrupt in any of that. Cleaves liked to say that we were acting as mere accelerants of an inevitable conflagration. A clever way to put things, maybe; pretty words to dress up our ugly business. But it made me think of an accused arsonist explaining to the court why he'd poured gasoline on a stovetop fire. "You see, your honour. That house was going to burn down anyway, so, really, I was simply acting as an accelerant of an inevitable conflagration."

The last raid I took part in happened near the end of that same summer of '23. The crew gathered around eleven o'clock at 63rd and Park, where we met the client, Mary McElhinney, aggrieved wife of Garrett, our target that night.

Mary led us on foot, walking stiffly, arms swinging high. A rich collection of bracelets on her wrists jangled in time with the steps. The rest of us marched behind. Give Mary a baton and one of those tall, plumed hats and she'd have passed for a drum major.

She took us to an apartment building with roses in flower boxes outside and a doorman on duty in the foyer. I thought the doorman might be a problem, but his expression on seeing our client turned grim and knowing. He opened the door wide to let us pass.

Accompanied by one of the Bisinheds, Cleaves rode up the small elevator with the client. Once they'd cleared the ground floor, Valentino nudged the other Bisinhed's shoulder.

"Know who that is?"

"Mrs. McElhinney?"

"Yeah, but before that she was Miss Mary Matthews. She's a Singer."

"What does she sing?"

"A *Singer!*"

"Opera? Broadway?"

"As in Singer sewing machines. She's an heiress, man! Now she's married to the top dog at the Chemical Bank. I'll tell you what. A lot of money's going down the drain tonight."

Up on the ninth floor, we paused as usual at the apartment door and once again, I fought the urge to take off. From inside, an angry female voice was making her conditions known. "Not before you get me another drink!"

"I said after." Upon hearing the male voice, Mary McElhinney stiffened.

"Not one more thing happens here until I get my goddamned drink."

Cleaves inserted the key, pushed the door open, and bellowed his uncivil greeting. We poured in after him and waited for whatever was going to happen to happen. In the event, it was something unexpected: a pantless Garrett McElhinney skipped over surprise and went straight to fury. He fired an empty glass at Dwight's head. A big man, he had a cannon for an arm. The glass shattered against Dwight's forehead. Blood flowed from the fresh cut.

Mary opened. "You lying bastard!"

"You think you can do this to me?"

"I can! I am!"

"I'll ruin you, you cunt!"

He went after his wife. Ronnie intercepted. Well matched in both size and strength, the two men wrestled on their feet, crashed against the wall, spat, and swore. Though older, McElhinney had the energy of a man who'd already been wound up but not allowed to spin.

Cleaves slapped Valentino on the back of his head. "What are you waiting for, dough brain? Take the pictures, will you?"

With Valentino's bulbs flashing, Garrett's woman, whose only problem a few seconds ago had been her empty glass, backed away and tried to hide her face. She scrambled to find her scattered clothes. Throwing a pillow off the mattress, she retrieved a black slip.

Valentino moved in for a better angle, but he ended up too close to the action and with an arm freed from Ronnie's grip, McElhinney snatched the camera at the soft bellows and flung it through the open window. By then his mistress had found her dress and pulled it over her head, but backward, bow in front, ribbons hanging at her knees. Frayed curtains of loose curls obscured her face. Black tears dribbled past her chin.

"What are you crying about, whore?" Mary screamed. She lurched three steps, swung, and struck with her handbag. The blow dazed the girl. Mary hooted, swung again, this time just missing her mark.

Crouching to the floor, the girl covered and curled into a ball. "I'm sorry. I'm sorry." She said it over and over again. Only moments earlier, she'd been adamant about that drink, but she wasn't much of a fighter.

I slipped around Garrett, who was still struggling with Ronnie, aiming to separate the two women. But Cleaves halted me. "Only if the client is losing."

Mary hooted again, then drove a toe into the girl's ribs. Ignoring Cleaves, I squeezed between them. Mary continued the attack, but now her fists landed on my head.

"Mary, stop," Mr. McElhinney said weakly. "Please." Ronnie was wearing him down, and now he was willing to be polite.

Mary stepped back. Hatred beamed from her eyes, bounding from wall to wall. She cracked open her handbag and reached a trembling hand inside.

The next moment, I remember distinctly. Most precisely, I remember the sounds. All those bracelets on Mary's wrist echoed like wind chimes as her hand sank into the bag. When it emerged, it was adorned by a small, nickel-plated pistol. She aimed the weapon at her half-naked husband, clenched her jaw, and squeezed the trigger.

A gun fired in a bedroom makes an unbelievable amount of noise. It also generates chaos and confusion, especially when that bedroom is crowded with nine adults. I know I don't have everything right, but I remember the cloud of gun smoke, the smell of spent powder, and Garrett McElhinney slumping to the floor, clutching his arm. I was aware of Valentino's voice shouting in Italian. And

Ronnie screaming and checking himself for wounds. What I don't remember, exactly, is grabbing the girl by the wrist or brushing by Cleaves, the still-bloodied Dwight, or the newsman, and running from the room.

But I do remember following the girl down a set of stairs. I urged her to hurry. On the seventh, we scurried across the long hallway to the second staircase, and on the fifth we boarded the unmanned service elevator. Once I'd closed the cage and the car lurched downward, I felt a little safer. I asked if she was okay. She nodded and leaned heavily against the car's rear wall, rattling the steel. The collar of her backward dress choked at her neck. She closed her eyes and caught her breath. She needed the rest. With those smears of colour on her face, the blue, blood red, and black, she looked like she'd been sneaking into her mother's makeup bag. One side of her face was already inflamed and swelling where Mary's pistol-heavy purse had found its mark.

The elevator seemed slower going down than it had going up. I loosened my tie and ran a sleeve across my sweaty forehead. Halfway down, I saw something familiar. Her hair, maybe. Something in those wild, storm-blown curls triggered a memory. Had we met before? I couldn't think where or when but she seemed so familiar. The elevator jerked when it hit bottom.

The girl remembered, too. Maybe she'd recognized me from the start. When she saw that I was trying to put it together, Jean Fox looked down at her shoeless feet.

"Damn you, Arthur Tormes," she said. "You're always catching me at my worst."

18

THE HARD PART ABOUT HAVING
YOUR FOOT IN THE DOOR

CLEAVES CANNED ME THE NEXT DAY. HE CAME RIGHT TO
Mrs. Lipoma's, flanked by the Bisinheds, Dwight with his head
wrapped in white gauze. He called me disloyal and unfit for the
job. I should have been relieved and I was. I slept well that night
and by morning the rash had disappeared. I could once again stand
to look at myself in a mirror.

But the effects of the job lingered. A few nights later, I dreamed
I was in bed with a woman, kissing and feeling around each other's
naked bodies in a promising prelude to something more. Then the
door flew open, harsh light flooded the room, and the Cleaves'
National Detective Agency announced a raid. Shocked, mouth
agape, I turned to my lover for an explanation, only to find I'd
been lying in bed naked with Agent Riley Triggs.

So, basically, in the mathematics of anxieties, I was in about
the same place. Now I felt more pressure than ever to find
something on Julian before my next debrief. I hoped something might emerge from Julian's meeting with Glenn Hoskin
Aviation.

❖

On the morning of his appointment, I opened the garment bag
containing my chauffeur's uniform, a forest-green tunic, trousers
with swirling yellow piping, brass cuff buttons, and a pair of
pins for my chest that granted me some imaginary rank. Made
for a much larger man, the tunic stretched nearly to my knees.
The sleeves swallowed my hands and the leather boots extended
to my lower thighs. I stuffed crumpled newspapers into the toes
and used a hand towel to fill the empty space after I tried the
cap on my head. In the end, I looked like a leafless plant, potted
in onyx.

"Couldn't you have bought me one that fit?" I asked Julian.

"It's a sharp uniform, Tormes. All the finest drivers wear one
like it."

The McFarlan, Julian's car, was a beautiful machine. Bright
red body under a black roof. Big chrome headlamps and polished
fixtures everywhere. Fenders like raised eyebrows over the front
wheels. The shape — long, then tall — reminded me of a cathedral, and the inside had all the mellow comforts of a gentleman's
study. It drove like a dream.

We crossed over to Long Island, through Queens to NY 24
and the open road. In the fields on either side of the highway, farm
workers detasselled rows of corn. I made a game of counting how
many pickers paused at their jobs to gawk as the McFarlan passed.

I found this part of the drive relaxing. The air out here was
cleaner and I kept the window rolled down the whole way.
Meanwhile, Julian, who was more focused on his business opportunity, listed the attributes of Glenn Hoskin's new bomber, the
DB-4. "Ninety foot wingspan, twin fins, and rudders."

"Do you think the parachuttagravepreresista can handle it?"

Julian ignored the question like I should have known better. "Two V-12 engines, each displacing twenty-four hundred
cubic inches, each driven by seven hundred horses." He paused
a moment to reflect on such an aircraft, the audacity required
to build it.

"It's the pioneers who reap the rewards, isn't it, Arthur? In this world, being second counts for nothing." He adjusted his tie. "I feel good about this meeting. I feel especially lucky today."

"Lucky like that woman said."

"Did you know Glenn Hoskin starred in a picture with Mary Pickford?" Julian's accent was particularly English, drawing out the word "starred."

"I didn't know that."

"It was called *Bright Skies Ahead*. Hoskin played a pilot. I tried to see it, but you can't anymore. I read the reviews, though, so I've got a pretty good idea what it's all about."

Glenn Hoskin housed his aviation company in a square brick building at the edge of an open field bisected by a paved runway. Behind the main building stood a barn-like structure that must have been the hangar. The Stars and Stripes hung limp on a white flagpole next to another with an empty windsock. At the front door, Julian paused, waiting for me to open it. Through the threshold, he stared straight ahead with that same expression — stern, rehearsed, triumphant — I had first seen that day in April when he stood atop the Harlem tenemen. To be honest, I shared his optimism.

Forgetting my ridiculous appearance, I announced Julian to the receptionist with some formality. But things turned sour before Julian even had a chance to lay his blueprints on the table.

"*He's* Mr. Julian?" she said. I confirmed it. What remained of the woman's eyebrows — two thin, curving lines like the backs of cornered cats — shot high on her forehead. Without another word, she disappeared into the back offices.

I sat on a bench until Julian's glare put me on my feet again.

We waited. I couldn't see the airstrip from the office, but several times I heard the bending sounds of takeoffs and landings. There were framed photographs on the wall, mostly of Hoskin aircraft but also one of a pilot. "David Rittenhouse," Julian said, admiring the shot. "He just claimed the Schneider Trophy. In a CR-3. Average speed, 177.4 miles per hour."

At the one-hour mark, the receptionist returned to her desk, red lipstick and face powder refreshed. She looked surprised, even annoyed, to see us still waiting.

"Mr. Hoskin has been called away on urgent business," she said.

I picked up the leather dossier, ready to leave.

"It's nothing for me to wait," Julian said. "When can we expect him back?"

"Well, I can't really say."

"Is there someone who *can* say? We had an appointment."

I set the giant chauffeur's hat on my head.

"Take that hat off, Tormes. We had an appointment."

"The business was urgent," the receptionist insisted. "Sometimes it happens. Maybe it's different where you're from."

"All right. Another day, then. Tormes, my planner, please."

"I think it best if Mr. Hoskin contacts you. I'll sure enough let him know." Except when she said "sure enough," she said "sho 'nuff."

I saw Julian's mouth harden.

"You let Mr. Hoskin know I'm just looking to sell an invention here."

"I will," she said. She gave me a glance as though hoping I'd aid her exit from this awkward moment. Maybe the uniform made her believe I wielded some power in this situation.

"You tell Mr. Hoskin that I don't want to join his club or marry his daughter or sit next to him at the theatre. You tell Mr. Hoskin, I'm interested in making money, just like him. That's *green* money."

Without replying, the woman picked up a pencil and bent her face to a bound ledger. She turned pages forward, pages back.

Julian buttoned his jacket and reached for his hat. "Bring the car around, Tormes."

"Right away," I said. I wanted to share in his outrage but sensed that to do so would only further illuminate the humiliation he was trying to obscure. Outside the offices, I affected a display of chauffeur's duties. I skipped around the hood to open the rear door and stood at crisp attention, hoping the receptionist and Glenn Hoskin and everyone else were watching from the windows, cowering behind split blinds. I glanced at the Black Eagle, hoping to share the joke, but he ignored my face and climbed back into the car.

19

I HAVE A FEW OF THOSE, TOO

SOON ENOUGH I LANDED A NEW JOB WORKING NIGHT SE-
curity at the Met Tower. I showed up at seven and for the next
twelve hours walked up and down hallways, checking door locks
and bathrooms and switching off left-on lights. I wore a brown
uniform with Met Tower shoulder patches but no metal badge. My
only weapon was a five-inch steel key ring that jangled on my belt
as I patrolled. It was pretty easy going. I lasted four-and-one-half
days.

On the fifth, Riley Triggs dropped by for an unexpected visit.
He was at the front doors when I went down for the one a.m. check,
unmoving on the other side of the glass, hands deep in his raincoat
pockets. Seeing him made me jump a little.

I invited him inside. He didn't budge. His glasses, speckled with
raindrops, sat lopsided on his face. He ordered me to quit the job.

"Can't have an attempted cop killer working in law enforcement," he said. "Hand in your keys. Tonight."

Lucky for me, Triggs had no objection when I was hired to wash
dishes at the Excelsior, a midtown restaurant owned by Tommy

Kippers, whose real name was Athanasios Kipouros. Like a lot of foreigners in those days, Kipouros went full Anglo in the lineups at Ellis Island. As Tommy Kippers, he'd done pretty well for himself. He drove a Lincoln. His kids went to private schools. The Excelsior was one of three busy restaurants he owned in Manhattan.

Though easy on the mind, the job took a toll on my body. The dishwashing station was downstairs in the cellar, tucked into a tiny, steam-filled box of a room. My shift began at five to six, and by the time the first sleepy customers had sipped their coffees, I was standing at the concrete sink, soaping the brushes, waiting for bins to drop down the dumbwaiter. In that cramped space, it didn't take long for the heat and humidity to build up and by most mid-mornings, it felt like I was breathing with half a lung.

For ten hours, I chipped, scrubbed, scoured, and wiped. Egg yolk, ketchup smears, melted cheddar, crusted cream sauces, blackened meat. I filled trash cans with heaps of beef gristle and bacon fat, potato skins, cigar butts, crumpled napkins, discarded newspapers, and gallons of spent grease. On busy days, the bins never stopped and when I finally went home, it was always tired and sore, my skin moist, puckered and reddened like a boiled tomato.

One evening in late October, I turned the corner on to 89th and saw a figure sitting on Mrs. Lipoma's front stoop. A light charge zipped through me when I recognized Jean Fox. It had been months since the messy night with the McElhinneys, and I never expected to see her again. But there she was, smoking a cigarette, flipping the big, colourful pages of a movie magazine. I made my last few steps slap hard on the sidewalk, but even when I stopped directly in front of her, she kept her eyes lowered.

"Hello," I said.

She looked at me with a smile for strangers. "Oh, hey there! What an unexpected surprise."

I sputtered something awkward, probably unintelligible.

"It's Jean. In case you've forgotten."

"I haven't."

She wore a white button-up sweater over a dark grey dress and sat on her folded black coat.

"Do you live around here?" she asked.

I pointed to the front door at the top of the stairs.

"In this place? You're kidding me."

"Nope."

"Some coincidence. I should play the numbers tonight."

"Why not?"

"Too bad I've quit gambling."

She closed the magazine, stood, and unfolded her coat. "It's the strangest thing! In a city this big, too." She slid her arms down the coat sleeves, began to button, and when she reached the top, her face became mock-serious. "Or is it really a coincidence at all?"

"Huh?" Because what else could it be but a coincidence?

"I came to thank you," she said. "For your ... you know ... that night."

"You don't need to do that."

"I absolutely disagree." From her coat's pocket she produced a few folded banknotes. "I should have done this weeks ago. Here."

"It's okay."

"You did me such a favour. Bigger than you can imagine. Take your reward. It's not much, but I hope it's enough to make us even."

"I'm not taking your money."

She folded the bills a second time and hid them in her closed hand. Jean looked different from the last time I had seen her. Younger and healthier. Like she'd recently emerged from a long illness with renewed vitality.

"But if you haven't eaten," I said, "we could go to dinner somewhere."

"Yes. Let's. My treat, of course. No arguments. Unless you have to work tonight? If you do, we could make it another time. I'm actually free most every night."

"I work days now. I lost that other job."

"I'm so sorry."

"Don't be. It wasn't your fault. I'm actually glad I got fired." I meant it, too. No way I could have quit on my own without creating trouble with Triggs. Getting fired was my only way out.

"I got a new job myself. Chemical Bank didn't want me around anymore but I got onto the switchboard at *The Sun*. Doesn't pay as much, but an hour at a newspaper's more exciting than a year at a bank. I mean, sometimes I'm so busy I don't have time to breathe! How'd you end up in a racket like that, anyway?"

"It's a long story."

"Yeah?" she said. "I have a few of those, too."

In a brightly lit diner we both ordered the special, grilled trout and scalloped potatoes. Jean struggled to work around the fish bones. I showed her how to slide a knife along the ribs to free the filet. "If you don't take care, the bones can snag in your throat."

"It's far more delicious this way."

"How did you find me, anyway?"

"Easy. I asked the Black Eagle of Harlem. It was my only clue, since you're not in the directories, which is a bit odd. I remembered the parachute jump and especially that little hesitation when I asked if you and Hubert Julian were friends. A telling pause, as it turns out!"

I nodded. So now Jean thought Julian and I were old friends, too. I didn't see any point in setting her straight.

"And how did you find Julian?"

"That was actually even easier. I went up to Harlem and asked around for the guy who jumped out of the airplane playing the saxophone. Found him in a teahouse, signing his own photograph. Which makes me a pretty good detective, I'd say." Her voice trailed, perhaps remembering her last encounter with that profession. "Or maybe a secret agent. Anyway, I stood in line behind about a hundred others, at least ninety-nine of them being girls. I guess he's enjoying the fruits of not killing himself."

"You have to admire his daring. Those jumps made him a real hero."

"I know! I've never seen anything like it. What's he all about, anyway?"

I chewed on my last slice of potato, then rested the fork on the plate. "I actually don't know."

"Aren't you old friends?"

"Even old friends can be mysteries to each other."

"Like Othello. Who never saw it coming with his supposed friend Iago."

"Yes, a lot like Othello," I said, though I'd never heard the name before. She probably knew this, but didn't challenge me. Even that early, Jean Fox and I were forming and fixing a multitude of unspoken barriers and boundaries.

"I still have his photo," she said. "Want to see?"

She passed over a five by seven, Julian leaning on a small wooden table, next to a globe mounted on a tripod, a model biplane resting in his hands, gazing beyond the lens to the limitless beyond, a hero with heroic dreams. It was a striking pose, actually.

"Would you mind letting me have this?" I asked, thinking of my next debrief with Triggs.

"Why? You think it'll be worth something someday?"

"You never know!"

She pulled out her pack of cigarettes. I got the match lit on the second try. It wasn't late, but I felt the evening winding down, as though Jean were on a timetable.

Setting her smoke in the ashtray, she reached for my plate and slid the fish carcass over — head, tail, the little white bones cleaned of their meat — laying it parallel to the skeleton on her plate.

"There," she said, nudging one head closer to the other. "Reunited in death."

"How do you know they were together in life?"

"Just look at those adoring eyes!" she said. "Though maybe you're right. They could easily have been total strangers."

The disappointment showed on her face.

"Doesn't matter," I said. "The important part is neither has to spend eternity alone."

She laughed a little polite laugh. But when the waiter approached our table to see about coffee or dessert, she shoved the dirty plates his way.

"Just get rid of these, would you?"

20

IT'S AKIN TO LANCING A BOIL

IN MID-NOVEMBER JULIAN ASKED ME TO DRESS UP IN THE oversized green chauffeur's uniform and drive him in the McFarlan to a series of meetings he'd set up with potential buyers for the parachuttagravepreresista. I told him I'd be happy to do it. It felt like too long since I'd brought anything juicy to Triggs.

"It's a long haul," Julian warned. "Newark, Cleveland, and Detroit."

"When do we start?"

But my enthusiasm counted for nothing. Julian slept all the way to Newark, then again en route to Cleveland. From Cleveland to Detroit I tried to talk, but he hushed me, saying he had to revise his presentation. In the end, it didn't matter. All three companies turned him down.

"They said the invention was too advanced," Julian said after the last meeting in Detroit. "I said, 'Of course it is, that's how you move forward, by adopting advanced technologies.' But they just don't understand. All the engineering smarts in the world and none of them have any clue."

Empty-handed and exhausted, we began the journey back to New York. Julian was in a sour mood, still uninterested in conversation. We drove straight through, fuelled by coffee and candy bars. We'd been on the road for ten hours, with six still to go, when he finally said something.

"Pull over."

"Here?"

"Here."

Here being the middle of a narrow bridge spanning the Susquehanna River in Pennsylvania. I did as asked and kept the engine running as Julian stepped out of the car, clutching the handle of the dossier containing the plans, blueprints, and technical details for the parachuttagravepreresista. So many years of work, zipped up in black leather. I joined him outside. It was past midnight, and cold. Light flurries swirled in the headlights. Then, without announcement or explanation, Julian reared back, swung his arm, and sent the flat case spinning high over the iron railing and into the dark waters below. When he heard the watery smack, confirming its landing, he returned to the back seat and for the rest of the drive to New York, he slept.

I met with Triggs two days later. Amazingly, even without useful information, he praised my work, though I imagine he derived the most pleasure from hearing about Julian's failures. Still, I was grateful for his approval and went so far as to mistake it for satisfaction, which wasn't the case. Over the years, I learned that receiving praise from Triggs, as rarely as it came around, was something akin to lancing a boil. Yes, there's some immediate relief, an easing of the pressure. But you also know that unless you scrape the cavity clean of poison, it won't be long before the swelling returns.

I arrived back at Mrs. Lipoma's to a minor commotion. Other tenants lurked in the hallway, peering in the direction of my shared room, where loud voices battled. I brushed past them and entered to find two burly immigration cops fixing cuffs around Sergio Pratti's wrists.

"I refuse to acknowledge your authority!" Sergio shouted while offering no resistance to their authority.

"What's going on, Sergio?" I asked. "Where are you taking him?"

The cops gave me stony, skeptical looks, but no answer. They were like Triggs — all of them were — thriving on an ignorance of their own creation.

"Looks like my time is up, man!" Sergio said. "Good luck to you, Arthur!"

"I don't understand!" I shouted as they led him past a line of smug onlookers. "How can they do this?"

"Don't mourn, Young Arthur! Organize!"

The deportation hearing convened two days later in a downtown court. I expected to arrive at a room packed with Sergio's anarchist buddies, agitating and disrupting, willing to sacrifice their own inherent freedoms for the sake of their Italian-born comrade. But the benches were all empty. Not even his parents showed up.

Men in dark suits took their seats at wide tables up front and when a bailiff gave the signal, two guards marched Sergio in from a side door. They hadn't given him a change of clothes or a razor. His hair was an uncombed, tousled mess. I caught his attention with a wave. Forever resisting, he winked a return.

Things got going with the government lawyer, who spoke against Sergio, outlining his seditious activities. He reminded the court that Sergio shared the same ideology as the men who'd bombed Wall Street, as well as Leon Czolgosz, the anarchist assassin who shot down President McKinley back in '01. Sergio bristled at the false association. He was strictly against violence, had denounced the bomb throwers in both print and speech.

But this lawyer didn't care. He presented Sergio's immigration records as evidence of his Italian birth. The judge nodded along approvingly, uninterested in Sergio's side of the story. The lawyer requested deportation and in the next instant, the judge whipped out the necessary form and signed the order on the spot. No deliberation. The gist: Sergio would be removed from American soil for good on a ship departing New York the next day. Back to the chaos of Italy, back to the pig farm, which, as far as Sergio knew, still suffered under his neighbour's curse. While the judge read the sentence, Sergio remained still. Not even a flinch. When the guards came to take him back to his cell, he raised a clenched fist in the air, holding it high as they ushered him out of the courtroom.

"Good luck, Mr. Pratti!" I shouted. "Be well!" But the door closed before he could return my good wishes.

Later, back in the room we had so recently shared, I began to organize Sergio's books and papers, plus boxes of letters, reams of stationery, and one of the two shirts he owned, still hanging out to dry from the day of his arrest. I thought I'd send them over to the Macelleria Pratti in East Harlem but as I read some of the titles — Malatesta's *L'anarchia*, *The Conquest of Bread* by Peter Kropotkin, and a collection of Emma Goldman's essays — I decided the elder Pratti would likely use the books as kindling to roast his porchetta, so I kept the whole lot, not just the political books but the novels and books of poetry Sergio still had from his aborted college years.

I sat down with one, *The Good Soldier*, but couldn't concentrate. Poor Sergio. How cruelly efficient the system had been with him! Arrested on a Monday, he'd be sailing back to Italy on the Thursday, twenty years of American life wiped out like his father's pig herd. Banned from ever returning, he'd never see home again. And why? Sergio was no criminal. He was the least threatening person I knew. In fact, the more we lived together, the more I came to believe that Sergio's anarcho-pacifism was a sham he used to cover his true cowardice. His unwillingness to throw a punch was less about non-violence than about fear of his receiving a harder one in return. That didn't matter. Because some government official (who'd probably already forgotten Sergio's name) decided he didn't belong here anymore. And that was all it took to get rid of him.

21

CERTAIN SUSPICIONS AROSE

JEAN AND I HAD TWO KINDS OF DATES: MOVIES AND WALKS. In those first few months, we saw *The Covered Wagon*, with Warren Kerrigan and Lois Wilson; Tom Mix in *North of Hudson Bay*; *The Green Goddess*, based on the play by William Archer; DeMille's *Ten Commandments*; and plenty of other good ones whose names I no longer remember.

We tried baseball once, the Yankees versus Jean's Tigers at the colossal new stadium. I didn't understand the game, but liked the sights and sounds, the trim green grass and sharp lines, the smack of a bat and ball. I liked the hot dogs they brought right to your seat. The game was a real slugfest, tied at six runs each in the fourth inning. The Yanks had men on base with the great Babe Ruth at the plate when I happened to look down and spot Triggs, sitting alone just three rows in front of us. I spent the rest of the afternoon pretending to be sick in the washroom. After that, we never saw another ball game again.

When we were low on cash or had already seen all the current movies, we chose to walk. We visited every neighbourhood in the city, all the little hives and enclaves where people ate and slept, studied, worked, and played. We avoided repeating the same route twice and when that became impossible, tried to notice at least one new thing along the way because Jean had a theory: the hours pass more slowly when you're seeing something for the first time.

"Theoretically, you could live forever if you could somehow wake up in a different place from where you went to sleep."

"Too bad that's impossible," I said.

"For now."

By then we were going out two, even three times a week, at least. Some would have called us boyfriend and girlfriend, but I couldn't afford to think that way. That is, I wouldn't use those words, at least. Because to call Jean *girlfriend* or for Jean to call me *boyfriend* would put expectations and requirements on the relationship. Basic, fundamental stuff like commitment and consideration and honesty. I had no problem with the first two, but the last was tricky. I was hiding some big secrets. And, since I couldn't be honest with her, she couldn't be my *girlfriend*. Avoid the word, I reasoned, and I could avoid the obligation to tell the truth. Which was the only way I could actually be with her. It was a confusing way to think about it, I know, and not an argument anyone would take to court, but with my undereducated, eighteen-year-old's logic, it all made sense.

With the amount of time we were spending together, it wasn't long before I figured out something important about Jean Fox. She had an unusually strong interest in death. First came that macabre wager she had proposed as we waited in the vacant lot for Julian to jump. Then her zeal while relating the story of poor Franz Reichelt, that gormless Austrian tailor whose wearable parachute failed the crucial test on the Eiffel Tower. She'd spoken of death wishes and deals with undertakers. More recently, on one of our longer walks, we paused in front of a pet store window and waited for a milk snake to make a meal out of the tiny brown mouse that had been dropped for that purpose into the aquarium. We stood watching for forty-five minutes but the snake never moved, and all that time the mouse cowered in a corner, a trail of black pellets tracing his frenzied failed attempts to escape.

"Just not my day, I guess," Jean said when I finally convinced her to give up.

The clincher came in November, a cool day with a biting wind, the kind of day you feel winter stretching its legs, readying to enter the arena. We'd just walked past the Natural History Museum and were about to cross 82nd when Jean changed her mind and redirected us south. Half a block later, she turned into the elegant Endicott Hotel and pulled me with her into the main lobby. Passing the concierge and reception desk and loitering bellhops in pillbox hats, we came to a long room, marble tiled and lined with palm trees stretching high to a glass canopy. It was full of hotel guests, a chatty crowd in gowns and tuxedos occupying rows of low tables. Waiters in tight gold waistcoats freshened coffees, lit cigarettes, fetched evening newspapers. Altogether, the scene made me feel outnumbered.

"Shouldn't we leave?"

"Not yet," she said. "See that?" She pointed to an empty table with four unoccupied chairs. "You're probably wondering why nobody sits there."

"I am now."

"Nobody has dared since the tragic day in 1904 when the broken-hearted Don Carlos Frederico von Bauditz ..." She concluded with a pantomime, forming a pistol with her thumb and forefinger and firing an imaginary bullet into her temple.

"Right there at that table. In front of everyone. You see, Don Carlos fell in love with a French girl, but she didn't love him back. He was heir to a fortune in Venezuela. Twenty-six years old. That's only eight years older than me."

"How do you even know this story?"

"Stay at the Endicott long enough and you'll hear it, too."

"You stayed here?"

She nodded. "For ten months."

I laughed a little awkwardly until I realized she was serious.

"I didn't know you were rich."

"Ha, I'm not. Not rich at all."

Certain involuntary suspicions arose. A number of uncomplimentary thoughts. Sometimes, the mind can't help itself. "So someone else took care of the bills?"

"Careful, Arthur."

"I didn't mean …"

"Yes, you did," she said. "And you're dead wrong."

"I'm sorry."

"You'd better be. The money came from selling my parents' house in Michigan. Of course, by then, it was my house because my folks were dead. Fourteenth of June, 1922, if you were interested in the exact date."

"Both of them?"

"Yeah."

"On the same day?"

"On the *exact* same day. At the exact same time. To the second."

"But how?"

"That's actually the screwiest part about the whole damn thing. Let's get out of here."

Outside, we paused at a corner until a traffic cop gave us the signal to proceed. We mounted the opposite sidewalk where Jean continued her story.

"What happened was, they fell off the observation deck at the Woolworth Building."

"My God," I said. It seemed too incredible. "Did they have some kind of a pact?"

"Suicide? No! Why would you think *that*?"

"I don't know. Isn't it a bit unusual for two people to fall off a building at the same time?"

"I guess it would be."

"Also, you were just talking about some Venezuelan guy shooting himself in the head, so …"

"Well, when you put it that way, I can see your point. But it wasn't like that. No. What happened was they were on the observation deck, fifty storeys up, posing for a souvenir photograph, and they just kept backing up. Back and back and then ..." She turned her hand and swiped down. "Over they went."

"Don't they have a railing up there? Some kind of barrier? They must."

"Not one that was high enough, I guess."

"It's ... how do you ... I can't imagine."

"I know! That's exactly it. It's so crazy that you can't even imagine it ever happening. It's just *too* damn bizarre."

"I'm so sorry," I said.

"Thank you. You're very considerate. Not many people our age understand. Actually, it doesn't matter how old they are. Genuine compassion is hard to find these days." She weaved her hand into mine again. "The accident really is the weirdest thing. I still can't get over how *weird* it is. I'm trying, but I'm starting to think maybe I never will."

I wondered if, instead of "*is* the weirdest thing," she meant to say "*was* the weirdest thing," but it wasn't the right time to raise a petty point of grammar. Instead, we drifted along for a few minutes, up Broadway and under the flickering RKO marquee. Jean squeezed my hand, her fingertips between my knuckles, and held it tighter and then too tight, and just when I was about to shake free, she released and added something like a conclusion to her story.

"The Endicott was pretty nice, actually. They did my laundry and every day a lovely maid named Beata came to change the sheets and clean the room. I couldn't have asked for more. But then my money ran out. That place isn't cheap. Ten months of staying there sucked up everything my parents had worked their entire lives to save."

22

I WAS FLOODED WITH
PARALYZING MISGIVINGS

WE ENDED THE NIGHT AT HER ROOMING HOUSE. ON HER stoop's lowest step, I leaned in, intending a respectful peck on the cheek. We had been out at least seven or eight times, and I felt confident a kiss would be well received. But Jean turned her face the wrong way, sending us both off course. I landed close to her nose just as her lips pressed against the middle of my chin. We held the misaimed kiss for several seconds, until she pulled back and passed her latch key into my hand.

"Know how to use this?"

In the vestibule, she gave me the hush signal and pointed to my shoes. Hands clasped, we padded down the hall and up the stairs in our stocking feet. I understood her caution — women's hotels had strict rules — and didn't even mind the sneaking around. In fact, as I think about it now, the forced silence feathered my excitement.

In her room, I left my shoes near the door and laid my coat on an empty stool. She drew close and we shared a proper kiss.

She pulled back. "Do you think my head is too big?"

"For what?"

I steadied an all-over tremor by holding her tight. The carpet was warm under my feet. More kissing plus touching and fondling, and then I took off my shirt and unlatched my belt while her dress sort of melted around her ankles. She unclipped her garters, then raised a foot to a stool to remove a stocking, and I stared at the beautiful cavern that formed behind her knee.

She tossed her empty stockings into the middle of the room, adding to a general mess. The floor was strewn with skirts, blouses, and dresses, plus books and movie magazines. Stacks of dirty dishes took most of the space on her dresser. At the back of a small writing desk littered with pens, ink, and notebooks with warped pages was a photograph framed in etched silver. A stolid couple posed soberly, wearing prewar fashions. The man, seated, had Jean's curly hair. The woman behind, one hand on his shoulder, was surely the source of Jean's round cheeks.

"They look like good people."

"They were," she said, turning her head for a look. "But there's something about that picture I've never figured out: Is she leaning on him for support? Or is she holding him down?"

"Can't it be both?"

"I try not to think that way," she said, and kissed me again.

Under layers of woollen blankets, the air grew hot and scarce between us. Jean's fingers followed the valleys between my ribs, pausing where my heart thumped an arrhythmic beat.

"Did you bring anything?" she asked.

"Like what?"

"Like we don't want me to get pregnant, do we?"

"Oh no," I said. "Of course not."

"Well?"

"I didn't know we were going to ... I don't have anything. Do —" I stopped short, wondering at the propriety of asking a girl if she keeps condoms in her room.

Not for the last time, Jean read my mind. "Top drawer of the bureau," she said.

I slid off the mattress, opened the indicated drawer, and rummaged through a mass of delicate fabrics and ribbons. But when my hand found the little tin box, I was struck by a signal of some sort, noisy like the static that interferes with a clear radio signal but also with lights, white and red and purple, flickering in my head. I steadied myself on the edge of the dresser.

"What is it?" Jean asked.

"Nothing," I said. The interference, whatever it was, passed and I returned to the bed. Then, a few kisses later, with the package open, the rubber ready to unroll, it came on me again, this time louder and brighter. It lasted until I felt something switch off and I was suddenly flooded with paralyzing misgivings. I slapped the side of my head, hoping to drive it away.

"Are you okay?"

"I don't think so."

"What's wrong? Don't you feel well?"

"I feel fine. But ..."

"But what?"

"I don't know about doing this."

"What do you mean you don't know?"

"I like you. Very much."

"I know that."

"And I want to ..."

"That's pretty clear. Or it was until now."

"I just ..."

"What's going on?"

"I don't know. Honest. I don't ..." I wasn't lying. At that very moment, I felt detached and unable to connect to the person I'd been only seconds before.

"Arthur?"

"I don't know! I just can't, okay?"

"Aww, Christ!" She turned to the wall.

I pushed myself upright, angry, confused, still wanting to have sex with Jean but somehow unable to so much as touch her skin.

A stillness invaded the room, the waxy quiet of an empty church. I felt Jean's boiling frustration next to me as she struggled to understand. There aren't many reasons why a man in my position — young, healthy, naked in bed next to an attractive, equally naked woman he adores — suddenly loses the nerve, but I bet Jean had a good list going in her head. A secret wife? A diseased pecker? A preference for men?

Among all those possibilities, the excuses and explanations she may have considered, I am certain she never managed to stumble on the true killer of our joy that evening; that is, my consuming fear of being locked up for the next thirty years.

Because while Jean was composing her list, I was also trying to understand how this promising evening could have gone so suddenly wrong. Everything had been progressing so nicely until that flicker and light in my head when I reached for the box of rubbers in the top drawer. The drawer. The bureau drawer. *Bureau!* Was that it? Jean had used the word *bureau*, which is meaningless in ordinary circumstance but a whiz-banger of a problem when the same word brought to my mind to not only a place to keep clothes, but the Bureau of Investigation. Hearing it must have evoked Riley Triggs who, after drifting through the walls into Jean's bedroom, snaked his way into my head and laid ruin to what should have been a perfect evening.

Frustrated and ignorant of any of this, Jean used what she did know to arrive at her own conclusion. She sat up and turned on her bed lamp. "Do you want me to explain? About that night?"

"What night?" I asked, confused.

"You know what night. *That* night. Isn't that what's ... bothering you? Because I can explain if it'll help."

"No explanations needed," I said. "Not as far as I'm concerned." Was I saying so for her sake? Or mine?

She continued anyway. "It's not so much about that night, but there were some things that happened before that. Things that sort of led up to what happened with McElhinney and his wife."

"What's happening here has nothing to do with that night, believe me."

"It was actually all kind of the same night, when I think about it. The same long night. A single scene in a much longer show. Lots of actors. Only one actress, though."

Did she think telling me all this would make a difference? It wouldn't. Not tonight, anyway. Not as long as that Bureau stood four feet away. (Why couldn't she have just called it a dresser?)

"I'm telling you, it has nothing to do with you at all."

"So what is it, then?"

"I told you. I don't know!"

"Then how can you say it has nothing to do with me?"

"Because I can, okay? Just accept that, will you?" I sat up on the edge of the mattress and scanned the floor for my scattered clothes. "I should go," I said. "I have to work tomorrow."

"All right, then," Jean said, giving up the fight. Maybe more readily than I would have hoped.

I found my underwear and pants, slid into my shirt, and buckled my belt.

"Hurry up, then," she said. "And don't make any noise on your way out. This wasn't worth an eviction notice."

For as long as I live, I will never think of that night with anything but shame and regret. But over the forty or so blocks I walked and jogged from Jean's rooming house to Mrs. Lipoma's, I expended enough energy to straighten out my thinking. I concluded that ending things with Jean was the only way. Maybe the sex part could be remedied by a change of venue (or the swapping of furniture), but I didn't see how it could work in general when I was unable and forbidden to share some fundamental facts about my life. Since arriving in New York, I'd gotten pretty used to lying. Mrs. Lipoma, Sergio, Triggs. And Julian, who'd barely heard a single truthful word from me. I felt no pangs of remorse about this. I couldn't imagine any situation where I would prefer to go to prison than lie to my old landlady. But it was different with Jean. To be with her, I'd have to be honest. But that same honesty could land me in jail, which meant not being with Jean, the exact opposite of what I wanted. So there it was. I wished it hadn't been so ugly at the end, but splitting up was the only answer.

23

WE ARE GOING TO MAKE HISTORY

WHAT FOLLOWED WAS A MOODY, MOPEY MONTH. I STILL worked regular shifts at the Excelsior but slacked off when it came to Julian. I told Triggs he was still recovering from failing to sell the invention. "He hardly leaves his apartment."

Triggs accepted the explanation. He knew about disappointment.

Then one afternoon after work, I rode the subway north to Julian's buffet flat, hoping to learn something new. The madam, his landlady, met me at her front door.

"He's not living here now," she said.

Oh no. "Where did he go?" I asked.

She shrugged. "Didn't say where he was going to spend his nights now. Could be at the Benson. Could be the Olga. Lots of folks these days live at the Olga. Suppose he could be there with them. Could have found some other woman to take him in." She spat. Her gob landed with authority on the brown brick wall. She paused to admire its shape and viscosity, then went back inside.

He wasn't at the Benson or any of the other hotels I checked. Then the clerk at the Olga confirmed that yes, Julian was renting room 221 by the week. But my knocks received no answer. I wrote out a message on hotel stationery and returned to Mrs. Lipoma's to wait. When I didn't hear from him, it was back to the Olga the next day. Again, Julian was out, and no, he hadn't left any messages. On my third visit, the clerk didn't even let me ask.

"Understand that Lieutenant Julian is a busy man," he said.

"Just one more note," I said.

Please, I wrote. *It's important. I have urgent matters to discuss.* Later, I realized that these words put me in a bind. If he responded, I would have to find something to match the desperate tone. What urgent matters could I possibly have?

But he didn't answer that note, either. Now it had been a month, and I was undermining any goodwill I'd built with Triggs. I lay awake that night in the gloomy half dark of my half-empty room, half-crushed with worry about finding him. How long could I lie to Triggs? What would happen if I had actually managed to lose Julian?

Happily, I never had to answer those questions. I finally found him, only days before a dreaded debrief with Triggs. By pure chance, I spotted him at the first table at Frank P's (in restaurants, Julian always liked to sit near the front). In his serious dark suit and simple striped tie, he looked like a banker. He was leaning forward over the table, concentrating hard on the man seated opposite.

I rushed over, as though afraid he might vanish.

"Hubert Julian," I said. "What a thing to run into you! It's been too long. Did you get my notes? Hope I'm not interrupting. I left you three or four notes in the last week. But you're here. What a thing!"

"Arthur Tormes," Julian said. "An unexpected surprise." He rolled a flattened hand to present his friend. "May I introduce Mr. Clarence Chamberlin."

I remembered the name. It was Chamberlin who had piloted the Avro for Julian's parachute jump back in April. He would become famous a few years later, but in 1924, he was really known only in aviation circles. And yet, on that day, he didn't look like much of a pilot. There was a kind of carelessness to his appearance. Shadowy grease marks stained his canvas jacket; a lopsided square of stubble showed where that morning's razor had missed its mark. His eyes were weathered and wrinkled, surrounded by an excess of skin.

Julian continued. "You'll be interested to know about the matter Mr. Chamberlin and I have been discussing."

"I'm sure I would," I said, sliding uninvited into the seat next to Julian.

"I'll begin simply by saying this. We are going to make history."

"Sounds interesting already. Tell me more?"

"I'm going to fly across the Atlantic Ocean —" here Julian paused for drama, a showman even on this tiny stage with its audience of two "— solo."

"Solo?" I repeated. "You mean alone? Is that even possible?"

"Oh yes," Chamberlin said. "With the right machine and the right skills."

"Preserving fuel, steering by the stars, some mechanical elements I probably already know half of," Julian said. "The rest won't be so hard to pick up. A lot of it is instinct."

Chamberlin nodded. "Sure. A lot of it is just your common-sense stuff." He puffed on a cigarette wedged deep in his finger crotch.

"You know, that's remarkable," Julian said, "Billy Bishop said the same thing when he gave me my first flying lesson. Word for word."

"But all the way to Europe?" I said. "Solo?"

Chamberlin's eyes drooped. His big forehead and small mouth lent a plotter's look to his face. "Not to Europe. First, New York down to Natal —"

"That's in Brazil," Julian clarified.

"Natal's where you cross. To Liberia. That's your shortest distance, point to point. Then you're on to Ireland, back across to

Newfoundland, and home." Chamberlin's finger drew a wide circle in the air, pausing at the points on his imagined world map.

"Pan-Atlantic." I whistled. I couldn't help but be impressed. And it was genuine, too. The solo trans-Atlantic was the next big thing for our generation. Our race to the pole, our source of the Nile.

Chamberlin began to recite the technical elements. First, the vessel. "A seaplane," he began. "Biplane. Two pontoons, airtight. Not as fast or efficient as your mono but more stable in the air. The route you take across the water and back more or less follows the shipping lanes. If you get into trouble and have to ditch, there's a chance they spot you."

"Doesn't matter. I won't be ditching. I've always had luck on my side. Are you waiting for someone, Tormes? You keep looking around."

"Was I? I didn't realize."

"There's still a chance you go down," Chamberlin said. "Might as well be smart about it."

Julian and Chamberlin were glossing over the danger and I went along for the ride. I could have warned them about the Atlantic hurricanes and the house-high swells I had endured on the *Diego Hurtado*. I might have mentioned the terrible feeling when you realize you're all alone, well beyond the reach of any rescuers, and that death may well come with the next wave. But why spoil the mood?

Chamberlin continued. "You'll need a radio compass, gyroscope, drift meter, charts, batteries for lights. Fresh water and food, of course. Better bring a fishing line and hooks, too, just in case. The engine? Twenty-five hundred horses, minimum. Twelve cylinders. That should give you a range of two thousand miles, give or take, depending on the wind. Where are you with the money?"

"I have about eight grand," Julian said.

"You'll need more. A lot more."

Julian nodded. "I'll get it. Money's the last thing I'll let stand in my way. I'll rob a bank if I have to."

He laughed and Chamberlin laughed, and I joined in their happiness. As they dived deeper into the details of this great adventure, I let myself be taken in, setting my skepticism aside. Because if Julian competed the flight, he'd be an instant global celebrity. They'd pin medals across his chest, name schools and streets in his honour. He'd feature on every front page of every newspaper and magazine, like a prizefighter or Hollywood starlet. If that happened, Riley Triggs and the Bureau of Investigation would spend tens of thousands to keep tabs on him, paying real agents to do the job. Which would mean Triggs would no longer have need for an involuntary recruit like me.

DEBRIEF WITH SPECIAL AGENT RILEY TRIGGS
■ MARCH 29, 1924

—Cold, Tormes?

—It's just that I thought you told me to be here at five and now it's seven.

—See? Nobody likes to be kept waiting. That's another lesson you can thank me for. Besides, it's not that cold.

—I can't feel my feet.

—Tropical blood. Makes you soft. You see it with the coloureds up from the south. And the Puerto Ricans, too. Certain wops, even. They never get used to the cold. Just like if I went down to the islands. A short visit I could handle, but to live there? No. My system's not made for that kind of heat. You need to be in the right climate so your system won't fail. People don't always understand that. Look, you take a shark. In warm waters he's the most feared fish in the ocean. He thrives down there. Bring him up here and a minnow'd chase him all the way back. We all have our place in this world, and that's where we all ought to stay. It makes a lot of earthly sense, if you think about it.

—...

—I hear you got yourself a new girlfriend.

—No.

—Jeannette Fox? Born 15 June, 1905, Port Huron, Michigan. Employed at the *New York Sun*. Unmarried. Parents deceased. Likes parties.

—Jean? Oh no, sir. That was just a casual thing. We went out a few times but nothing more. It's over now.

—Yeah, a few more than a few is my understanding.

—Now that I count, sure. Seven or eight times. But like I said, that's history.

—I just hope she's not still fucking that guy from the Chemical Bank. You know which one I'm talking about, don't you?

—...

—The one with the crazy wife? You know? Bang-bang?

—I know who you mean.

—Don't get tough with me. All I'm saying is that someone could get hurt. I'm watching out for you, Tormes. Remember that.

—...

—What do you have on Julian?

—I got a good look at the plane. It's a Boeing Model C. One of those seaplanes with the pontoons instead of wheels. I wouldn't say it's a very fit plane just now. Clarence Chamberlin, the mechanic —

—Is Chamberlin a coloured?

—He's from Iowa.

—Go on.

—Chamberlin is going to put in bigger gas tanks and navigation instruments and the like. But I don't know. I figured he would buy a new plane, all the most recent technology. But this one is old, left over from the war. When Chamberlin started the engine it made an awful racket and spewed black smoke.

—Do you still think he can do it?

—I have to say that seeing that plane gave me some doubts.

—How's he going to pay for it?

—He needs eight thousand more dollars. He said he'd rob a bank if he had to.

—He said that?

—Yes, but he was joking, sir.

—Did he say which bank? When?

—I'm sure he doesn't really plan to rob a bank.

—So? Where's the money coming from?

—He's going to sell the McFarlan, and then he plans to get the rest with a direct appeal.

—To who?

—The people.

—His people?

—Any people. I volunteered to help him.

—And?

—He agreed.

—Why would he want you?

—I couldn't say.

—Does he suspect something? Did you blow your cover?

—No.

—So you just volunteered. And he agreed?

—That's right.

—Right now for him, fundraising is the most important thing. And he wants *you* to do it? The turd I crapped out this morning is more qualified than you to raise eight grand.

—...

—...

—He wants me to find sponsors.

—Okay. Do that. Do a good job, too.

—Yes, sir.

—Fundraising's a place where someone without a head for numbers can go wrong. That would be useful.

—...

—...

—Agent Triggs? Could I ask a question?

—Ask away. Don't know if I'll answer.

—In the event of ... say Julian crashes. I mean, say he ... dies.

—Say he does.

—What happens to me?

—...

—...

—We'll have to see, I guess.

24

WE MANAGED TO WRIGGLE AROUND OUR SECRECIES

THAT WEEKEND, I TOLD JEAN ALL ABOUT IT.

"The Atlantic?" she said. "City or ocean?"

"Incredible, isn't it?"

We were on our way to the Rialto for an early afternoon double feature, *Safety Last!*, starring Harold Lloyd and Mildred Davis, followed by *Our Hospitality*, with Buster Keaton, always one of Jean's favourites. Seeing a movie had been her suggestion. She called a few days before, the first we'd talked since the break-up.

"There's no point being angry with each other, is there?" she began.

"No, there isn't," I said.

"Sometimes things don't work out. Sometimes we don't know why. So what?"

"Exactly. So what?"

"And we both like movies, right?"

"Yes we do."

"So why shouldn't go see a movie, then?"

Plenty of reasons, I thought. But instead: "I couldn't agree more."

Along the way and as we took our seats in the theatre, I told her about Chamberlin, his plans for the biplane, how Julian planned to follow the shipping lanes from Brazil to Liberia, how I was going to help him raise funds for the flight.

"He's brave," she said. "I'll give him that. Those jumps took real guts. For most people it would be enough. Do you think he can make it?"

"Why not?"

"Well, for one, it's crazy. For two, it's dangerous. For three, it's never been done before."

"There's a first for everything."

"You should talk him out of it,"

"Why would I do that?"

"You're his friend, aren't you?"

"Well, sure. But he wants to make history. I could never tell him he shouldn't try."

"I wonder if that's what Franz Reichelt's friends thought?"

"This has nothing to do with Franz Reichelt," I said. "Besides, I'm not so much his friend that I can talk him out of something he's determined to do."

"God, do you know how deep the ocean is out there? That poor bastard could sink for days before hitting bottom. If the sharks or giant squids don't get him first."

Safety Last! came as advertised and we were in stitches from the start, right up until the big finish, when the Harold Lloyd character escapes from the police by scaling up the wall of a downtown skyscraper. He almost falls about twenty times and in twenty different ways, all for thrills and laughs, but when he scrambled up to the top ledge, about thirty storeys above the street, I wondered if the scene would remind Jean of what happened to her parents on the Woolworth tower. But when I looked, her eyes were glued to the screen. She was laughing as hard as anyone in the theatre, all the way to when Lloyd lands in Mildred Davis' waiting arms.

Between features, they ran a short spot warning about the dangers of cheap home brews and bathtub gins (*Beware! Blindness Is No Bargain!*), followed by something lighter, a reel from last years' college football season, including highlights of a big game, Wolverines versus the Golden Gophers.

Jean threw an elbow into my ribs. "Look," she said, "that's Michigan! Go Blue!" She leaned forward in her seat, brought her hands together, and steadied her chin on her fingertips to concentrate. On the screen above us, cheerleaders in matching sweaters bounced and flipped and tumbled, rousing the fans. Bands marched up and down the field. Spectators in long coats smoked, doffed their hats, and waved wildly for the camera. Then came the game highlights. Kickoffs and returns. Long runs and scores. Fumbles and scrambles in the mud. I didn't understand the rules, but when I turned to Jean to ask who was winning, thick streams of tears were streaking down her cheeks.

"Are you okay?

She shook her head, too upset to speak. I tried soothing strokes on her forearm and when that didn't work, I wrapped an arm around her shoulders, hoping to quiet the trembling.

As the second feature began, the movie music had to compete head-on with Jean's wailing, which had grown louder since the end of the newsreel. An unsympathetic audience shushed and complained. I felt her clenching and fighting with herself, trying to stop. Soon, a flashlight beamed down our row. I helped Jean to her feet, gathered our coats, and led her out the side exit.

Mrs. Lipoma's was closer, so I took Jean to my room, the first time she'd seen my dingy quarters. I gave her the wobbly desk chair and sat beside her on my bed, holding her hand, until the tears finally slowed. Did I ask what the matter was? No, of course not. Instead, I put water on for tea. Jean remained seated, her breathing growing gradually more normal, while I stirred sugar into her cup. I tried to talk to her without talking about anything. She thanked me for the tea, calmed by its warmth and sweetness, and after she'd drained her cup she went to the bathroom to wash her face and fix her wild curls.

When she returned, instead of taking the chair again, she bent to my face and kissed me. A long, deep kiss, clear in its intent. I waited for the same debilitating flicker of light but thankfully, it never came. I reached for the top button on her blouse. We did not leave my room until Tuesday, when we both had to go to work.

All in all, I would say that this was a strange sequence of events. Jean's phone call, the movie, the newsreel, the tears, a weekend in bed. I'd convinced myself that any kind of relationship was impossible. In that way, nothing had changed. And yet, we were at it again.

It wasn't just me. At that point it was clear that Jean was also incapable of total honesty. We both harboured our individual secrets. Maybe this should have been more of a problem, this apparent obstacle to mutual trust. But it wasn't. In fact, it seemed like our being together would actually depend on maintaining the integrity of those secrets. This was how I saw it and I think she felt the same way, though of course I had no way of knowing and no way to ask.

Maybe I was too young. Maybe I was too eager for love, too hopped up on sex, to understand the peril of such an arrangement, how some conditions just aren't negotiable. Possibly. Probably. I don't really know. But on that weekend and on many nights and days that followed, we managed, without effort or strife, to wriggle around our secrecies. At the time, it was just sensible for me to accept Jean's secrets if it meant I didn't have to reveal any of my own.

Thinking about all of that now, I wonder how in the world I could ever believe such an arrangement could ever last.

25

I FELT THE PECULIAR, PARADOXICAL ALIGNMENT OF OUR INTERESTS

TO SELL THE MCFARLAN, JULIAN HAD ME PLACE ADS IN A few papers. We got a few bites, including one from a Bahamian dentist and his wife out on Long Island. For the road test, the couple climbed in back with Julian and I drove them through Astoria and then back to Manhattan by the Queensboro Bridge. In the back seat, Julian and the couple conversed amiably. Sunshine gleamed off the chrome accents; I was glad for the extra time I'd spent polishing the windows and mirrors.

On the bridge, we overtook a hearse covered in white carnations, and as we passed over Blackwell's Island I eased up next to a long, cream-coloured Rolls convertible. A pair of snappily dressed men chattered in the front seat, something to do with a small photograph in the passenger's hand. The passenger turned and scanned our party. Our eyes met and his mouth flinched into a dismissive smirk.

Julian ordered me to pass. "Let's show our friends how the car performs when you open her up," he said.

I glared at the smirking man and hit the accelerator, but too hard. The transmission skipped and the power drained from the engine. We had to pull over to restart. In the end, the dentist paid less than Julian had hoped.

In mid-April, Julian hit the road to fundraise. North to Syracuse. West to Chicago. South to Durham and Atlanta. I made the arrangements: train tickets, hotels, confirmations. I set up accounts at different banks all over the country to make it easier for locals to donate. As Julian put it, "Geography should not be an impediment to breaking barriers!"

Good idea, I thought, and once again felt the peculiar, paradoxical alignment of our interests. I had no guarantees from Triggs, of course, and I still wasn't at all sure what Julian's success or failure would mean for me. Until I knew more, it was best to keep up appearances with unwavering support.

While he travelled, I stayed back in New York and tracked him through out-of-town newspapers. It should have been a big story from the start, but the Negro press paid little attention, running tiny items among other tiny items. Gradually, too slowly for my liking, their interest increased. Finally, Julian made the front page of the *Norfolk Journal and Guide* with this headline: "Plans to Fly Around the World in One Month's Time."

Slightly inaccurate, I thought, though not likely a mistake that would hurt us. I read the smaller headline below. "Lieutenant Hubert Julian to Be to the Air What Magellan Was to the Sea."

Terrific analogy, I thought. I put down a dollar for ten extra copies and while the vendor made out the receipt, I read the rest of the article, pleased with Julian's first quote. "My life is consecrated to this venture. I will sacrifice it for my people's good."

Very well put. Dramatic, determined.

The quote continued. "There is a hard and fast rule against colored men in the air service and the aviation schools and since I have demonstrated to the world at large that a colored man can become a successful aviator, I intend to open up to members of my race an opportunity in this very lucrative field."

Just great stuff. Proof of his character and generosity, his noble mindedness. The readers of Norfolk could have no doubt that Hubert Julian was a man worthy of their donations!

But then, "I was born in Trinidad and my father was a wealthy cocoa planter. I went to McGill in Canada and received my medical degree. They were short on surgeons in the aviation corps and, as I had already become an aviator, I was sent to France. I was shot and was contained for some time in a hospital at Nice. After my discharge, I qualified as a pilot and was a first lieutenant when the war was over."

None of which was true. Not McGill, not medicine, not France, not the rank. To fit so much bullshit into so few sentences was the real achievement. But why? His story was compelling enough on its own. He didn't have to lie to get onto the front page.

"Why?" I asked when I saw him next. "The lies will only hurt us if someone gets around to asking a few questions."

"What questions?" We were in his living room, bundled in winter coats. Something was off with the furnace.

"Questions! Any question! At McGill or in the Canadian aviation corps."

"I tried to join the army, but my father fixed it so I couldn't."

"Or in that hospital in Nice."

"Nobody's going to call anybody in Nice," he said. He had me there. A cross-Atlantic fact check, a considerable expense for a smaller newspaper, seemed pretty unlikely.

"There's a paper trail," I said. "How are you going to respond?"

"Does it matter?"

"In general, people don't like liars. It could sink us."

"Nobody's going to remember a few fibs once I've crossed the Atlantic. Hell, Tormes, in this world we're surrounded by liars. Everywhere. Here's an advertisement for reducing cream. You think rubbing this grease on your belly will shrink it? Salesmen, preachers. Every politician ever elected. Who remembers what lies Jefferson told? What truths Napoleon stretched?"

"I don't think Napoleon ever stood for election," I muttered. "Mind if I put a kettle on?"

He trailed me into his kitchen, which smelled of recent and vigorous cleaning, and concluded his argument over the rushing water.

"People need something to believe in. I have to convince them I'm worthy of their belief before they'll invest in me. Now, I dress well and have a compelling way of speaking, but that goes only so far. I add a little seasoning. So I told them I was a doctor. So I told them I'd been wounded."

I lit the gas and laid the kettle on top, pulled his pot down from an upper shelf. Julian waited for me to deliver my next point, which would have been something about offending actual veterans. But I was suddenly snagged by my own hypocrisy. Lying too much? Hell, I'd been lying to Hubert Julian since the day I met him. And not just Julian. I'd lied to Triggs about Jean and lied to Jean by not telling her about Triggs. In fact, I was lying to Julian right now.

I spooned tea into the pot and shrugged capitulation, dropping the argument mid-round, like a boxer on the take. But Julian refused to accept my surrender.

"You know what I think? I think those people in Norfolk might have suspicions. They might wonder about McGill or Nice or France. I wouldn't doubt it at all. You ever play the numbers with Casper Holstein?"

"Gambling's for suckers," I said.

"And God knows I've said the same to many friends who play with money they cannot afford to lose. But you know what? The man who plays Casper's numbers buys something."

"A chance at a big payoff."

"An unlikely chance. But no, that's not it. What that quarter or dollar buys — what it *guarantees* — is this: a night or two of imagination, some good hours playing out the dreams of his life.

His sweet, private dreams. Getting the bear off his back. Or maybe a down payment on a car. Or just a new pair of fancy shoes he can wear next time he goes out on the town with his best girl. It's a wonderful dream. All his own. And all for the price of a single play. Now that's a pretty damn good deal, wouldn't you say?"

"Maybe," I said. "But dreams are dreams. Your lies are being recorded in ink. I'm telling you, it's going to hurt us eventually. You should stop."

26

SPARE YOUR SKIN!

WE CARRIED ON. JULIAN DELIVERED SPEECHES AT RALLIES in Philly, Newark, and New Haven. Donations, some large but mostly small, flowed steadily. He repeated the lies he had told in Norfolk but I kept quiet, having decided that his methods were his methods, the consequences his burden.

I began to devote more of my free hours to prospecting sponsorship, thinking that if I could nab just one, neither Triggs nor Julian would have reason to gripe. I made a long list of companies who advertised in Black newspapers or on billboards in Harlem. Realtors and shoe shops, dance schools and haberdashers. An outfit that taught people how to win at card games. Another that promised to fix bad posture. Each night, I typed, addressed, stamped, and mailed a dozen or more letters. None of the recipients were interested; most didn't bother to respond.

I sharpened my strategy, narrowing my targets. I visited the Fair Weather Life Vest Company, thinking Julian made the right kind of spokesman, someone who understood the value of a reliable life vest. Interesting idea, they said. But not so interesting to cut a cheque. I pitched Standard Oil with an offer of exclusivity: "Standard: Official Fuel of the First Solo Trans-Atlantic Flight."

"What did they say?" Jean asked later.

"They wanted no part of it," I said. "They reckon that if Julian crashes —"

"Which he probably will —"

"They reckon that if Julian crashes, someone's bound to blame the gasoline."

Jean and I had intended to see a movie that night but when I arrived at her building, she could see my exhaustion and kindly led me back upstairs. Now we were on her bed, Jean propped against a pair of pillows, my head resting on her stomach.

"I see their point," she said.

"Why would anyone blame the gasoline?" I yawned. "The weather, the pilot, the machine, but the gasoline?"

"Don't be so sure," she said. "The sanest people you know will go nutty when people they love die. Who's next on your list?"

"I need to make a new list."

I shifted my head until the tip of my nose barely touched the curving underside of her breast. Sometimes I liked to touch her that way, with accidental, even undetectable lightness. I closed my eyes while Jean ran her fingertips across my head. I heard the rustling sound of my hair being reordered. Her fingers moved to my face and traced soothing shapes over my cheeks, nose, and lips. I wanted to sleep. I wanted to be with Jean and sleep at the same time.

"I have an idea," she said.

"I'm just so tired."

"Not that," she said. Her fingers moved to my jaw and pushed at the skin and stubble like a sculptor pushes at shapeless clay. "What about a razor company? Gillette or Ever Ready or GEM?"

"What would he need a razor for? No one's even going to see him until he gets to Africa."

"*If* he gets to Africa, which would be a miracle."

"So you've said."

"So that's it, dummy."

"I don't get it."

"What's more like a close shave than a flight across open ocean?"

The next day, in letters sent to every razor fabricator in America, I repeated her exact words: *What's more like a close shave than a flight across open ocean?* Only four days later, I received a response from GEM, special delivery, promising five hundred dollars for the exclusive right to have the brand name painted on the fuselage.

That was Jean Fox. My girlfriend.

27

I FELT AMBUSHED

I COULD HARDLY BELIEVE IT. FIVE HUNDRED DOLLARS! Electrified by the good news, I rushed over to tell Julian. He whooped and slapped my back. We celebrated at Frank's on 125th. Baked breast of lamb. Stewed mushrooms and fried sweet potatoes. Julian even used the secret word, and the waiter brought me cold beer in a chilled mug.

A week or so later, we met to discuss our next steps. Things were moving pretty fast now. On the Harlem-bound subway I reviewed the statements. Including the GEM money, we had close to four grand, almost half of what we needed to buy the Boeing outright. With only two months left before the July 4 target, time was tight. Labour Day might be more realistic.

I stopped at the first kiosk outside the 125th Street Station, where the latest magazines hung on a line like laundry. I scanned the fresh newspapers stacked on the ground and lower shelves. My eyes caught a familiar name in the headlines. Hubert Julian had made page one again, this time on the latest *Defender*, perhaps the most important paper in Black America in those days. Things are really going his way, I thought. And then took a closer look at the headline, all-caps and five columns wide.

LIEUT. JULIAN AN IMPOSTER, SAYS WIFE

I felt ambushed. With no one else around, I looked to the news agent, thinking that somebody owed me an explanation. Wife? Yes. I remembered that rent party (it would have been about a year before) when Julian had said something about a brief marriage to a woman in Canada. But she'd died. He missed her every day, he had said.

I paid for the copy and read the full article. This supposed wife's name was Edna Powell and yes, she'd come from Montreal, crawled out of her grave and down to New York to denounce her runaway husband in the press. She alleged abuse and abandonment. She produced a letter from Julian, reprinted in the *Defender*, in which he confessed to infidelities. She said she had filed for separation but Julian had refused to see her.

With the newspaper jammed into my pocket, I proceeded to Julian's apartment, stomped up the stairs, and pounded on his door. Still buzzing about the GEM win, he welcomed my scowling face inside. Before I could show him the front page, he disappeared into his little kitchen, returning with a box, plates, and forks. "Lady downstairs makes a tasty key lime," he said. He opened the box, releasing sweet fruity smells. "Sit down and let me cut you a five-hundred-dollar slice."

I did not sit. "Maybe you should save it," I said. "In case the missus drops by."

"The missus?"

Part of me savoured that moment. I liked the power that came with holding onto information Julian did not have. I let his ignorance linger a beat or two more before producing the *Defender*. "I'm talking about Edna Powell Julian. Your wife."

He set the pie on the table and snatched the paper from my hand.

"Is this the wife you told me about? The wife who died?"

"Let me read, would you?"

"I guess she pulled through in the end."

"Oh please, Tormes."

"She claims you're an imposter. Not even a pilot."

"She's lying, of course. Anyone can see it."

"So it's true? You're married? And you just left her? Abandoned your own wife?"

But Julian was still reading or re-reading, his frown hardening as he moved down the column and on to page three, where the story continued. "Colossal faker? Charlatan? How can she say those things? After everything I did for her. The woman should be thanking me. And here. What? I never once beat her. Another lie! I'll sue her. The *Defender*, too. It's slander!" As he ranted, his accent shifted island-ward, the words delivered faster, the inflections more vigorous.

"Why didn't you tell me any of this?"

"I don't need to share every detail of my life with you."

"This kind of thing? A wife you abandoned? Yes. You do."

He crumpled the paper and tossed it into the garbage bin. "Me and Edna were together for a few months. That's all. I practically forgot all about her."

"Jesus, Hubert. This isn't some lie about the army. This is a moral issue. It's going to kill us, especially with women."

"Us?" he said. "Last time I checked, *I'm* the pilot."

"Yesterday you were a heartbroken widower. Today you're a heartless wife deserter. You wouldn't let her into the apartment? Is that true?"

"That's one more lie they told. First thing tomorrow, I'm calling a lawyer."

"Suing won't help you now."

"Everybody in the world's got marriage problems."

"Problems? You've been telling people she's dead! I told you —"

"Don't. Do not say it."

I sat down and tempered my voice. "All I'm saying, Hubert ... is that this thing could be a whale-sized problem."

Now Julian sat, too. "I was young. She was young," he sighed.

"She hired the Boulin Agency," I said.

"Boulin is low-life scum."

"He's good. My old boss, Cleaves, admired him."

"That she hired Boulin tells you just what kind of woman she is." Now he returned to the kitchen and retrieved the paper from the bin, uncrumpling and brushing off some coffee grounds. (He'd made the front page, so of course he wanted a copy.)

"You know what? I'll say a few things about her, too. I'll correct that record. You think living with her was a picnic? It wasn't. And let me ask you this: Who do you figure the people will believe? What would they prefer? To see a Black man be the first to cross the Atlantic? Or to destroy him — and along with him the hopes of our race — because of some fib?"

"The woman wants her pound of flesh."

"She can't have it. And besides, half of whatever I give her will go Boulin's way. That's how he operates. He's a leech."

"Give her the money. Give her the alimony she wants. Make her promise to keep her mouth shut. Make her sign something." From divorce raiding, I knew such agreements existed.

"Twenty-five a week is a lot of money. And the two-hundred-fifty on top of that? I'm trying to buy an airplane, remember? No, Tormes, I don't think so."

"Give it to her and be done with it. Do you really want this hanging around your neck?"

Julian paused. He leaned on the door frame and looked to the ceiling. He looked at me again. "Are you sure?" he asked.

The truth? I wasn't sure. Keep quiet? Give in? Fight her? I didn't know the woman, couldn't guess how she'd act one way or another. How aggrieved was she? How vengeance-minded? But still riding the tailwinds of the GEM sponsorship win, which (thanks to Jean) gave me the illusion I was capable of intelligence and sound decision-making, I stayed firm.

"Give her the money. You know the papers," I said. "If you're going to buy the plane, you need the public behind you. If you fight her, you'll be headline news for weeks, even months, and not for good reasons, either. You pay up now, we move on, and whole thing is stale bread in a week. Then we'll raise the rest of the dough for the Boeing while Boulin buzzes off to other dung heaps."

Julian thought about what I had said, glanced again at the *Defender's* front page, and then re-crumpled the paper and dropped it into wastebasket. This being his way of acknowledging, as he rarely did, that I was right.

28

HE PRACTICALLY MURDERED
THOSE SPIKES

THE CHEQUE FROM GEM IMPRESSED CLARENCE Chamberlin, and he agreed to let the Black Eagle take the Boeing from the hangar in Washbrook Heights to a lot on 135th Street, where we put the plane on display for all to see. It was an answer to an unspoken prayer. The papers, having forgotten about Edna Powell, sent photographers, prompting scores of curious visitors to line up along 135th and pay half a dollar for a closer look at the history-making aircraft.

To help his own cause, Julian painted a message on the fuselage: *This Plane Is the Property of the Negro Race, Donated by Them for Their Future in Aviation.* He named the craft the *Ethiopia I* and coloured the tail in green, red, and black. The lines continued to grow, the money accumulated, and by my next debrief, I told Triggs I believed Julian stood a decent chance of raising the money needed in time for his planned takeoff on the 4th of July.

"Though August first might be more realistic," I added.

The Black Eagle practically lived with the Boeing, watching over it like a mother robin guarding a precious single egg. Arriving at sunrise, leaving after dusk, he dressed each day in his pale-blue aviator's uniform, brass buttons and stiff boots polished, garrison cap tilted smartly over one eye.

His strongest support came from West Indian ex-pats, and Julian catered his pitch accordingly. He laid out a map on the *Ethiopia*'s lower wing and with a hovering finger traced his route down to Brazil, over to Africa, up to Europe, and back. But depending on the audience, the plan could change. With a Bajan family, Julian steered the finger over Bridgetown. He assured a Jamaican woman he would fly directly over her mother's house in Port Antonio and even used his watch to calculate the hour. "Should be there about eight in the evening," he said.

"Oh no. It'll be too dark and her eyes are bad."

"Then I'll put on the gas and be sure to arrive before sundown."

With women who came alone, he drew his mouth closer to their ear and promised perfumes from Paris, which sometimes prompted a second donation. For a few dollars more, he strapped into the seat behind the controls, started the engine, and made the flaps and rudder wave.

Each afternoon, I checked in with the banks then went to the lot to report on the day's take. One Wednesday night I arrived just as Julian was wrapping up. Maybe the late-day light flattered its appearance, but I thought the Boeing looked magnificent. Fit, strong, capable. Clarence Chamberlin had done a fine job fixing it up. I ran my hand along the wood propeller, its polished, carved curves. It was an honour just to touch it. If Julian completed his flight in this Boeing, some museum would acquire it and display it forever and for all the world to see. Like an ancient urn or the mummies they were always digging up over in Egypt.

I helped Julian unfold the heavy grey tarp he used at night so that nobody got a free look. We pulled lines looped through grommets, tied them off, and secured them with railway spikes. I was hammering away, enjoying the rhythmic clanging, when a man entered the lot, asking for Lieutenant Julian.

"You have to come back tomorrow," Julian said without raising his head. "The *Ethiopia* is covered for the night."

"I'm not here to see the plane," the man said. He wore striped trousers and a long, unbuttoned blue raincoat. Skinny and slight shouldered, he did not present a physical menace. But the way his eyes stared dryly from behind rimless glasses left me uneasy.

"My name is James Amos," he announced. "United States Department of Justice." He stepped from shadow into a streetlamp's first glow, stopping about ten feet from where we stood, the hammers and spikes still weighing down our hands.

"I know who you are," Julian said.

I knew the name, too. A lot of people did, for better or worse. One of the few Black agents in Hoover's Bureau, Amos had been part of the same Garvey task force as Triggs. Before that, he'd been a bodyguard for Teddy Roosevelt.

None of this made an impression with Julian. "What do you want?" he said.

"Just a friendly visit," Amos said. "I see you've been conducting a little drive for funds in the community."

"That's right. Though I don't see why that's your concern. Or the government's."

"Well, Lieutenant, it is. It's definitely a concern. There is a law against collecting funds through the mail for fraudulent purposes. Just like your old pal Marcus Garvey."

"There's no fraudulent purpose here," I said. "I opened the accounts. Every penny goes straight to paying off this aircraft. I can show you the statements."

"And we never used any photo in any publicity," Julian added.

"But you will fly this airplane? Across the Atlantic? On Independence Day?"

"Of course I will."

"Well, that's fine, then. So long as you do what's been promised — that is, so long as those funds go where you say they're going — you have nothing to fear." He took half a step back before continuing. "But I beg to inform you that if, for any reason, that promised flight doesn't take place on the promised date, you can expect consequences."

"What kind of consequences?" I asked. I was thinking about those accounts and my signature on all the papers.

"That, friend, would be for a judge to decide," he said. He avoided specifics. Better for him. An undefined threat fertilizes fear; the scariest monster is the one you can't see. In the closet. Under the bed. I understood the strategy from the way Triggs used it with me. In fact, this Amos reminded me of Triggs in a few ways.

"Of course, you could always give all the money back," Amos said. "With signed receipts from every donor, we'd have no reason to prosecute." Then he touched the bill of his fedora. "You all have a good evening."

Once Amos cleared the lot, Julian loosened his collar. His breathing deepened. A sheen of sweat appeared on his forehead.

"Are you okay, Hubert?"

The Black Eagle swallowed and gazed into the darkening sky, his face twisted. He looked like he'd just realized he'd been standing in quicksand. It didn't last long, less than a few seconds, but I was sure I'd never before seen him look so rattled.

"Hubert?"

"Fine," he said. "Of course I'm fine. Why wouldn't I be?"

"'Cause of what Amos said?"

"You can see what he's doing, can't you? Same as Boulin and my ex-wife. It's obvious now, isn't it? They can't stand to see me winning. Hell, Boulin probably sent him over." He picked up the end of a rope. "Let's get this tarp down and go home."

We pulled, looped, and tied. I worked slowly, wondering if Amos was really Boulin's doing. Maybe. Boulin definitely had connections somewhere in the Bureau. But in my mind, I pictured Riley Triggs as the more likely mastermind. Maybe he was worried that Julian's pan-Atlantic flight would succeed, that his power and popularity would put him out of Triggs' own reach and someone else — maybe Hoover himself — would take the glory for bringing Julian down. But if that was so, Triggs could have ordered me to dial back the fundraising. Or to lose the cheque from GEM. Then again, maybe he actually *wanted* Julian to land safely in Africa and get famous. Big game might be more dangerous, but they also make for bigger targets. Such confusion. Sometimes, I wondered if Riley Triggs actually had a strategy.

There was something else that bothered me. I had no reason to ever trust the man, but for Triggs to send James Amos suggested he'd had lost faith in me.

In the sulphur-lit gloom, we moved down the tarp, swinging our hammers. Julian finished his side ahead of me, made the turn around the tail, then knocked down a few more spikes with powerful arching swings. He was practically murdering those things. Two big knocks and the head was flush to the ground. What would he do with that hammer if he knew I'd had a part in bringing Agent James Amos to the lot?

The last spike driven down, we tossed the tools into an open box.

"What are you going to do?" I asked.

"Go home," he said.

"I meant about Amos, about what he said."

"Amos can rot in hell with the rest of them. I'm going to raise the money, and then I'm going to fly."

I remembered Julian's father, a rich man in Trinidad. Plenty of people fund their dreams with family money. It seemed like a sensible idea, but Julian shook me off, shocked at the suggestion.

"I wouldn't do that," he said.

"A loan, even. To be paid back, with interest."

"This is something I have to do on my own."

"I get the pride, Hubert. But what if you don't raise the money in time?"

"All my life, people like Amos have been trying to get in my way. Guess what? Every one of them failed."

He kicked the tool box under the tarp. Sharp stones scraped against the metal shell.

"We're a ways off what you need, money-wise," I said. "Shouldn't you at least consider returning the donations? You could start again. Next time, when you advertise, you leave out the date."

He rolled his sleeves down to his wrists, slid his arms into his suit jacket, and placed his hat at the preferred angle. Looking at him, you wouldn't have guessed he'd just pounded in a dozen railway spikes, much less faced the threats of a federal agent.

We started together toward the sidewalk. "I'm just saying, Hubert. He probably meant what he said. I mean ... Garvey."

"Those charges were trumped up."

"You think that matters now? He's still headed for the jug."

He gave me a sudden hard slap on the back. I lurched forward.

"Don't worry, Tormes," he said, smiling. "I'm lucky, remember? Too lucky to ever go to prison."

We proceeded in our separate directions, destined for our separate homes. At Seventh, next to a fruit stand and the first strawberries of summer, I waited for traffic. I wondered about Hubert Julian and his notion of luck. I wondered if it made him the most confident man I'd ever known. Or just the most deluded.

29

YOU CAN'T PUT A PRICE ON FREEDOM, BUT THERE IT WAS

JULIAN EVEN GOT LUCKY WITH THE WEATHER. JULY 4TH, 1924, was a windless day, the sky crystal blue and haze free, perfect conditions for flying. I arrived at the lot several hours before take-off. A small crowd had already gathered to witness his preparations.

Julian was dressed for flight: the familiar airman's suit and high cordovan boots with tiny silver spurs on the heels. He was leaning against the *Ethiopia*'s lower wing, unhappy with an article in the *World*.

"The most sensational story of the year and they dump it on page five! *And* they got the facts wrong. Fifteen hundred short? How much is it, really?"

"Fourteen hundred and twenty-eight dollars," I said.

Unfortunately, the *American* and the *World* were the only two papers to run anything about him at all. The other dailies ignored him. He folded the newspaper and tossed it to the ground. "I can't catch a damn break."

"I talked to a lot of editors. They all said they'd talk to you once you landed."

"Did you mention the parachuting?"

"Of course."

"Did you tell them I was trained by Billy Bishop?"

"Nobody knows that name here."

"Idiots."

"But didn't you see the *American*? The writer there called you the Booker T. Washington of flying."

He shook his head. "How do they get away with it?"

"Their loss," I said.

And I meant it. The Boeing looked good. Earlier, Chamberlin had pronounced the engine ready. The GEM Safety Razors logo glowed with fresh white letters large enough to see for miles. If everything went well, that logo would make front pages in Trinidad, Brazil, Liberia, France, and England. I should have asked for more money.

Because as it was, we were still short. We had sweated for every penny but donations in the last weeks had slowed. As the clock struck eleven, Julian still owed $1,387. I accosted every newcomer, anyone who came within shouting distance to the lot. I sold autographed photos and round buttons with a picture of Julian in his leather helmet, the bug-eyed goggles resting easy on his crown.

Some people bought one or the other, and Jean Fox contributed five dollars and a good-luck kiss, but with only thirty minutes before his scheduled takeoff, we were still several hundred short.

Moved by the same desperation, Julian climbed to the *Ethiopia*'s upper wing, spreading his arms for quiet.

"Folks, I'm a little short on the cash I need to buy this plane outright and make my historic journey. Now, I know you're all proud people and you want to see me succeed. But I need your help here. I need you to reach on down deep into your pockets and pull out whatever coins or bills you can find and donate them to this great cause of Negro aviation."

This was not how either of us had imagined it. If only Edna Powell had stayed in Montreal. And what a shame we'd had to rely so much on individual donations. Three weeks back, I'd thought of taking out a loan, using the Boeing as collateral. Julian initially liked the idea. In half-a-dozen banks, I'd barely got past the guard at the front door.

"Told you," Julian said. "Stupid idea."

At one o'clock, Julian announced an hour's delay. The crowd, which had grown tenfold over the last thirty minutes, groaned but remained in good spirits. Vendors cleaned up selling hot dogs and drinks. I spotted Clarence Chamberlin watching from the back fringes. His relationship with Julian puzzled me. I would not say they were great friends — in fact, as far as I knew, Julian didn't have any close friends — but they shared membership in an exclusive brotherhood of adventurers. And yet, as the delay stretched on, Chamberlin looked a little embarrassed, standing with both hands in his pockets between the plane's two owners, a couple of gloomy businessmen from Newark who'd been waiting months for the rest of their money.

I shuffled through the still-expanding mob in their direction. I thought I might be able to talk to them, maybe convince one or the other to make a deal. I asked Clarence for a word.

"A proposal — let Hubert fly now. When he gets back, he'll pay them twice what he owes."

"Is this coming from him?" Clarence asked.

"It's an outstanding rate of return."

He smoothed his wispy hair. He had one foot on the curb, the other in the dry mud of the gutter. "They won't do it."

"You haven't askcd."

"You don't get it, Arthur. These men don't reckon he'll be back to make good on any offer, no matter how sweet. They want it all now."

"Are you saying the plane is unfit?"

"The plane's as fit as she can be. But you know it's a long shot. Hubert knows it, too."

I don't think Clarence meant to sound cold. He simply knew better than anyone how things could go wrong.

"I'll speak with them," he said. "See if they might knock off a few dollars."

I turned to take this promising news back to Julian, who was still appealing for generosity from his perch on the Boeing's wing. The sun had arched past its peak and now the clock neared two. The idea had been to roll the Boeing into the East River from a concrete ramp, and if we didn't get it there soon, we'd lose the tide.

"Well?" Julian asked.

"You still need eight hundred and forty-three dollars. But Clarence is going to talk to the owners."

If my news granted Julian any hope, the appearance of Agent Amos snatched it right back. Even among so many people — twenty-five thousand, by one estimate — Amos was easy to spot. It helped that he was the only spectator in the company of four uniformed cops. He wanted Julian in cuffs before the end of the day. What tremendous weight that skinny bureaucrat carried! Some people claim you can't put a price on freedom, but there it was for the Black Eagle: eight hundred and forty-three American dollars. The sum difference between liberty and prison.

"My ideas are exhausted," Julian admitted. "This is terrible timing."

"Have you tried selling your shirt?" I'd meant it as a joke. But in the next instant, Hubert had his suitcase open.

"Who will give me ten dollars for this shirt?" he shouted, holding the white garment aloft. "Handmade of the finest cotton. Stitched by skilled tailors. I insist on the very best, you all know that. Make it five!"

He showed the pearly buttons and collarless neck. In the high sun, the fabric sparkled. Hubert stood taller. The silver spurs on his boots tinkled.

"The flight will go on! Shirted or shirtless I will sail! In thirty-one days I will return either in my shirt — or on it!

"Ladies and gentlemen, I am going to break records!

"How about this suit? Just thirty dollars for this handsome wool suit."

They cleaned him out, emptying the suitcase of everything but his underwear. Even the socks went to a collector. I went back to Chamberlin with the cash. His partners had seen everything and were willing to move. They figured they could extend some credit to a man who wanted to fly so badly he'd be willing to do it naked.

"You're a great man, Clarence," I said. "If the world remembers you for anything, it will be because of what you've done on this day."

❖

With the help of many volunteers, we rolled the Boeing to the banks of the Harlem River, arriving just before four o'clock. The tide had already retreated. After brief deliberation and a plea, someone produced a dolly and the volunteers surrounded the fuel-heavy plane and began pushing and pulling to get it through the thick mud and into the river.

Once the plane was floating, Hubert hauled himself into the cockpit. I stood on one of the pontoons and wished him Godspeed.

"Don't need it," he said. "I have my own luck, remember?"

He started the machine. A puff of black smoke brought cheers from the crowd. The engine sounded strong, the rumble smooth. The propeller whined and pulled the plane a few hundred feet off shore where Julian pointed it south. He gave it some gas, and it rode over the light chop, river water spitting a high tail. The engine worked harder, and the plane responded with more speed. The pontoons bounced on the waves a final time and when Julian pulled back on the stick, the *Ethiopia I* separated itself from the Harlem River.

Julian turned and saluted. Now the crowd let it out, cheering so loud I was certain he could hear it over the engine. I turned in time to see Amos in the throng, dismissing his cops and backing away.

For the first time since my involuntary arrival, I liked that I was living in New York City. Amazing how many people had contributed their dimes and quarters to see this happen. I shouldn't have been surprised. Rich folks didn't care. They'd been to Paris. They'd

seen the pyramids in Egypt. For them, it wasn't such a thrill to see
a plane hop off, even one destined to make history. Not so for the
common man, who will gladly part with that dime or quarter if
it translates to something worth seeing. Hubert Julian taught me
that.

He was only about a thousand feet off the ground when the
plane began to tilt to the left. I knew something was wrong when
I saw Julian stand up in the cockpit. The engine, moments ago
sounding steady, now strained with the effort. He looked over the
wing and turned to the tail, trying to pinpoint the trouble. But his
vantage point blinded him to the real problem: the left pontoon
was partially detached from its struts and hung, like a broken foot,
below the fuselage. He'd have to turn back, which was probably
the intent when Julian sat back in the seat. Seconds later, the strut
gave way and the pontoon broke free. Amid a chorus of gasps in the
crowd, it plummeted to the river's surface like a bomb.

To correct the imbalance, Julian swung the plane hard to the
left. But with the shifted weight he pushed too far and instead of
going left, he knifed up and then right until the *Ethiopia I* was
flying on its side and also losing altitude. When he sped past five
hundred feet, even people who knew nothing about airplanes could
tell there was nothing he could do to pull out of the descent.

The top right wing hit the water first, snapping off on contact
and spinning madly in the air. Then the other wing and the still-
attached pontoon dug in, and the crippled craft cartwheeled head
over nose. Four, maybe five, times. It was hard to tell in the blur
of river spray.

When the water settled, the Boeing was bobbing unsteadily,
riding low in the water, miraculously upright. Julian slumped in
the cockpit, not moving. Both left-side wings were broken and
bent. Half of that beautiful carved propeller spun a final few rota-
tions. The rest of it was floating somewhere downstream, among
other bits and pieces of river trash.

DEBRIEF WITH SPECIAL AGENT RILEY TRIGGS
■ JULY 24, 1924

—Over here, Tormes.

—Agent Triggs. I almost didn't recognize you.

—Is your memory that damaged?

—You look … different. I hope you're not sick?

—I've lost a few pounds, that's all. The new Bureau wants its agents to look like Hercules. I'm eating carrots and celery three times a day. Prune juice and barley tea. Get this: those are my fucking treats. No meat, not even bacon. I'm farting all the time. Some days, I move my bowels five or six times. Tiny little shits, like a terrier's.

—Would you like to hear about —

—Twenty-three years I've been with the Bureau. I have a good record. Not perfect, but good. Solid. So I wasn't any Olympian, but I could handle myself when I needed to. Not good enough for him. I buy the most expensive paper, it's like a wire brush on my ass. I hear the best thing is a swan's neck. The down is supposed to be soft and resilient, but a swan's not something you can keep next to the toilet. But you'll want to forget about my problems and mind your own business. I just farted now. I hear your chippy's moving up the ranks.

—Jean?

—Who else? If you were sticking it in somebody else, you can be sure I'd know.

—She got promoted at the newspaper. She's now secretary to the foreign news editor.

—…

—His name is Mr. Landarer, in case you needed to know.

—Landarer? Phil Landarers?

—I don't know his first name … Oh, I get it now.

—I don't bother with the foreign news. You'd better hope Phil's pecker is one of the few in this world that's smaller than yours.

—…

—What do you have for me? Is Julian still alive?

—Still in the hospital. I went for a visit yesterday. He's awake now and talking. The doc says he's going to be fine.

—Hard to believe he survived.

—He certainly is lucky, sir.

—I'd have bet money, a crack-up like that, he'd be a dead man.

—Would you have preferred that to sending him to prison?

—Can't send him to prison until I have a charge. Maybe you don't understand that this is why you're here and not in Sing Sing.

—Then why send that agent?

—What agent?

—Amos. Who threatened him with mail fraud charges if he didn't take off.

—Jim Amos? He went to the lot? He talked to Julian?

—Didn't you send him there?

—...

—...

—You leave that to me, Tormes, understand? You stick to what matters to you. What's Julian's excuse?

—For what?

—The crash. Did he ditch on purpose?

—The pontoon fell off.

—Convenient place for the pontoon to fall off where it did.

—...

—More convenient there than a couple hundred miles out to sea.

—...

—Makes you wonder if that wasn't the plan all along.

—Does it matter? He didn't make it. Now Julian won't be leading any Negro revolution.

—For now, at least.

—...

—We'll see what happens next. What you don't understand, Tormes, is that failure can be as powerful as success. More powerful, even. Look at Moses, or Robert the Bruce, or the Giants who came back from two games to none to take the '21 series.

—...

—I can't ignore this, and you know what that means? That's right. You can't ignore it, either. So get back to that hospital. I want to know who visits him. Who's paying the bills? I want more information, not less. Your reports have been too thin lately. Don't make me say that again. Julian's going to have to follow this up. He's got their sympathy, now he needs to win their confidence. That can't happen.

30

REFUSING TO HELP COULD BE
TAKEN AS A LACK OF FAITH

THAT SAME NIGHT, ANOTHER STRANGE DREAM. I WAS IN A wide, open field, chasing madly after a flock of white swans. Triggs was there, squatting on a toilet, wool trousers bunched at his ankles. All the while, as I lurched and dived at the big white birds, he mocked and berated and screamed at me to hurry up.

Riding the train out to the Flushing Hospital the next morning, I thought it might lift Julian's spirits if I told him about the dream. But I arrived to a cheery room full of flower arrangements and cards propped up on every flat surface. Even with half his body bound in bandage and plaster, his mood was bright. When I came in, he was recounting his rescue to a trio of orderlies.

"... but they weren't rescuers. In reality, they were rum-runners," he said, "waiting for a seaplane like mine. When their boss realized I wasn't their delivery man, he told them to do away with me. 'Throw the Black bastard back,' he said. Luckily, they dumped me on shore instead."

As the orderlies filed from the room, they looked at me hard and disapprovingly, as though I'd been in league with the rum-runner who'd valued the bottle over the man.

"What was that about?" I asked once they were gone.

"Just a bit of breeze shooting. Those gentlemen are concerned that I'm being treated right in here."

"I thought it was a Mr. Hess who pulled you out in his motor-boat. That's what it said in the *Times*."

"I don't think those fellows are subscribers," he said.

In September, with his body healed and whole again, Julian returned to Harlem. I don't know if he expected a hero's welcome but if he did, he was disappointed. There were some unflattering articles in the press that fouled his mood and filled him with anger that had no outlet. This, until he ran into Hubert Boulin on Seventh Avenue.

I got to witness the whole bout, right from the opening bell. In the parlay, Julian accused Boulin of finking to James Amos. Also, in a voice loud enough to attract attention from across the street, of dressing like a shoe salesman. Boulin denied the finking charge and told Julian to take another dive in the Harlem River. Then they went at each other. Boulin landed the first good punch, a smacking left hook. Julian fell back and thudded against the pavement. But he leaped to his feet and the rest of the brief fight went his way. By the time a cop intervened, Boulin's eye was swollen to the size of an orange. Both men were arrested, both fined. I congratulated Julian on getting his revenge. He chewed me out for not warning him that Boulin led with his left.

To earn money, Julian demonstrated parachuting and performed stunts for paying audiences. He rented his planes with irksome terms, especially the extra-high deposits the plane's owners demanded of him in particular.

"Why do they charge you so much more?"

"What do you think?" he replied.

"Because of your crash?" I said.

"Try again."

I followed him to the airfields. Long Island, New Jersey, Hartford, Connecticut. I was on the ground when he buzzed New York's city hall, spinning loop-the-loops at a rally for Mayor Hylan's re-election bid. On Thanksgiving Day, 1925, I was in Philly when he flew over the stadium hosting the annual Penn–Cornell football game.

He began to talk out loud about another attempt to cross the Atlantic and told the press he'd commissioned a twenty-thousand-dollar amphibious plane from Columbia Aircraft, aiming to take off for Liberia on Labour Day.

If this meant more fundraising, I wanted no part in it. Except, as I thought again, Julian might interpret my refusal to help as a lack of faith. He might then push me away, something I couldn't afford. I decided I would make an offer to help but not without pointing to my failures the last time, how he'd been reduced to selling his own shirts when I came up short.

But Julian never asked for my help, instead putting himself personally in charge of raising the twenty grand. He went first to the NAACP, who turned him down flat (the NAACP had always hated Garvey and held his former allies in lowest regard). But even without their help, Julian still managed to raise enough to bring the plane to Harlem. As with the *Ethiopia*, he planned to charge people to see it. Except before he raised a single nickel, vandals hopped the fence and went at the machine with crowbars and axes. The plane was ruined, postponing the dream until the following February (we're in 1926 now), when Julian told a reporter from the *Amsterdam News* about the Bellanca he intended to buy for another attempt to cross the Atlantic.

31

I BASICALLY EXECUTED
THE POOR SLOB

FOREIGN NEWS FOR *THE SUN* MEANT EUROPEAN NEWS, AND
Jean's boss, the worldly Mr. Landarer, made her come into the
office early to help him sort items from the overnight wire. Most
days she got off work right around the same time I had to go in,
because believe it or not, I got promoted, too. In booming New
York, Tommy Kippers had trouble hanging on to employees, which
made room for me to move up. He gave me the late kitchen shift.
I cooked a little, brewed coffee, and kept watch for trouble in the
alley whenever Owney Madden's men showed up with the liquor
deliveries.

With Jean working early and me working late, we saw a lot less
of each other. I didn't like it but Jean didn't mind the sacrifice.
It was better all around for her. Better pay, more responsibility.
Landarer had been to over forty countries and had all kinds of en-
tertaining stories, she said. Not that I thought there was anything
going on between them. That was just another way Triggs worked
me. He knew a lot about Jean and me. And right from the start, too.

Not seeing Jean as much gave me more time — too much
time — to think about how Triggs had learned so much. On

solitary nights, ruminating with the aid of a glass of rum or whisky, I could step into it up to my waist. Jean and I were certainly the product of strange coincidence, though just *how* strange, I didn't know. The vacant lot, the divorce raid. And the way she found me at Mrs. Lipoma's, all of it based on a tiny snippet of conversation she'd heard months before. That seemed like a long shot, too. Sometimes, I threw off the constraints of reason and even allowed myself to wonder if Jean was working for Triggs. Maybe as an agent. Maybe he'd foisted a deal on her like the one he'd foisted on me. My view of the world was increasingly tinted by paranoia; I had all kinds of bizarre ideas and explanations. Complete lunacies, planted by Triggs for his own amusement. I vowed not to let them affect my feelings for Jean and I think I kept my word to myself. Still, it'd have been better overall if those thoughts hadn't come around as often as they did.

We were at a small park not too far from her place. We would go there sometimes, especially on warm nights, and sit together on one of the benches while neighbourhood kids fought over the monkey bars and the one swing that wasn't busted. On that evening, find-ing the park empty, we'd decided to have a go on the teeter-totter. I moved a little one way and she moved a little the other until we achieved balance, allowing us both to sit with our legs dangling freely and pleasantly in the air.

I had just told her about Julian's latest plans. Jean wasn't impressed.

"Where's he *not* going this time?"

"Liberia," I said.

"Oh, please."

"You shouldn't be so cynical," I said. "It's been two years, a long time in an advancing field like aviation. And Giuseppe Bellanca's a legitimate builder."

"If he can only find a legitimate pilot."

"That's not fair," I said, though mocking Julian helped dampen suspicions about a Jean–Triggs collaboration. "He can fly. He did a loop-the-loop over city hall."

"Why do you always defend him?"

"He's a compatriot." And then, putting on what I still carried of my old accent, added, "We islanders need to stick together in this strange and hostile land."

"Right," she said, unconvinced.

I said nothing. Why aggravate one lie with more lies? Jean Fox was a wonderful, beautiful, and, most of all, tolerant woman, but I worried if I wasn't driving her pretty close to her limits. I made a hasty lane change and asked if she had any scoops from *The Sun*'s foreign desk.

"Jonas Windermere called in from Mexico this morning," she said. "They killed Pancho Villa in Mexico. They shot him with dumdum bullets. The kind they use to kill elephants."

I thought about what bullets meant for elephants would do to a human body, and then we were quiet, suspended above the playground sand on the ends of the teeter-totter. Our silence blended seamlessly with the growing darkness. It gave me the false but agreeable sensation that Jean and I were alone, that the city's millions had made the collective decision to leave the town to us for the night.

Jean must have felt it too because she didn't bother to lower her voice when she released a sigh and said, "This seems like a good time to tell you about how I lost my virginity."

I felt my end of the board sinking and shifted to bring us even again. "You don't have to."

"I know. But it's a nice night and we're having a lovely time, and besides, I want to tell you."

"I'm not really sure I want to know," I said. "Though it's definitely a nice night."

"Good," she said. "First, the setting. Port Huron, Michigan. A funeral. More specifically, my parents' funeral. Not the actual funeral, but the visitation. Where the open coffins were laid out, my father in one, my mother in the other, with flowers arranged in front and back. Were you going to say something?"

"It doesn't matter," I said. But I was thinking about their bodies and what they would have looked like after a fall from the top of the Woolworth Building. Worse than being shot with dumdum bullets. Open coffins? It seemed impossible.

Jean continued. "The Longs and my parents were old friends. Mr. Long was pretty upset, actually, which is something I didn't understand. I mean, he still had his wife and kid, and for all I knew, *his* parents were still alive. But I've learned since. Death hits different people in different ways.

"Anyway, I must have talked to a thousand people that night. *I'm so sorry for your loss, Jeannie. Such a tragedy, Jeannie. Is there anything we can do to help, Jeannie?* I hardly knew anybody; some of those people were complete strangers."

"They called you 'Jeannie'?" I asked.

"Everyone did," she said. "I thought I was doing pretty well. Holding up, as they say. But then it just started to annoy me so much. Like a pebble in your shoe or gristle in the teeth, you know? Sharing this time and this place and these awful, screwy feelings with all these people, these total strangers. It left me cold and wanting to get out of there.

"So that's when I went over to Charley Long. We were in the same class which, I don't know, gave us a connection even though we ran in different circles. Charley's awkward, kind of small-minded, actually. But I knew he was sweet on me. He was always bragging about this job he had lined up at the factory where they make Fibravin."

"I've never heard of Fibravin."

"It's a cereal," she said. "The only reason to eat it is if you're bunged up to the throat."

"That never happens to me."

"Better for you, then.

"Anyway. With all these people around, talking in quiet voices, staring at me like they thought I'd burst into flames,

I grabbed Charley's hand and led him upstairs. I didn't really have a plan or anything. We just sort of ended up in an office with a leather couch. I closed the door and that's when it happened. Just like that. No discussion. Nothing. It didn't last long. Didn't even bother taking off all our clothes. Afterward, Charley cried.

"What do you think? Crazy, eh?"

I didn't know if this was crazy or not. Or if she just wanted me to think it was crazy, to confirm her worst suspicions about the way I thought of her. I remembered my mother's funeral, the few people standing around her grave and the charity minister who talked about the wages of sin. I think I understood why Jean did what she did. That need — not for sex but for whatever it is you think you're getting from the sex — can be very powerful, especially when you're feeling raw and weakened.

"People do crazy things in crazy situations," I said.

"I still don't know what I was thinking, but can I tell you something else? When I picture that night, I can't see it going any other way. Like everything plays out exactly the same. Leading him upstairs, finding that office, everything. What's battier still is that I kept seeing Charley. Because we'd done what we'd done, he just assumed we were sweethearts. I don't blame him. That's usually how it works. He wanted to go to dances or play bridge with other couples. Bridge! We were seventeen, for God's sake.

"The only part I wanted was the sex part. He'd come by my house, which, of course I had all to myself, and we'd go right at it. I can't say I didn't like it, but well, I can't say it left me satisfied, either. And even then, after every time, after he'd gone home and I was alone again, I told myself, *That's it, no more. That was the last time.* But it wasn't. It went on the whole summer, every day, more or less. Then one day Charley showed up at my front door with his great-grandmother's ring, and I knew I had to end it.

"I said, 'I'd sit on a pole for the rest of my life rather than spend it with you.'"

"Harsh."

"I basically executed the poor slob. He went home crying and told his parents everything, I mean *every*thing. His mother came over, same night. She was nice at first, but then she started yelling and calling me some names I'd rather not repeat. I was cruel as hell, no question. I didn't deny anything. And I don't know why I thought Charley would comprehend something so incomprehensible, but when he didn't, I hated him for it. I mean I really hated him. I know that wasn't fair."

She took a deep drag on her cigarette and exhaled a weary bloom of blue smoke. It was late now.

"I don't blame Charley and I don't blame Mrs. Long. She had her ideas about the way things should be. I'm glad I told you all this. I've never told anyone."

"Really?"

"Really."

"Why now?"

"I don't know." She flicked her cigarette to the ground. It sparked and bounced on the packed dirt. "But I love you. And I trust you. And I wanted you to know. I'm getting cold. Let's go now."

When I think back on that night in the park, I feel like Jean had expected me to match her confession with one of my own. That she sensed, after three years, I might be ready to unload in the name of love and trust. I truly wanted to be worthy of her trust. But I wasn't prepared to take on the risk. That is, I told myself that maybe someday, once Julian was neutralized and Triggs was out of our lives and I was free of it all, I would make a complete and thorough confession to Jean. Tell her everything, from start to finish. But no, not yet.

And so I said nothing, somehow believing that the lies of the present could be justified and forgiven with a promise to tell the truth in the future. Soon enough, I'd find out how wrong I'd been.

32

ALL I HAD TO DO WAS
HIT THE BRAKES

IN EARLY 1927, JEAN MOVED UP AGAIN AT *THE SUN* AFTER
the social reporter got married and had to quit her job. They hired
Jean to take her place. She wrote three or four pieces a week because it was always one season or another in the social pages. Deb
ball season, engagement season, wedding season, and even a season
they just called *The Season*. She attended openings for operas and
philharmonics. Galas to raise money for museums. Black-tie balls
on the eve of fox hunts. She covered graduations at Columbia,
Princeton, and Barnard College, and when certain ships arrived
from Europe, she ran down to the 32nd Street pier to list the
listable passengers and the sights they'd seen overseas.

Deadlines were a strain but she liked the job, and the money
was good enough that she started to save for an apartment. I suppose the job also gave her a glimpse of a life she might have led if
things had turned out differently for her. If she'd gone to college
like her friends, if she'd met and married a man with money or
prospects. I could tell by the way she talked about those parties and
balls, the fine food, the decorations and dresses, that a part of her
yearned to cross over into that world.

Around then, she started to take a drink now and then, her first since she'd quit booze cold after the night with the McElhinneys. She began to dress differently, too. No more frills or lacy accents, no more girlish polka dots. Just solid colours, mature darks and stripes. She wore more restrained necklaces, and her earrings no longer dangled but were fixed and unmoving on her lobes. On one shopping excursion, she found something for me: a grey fedora with a black band. I tried it on. It fit a little loose, but I liked it.

"There," she said, adjusting. "Now you look like a grown-up."

On her twenty-fourth birthday, a warm mid-June night, I went downtown to meet her in a coffee shop not far from *The Sun* offices. We would dine at Gladys', then move on to The Nest for dancing to the Luis Russell Orchestra. If I had any money left after that, we'd finish the night in the early hours of tomorrow at Club Hot-Cha.

I laid the fedora on the table and began to read that day's *Amsterdam News*, looking, as always, for Hubert Julian's name. I found it in an unexpected section: the wedding notices.

This wasn't a grave development. A married Hubert Julian didn't present any greater or lesser threat than he did as a bachelor. And yet I felt that panicky gut-punchy feeling of having missed something important, a bill payment or a court date, say. I had a name, Essie Gittens, but I urgently needed to learn more about this woman. When Jean arrived a few minutes later, I insisted we go straight to Harlem for a visit.

"To congratulate him."

"But our reservation is for seven."

"They'll hold it."

"You don't know that."

"So we'll go somewhere else."

"I don't want to go somewhere else. It's my birthday."

"I know. And it's going to be a great time. It'll be a short visit, I promise."

"They didn't even want you at the wedding. What does that tell you?"

"Very little."

"Go tomorrow," she said, voice rising. "He'll still be married then, won't he?"

She was right, of course. But I couldn't see reason through the compulsion. "Why are we wasting our time arguing about this? Let's just go, say hello, and get on with the evening?"

"I don't understand why it has to be now?"

"Because it does."

"That's not an answer."

"Can we please just go?"

"You go," she said, fixing a cigarette into her holder, a recent acquisition. "I'm not stopping you."

"Jean."

"This is ridiculous. You want me to go with you? It's simple. Just tell me why it's so important to ruin our plans for my birthday so you can meet Hubert Julian's new wife."

"It would take too long to explain."

"Better to start now, then."

"Jean. Please."

"You're hiding something, Arthur. Tell me what it is now or I'm going home."

I rubbed my eyes with the knuckles of my forefingers. I knew there was nothing I could say to change Jean's mind. Over the years we'd been together, there had been dozens of cancellations and postponements as I carried out my obligations for Triggs. Jean had always been accommodating, even when I didn't (or couldn't) explain. I was going to lose here. I was doing damage. I hated myself for being unable to resist. It was as though I were behind the wheel of a very fast car, heading straight for a brick wall. To save myself, all I had to do was hit the brakes. And yet. And yet!

Jean went home, angry, hurt, and considering her options. I hopped on the A-train to Harlem and rode the whole trip bent over, hands clutching my face, feeling nauseated. If there was anything at all good that came from the awful exchange with Jean, it was this: the crazy suspicion I had of her collaborating with Riley Triggs was forever scrubbed from my mind.

33

YOU MEET A MAN WHEN HE'S SIXTEEN, YOU'VE SEEN HIM AT HIS WORST

I STOOD IN FRONT OF JULIAN'S BUILDING ON WEST 128TH Street, not yet ready to go inside. I needed time to generate the cheer and happiness newlyweds expect of their friends. I paced, circled the block, found a barbershop known to sell rum in hair tonic bottles, downed a few shots, and had my mood temporarily lifted by the time I reached their apartment.

The former Miss Essie Gittens greeted me at the door.

"Are you really Arthur?"

"How do you do, Mrs. Julian."

"I was expecting someone older. You look far too young to have been Hubert's classmate."

"Just one of those faces, I guess."

She was a very pretty woman, slender and light skinned, with short hair that clung to her forehead in a fashionable way. She gave me an effortlessly forceful hug. When she stepped back, I perceived a determined squint, as though she were trying to bring me into better focus.

I had a long look around their impressive new apartment.
Large, naturally bright, painted and papered with warm colours.
The kitchen, accessed through a swinging door, featured a four-
burner stove next to a double sink. A squat electric refrigerator —
one of the early home models — rested on four curving legs. New
furniture filled the living room, with smartly matched upholstery
on the sofa and twin armchairs.

"Hubert's just dressing," Essie said. "Let me get you something
to drink. I asked, but Hubert couldn't tell me what you like to
drink. Tea? Coffee? We have a little rum, too."

"I'd take a glass of rum," I said. "After all, we're celebrating,
aren't we?"

She began to turn to the kitchen but swung back and after
starting to say something else, said, "Maybe we should wait for
Hubert. Come. Let's sit."

I took the sofa. Essie crossed the room, covering the short distance with steps that suggested stowed energy, as though she were
about to break into a sprint. She sat in an armchair, crossed one
lively leg over the other, then switched.

"I don't know what's keeping Hubert. Should I check? No.
We'll wait."

"Sure. Let's wait. Why don't you tell me about the wedding?"

"We had a small ceremony. We wanted it quiet." She smiled
through the rest of the story. I could tell how much she enjoyed
saying *we*.

Julian appeared from the bedroom. He looked sullen and di-
shevelled, like he'd just risen from an unsuccessful nap. No tie,
collar open on his untucked shirt. Socks bunched at his shoeless
ankles. Swollen eyes, chin darkened with stubble. A man should
feel free to look any way he pleases in his own home, but this was
an unusually unkempt look for Hubert Julian.

"Hello, Tormes." He slumped into the second chair, gripping
the armrests like they wanted to fight. Breeze through an open
window ruffled the top pages of a mound of newspapers on the
floor next to him.

"I was just telling your friend about our wedding," Essie said, rising. "Now I'll get those drinks. What about you, Hubert? Nothing? What about some lemonade?"

Julian waved her away.

"Suit yourself," she said, then skipped into the kitchen.

I waited to hear clinking of glasses, the pop of a bottle uncorking. Instead, I sensed Essie's presence behind the kitchen door. I pointed to the newspapers. "Catching up on the news, Hubert?"

Essie reappeared. "I'm afraid there's no rum!" she said. "We've had so many well-wishers come to our home lately, we must have run out."

"I happen to have some here," I said, pulling out the tonic bottle.

For a half second, Essie's mouth flinched into a frown. "I'll get you a glass, then."

I turned to Hubert. "Did your folks come up from Trinidad?"

"They couldn't make it."

"Travel is so expensive," Essie said, passing me the glass. "Even in tourist class. You know what? I think I might ..." And she was in the kitchen again.

"Father's too busy," Julian said once Essie was behind the door again. "Especially this time of year." Then he stared at the armrest until Essie returned with a cup of tea.

"So tell me. How did you two meet?" I asked, pouring.

"Back home," Essie said. "We were just kids then. But you know what? You meet a man when he's sixteen, and you've seen him at his worst."

"You never forget your first love," I said, trying not to think of Jean as the word *love* came out.

"Not when he's this handsome!"

I couldn't imagine Julian as a teenager, much less in infancy. Part of me assumed he'd sprung from the womb as a full-grown man swaddled in a bespoke suit with a silk bow tie.

Essie brushed an adoring hand down Julian's cheek, but he did not stir. I looked down at the newspapers again and realized the source of his lousy mood: Charles Lindbergh, who weeks ago had electrified the world by crossing the Atlantic in the *Spirit of St. Louis*.

"Tell them what happened when you left," Essie said.

"Left for where?" I asked.

"For school," Essie said.

"In England," Julian said.

"No, not England —"

"It was England," Julian insisted.

Essie continued: "Anyway, this one figured I'd be in tears to see him go. Instead, I just got angry. Why'd he need to go to another country for? I smacked his face so hard. It must have been second term before it stopped hurting."

"Is that true, Hubert?" I asked.

"She had a temper, that's true. But I tamed her."

"Who tamed who, dog!" Essie replied, and laughed, trying unsuccessfully to share the joke with her husband, and it didn't seem to me that this matter of taming had been settled.

"We should have a little something to eat with this drink," Essie said, springing up. She didn't like being still for too long.

I nodded again at the piled newspapers. "Anything new on Lindbergh?"

Julian shrugged. "Probably. Who cares?"

"Seven hundred thousand people went out to see him in Brooklyn the other day."

"The man can't go a day without someone throwing him a damn parade," he said.

"Hearst had a gala at the Ritz," I said. "Charlie Chaplin was there. My girl ... Jean covered it for *The Sun*."

"And never once has he said one kind word about those of us who came before him," Julian said. "Whose trials and tribulations paved his gilded runway. Not once."

"Unfair," I said. "Really very unfair."

Essie returned from the kitchen with a sandwich plate full of sugar cookies.

"Charles Lindbergh just has to have *all* the attention," she said, laying the plate on the coffee table. "And don't the newspapers just love him? Oh, that shy smile and wavy yellow hair."

"He sure got lucky," I said.

"He lives with his mother, you know," Essie said. "A grown man! If a flyer like Hubert lived with his mother, they'd call him all kinds of awful names."

"You think they need me to live with my mother to call me names?" He slumped a little more. He didn't drink, but his mood seemed liquor dampened.

"Give Hubert a sliver of Lindberg's backing …" Essie said. "That man just strolled into a bank and they wrote him a damn cheque. What happened when you tried the banks, Arthur?"

"They turned us down," I said.

"I'd bet Lindbergh had connections with the bankers. They all do."

"Sure," I agreed and bit into a cookie. The sweet grains crunched in my teeth. "You're probably right about that, Essie. You know, I've heard before that St. Louis banks are a much looser bunch when it comes to loaning money."

"Son of a bitch," Julian said, rising from the chair. "More luck."

An hour later I was at Jean's rooming house, full of apologies and a bouquet of white roses. She slammed the door in my face. I went back the next day and the day after that. On the fourth day, she relented and let me inside. We sat in the common room, where residents were officially allowed to entertain male guests. It was a long conversation. I nodded a lot. It was easy for me to concede that I'd been in the wrong. I'd never thought I was in the right in the first place. That she took me back only showed that Jean Fox understood secrets. Plus, I made a promise: no more cancellations, no more postponements. I would never allow Hubert Julian to interfere with our relationship again.

"Never again. I promise," I said. But as we ended our talk with a long, satisfying, loving hug, I was sure that it would be all but impossible to keep that promise.

DEBRIEF WITH SPECIAL AGENT RILEY TRIGGS
■ APRIL 10, 1928

—What's wrong, Tormes? This bench not to your liking?

—No, it's fine, it's just —

—Nice day to be outside in the park. You get to see the new buds on the trees. The daffodils. The world is a beautiful place. You gotta enjoy it while you can.

—We don't normally meet in places that are so public.

—What's normal? Here you get a perfect view of the ball fields. What's better than that? Season opener tomorrow. Do you like baseball? Or are you still too much of a foreigner?

—Sure. The Yankees had a pretty good season, didn't they? Waite Hoyt. Lou Gehrig. That Babe Ruth. Sixty homers. Boy!

—Shows you what a fat guy can do.

—I never underestimate what a fat guy can do.

—Are you talking about me?

—Not at all, sir.

—I love my steaks and I love my cream pies, and I don't even mind a cold de-alcoholized beer now and then. The world can tell you to do this and the world can tell you to do that. Fall in line, even when you know better. When it comes to what's for dinner, I like to be my own man.

—You were getting too skinny, anyway. This, the way you are now, it suits you better. The longer hair, too. Did the Bureau change its policies?

—...

—...

—The Bureau's policies are none of your damn business.

—Of course they aren't.

—What's going on with our friend, Julian?

—All quiet. Still.

—Really?

—Really.

—No fights?

—None that I know of.

—What do you mean by that?

—Just that I haven't heard of any.

—Why wouldn't you have heard of any? You always watch him, don't you? You're supposed to know.

—It's just that I can't track him *all* the time.

—What else have you missed, Tormes?

—Nothing. I swear. But I was thinking that if I had some help. Maybe a second man. You know, someone who can be there when I can't. Do you think that's possible?

—Of course it's possible. We're the Department of Justice. We can do anything we want.

—It would really be helpful.

—I'll give it some thought. Guess what? I just did. The answer is no. You're on your own. What else about Julian? Any other new ventures?

—He's got a few exhibitions booked. I think maybe …

—What?

—Well, I think maybe he's done.

—Done what?

—With trying to break records. Maybe marriage is what changed him. Maybe he's decided to settle down and try something safer.

—It's possible.

—Lindbergh's flight might have been a factor.

—Charles Lindbergh is a national hero.

—Julian thinks it should have been him.

—He's dreaming.

—…

—Because this country is a country with certain ideas about who is and who isn't an American hero. You have to be a certain type, and one thing I can say is that Hubert Julian is not that type. You really think he's done? Just quit the fight.

—I do, sir. And maybe whatever threat he posed to the U.S.

—Huh. I thought he had bigger balls than that. I'm not surprised. But I thought he had bigger balls.

—I've never actually seen his ... you know, genitals. But what I'm saying is that maybe he's not actually the threat you think.

—Don't tell me what I think.

—I didn't mean ...

—A guy like that is always up to something, always biding his time. You'd better hope he is.

—But what I'm asking is ... what if he *isn't?* What happens to me then?

—I don't think you want me to answer that question.

—...

—...

—Keep watching him. Keep me informed. What about you, Tormes?

—Me? You already know everything about me.

—Still with that girl?

—I see her now and again. Very casually. Really, it's nothing to me.

—Still keeping quiet about our arrangement?

—Absolutely.

—Good. I'd hate to see her suffer because you can't keep a damn secret. A jailbird might only serve two days, but for women on the outside, thirty years is really thirty years. Some women, they're loyal. They'll wait it out. But from what I know about your broad, she's not the waiting type.

—...

—...

—...

—Anything else you want to tell me?

34

VAGUE DETAILS OF A FUTURE
HOVERED IN THE AIR

TRIGGS' EYES HAD NARROWED AFTER I ANSWERED HIS
final question with a decisive "Nothing." I didn't have a clue how,
but Triggs always seemed to know things about me, private things.
He liked to remind me that privacy was a fantasy, something I
could only wish for, like the power of invisibility or time travel
(something I wished for often). And now I was afraid he'd discovered what I'd left out of our briefing. Specifically, that Jean Fox and
I were engaged to be married.

It had happened only a week before. Jean had just moved into
her new apartment, a two-bedroom on the sixth floor of a midtown
building. She was showing me around, beginning with the kitchen
and its double sink, four-burner Hotpoint, and Monitor Top fridge.

"I can grab some little things from the restaurant," I said.
"Spatulas, colanders, pie pans, depending on what they have lying
around."

"Thanks. But no thanks."

"Why not?" When she lived at the rooming house, I used to
bring her glasses, coffee mugs, forks, and knives, pilfered gifts she
gratefully accepted. "I'd like to contribute."

"And you will," she said. "But my new home is going to be pure."

"What's 'pure'?" I asked.

"I'm a self-sufficient woman. I don't want to spoil a pie because I used a stolen tin to bake it."

"I'm the assistant manager now. If I take things, it's not stealing." Which wasn't true, but I'd seen other managers help themselves to Tommy Kippers' inventory. "Besides, it's a good quality tin. It cooks the crusts nicely. Never too soggy or burnt. Why waste your money?"

"You worked too hard for that promotion to get fired over some lousy pie tin," she said.

I saw her point. Also, I had managed to keep my promise to her about Julian. I was still spying on him, which Jean didn't know, of course, but so far hadn't let that come between us.

"This is the living room," Jean said.

Excepting a bookcase she'd already filled, she'd yet to bring in much furniture. She shared her plans for future additions: a sofa, two chairs, a coffee table in the middle, curtains, an area rug. The absence of furniture contributed to a neatness and made for a notable contrast with Jean's old room, which often made me think of a flood zone after the water's receded.

We moved on to the dining nook. She had found a used table and bargained on the price because there were no chairs to match and the maple top was battered with gouges and stains. But you could see that it had once been beautiful and could be again, and Jean showed me sheets of sandpaper and jars of varnish she would use to restore it.

As she spoke, I felt a yearning to be part of her plans, to ponder a life without the harassing presence of a federal agent. I had never realized, before that night, how plans are a kind of lifeline. They tether us to a future, show the ways forward. Doesn't matter how practical or fanciful, a plan gives a person something worth sticking around for. Jean wanted a dining room table she could show off to guests and, maybe down some dreamed-of road, use for family dinners, birthday parties, card games. I envied that simple luxury.

She took me the bathroom next. "I've already had three extra-long baths. It's my favourite thing so far. Used to be I couldn't take more than ten minutes before one of the girls would start pounding on the door. But now? I light a candle and soak in the dark like a queen until the steam lightens my head like a balloon."

"It really does seem like a great way to get clean."

"It is! I get so relaxed I sometimes imagine myself as a corpse in the morgue. Except in my imaginings, the morgue is top notch, the Versailles of morgues. Everything clean, marble walls and floors. Pure white. Then I imagine this crusty coroner with giant eyebrows and his young assistant who sort of looks like you. They look me over. They measure and prod around, trying not to be aroused."

"It would be hard."

"Exactly."

"And then the coroner says," here she lowered her voice, to something more crusty coroner-like, "'No foul play suspected, but these corrugations on her fingers and toes are indications of recent and lengthy submersion in water.'

"And his young assistant says: 'Did she drown?'

"And he says: 'No water in the lungs. Plus she smells too good. It's a clear case of Overbath!'"

"I've never met anyone who loved a bath so much," I said.

"I'm going to paint the room in that blue colour that has a bit of green in it. So it looks like the lake."

We stood for a moment, beholding that magical bathtub, staring into the flawless white. A bathtub had never been a source of much emotion for me, but I absorbed Jean's happiness and for the first time since that late night on the *Barbara Lynne*'s decks, some vague sense of a future hovered in the air around me.

"Unless you'd be available to do the painting?" she said.

"I'd like to do that for you," I said. "Let me paint the whole place. Any colours you pick. Two or three coats. Whatever you want. I want to be part of this."

"I'm glad."

"Also, I think we should get married."

She wrapped her arm around my waist, still staring into her bathroom, and the walls that would soon be painted to look like a lake.

"Of course we should," she said.

Sometime right around that exact moment probably, I should have told Jean the whole story. There had been no announcement, no date set or hall rented, but she was my fiancée now and no one would say she didn't deserve to know everything. It had been five years, and we loved each other, and I think I can say that we were happier than we ever were. I should have honoured that happiness with honesty.

Except no. While Jean had been busy shaking the ghosts of her past, I remained bound to mine. When I think back, I believe I actually knew I couldn't continue with the lies and the omissions, but by the time I suggested marriage (that it was more of a suggestion than a true proposal probably says something), I had fooled myself into thinking otherwise. Could I fulfill the terms of my secret deal with Triggs, avoid Sing Sing, *and* build a life with Jean Fox? Somehow, incredibly, I believed I could.

It helped that Triggs had been less demanding lately. Rather than the usual in-person briefings, he had me post weekly reports. Then, when we did meet, he was detached and distracted. Whatever fuelled his pursuit of Julian no longer burned so intensely. And yet, there was never a hint of letting me off the hook. I was still an unhappy passenger on an unhappy boat, but at least now I was cruising in calmer waters. Not ideal, but it could have been worse.

Which probably explains why I said nothing to Jean. Because why risk everything with a confession?

35

HE EXPANDED HIMSELF

IN ALL THOSE YEARS, HUBERT JULIAN ONLY EVER CAME TO see me at Mrs. Lipoma's one time. It was on a Saturday night in March of 1930. I wasn't even supposed to be home, but Jean called last minute to cancel our date.

"Not my fault," she said.

"Who do I blame, then?"

"D.H. Lawrence."

"What'd that prick do this time?"

"He died. And now my editor wants an obit for the morning edition."

About six months before, Jean had moved on from the society pages to obituaries. She loved the new job and you could read the passion in her writing. Once, when a famously portly New York socialite croaked on the eve of her annual trip to France, Jean wrote, "Alas, the *Normandie* sails a little lighter, today." A former player for the Giants, a slugging centre fielder, "saw the curveball no batter can hit." She even wrote celebrity tributes in advance. Like for Arthur Conan Doyle, expected to pop off any day now: "Death! The one mystery even the great Sherlock Holmes cannot solve."

No one had ever applied such verve and energy to obituaries, and her pieces prompted a flood of letters, some outraged but far, far more in favour, so many that advertisers noticed and began to buy space on the obit page, previously a no-go zone.

Julian arrived shortly after ten p.m.

"Tormes, I have big news." He was dressed formally. Tuxedo, white tie, a long, heavy coat with mink lapels. A few final snow-flakes glistened on his shoulders and on the rounded peak of his hat.

"You look sharp," I said.

He ignored the compliment (because I'd only stated the obvious), pulled off his gloves, and twisted out of his coat. He looked for a closet and then to the wall for a hook. Finding neither, he tossed the coat on my bed. I invited him to sit.

"With what I have to say, I'm going to stand," he said. He turned left then right, looking for a route to pace. This was clearly the worst kind of forum, far too small and modest for his big announcement, but he'd already come all this way. Finally, he stopped, then expanded himself by laying hands to hips.

"Well?"

"I'm trying to think, man! Where do I begin?" He sucked in several deep breaths. I considered offering a taste of rum, though part of me feared he might accept. "Right. Okay. It starts yester-day. I received a visit from a man named Bayen. *Prince* Malaku E. Bayen."

"Prince?"

"Correct. A prince of Ethiopia. He came to see me. A very distinguished gentleman. Poor Essie almost fainted. I could hardly believe it myself. But hear me out, Tormes. This prince asked me, on behalf of Ras Tafari — I should have said this part first, the prince is Ras Tafari's cousin. Also his advisor. You know who Ras Tafari is? The emperor designate of Ethiopia. So what his cousin, the prince — speaking on behalf of Ras Tafari — what he asked

me to do is perform a parachuting exhibit at the emperor's coronation. In Ethiopia. In *Africa*."

He held out his hands, wide and open, like a circus tumbler
who'd just stuck the landing.

"That's fantastic news, Hubert."

"It certainly is."

"What was this prince's name again?"

"Bayen," he said. "Malaku Bayen."

"How do you spell that?"

"*B-a-y* — what does it matter how the man spells his name?"

"Just curious. Is it *e-n*? Or *a-n*?"

"Forget about spelling. I haven't told you everything. He's also
asked me — again on behalf of the emperor-elect — to take com-
mand of the Ethiopian Air Force."

"The air force! But you don't … Amazing!"

"I know. It really *is* incredible. The honour of a lifetime.
Though when you think of it, I'm the logical choice. Ras Tafari
will be crowned in six months' time. He's got plans to modernize
the whole country, and he wants Negro men to show the way. This
air force is a big priority. Tafari must have read about me. I was just
at dinner with Bayen, finalizing the deal. Henry's Restaurant, on
109th. You probably don't know it, but it's among the best in the
city. The coquilles à la Valéry are a marvel."

I didn't know what that was. "Sounds delicious," I said.

"The prince is a remarkable man, Tormes. You meet these kinds
of men so very rarely. The kind who by the way they treat you
make you realize you've arrived. I told you he's studying medicine at Howard, didn't I? Maybe I didn't. Howard University,
Washington, D.C. I think I will sit now."

Julian pulled the white scarf from around his neck and extended his legs, setting his heels on the room's bare floor. He laid
his hands over his belly in a satisfied way.

"The emperor's private pilot," he said. "I'll take him up to inspect his empire." He stood and once again tried to pace. Finding
no more room than his last attempt, he instead tilted his head up,

looking past the peeling paint to imagine himself piloting a golden biplane, the emperor in the second seat, just the two of them floating above rich farmland, green mountains, thick Abyssinian forest.

"You know, Tormes, some days I wish I were a drinker. I'd have downed a case of champagne. Prince Bayen ordered wine with dinner. Essie drank, too. Why not? A night like tonight makes me question the point of Prohibition. I understand the need to cut off the common drunkard, to save him from his own vices, but shouldn't a man like the prince be able to enjoy himself? We had a terrific time, all three of us."

"What happened to Essie?"

"I sent her home in a cab. Then I practically ran over here. Can't believe I remembered where you lived, but my mind is sharp tonight. And I haven't even told you the best part."

"What you've told me sounds pretty good so far," I said.

In fact, I was thinking of how this news, if true, would play with Triggs. As Julian detailed the offer, I wondered how he could be a threat to the United States if he was living and working way over in Abyssinia?

"Well, get ready because there's more." He paused and turned to face me, then lifted a foot to my wobbly desk chair. I'd seen the pose before. The Black Eagle in full flight suit, foot resting on the lower wing of a biplane. He'd used the photo to raise money for one of those flights that never happened.

Now he smiled like he was about to sell me something.

"As an officer in the Ethiopian Armed Forces, I will naturally have a substantial budget for expenses," he said. "Including a salary for an aide-de-camp."

"Sure, why wouldn't you? Sounds like a terrific deal."

"You don't get it?"

I didn't. And even now I know I could never have predicted his next sentence.

"I want *you* to be my aide-de-camp," he said. "In Ethiopia."

I don't believe I need to list the terrible thoughts careening through my head at that moment.

"Why aren't you saying yes?"

"You want me to go to Abyssinia with you?"

"Ethiopia, Tormes. They prefer to call it Ethiopia. And yes, I want you to come with me. Who else? I've known you for a few years now. You've proven yourself to be a reliable man."

"No. Me?"

"Who else but you?"

"Wouldn't it be more fitting if your aide were Ethiopian?"

"Not at all," he said, lowering his foot from the chair. "I don't speak Amharic. That's what the Ethiopian language is called. I wouldn't be able to issue any orders."

"I don't speak Amharic, either."

"That's less important."

"I don't know what to tell you."

"It's the opportunity of a lifetime."

Not for me, I thought. Not for my lifetime. I knew about bat-men in the army, like butlers for officers who shined shoes and brewed tea and trimmed nose hairs with tiny scissors they stowed in a special leather kit. Was that the sort of thing he'd have me doing?

So what to say?

The question wasn't mine to answer. Julian's stare urged a response I could not give, to come to a decision I did not have the power to make. I already missed what my life had been before Julian knocked on the door that night. I missed my beautiful fiancée. I missed how much we were in love. I even missed the current, low-intensity version of Triggs. I'd grown accustomed to it, despite the constraints he imposed on my life.

"Can I think about it?" I said, finally. But I wasn't thinking about his job offer. I already knew I didn't want it. That part was easy. Instead, I focused on what would happen on Monday afternoon, just two days from now, when I would meet with Agent Triggs for our next debrief.

DEBRIEF WITH SPECIAL AGENT RILEY TRIGGS
■ MARCH 6, 1930

—You're going.

—I can see you're excited. But let's talk about this. What if we sat down somewhere warm? What if we just talked for a while?

—Nothing to talk about.

—All I'm suggesting is that there could be some options to consider.

—Like what?

—Would you like to sit down, maybe? Remember that bench by the ball fields that one time? That was nice. It's too cold now, but how about that coffee shop across the street?

—Yeah, we're fine here. You'll get used to the stink after a while. Besides, this meeting is over. You're going to Abyssinia.

—But … I don't understand.

—What don't you understand?

—If Julian's over in Ethiopia, how can he threaten America?

—Who can say what he'll get up to over there? Who can say who he'll meet? What kinds of plans he might cook up? Commander of an air force? Point is, you never know. We both know Hubert Julian has a difficult relationship with the truth. I've seen it in your reports. You've called him a mystery. Or am I wrong?

—No, you're not wrong, sir.

—Your word. *Mys-ter-y.*

—I know. I remember.

—You solved that mystery? Didn't think so. You're going.

—…

—What's the matter, Tormes? If you're in Africa, you're not in Sing Sing. That's got to be good, isn't it? Though you're going to want to watch out for flying spears when you're over there.

—Please. Can't we talk about it? I'll buy the coffee.

—You're going to want to watch for the head-shrinkers, too.

—What if you let me stay here? What if I spied on someone else for you instead?

—Not interested.

—You must have other cases. I could help out with those, maybe?

—What is it, the girl? Is that it, Tormes? Christ. You knew that wouldn't last. Didn't you?

—...

—You didn't? Ha! That was dumb.

—I could do so much more for you here. What about unions? The Reds? I've heard the American Legion is jumping with radicals.

—Your job is Julian. You shouldn't have fallen for any broad, Tormes. A man in your impossible situation.

—...

—...

—How am I supposed to explain this to her?

—Do I care? Tell that little lady whatever you want. But keep our arrangement out of it, understand?

—...

—Frankly, I don't get it. She's decent looking, I guess. And what do I know about what happens between you two in the sack. Maybe she's got some tricks to jet your juice. Skirts today know more things than when I was making the rounds. Even still, why bother? I used to think shit like that mattered. But it doesn't. It's a damn distraction.

—...

—...

—I just don't understand.

—That's because you're a fucking idiot.

—I've been following him around for seven years already.

—And yet you didn't see the thing with Abyssinia coming. You're going to want to be using your instincts better. A good agent needs good instincts. I always had the sharpest instincts. Never failed me in the field or in the office. I learned to trust them more than I trusted so-called evidence. Evidence is fine, I'm not saying it's not useful. But it can be screwed with. Rely on it too much and an agent becomes careless and soft and he's no good. Not everyone saw it my way, though.

—...

—The fact is, you should have been paying more attention. What if Julian hadn't made you his chief bootlicker? What then? He disappears to Africa. The Bureau of Investigation is forced to launch a manhunt. Do you know how much a damn manhunt costs? A lot more than it costs to keep you in Sing Sing for thirty years. Now, think about where I'd rather spend that money.

—...

—Then go pack your bags.

36

I DUG PAST THE LOOSE DIRT AND RUBBLE

JULIAN CALLED THE FOLLOWING SATURDAY, WANTING TO see me that same night.

"Be here at seven."

"I've got plans," I said. Jean had long ago invited me to *The Sun*'s annual Pulitzer Prize Gala.

"See you at seven. I insist."

At seven I was still struggling with the bow tie of my rented tux. Then a strap on the cummerbund snapped. And yet Julian said nothing when I arrived. Not about the suit, not about being forty-five minutes late.

"This way," he said. "Let me show you."

He led me to the dining room table, empty except for two squares of paper. "Here they are."

"What is it?"

"The tickets to Le Havre, the first leg of the journey. Just received them today from Bayen. Go on now, have a look."

"They're a lot bigger than I would have thought."

"The S.S. *Europa*, man! She's brand new! State of the art. Departing in four weeks less a day."

"I can see that," I said. "But why did I have to come to your apartment?"

"To see the tickets! Go ahead, now. Touch them!"

Jean was already dressed when I arrived at her place, an hour late. She wore a shimmering, full-length, oxblood-coloured gown with thin straps that ran like lizard tongues over her bare shoulders. Long bells moulded from silver threads dangled from her ears, and when I kissed her I smelled subtly sweet perfume.

"You fill up that dress pretty nicely," I said.

"Why, thank you," she said, twirling. "What's wrong with your tie?"

I dropped my hat on the table, dipped into the kitchen, and opened the refrigerator for ice. On the counter, I chiselled chunks from the frozen block and poured two drinks, gin martini for Jean, rum for me. Through my restaurant connections I could always get the real stuff. By 1930, Prohibition enforcement was a bit of joke, but I took pride in properly stocking my fiancée's liquor shelf.

"Do we have time?" Jean said.

"Probably not," I said, handing her the drink.

I sat on the sofa, the latest addition to a living room that now included one armchair, a coffee table, and a radio set. She'd found chairs for the dining room, but the tabletop remained unfinished.

Jean lit a cigarette and raised her glass to her lips. She approved of my mix, then set the glass on the table. Without looking at me, she released a smoky sigh and said, "Just tell me."

I can only guess at what she thought was coming next, but I can guarantee it wasn't anything close to what actually came out of my mouth. "I have to go to Ethiopia."

"Okay." She drew out the word, waiting for more.

"Next month," I said. "Four weeks less a day."

"Why do you have to go to Ethiopia?"

I tried to speak but couldn't find my voice. I kept picturing Julian, the joy he'd taken in fingering those ship tickets. And also

Triggs. *You're going.* Those words slithering from his mouth. I sighed. Tears gathered behind my eyes.

"I have to go because Hubert Julian is going, and he wants me to be his aide-de-camp."

"Julian. Again. We had an agreement."

"We did. I know." I stood. Sat down again. "Julian's been offered a job running the Ethiopian Air Force. And also they want him to show off his parachuting."

"Who wants him?"

"Ras Tafari. The next emperor. He has a budget, you see. For staff. And he wants me to be his aide-de-camp."

"For how long?"

"For as long as he's there."

"Is his wife going?"

"No."

"Why not?"

"I don't know."

Jean clutched my hand. She held it against her thigh and the gown's silky material. "Well, it's easy, isn't it? Just tell him you can't go."

"I can't do that."

"He can't *make* you go to Ethiopia. This is America, Arthur. Tell him no."

"I can't."

She released my hand, unclipped her bell-shaped earrings, and tossed them on the table. They bounced like dice and slid to the floor.

"I should tell you," I said. "There are some things you don't know."

"I've got a pretty clear feeling there's a lot I don't know."

I covered my face with my palms and rubbed hard, smearing the first tears into my hair. I searched out air with short breaths. Three, four, five times I sucked in, but my lungs weren't up to it. They felt half rolled up, like a paper bag.

"What are you trying to do? Make yourself pass out? I'll still be here when you wake up."

"It's not Julian."

"Who is it, then?"

"The Bureau of Investigation."

Over the next half-hour, while Jean drank and smoked and stared at me with varying combinations of shock, disbelief, and anger, I told her everything. I mean *everything*. I dug deep, past the loose dirt and rubble, to the very core. I started in 1923. The *Barbara Lynne*, that prison in Oswego, Riley Triggs, and how I'd agreed to spy on Julian in place of twenty to thirty years in jail.

"Oh good Lord," she said at a pause.

"I know."

"Hubert Julian? A threat? To America? How?"

"I don't know. Triggs has this idea."

"Do you agree with him?"

"Not really. I'm not sure, actually. But honestly, after seven years, I don't even know what a threat from Hubert Julian would look like."

"Tell Triggs to find someone else."

"I tried. It doesn't work like that."

"What am I supposed to think? What am I supposed to do?"

"I thought maybe you suspected."

"Suspected? How?" She lit another cigarette. "Okay, maybe something. Something with you and Julian. I thought maybe you were queer for each other, but even then it wasn't because I thought you were a fairy but just because I couldn't figure out why you cared so much about every little thing he did. But then you made that promise to me. It was *your* idea ... What now?"

"I'm so sorry."

"I should fucking hope so! We were supposed to ..." She stood up with the near-empty glass in her hand. "I'd like another drink."

"There's more I need to say."

"No. Actually, I don't think there is, Arthur."

"But —"

"Get me the damn drink, would you?"

I threw together her martini in the kitchen. When I returned to the living room, she was at the radio, bending to the glowing orange dial, waiting for the tubes to warm.

She sipped, then passed the glass back. "Too much vermouth. Try again."

I went for the gin and added a squirt. Jean twisted the radio's knob until she landed on big-band music. A live broadcast relayed to New York from Chicago.

"No drink for you?" she said.

"Doesn't seem like such a good idea."

"A bit late to be taking on virtues, isn't it?"

She listened to the music, one number after another, her gaze fixed on the orange dial as though she were watching a disappointing movie. After a while, I thought I saw a change in her face, the movie mercifully ended. The music and gin combusted inside her, and over the next few minutes, through clarinet, trombone, other solos, I thought she was building to something. I couldn't say what. I sat on the couch and waited, bracing myself, resolved to love her regardless.

The announcer told us about Polident toothpaste and Texaco gasoline, and Jean's face changed again. Whatever it was she'd been building toward vanished. With a flick of the knob, the radio's orange light dimmed, and she slid back next to me on the couch.

"Show's over, I guess," she said, fisting the gin bottle and emptying it into her glass. She tried to kick off her shoes but they were too tight on her feet.

"I feel like I should tell you everything," I said.

"I don't want to hear any more."

"I don't have any choice here."

"You say it like you're blameless."

"Aren't I?"

She gave me a mean look, her eyes glossed with tears. "I really don't see how that could be true."

"Please. Can you listen to me?"

"Enough, Arthur."

"Jean."

She sipped the drink and left the gin to burn in her mouth before swallowing. "Honestly. It's fine," she said.

"It's not fine."

"Why don't we just get on with the rest of our evening?"

"The gala?"

"Screw the gala," she said and then twisted her body and pulled her legs up to the sofa until she was on all fours. Her face was very close to mine. "Really, Arthur. I've always known that in this life, nobody owes anybody anything. Why don't you kiss me?"

"I'm confused," I said.

"Good. Be confused. Whatever makes it hard for you."

She kissed me. The air between our lips felt broken. She shot her hand down to my crotch.

"See? I knew it would work. Bedroom? Unless you just want to fuck me here? Pull the sofa back from the wall and you can fuck me from behind. Keep the curtains open, too. Then all my neighbours can see me being fucked."

"Jean."

"What? What's there to lose?"

"I don't —"

"Okay, fine. Bedroom, then. You go. I'll be right in."

She shut the bathroom door, leaving me alone in the now-quiet living room. Among the many good things about being with Jean was that it allowed me to forget a little about Triggs and Sing Sing. She alleviated that sense of fear that always came on me when I thought about the future. Whenever I imagined this night, one of the upsetting parts was realizing that I would no longer have her to lessen the fear.

But it didn't happen that way. Now that Jean knew everything, instead of intensifying, the fear disappeared. I realized, as I made my way to the bedroom, that I wasn't afraid of going to Africa either, even with its indefinite date of return. Why should I be? I had no control. What happened in this apartment or in Ethiopia or anywhere else in the world had nothing to do with what I wanted or didn't want. Fearing something you can't control, like the weather or kidney failure, say, is a waste of energy.

I lay down on her bed in the dark, but when Jean came in she turned on all the lights. I guessed that she wanted me to see everything, to sail to Africa with the memory vivid. Without looking at me, she went to work on my trousers, unbuckling and unzipping and tugging. She pulled my unsure prick from its nesting place and then paused. She was looking at her forearm, her light skin against my darker stomach.

"What are you, anyway?"

"What do you mean?"

"I mean, where are your people from? Before Trinidad. Is it Spain? I always figured Spain."

"Why?"

"Because of the Rio Tormes."

"Tormes was my mother's name."

"Was she Spanish?"

"Maybe. I never had the chance to ask her about it."

Jean's eyebrow flinched. "Huh."

She wasn't going to believe much of anything I said tonight. Even still, "There's something I should tell you about my mother. When I said she was a teacher, she wasn't."

"Who cares, Arthur."

"Also, she didn't actually die of —"

"Really, just fucking shut up, okay?"

She raised her red gown to her hips and reached to pull me inside. I was stiff, not just in the prick but seized all over, a kind of mortification. As Jean rose and fell, she pulled her shoulder straps down her arms and now the dress was bunched at her middle. I wanted to touch her breasts but felt like I needed express permission. I reached for them anyway. She began to move faster. She was familiar and yet different, just enough to notice. Like the difference in two accents from the same language.

"Don't you dare stop," she said.

"Stop what?"

She didn't want to hear it. She clamped a firm hand over my mouth, crushing my lips against my front teeth. It forced my heavy breathing through half-covered nostrils, producing snotty wet noises, an ugly accompaniment to her pleasures. Still, she continued, faster and more deliberate, oblivious to my sloppy breathing, until she found the spot. After she came, she released her syrupy limbs and let her body deflate next to me. I climbed atop her, closed my eyes, and did not open them until I finished.

We lay together under all the glaring lights in her bedroom. I felt tremors coursing through her body. I made efforts to slow my breathing but didn't wait for my pulse to return to normal. I stood and buckled my belt and tucked in my shirt and then looked down at Jean on the bed. Her beautiful gown was still bunched in thick red folds across her middle. Below it, wetness reflected light on her skin and in the curls of her hair.

PART TWO

When a man achieves greatness, there his troubles begin.

> — **HUBERT JULIAN,** in *Chicago Defender,* December 6, 1930

37

AWAY FROM THE SEA, THE
HEAT PUNCHED HARD

HUBERT JULIAN AND I SAILED ON THE *EUROPA* TO LE HAVRE, where we caught one train to Paris, then another to Marseille. In Marseille we climbed aboard a different ship that called on several ports in the Mediterranean before funnelling through the Suez Canal and into the Red Sea. Finally, on May 31, 1930, we tied up in the Port of Djibouti where gulls and petrels paddled through the calm, oily water and the heat-stilled air smelled of spent diesel and rotting fish.

Malaku Bayen, sporting a broad topee against the sun and heat, greeted us at the foot of the gangplank. Two uniformed men lurked a few feet behind. "Welcome," he said. A handshake for Julian, a cool nod for me. In jaunty, diplomatic tones, he asked Julian about the trip, if he'd enjoyed the views, if he'd experienced any rough seas.

"Everything was fine. Really. An exceptionally smooth crossing."

Bayen pointed to his car, parked with others in a nearby lot. "To your hotel, then?"

But Julian wasn't ready. He was too busy looking around, taking in the scene like he'd waited his whole life to see the eastern edge of the African continent and this sun-whipped, salty city of low white-washed buildings, warehouses, and precious few trees. Beyond a concrete breakwater, anchored cargo ships waited for an available berth while closer in, fishing boats bobbed on red-and-white moorings, their metal riggings clanging flat tones. Longshoremen rolled barrels into freighter holds and fishermen lugged tackle and nets to or from their skiffs. Men in white shawls crossed in the other direction, leading mules loaded with grain, firewood, bricks. We'd arrived on a market day and vendors beckoned from under faded canopies, offering deals on hides, spices, flowers, fruit, cloth, coffee, housewares, and precious stones. From somewhere in the city, a minaret blared a call to prayer.

"Beautiful, isn't it?" Julian said. "Truly wonderful." He touched a handkerchief to the corner of each eye.

Bayen's driver brought us to Place Menelik and our hotel, which shared the city square with government offices, a police station, and a clutch of sleepy shops and cafés where tables of Arab men sipped frothy coffee from small glasses. Here, away from the sea, the heat punched even harder, but Julian remained unbothered.

"Look at that, Mr. Tormes," he said, pointing first to a man in a priestly looking robe and then to a camel tied to a post. In the hotel's arcade, he joked with the porters, embraced the manager, clowned around with a bunch of shoeless kids who'd swarmed him. In his Montreal French, still fluent after so many years, he bantered and teased and handed out pennies and nickels from America.

The next day at dawn, Bayen rushed us down to the train station, where I wheeled Julian's trunks to the luggage car. By the time I'd delivered the last one, my shirt was soaked in sweat and I needed a rest. It wasn't even eight o'clock, but the intense heat had me out of sorts. I was slow; my brain felt enveloped in fog. Also that morning, I'd taken my first dose of quinine.

But I couldn't rest yet. A conductor's whistle blew a warning, and passengers began to move. Bayen led us to the first-class carriage, where he whipped out an arm like he'd made the car appear especially for Julian. The Black Eagle approached with lively, grand strides and climbed in. I started after but Bayen wouldn't have it.

"This is not your car, Mr. Arthur." Bayen's English was flawless, his accent plainly American, and yet I squinted and stared at him as though he'd been speaking Japanese. I tried to enter the car again but Bayen lowered his cloaked arm to bar my way. He pointed a long finger in the direction of the distant caboose and said, "Your carriage is down there."

I reached into a pocket for my little green ticket and through the brain fog I read the French: *troisième classe.*

"I see," I said, and started down the platform.

As I passed his window, Julian poked his head through the wide frame. "Enjoy the trip, Mr. Tormes!" Behind him, a man in a red coat poured coffee from a carafe.

"Enjoy your coffee," I said. "Don't burn your tongue."

"Don't be upset, man! It's just protocol!"

I squirmed through the shuffling crowd to reach my car. My seat was a hard bench nailed together from mismatched slats. I sat next to a man who'd already fallen asleep against the window. No men in red coats, no coffee.

Four hours later, we stopped in Ali Sabieh, where the compartment filled with men and women clinging to bundles wrapped in rope. Their children squeezed into empty spaces on the floor. My companion woke in time to disembark and I slid to the window, freeing a space for a lady and the two boys she stuffed between us. For a long time, the kids stared at my face, the only white one on this part of the train. When I offered a smile in return, they shifted in tandem toward their mother, clinging to the excess cloth of her dress.

And on we went. To Guelile and to Dewele, where customs officials inspected luggage and demanded ten thalers to update a visa that was supposed to be valid for another twelve months. We crossed the border into Ethiopia and then stopped at Adele, where

I left my seat to drain my bladder into parched desert sands. When I returned, someone had claimed my place on the bench. The boys peered up at me, this time all smiles.

The conductor blew his whistle and the train resumed its chugging course. The engine didn't have much guts and progress was slow, sometimes at the pace of a slow jog. Shifting from one foot to the other, I found the lack of speed frustrating, at least until we actually did accelerate and the train began to sway on its narrow gauge, leaning to one side and holding a worrisome tilt before shifting back.

We came on near-desert land, where sand swirled under a close sun. The grit invaded the car and soon my eyes were red and swollen, my throat bone dry. Passengers who knew better had already wrapped scarves over their faces and drank from water flasks. A man beside me poured a few ounces into my cupped palms. I bowed my head a little at the kindness and made a note to learn the words for "thank you."

We arrived at a deep gorge spanned by a wooden bridge then hugged tight to cliffs as the train fought its way up a severe grade. On the descent, the brakes screeched continuously, sounding like a large animal in embarrassed distress.

Back on flatter land, we spent a long time passing a range of distant rounded mountains. Closer to the tracks were several anthills: steep, roughened dirt cones built by tiny insects and yet still magnificently taller than an average horse. On the banks of a muddy lake, I watched gazelles bend their antlers to rip at sweet shoots and grasses. Not long after, one ostrich stood before another, flapping a friendly wing. A troop of long-tailed monkeys contemplated our passing from the naked branches of a tree. I thought of Jean Fox, how much she would have enjoyed these strange new sights.

At the end of the long day, we put in for the night in Dire Dawa, a town built especially for the railway. I spotted Julian and Bayen on the platform, chatting under a shady awning. We'd been inside a crowded train for ten hours, but Julian looked well rested, even energized. He commented unfavourably on the cakes they'd served after Adele.

"Felt like yesterday's batch."

"I'd have eaten them even if they were last year's," I said.

Bayen sneered, like hunger was confirmation of my weakness. He pointed to a two-storey brick building with a small garden in front. "You may take Lieutenant Julian's overnight bag to that hotel. Room 34."

A simple-looking place, but I didn't much care. I only needed food, a decent bed, and a bath.

"And my room number?" I asked.

"You are not lodging in that hotel," Bayen said. "Follow my man. He will show you."

After dropping Julian's baggage, Bayen's unspeaking man led me down a couple of blocks of dirt road, past a line of bougainvillea bushes with their purple blooms, to a low, mud-bricked structure. In a tiny, airless room I collapsed onto a rickety bed made of strapped-together boards and a sack half stuffed with dried straw for a mattress.

Julian was already in the station when I arrived the next morning. He looked fresh, his face clean shaved.

"Restful sleep, Tormes?" he asked.

I rotated my cramped shoulder. "I feel like I spent the night hung up in a dungeon."

"This isn't Manhattan, is it?" he said, laughing.

After another night's stopover, this time in a place called Awash, the train climbed up to the central plateau and we arrived, finally, in Addis Ababa. A contingent of four imperial guards greeted Julian on the platform and then escorted us to the Hotel de France, the city's finest, our rooms courtesy of Ras Tafari's imperial government.

I lugged Julian's trunks up to the sixth floor and a bright, well-furnished suite. Julian picked up a table lamp, put it down, ran his hand along the thick bed spread. He nodded, quietly humming with approval. He opened a set of double doors to a north-facing balcony overlooking the hotel's gardens. From that perch, he could see the tennis club, the polo grounds, and the silvery dome crowning the new cathedral where the emperor's coronation would take place in November.

I hoisted his last trunk to a closet shelf.

"You need to sleep," he told me. "I can see that. It's been a long few days. Why don't you unpack the trunks, set up my toiletries, hang the suits in the closet, and lay out my pyjamas, slippers, and housecoat. Then let's call it a day."

My own room, a few floors below, was dark, cramped, and generally beaten up. Inside, I opened a window to flush the staleness. On this side of the hotel, the view was of a lopsided grid of narrow streets crammed with shacks moulded from mud and bundled sticks. Some roads were paved or cobbled, but most were packed with dirt that lifted and fell with passing feet and hooves. Hundreds of cooking fires laid out a cover of haze that smelled of burning spices. In the distance, shadowy hills rippled with eucalyptus trees.

I kicked off my shoes, unbuttoned my shirt, and got to work unpacking my own trunk, including the typewriter I'd carried across an ocean, two seas, and half a desert. I set it on the little desk and sat down feeling a kind of loneliness that reminded me of those nights I'd spent in the Oswego jail.

I wanted to write a letter, to connect to someone, even if only for a page or two. Mostly, I wanted to write to Jean. I could tell her about the trip and the interesting things I'd seen, the gazelles and the monkeys and the shape of the land. But she'd been totally clear in that regard: any letters that came her way from me would be dropped — unopened — into the incinerator.

So who, then? Tommy Kippers? The boss and I had parted on good terms. The restaurant business was hurting; he'd been looking to cut staff anyway. But writing to Kippers — or to anyone else — would mean explaining why I'd come to Ethiopia, and I had no appetite for confessions that night.

Which left Special Agent Riley Triggs. We'd been in the city for less than half a day and I had nothing new to report to him. Other than Bayen and a few hotel and train workers, Julian had spoken to no one. Nor had he performed any of his new duties as Air Force commander.

And yet, a few minutes later I was at the desk, rolling a sheet of paper into the machine, and pecking out the familiar heading of my report. Why not? It wouldn't be the first time I'd made something from nothing, would it?

I didn't get far before someone knocked on my door. A note had arrived for Lieutenant Julian. I figured as aide-de-camp it was as much my job to open notes as it was to carry his bags. Besides, if it was nothing important, I could let him know in the morning.

But after reading, I rebuttoned my shirt, laced my shoes, and went straight back up to Julian's room. This news would not wait until morning.

38

SHE LOWERED HER VOICE TO
A CONSPIRATORIAL LEVEL

THE NOTE CAME FROM AN OFFICIAL NAMED TESSEMA WHO, in the name of Ras Tafari, had summoned Julian to the gebbi on Mount Entoto, the complex where the emperors of Ethiopia had held court since Addis became the national capital. With hours yet to go before the appointment, Julian paced the boards of his suite, fretting as he tried to decide between the blue aviator's uniform, cut for him seven years ago and fashionable in its day, and the dark suit he had made before we left New York.

"Pinstripes are fine in America, but at the court of the Lion of Judah?" he wondered. I didn't bother to venture an opinion. After flipping and flopping about a thousand times, he went with the blue uniform.

"I don't want to give anyone reason to doubt my purpose," he reasoned.

A car collected us at the hotel and we were off, zigzagging through a confusing series of narrow streets packed with mules, cars, carts, and people going about everyday business. We cut through the diplomatic quarter and houses protected by high walls and men with rifles. A road banked by flowering shrubs led up a hill to the gebbi's main entrance. There, a guard led us ceremoniously to the main palace and its great hall, an open salon with a polished floor and tall windows that overlooked the rooftops of Addis Ababa.

I stayed back as Julian presented his invitation. Once inside, I leaned to him. "You should drink some water," I said. I retrieved a glass from a tray, but his hands were too unsteady to hold it properly and I took it back. In seven years, I had never seen him so excited, so taken by his own emotions. The Black Eagle of Harlem was positively vibrating.

"Are you okay, Hubert?"

"Fine. Obviously, I'm fine. Why wouldn't I be?"

"You're sweating."

"This is a great honour for me," he said. "Give me your hanky, would you?"

After a short wait, a servant conducted Julian into the palace's inner rooms. He walked through one set of carved doors and then another, each opened in their sequence by a liveried footman. Leaning in, I caught a glimpse of the crimson throne and the two seats, one for Ras Tafari, the other for Menen, his queen. Next to the throne, a servant stood ready with a pillow. Later, I learned his purpose: to place the pillow before the emperor's high chair and thereby save His Majesty the indignity of dangling feet.

I retreated to a small room to wait with other aides. I met the French trade commissioner's assistant, the secretary from the Italian naval delegation, less official types, too. There were merchants, traders, and a German pharmacist who'd once been a stage actor in Hamburg. They seemed at ease here, drinking coffee, smoking, playing cards. From what I could understand they preferred their talk small — weather, horses, tennis games — their conversations marked by a kind of unlively slowness, as if everyone knew they needed to spread the topics thin.

After mingling for half an hour, I found myself next to a woman with neatly styled dark hair and the kind of clear, fair skin you see in advertisements for beauty soaps. She was short, a few years older than me, with a stature that made me think she would be hard to knock over. I asked her what was supposed to happen at these things.

"You're looking at it."

"Card playing? Smoking?"

"Oh, we gossip, too. What legation are you attached to? Wait, allow me a guess. Greek? No? Syrian?"

"My name is Arthur Tormes," I said. "I'm with Julian. Lieutenant Julian."

"Oh," she said. "So you're with *him*."

"I'm his aide-de-camp."

"A white man working for a Negro? In America? That's somewhat unusual, isn't it?"

"You see it from time to time. It happens." She stared at me in expectation of a more fulsome answer. "I didn't catch your name."

"It's Dunckley," she said. "Mrs. Russell Dunckley. My man is with Coward and Sons of London, the coffee traders. He's not a Coward, before you ask. But he's in Nairobi, so I'm here on the chance there's something to learn."

"About coffee?"

She shrugged with her eyes. "If I'm really honest, I don't know why I come. Boredom more than anything, I suppose."

She asked me more about Julian, and I explained that Ras Tafari wanted him to run his air force.

"Impressive," she said. "Though not a demanding job in Ethiopia."

"What do you mean?"

"Well, for one thing, there are only three planes in the imperial force."

"Only three?"

"Theoretically. But in actual fact only two, since one is a new Gipsy Moth. Ras Tafari prohibits anyone from flying it. Not that he hasn't put the other two to good use."

She paused, waiting for me to ask. Which I did. "How so?"

"Well. It happened a few months ago." Her eyes widened and her voice dropped to just above a whisper. Mrs. Dunckley was a woman who liked intrigue, even if it had to be invented. "There was an uprising. In the north. A rival by the name of Gugsa Welle, also husband to the late Empress Zewditu, had amassed an army in secret, believing he'd claim the crown all for himself. A good old-fashioned palace coup. Except Tafari got wind of his plans and dispatched Captain Maillet over there to drop a few grenades on Welle's troops." She flicked her head toward a roundish figure stuffed into a French military uniform.

"What happened?"

"Welle's men were brave fighters, but they'd never before faced an air attack. They were scared witless. Ran for their lives. Gugsa Welle fought on but in the end, they shot him dead as he rode atop a white charger. How glorious! Now he's set up to be a martyr to the conservative cause."

"And Zewditu?"

"Also dead. Two days later."

"Suicide?"

"Sadly, no. Not quite so romantic, I'm afraid. Diabetes. The old girl had a weakness for sweets, you see." Mrs. Dunckley lowered her voice again. "There've been rumours that Tafari poisoned her. No one has any proof, of course, but you can see how it's a perfectly logical explanation."

"Certainly," I said. And then, "Do you happen to know how to spell Zewditu?"

Addis Ababa, Abyssinia, May 22, 1930

TO: BOI Special Agent Riley Triggs

RE: JULIAN, HUBERT (a.k.a. THE BLACK EAGLE
            OF HARLEM)

FILE NO: 30-20

By now you have received report with details of
JULIAN's first meeting with Ras TAFARI. JULIAN
remains fascinated with Emperor Designate, talks of
little else. Full of praise for the king's mind, manners,
great interest in aviation, progress of Abyssinia, Africa
in general, etc.

    Less clear to Your Informant were Emperor
Designate's feelings toward JULIAN. However, these
clarified later this very afternoon at festival in the city.
The Emperor Designate, curious to see parachuting
demonstration, asked JULIAN to jump from height of
5,000 feet. Target was infield of the city's hippodrome.
Grounds decorated for occasion with national flags on
staffs. Ras TAFARI watched from large grandstand,
accompanied by elites, ambassadors, important visitors,
etc. Lower-ranking officials and other observers on
smaller grandstand. Regular Ethiopians, three and four
deep, surrounded field. No seats.

    JULIAN, eager to know TAFARI's reaction to the
jump, instructed Your Informant to pay close attention.
The pilot, MAILLET (French, referenced in previous
reports), took JULIAN up. At first, plane flew much
higher than 5,000 feet. Your Informant wondered if
Frenchman trying to sabotage jump to cause JULIAN to
lose favour with TAFARI. However, plane later brought
lower.

    Jump went very well. Exceptional success. JULIAN
landed on target, only 10 yards from Emperor's
grandstand. A one-in-a-thousand shot.

    Crowd erupted, elated. Moments later Ras TAFARI
climbed down from grandstand to shake JULIAN's

hand. Very rare honour. Applause continued. JULIAN
overcome with pride.

Several more honours bestowed. JULIAN made full
colonel in Imperial Air Force. It was explained that
promotion could come only if JULIAN agreed to accept
Ethiopian citizenship, which he did, renouncing British
rights in same breath.

Later, at well-attended ceremony in the palace,
TAFARI used old Coptic Bible to swear in JULIAN.
Then he pinned medal to JULIAN's chest. The Order of
Menelik II, country's highest decoration. Heavy cross
in red and green with gold trim dangling from ribbon.
Another rare honour, very unexpected. JULIAN saluted
by officers of the Imperial Army and veterans of Adwa.

TAFARI signed over six servants: three men, three
women. Their jobs: JULIAN's laundry, cooking, polishing
boots, sewing buttons on new uniform when it arrives (to
be studded with lions and crowns and other symbols of
Ethiopian might). TAFARI requested JULIAN to perform
at Coronation, set for November 1. Emperor also loaned a
car. Italian Fiat, chauffeur included.

END OF REPORT

39

HE BECAME A MAJOR ATTRACTION

SOON ALL OF AFRICA HAD LEARNED OF JULIAN'S PARA-chuting triumph and each day bundles of letters arrived for him at the hotel. Admirers wrote from across the continent: the Gold Coast, Rhodesia, Kenya, the Congo; schoolboys requesting auto-graphed photos, or advice on training to be a pilot.

"It shows how African boys are thinking of the future," Julian said. "In America, only Babe Ruth and Roy Rogers get this kind of mail. Meanwhile, the heroes here are actually contributing to human progress."

I sat at the typewriter while he dictated the replies. "Something like, 'You can do anything anyone else can do. Just get up, brother, and try. If you fail the first time, don't quit. Try again. You'll make it.'"

With all the new servants at his disposal, correspondence was one of the few duties I had left as aide-de-camp. Another was teach-ing English to his pilot trainees, mostly vocabulary and expressions related to aviation. I also accompanied Julian to social events and in that respect, I was busy. Every legation and club wanted him on their guest lists. Private homes opened their doors and Julian met all the important and interesting people in Addis: the traders, diplomats and physicians, the missionaries and educators. Ex-pats and Ethiopians alike demanded to know more about his life and how he'd captured the emperor's attention by flying and jumping in Harlem. He tensed his hands into claws to show them how he kept the fear outside. They wanted to know what had really happened when he tried to cross the Atlantic.

"It was the size of the crowd that did me in," he said. "There were so many photographers and writers, so many admirers who wanted to shake my hand and wish me luck, that I had no choice but to postpone the takeoff until the tide receded. That's what caused the unfortunate disaster. Will I make another attempt? I'm too focused on my duties here, but I wouldn't rule it out."

He repeated the old stories about McGill, medicine, France, and his apprenticeship in Montreal with Billy Bishop. Speaking English or French, sometimes both, he could keep a small audience entertained for hours. I don't think it's an exaggeration say that in the summer of 1930, with the exception of Ras Tafari, of course, Hubert Julian was the most popular man in Ethiopia.

On one of those golden nights, we attended an outdoor performance by Prince Hadji Ali. His act was built around Hadji's special anatomy, specifically a second stomach, tucked somewhere behind the first, that allowed Hadji to swallow all sorts of things — keys, watches, coins, a light bulb, even a live mouse — then bring them back up at will. A talent like that travels and the prince had a long resumé. He'd headlined shows in music halls from England to Egypt, played vaudeville all over America. He'd been among the last to perform at Russia's Winter Palace, and between tricks he told the Addis crowd how he'd seen the sadness of the tsar and tsarina, as though they knew, in their hearts, that a bloody end was drawing near.

At the show's thrilling climax, the prince downed a jug of water followed by a pint of kerosene. Then, his lovely daughter, the slinky Princess Almina, her scanty outfit adorned with bells and cymbals, set light to a small bundle of sticks on the stage. With great flourish of arms and folds of robe, Hadji spat the kerosene up into a long stream that arched and landed on the smouldering bundle of sticks. Flames whooshed, rising five or seven feet and dangerously close to the canvas canopy. After a few anxious moments, he spread his arms again and calmly heaved up the water, dousing the flames until the fire was extinguished. After, while driving back to the hotel, both Julian and I agreed: we'd gladly pay to see the prince perform again.

Back in my room, I flopped onto the narrow bed and clicked off the lamp. In the deep darkness of my confinement, I felt strangely content. Yes, content. And for a few reasons. Being far away was helping to cool the burn of losing Jean. I also felt insulated a little against the oppressiveness of Riley Triggs. I wouldn't say that I felt free (in fact, I still had the compulsion to look for him whenever I entered any room). But knowing he couldn't demand any face-to-face meetings or show up unannounced to threaten or intimidate or otherwise screw up my life made me feel less *un*free.

After seven years of spying on the man, I found myself rooting for the Black Eagle. This was a relaunch for him, the kind of fresh start he'd wanted when he left Trinidad for Canada and again when he moved to New York City. What made it different this time was that people here were on his side. The emperor's support counted for a lot, of course. A friend of Ras Tafari was a friend everyone wanted to call their own. I suppose I wasn't immune to his star power. I got caught up in it like everybody else.

Also, Julian seemed changed by this place, though it was hard to say how, exactly. He was definitely happy. As happy as I'd ever seen him. As happy as I'd ever seen any man, really. In a city with not much to do, only two movie theatres, the Black Eagle was a major attraction. Whenever he walked into a hotel lobby or restaurant, a small buzz coursed around the room. You sometimes got the sense they were waiting for an excuse to bust out a round of applause. He still focused on his own grandness. He still lied on occasion. So maybe he hadn't changed that much. Maybe in that equatorial land, where the days and nights were equally long, I was just *seeing* him differently.

Certainly, I was paying more attention. Or rather, I was paying a different kind of attention. In New York, I had listened to his talk and hoped to pick out something incriminating. Here I just listened. I realized, as I hadn't before, that his personality had a cumulative effect: the more he talked, the more you felt compelled to listen.

Sort of like the way we were compelled to watch Prince Hadji, I thought.

Except the prince was only in Addis for a week. Soon he would move on. To Nairobi, Salisbury, and then Cape Town and Johannesburg. A professional like Prince Ali Hadji knew how it worked. You can't play one town forever.

40

IT'S NOT SO EASY TO FIND A WORTHY OPPONENT

TO KILL TIME ON FREE AFTERNOONS, I OFTEN WENT DOWN to the tennis club. It had six clay courts ringed by ivy-covered walls, an emerald sanctuary for the displaced tennis players of Addis Ababa. I didn't play and no one ever asked, but even if they had, I wouldn't have known what to do with a racquet in my hand. Whack at the ball, sure. But where to? And how hard? Where to move? And how did you avoid tangling with your partner? Tennis in clubs seemed like a game you could learn only if you were born into it.

I liked to watch, though, especially a long rally — the slow rhythm, not quite clock-like but steady and soothing. And the pock sound on a sweetly struck ball, the grunted umph! with each hard shot. I liked the way the kids crouched at the net and scurried after mis-hit balls.

Mrs. Dunckley, the coffee-trader's wife, was one of the better players. She had a quick pivot and glided effortlessly from one line to the other. On serves, she hit with authority, her little body arching to the sky with the toss before whipping the racquet forward. She always wore an all-white outfit, which added to the elegance of her game.

One day, she was playing against Mrs. Modin, the Swedish ambassador's wife. The younger woman had just broken serve, leaving
Mrs. Dunckley down three games to none. On the next point, the
Swede dared to charge the net. Mrs. Dunckley responded by drill-
ing her return into the woman's left breast. The game stopped. Mrs.
Dunckley apologized while her opponent bent over to catch her
breath. She recovered but for the remainder of the match elected
to play safe, holding firm to the distant baseline. In the end, Mrs.
Dunckley won out, claiming a come-from-behind victory.

"You put a lot of spin on that backhand," I said when she came
to the sidelines for a towel. I imitated her stroke with my empty
hand.

"You're here again, I see," she said, dabbing her neck. "And yet
I never see you playing."

"I'd only embarrass myself," I said.

"Too bad," she said. "Maybe someday you'll change your mind.
I find it's not so easy to find a worthy opponent."

The next day, after another win, Mrs. Dunckley invited me up to
the clubhouse bar where we took a table overlooking the courts.
I wanted beer but she ordered us gin and tonics instead. "On a
humid day, you'll find it infinitely more refreshing," she said.

She asked what I'd seen of Ethiopia, if I'd visited Lalibela. "The
churches are the main thing, of course, but at dusk you walk up a
long hill.... You'll never see a sunset like it. Magnificent."

We sipped our drinks and watched the languid warm-ups of
a pending doubles match. I asked Mrs. Dunckley if she usually
played with her husband.

She shook her head. "Mr. Dunckley lost his feel for the game
some time ago." She brushed at the skirt's pleats, as though trying
to flatten them.

I wished I knew something more about tennis. The name of a
champion or two, or a few of the all-time greats, something to hold
up my end of the conversation.

We drained the last of our gin and tonics. Mrs. Dunckley looked at me for a long moment and I thought she might be about to suggest another round. Instead, she uncrossed her legs, leaned forward, and lowering her voice to that conspiratorial quiet she liked to use, she invited me — unambiguously — to visit her house later that afternoon.

My first response? To uselessly tip my empty glass into my mouth. Her dark hair, pinned up for exercise, now fell loose in places and stuck to her sweat-damp neck. The excited flush in her round cheeks intensified the green of her eyes. She regarded me over flat blue sunglass lenses, waiting for my answer. I won't say I wasn't interested, or tempted.

But there were considerations. I feared inserting myself into one more thing that would only complicate my circumstances. Also, I was still thinking a good deal about Jean Fox. Maybe not as much as last week or the week before that, but enough to leave me hesitant. Plus, I remembered that Mrs. Dunckley had a husband, even if, as she had said, they no longer played tennis together,

She read my face and shifted easily from cool insinuation to cool indifference. The waiter arrived. I reached into my pocket.

"Please, let me get these."

"They won't take cash," she said, signing the chit. "Perhaps another time."

41

I'D WALK TO THE LIP OF
AN ACTIVE VOLCANO

IT MUST HAVE BEEN A FEW NIGHTS OR EVEN A WEEK LATER
that Julian had a dinner scheduled and left me with the night
to myself. I decided to have a drink in the Imperial Hotel's bar,
hoping for a relaxing evening and to catch up on the news from
America. When I arrived, only two other tables were occupied. At
one, a pair of Ethiopian men in suits discussed the finer points of
a document they passed back and forth. At the other, two dowdy
white couples played bridge, mumbling bids and squinting at their
cards in the dim light.

Selecting a table far from the bridge game, I tossed my hat onto
one chair and slouched lazily into the other. I ordered a beer and
began to pick through stacks of old newspapers left by previous
patrons. A full three years had passed since Charles Lindbergh
landed in Paris and yet aviation news remained worthy of boldface
front-page headlines. *Graf Zeppelin Approaching New York After
Floating North from Brazil. British Planes Bomb Rebel Strongholds
in India.* My beer was not quite finished when I turned to the front
section of a weeks-old copy of *The Sun*, Jean's paper. More news
about pilots. The brave girl flyer, Amy Johnson, had successfully

landed her de Havilland in west Australia after taking off from London nineteen days earlier. I paused my reading to ponder Amy in her single-engine machine, trapped into that tiny cockpit for days with nothing but endless sky and ocean and untamed desert and jungle below her. Good for her, though to me, it sounded just short of torture.

And then, among the packed-in briefs on the social pages, I saw an announcement that caused my heart to capsize. *The Sun's* roaming foreign correspondent, Jonas Windermere, was keeping it in the family by marrying the paper's own obituary writer, Miss Jeannette Fox, twenty-six, daughter of the late Beatrice and Roland Fox, formerly of Port Huron, Michigan.

I folded the paper with a snap then swore loud enough to halt the bridge game. All four grey heads turned my way. After a moment, I went back to the page.

Windermere had proposed to her at Luke's, in midtown, having arranged to hide the diamond ring in a raw oyster. The article quoted Jean, my former fiancée: "He figured because I didn't choke on the thing, we were meant to be."

This was still several years before his books were bestsellers and well before Tyrone Power starred in the movie about his life, but I remembered the name Jonas Windermere from when Jean worked the switchboard at *The Sun*. I checked the date. Assuming no glitches, no tornadoes, landslides, plagues, or lightning strikes, Jean — Jeannette — Fox had walked down the aisle on June 21, just eight days ago. The newlyweds were due to depart for San Francisco on June 23rd, followed by a ten-day honeymoon at sea en route to Hong Kong, Jonas' next assignment.

The waiter arrived to ask if there would be another beer. I waved him off. I didn't want to get drunk. I didn't know what I wanted. To smash something. My own head would be a good start. I thought back to my divorce-raiding days, finally understanding those pitiful jilted spouses who tagged along with our crew on raids. Painful to them, embarrassing to everyone else, at least they could say later that they got their shots in. Stuck here in the middle of Africa, I would never know that satisfaction. Instead, I raised my hand for that second beer, adding a double shot of whisky to my order. Jean Fox. Married. But now she called herself Jeannette. Since when? This annoyed me, too. To be the last to know about such a fundamental change in her life.

The drinks arrived. I drained the whisky in a single throw. "Another?" asked the barman. "No," I said. I definitely didn't want to get drunk. I picked up the paper again. My hands weren't working quite right; they struggled to turn the pages. The article remained in the same spot. I tossed it to the next table with a clumsy throw. It split apart and half the pages ended up on the floor.

Did I have any right to be angry? Not with the way it had ended between us, which was all my fault. Immersing myself in a pit of regret, I kept asking what I could have done different. Damn Triggs. Damn the *Barbara Lynne*. Damn it all. Now Jean was married and sailing to China. And good for her! I should send my congratulations, a nobly composed note wishing every happiness for the future. A note to Jonas, too. Why not? Everyone should be happy. Maybe I'd do that. Not tonight, though. Tonight, forgetting restraint, I only wanted another double shot of whisky. And then another after that. And when I'd had enough, I'd walk to the lip of an active volcano and jump right in.

While I waved at the waiter, Julian came into the bar with a pair of men I'd never seen. Spotting me and my state, his face twisted disapprovingly. He pointed his malacca cane deliberately across the room to an empty table near the bridge players, then hollered at the barman for a bottle of Cinzano for his pals, plus Vichy water for him. In the next instant, the bottles and glasses arrived at Julian's table and it was like he couldn't ask for better service, even if he owned the place.

42

THE EXCUSES EASED IN

I SLEPT FITFULLY THAT NIGHT. AFTER A LATE BREAKFAST that went unfinished, I directed myself back to the tennis club. My head was throbbing, my stomach swirled, my thoughts were a jumble. I was full of turbulence and wanted it purged.

I spotted Mrs. Dunckley on a courtside bench, wiping sweat from her neck after her morning game.

"Good morning, Mr. Tormes."

I wanted to make this happen and the sooner the better. "Okay," I said, "let's go."

She looked up at me, continuing her ritualized dabbing.

"How nice to see you again," she said. "Go where?"

I shrugged. "My hotel?"

She glanced past my shoulder, then behind. I did the same. A few players occupied the courts; others spun their racquets on the sidelines. I'd met some before, but they were nothing to me.

"That's not possible," she said.

"That's not what you said yesterday."

"Yesterday, I invited you to my house."

"Okay, then. Your house. Let's go."

"It doesn't quite work like that." She inserted her racquet into its brace, two stacked trapezoids fastened with wing nuts and bolts at each corner. She circled the brace, tightening the nuts. This wasn't happening in the straightforward, automatic way I'd expected.

"What do you mean? Why not?"

She paused, as though to reconsider her invitation. She saw that something had flipped and that I was acting recklessly. Apparently, there were reckless people in her crowd. She had to figure what brand I was bringing to her, if it was the kind she could contain.

"Because it doesn't, Mr. Tormes." Her tone told me I would get nowhere on my current tack.

I took a breath and softened my tone. "As it happens, I'm pretty used to following rules," I said. "Tell me how yours work."

She smiled. From her tennis bag she produced a card. "My address. There's a little map on the back to direct you. Friday. Three o'clock sharp."

The Dunckleys lived in a wide white-washed bungalow fronted by crowded beds of flowers in full bloom. Mrs. Dunckley herself answered my knock, wearing a simple house dress made of thin cloth. We went straight to the bedroom. With the window blinds closed, the only light came from a single table lamp whose shade gave everything a yellowy hue. We crossed a floor rug made from a stretched-out animal skin, its sand-coloured fur brushed flat. She asked me to unclasp her pearls, then let them fall into a small wooden bowl on the bed stand next to a stack of books, a glass medicine bottle, and a large photograph framed in ebony.

For a brief, troubling moment, I thought the man in the picture was Agent Riley Triggs. My face must have turned a colour because Mrs. Dunckley asked if something was wrong.

I blinked. The photograph was not Triggs at all, but Russell Dunckley. The eyes had tricked me. There was something similar in their narrowness. Otherwise, her husband looked nothing at all like Triggs. His face was thinner, his hair darker and much thicker though the photo was old, too. The high, rounded collar suggested prewar.

"It's nothing."

She drew close and kissed me. "Good."

Mrs. Dunckley's hands pulled on my belt. I involuntarily glanced at the photo again. Her husband seemed to be leaning forward, a slightly bewildered look in those close-set eyes. My belt slid through the loops and landed on the floor. I wondered if there could be an arrangement between them. Maybe they were Catholic, unhappy with each other and yet prohibited from splitting up by religion. Or maybe divorce meant a lost inheritance or allowance for one or the other.

As my trousers fell to the rug, I settled on an arrangement. No point concerning myself with the specifics. Yes, an arrangement, I thought. You heard about those things all the time. I wondered if they still loved each other. If — despite the location of her hands at that exact moment — she still loved him the way I hadn't stopped loving Jean Fox.

She told me to sit on the bed and dropped to her knees. My prick hardened and I forgot about the photo. I shuddered at the first up and down explorations of her tongue. As she positioned herself, I tried more forgetting, this time trying to rub Jean Fox from my mind. Jean on her honeymoon, travelling by boat to China, probably having an afternoon fuck, too. Maybe I felt some guilt, an artifact of my earlier life. But with Mrs. Dunckley's head bobbing at my crotch, I quickly developed a victim's sense of entitlement. The excuses eased in. I hadn't asked to come to Ethiopia, had I? The choice hadn't been mine, had it? Why feel guilty about something I couldn't control? Instead, I felt suddenly superior.

We tore into each other, grappling and grasping. Flipping one way, then the other. I tasted her sun-warmed, tennis-salty skin. I caught a rush from sniffing the scented powder sprinkled between her breasts. I continued down, slowly, but wasn't far past her breasts when she brought me up to her face again.

"You don't like that?"

"Certainly I do," she said. "But that's beside the point."

I didn't know what she meant and didn't get to ask because with her racquet-gripping hands she began to yank at my cock. She cupped the underside of her breast and ordered me to bite her nipples. For a woman who'd insisted on waiting, she was incredibly impatient. We negotiated territory, reaching for bedposts and table legs, digging into the sheets to keep from spilling to the floor. We spilled anyway. I landed ass first with a thump. Tremendous pain. "Fuck!" I said. "Yes, fuck!" she said and then smothered our obscenities with kisses.

Good, I thought, because I wanted this, too. I wanted to wear myself down on her compact little body. By the end of this, I wanted to be too exhausted to move. If I ended up bruised or unconscious, all the better.

Later, dressed and seated in the parlour, I rested while Mrs. Dunckley spoke to Aric, her butler, in Amharic. He disappeared and returned with cool drinks on a wooden tray. Hardly any Europeans spoke the local language, in part because all the important Ethiopians spoke English or French. Beyond a few words, Amharic was generally unnecessary and no one I'd yet met had bothered to learn much. But Mrs. Dunckley's words flowed fluently.

As we finished the drinks she explained some of her decorations, things collected over seven years in the country. She described each piece — shields and skins, masks and pottery; their origins and meanings. I listened, my drink refilled, as she told me about her travels, how she'd explored Lalibela's rock-hewn cathedrals and touched the hardened niches left by the hooves of St. George's horse when he escaped up its sheer walls. She recounted a trip to Axum to see the obelisks used to mark royal graves and another when she retraced the route Pêro da Covilhã followed, trying to find the Kingdom of Prester John. In Magdala, she had stood in the very spot where Emperor Tewodros II shot himself rather than surrender to invading British forces.

"And the pistol he used to blow a hole in his head? A gift from Queen Victoria. How do you like that for irony?"

Her stories made me feel pleasantly far away. "Where else?" I asked.

"Not long ago, I toured Danikil, a place so infernally hot that half our party fainted. But I wasn't going to miss it. I soaked a kerchief in cool water, tied it round my neck, popped open an umbrella, and willed my legs to keep me going. Absolutely worth it. Another time, down in Awassa, I came close to being ganched by a wild boar before my shot found its mark."

I believed the story about the wild boar. I could see her out in the bushland, rifle raised, sights fixed on the charging beast. The more I learned about Mrs. Dunckley, not only that day but in the weeks and months that followed, the more she seemed like the kind of woman who knew what to do if she aimed to kill something.

43

I'D BEEN GETTING CARELESS WITH CONSEQUENCES

I WENT BACK TO HER HOUSE THE NEXT DAY AND MANY DAYS after that, but then Mrs. Dunckley's husband returned to the city and remained for two weeks. He finally left again on a Monday after breakfast. I was at the house before lunch.

It was mostly sex but it wasn't all sex. I agreed to her request to stay away from the tennis club but sometimes we walked through her gardens, the beds of violet and gold pansies, roses, and carnations. We visited the stables and the thoroughbreds she raised. Sometimes she invited me to spend the night and though the danger occurred to me (what with all the servants who came and went and saw me in the morning), I figured the risk was hers to take, not mine. One night, after we'd finished, she poured gin-laced punch from a jug and said, "Tell me, what is it you do for Colonel Julian as an aide-de-camp? You don't have to say anything if it counts as a military secret. I'm a great respecter of rules."

Her voice took on a little of that intrigue, and with my usual paranoia I wondered if Mrs. Dunckley might be working for Riley Triggs, a nutty thought that passed immediately.

"Oh, you know, aide-de-campy stuff."

"You seem to have quite a lot of free time. Not that I'm complaining, of course."

"He has all these servants who take care of most things. But I'm teaching the pilots some English. I handle his correspondence. Also, he's having a party soon and he wants me to draw up the guest list, send the invitations, hire a band. Also I have to choose the wine because he doesn't drink."

"Sounds like you're indispensable."

"Listen, a spelling mistake on an invitation could start a war, so —"

"How long have you been working for him?"

"Since we left for Addis."

This came as a surprise. "I had the impression you'd been with him much longer."

I shifted my leg until it aligned with hers. Her skin was warm and still a little damp. "You're not wrong. But I haven't been working for him. You see, I'm spying on him. For the U.S. Bureau of Investigation."

She turned to face me more directly. "I don't believe it."

"It's true," I said. "Since 1923."

"Seven years? What's he done?"

"Nothing," I said. "But someone at the Bureau thinks he's a communist. Or an anarchist. Anyway, a threat to America."

"Is he actually a communist?"

"If he is, he's not so good at it."

"One doesn't need to be a good communist to be a threatening communist."

"I don't really make those decisions."

She refilled our glasses. "Should you be telling me all this?"

Probably not, I thought. But lately, consequences were becoming less of a consideration. "I don't know, should I?"

In response, Mrs. Dunckley pulled herself upright and leaned elbow first on my chest. She shifted her weight and began grinding the hard point of her elbow, determined little circles like she was trying to make powder from my rib bones.

"That's no answer," she said, releasing her elbow from the divot in my chest. She clawed my ears, yanked my head up, and kissed me. She swung her leg over my hips and in the next wriggling moment, I was inside her again.

"Oh God. Arthur," she said once she'd found her spot.

"Oh, Mrs. Dunckley," I replied. Because she hadn't asked me to call her Fan.

44

SHE FIRED A WARNING SHOT

JULIAN'S PARTY WAS SCHEDULED FOR A SATURDAY NIGHT in late July. "I want to show Addis society a good time," he declared. We conferenced with the hotel manager one rainy morning. "We'll need white tablecloths, with candles and flowers at the centre of each table. You get the idea." He laid an arm across the manager's shoulders as the costs were added up.

"He'll definitely overcharge us," he said to me, as though the manager had lost his hearing. "But it's the same everywhere. The Ritz, the Plaza, they all gouge. No point in beefing." Even with the inflated prices, Julian spared nothing. All told, it would mean a big bite out of his government salary.

He kept me occupied with preparations. I ordered food from a Greek trader who had the right sources: cured meats, pickles, hard cheeses, pâtés, crackers. I ordered tej and wine and pricey French cigarettes because people preferred them over Arab tobaccos. I set the menu with the hotel chef and hired an orchestra, requesting the latest from New York. "Something people can dance to," I said. I was kept so busy, I had to cancel three visits to Mrs. Dunckley. The last of them was especially painful because it was our last opportunity to meet before her husband was due back in Addis. My best chance to see her again would be at the party, and I insisted Julian include the Dunckleys on his invitation list.

Party night arrived and shortly after eight, guests began trickling in. Julian welcomed the Japanese ambassador with a bow and shared a laugh with an Indian army major. When his rival, Captain Maillet showed up, uninvited, Julian had a word with the manager and the French pilot was quietly asked to leave. I occupied myself with the staff, directing waiters and their trays of drinks and hors d'oeuvres to the newly arrived and the underserved.

The four pilot trainees arrived together and stood in a cluster. They were all good men, but a competitive bunch. With only two Fokkers available (the emperor still stubbornly refused to let any-one fly the Moth) and one always reserved for Julian, the pilots knew not all of them would have a future in the air force.

They introduced their wives and as I repeated the names and used my few words of Amharic to thank them for coming, Julian joined the group. "See, Tormes? Fly boys in Ethiopia get the prettiest girls, too, just like in America."

The joke produced polite smiles but no laughter and then Dawit, the group's most eager student, started talking about the new Boeing Model 200 Monomail.

"With an innovative all-metal cantilever wing," he said.

"Is that a fact?" said Julian. "I hope you ladies enjoy dancing. The orchestra will be playing all the hits from America."

Then Abel asked about the new Blériot-Zappata 110. "She has a very large fuel capacity, six thousand litres! And there's a space for a second pilot. Do you think they have a chance to break distance records, Colonel?"

"Why not?" Julian answered. "Why not? Make sure you get something to eat, gentlemen. I told the chef to go above and —"

"Colonel Julian!"

It was Russell Dunckley. He had approached our group from behind, as though stalking us, waiting and watching for the right moment to attack. Mrs. Dunckley, a lesser member of Russell's hunting party, followed half a step behind.

"A pleasure to finally meet you." He had a loud voice, the kind that replaced sincerity with volume. His hair was a tired grey, his face puffed and sagged like wet dough. A drinker, I diagnosed. Drunk now, in fact. A narrow tract of ruddy scars ran from the temples to the hinges of his jaw. A similar series followed the folded white crest of his collar. The spots seemed coated in a sheen, like egg wash on a sweet roll. From returned soldiers I'd met, I recognized the marks and pattern of mustard-gas burns. That his voice was clear and unhindered by scars in the throat meant he'd managed to fix a mask in time, but those early models didn't protect the skin very well.

"Nice to see you again, Mrs. Dunckley," I said and shook her hand, hoping to feel some secret tenderness. But she was cautious, called me Mr. Tormes. She wore a quiet blue gown with heavy jewellery and more makeup than usual.

Russell snatched a glass of tej from a passing waiter and sampled. "This is the good stuff," he declared and then, after the waiter had moved on, "Sure you won't try a little, dear?"

"Thank you, no," she said, her smile cautious.

"I keep trying to get her to drink, but she's sober as a nun. Won't even let me keep liquor in the house. A regular Harriet Bloody Glazebrook, this one. What about you, Colonel?"

"As commander of the Imperial Air Force, I am required to remain flight ready at all times."

"So that's a no. Well. More for the rest of us, right, Mr. Tormes? Cheers!" He laughed with his mouth wide open, then raised his glass and while joining his toast, I noted a small change in Mrs. Dunckley's expression, from dutifully stony to slight ridicule, even contempt. It made me wonder if she might be open to stealing away to a darkened corridor or broom closet. But then, in the next instant, as though angered by her own intemperance, her face snapped back. Unquestioning and endlessly patient.

"How are things in Nairobi, Mr. Dunckley?" I asked.

"Same as always," he said. "But how did you know I was in Nairobi?"

"I don't know," I said. "Your wife must have mentioned it."

"Did I?" Mrs. Dunckley said. "I don't think so."

"Yes. It was at the club," I said. "Or have you forgotten?"

"I suppose I must have," she said. "Or perhaps you had a lucky guess. Kenya and coffee, you know."

"Do you play tennis, Mr. Tormes?" Russell asked.

"I don't," I said. "But I enjoy watching. Your wife's game is quite strong."

"Very good for a woman," he said. "Keeps my game sharp."

"Oh," I said, peering at Mrs. Dunckley. "I had the impression you no longer played."

"Then you've been misled," he said. "Just this morning it took three sets for Warren Bruder to best me."

A waiter breezed in with a full tray of fresh drinks. I exchanged glasses. To a soft round of applause, the bandleader took the stage and launched into the first set. I recognized "Ain't Misbehavin'," one of my requests. The clarinetist stood for his solo. His body remained stiff, formal as an imperial guardsman, everything except for his fingers, which raced up and down the silver keys.

"Colonel Julian paid a bundle for this band," I said. "We should put it to good use. How about a dance, Mrs. Dunckley?" I wanted to touch her in front of people. I wanted to pull her close, have her feel my hardness through that elegant dress material.

"I'm afraid I don't know those American steps," Mrs. Dunckley said.

"Who the hell does?"

"We've been in Abyssinia too damn long," Russell said. He drained his tej and grabbed a new glass, this time selecting whisky. He began an account of their early days in the country, so boring, full of complaints and pomposity that I wondered if he and his wife also travelled separately. Mrs. Dunckley's eyes were set on her husband the whole time. He was drunk enough that he wouldn't possibly notice her look at me. And yet, I never got a glance.

Now Russell Dunckley wanted to know how one commanded an air force with only three planes.

"It's not how many; it's how you use them," Julian said. "But it won't be such a small air force for much longer. As it happens, I've recently brokered a deal with an American company to purchase new planes for the emperor."

This news came as a surprise to both me and the pilots. We turned to Julian to learn more.

"Tell us more," I said.

"Details will be released in time, but be assured, Mr. Dunckley, that we'll be more than capable of fulfilling our duties in defence of the Empire."

"Can't see anyone wanting this country, anyway," Russell said. "Hell, I've been here seven years, feels like seventy. Haven't seen anything worth a damn invasion."

"No?" Julian sucked in a deep breath, but Mrs. Dunckley spoke before he could get going.

"Tell me, Colonel. How does your own government feel about you working for the military of a foreign power? Given the American stance on Negro enfranchisement, I should think the government would look unkindly on your commission."

"It's certainly a concern, Mrs. Dunckley. But to this point, my work here has been free from interference."

"No interference that you know of," she said. "Isn't it possible that you're being watched here in Addis? It certainly seems like something the American government would do. Don't you agree, Mr. Tormes?"

I nodded and stalled with a sip from my tej, all the while thinking *Don't, don't, don't, don't.* But thankfully, she didn't continue. This had been a warning shot, fired across my bow.

"The United States will have to learn," Julian said. "Just like the Italians and French and Brits are learning. We Ethiopians know what they're up to. We've seen it for centuries. And here we find ourselves enveloped once again. And yet, we've resisted and thrived. Where else in the world does a white man need a Black man's permission to do as he pleases? It bothers your newsmen. I see how they write about the emperor, calling his face effeminate."

"Well, you can't put that on me," Russell said. "I am merely a humble coffee trader. We should say hello to some friends, if you'll excuse me."

But Julian wouldn't let him go. "The emperor has embraced reform. He's opened schools and hospitals. He's sent young men to be educated abroad. They're bringing new thinking —" But the sentence died when the music suddenly stopped mid-tune. Hotel staff left their trays and formed a review line at the room's edge. The emperor-elect and his wife were about to enter. Caught unprepared, Julian rushed to the doors. He wanted to be first to welcome their majesties to his party.

45

THE MOMENT WAS
WRONG FOR LONG AND
COMPLICATED REVELATIONS

ANOTHER WEEK PASSED AND THEN RUSSELL DUNCKLEY
took off for Dar es Salaam. Mrs. Dunckley sent a note the same
morning. In my reply I told her I would come as soon as possible.
Instead, I spent the day writing a report to Triggs, including the
details of the party. Around four, I bathed and dressed, taking
my time. The truth? The report could have waited. I was trying to
prove something.

Outside the hotel, I climbed into a familiar cab. The driver
didn't need to ask my destination. We zipped past the same homes
and huts where idle vendors offered goods made from leather:
shoes, bags, whips. I wondered what Mrs. Dunckley had in store
for the afternoon. We had constraints, but all in all this was a
simple thing. No romance, no wooing. We were unhindered by
emotion or uncertainties. This was very different from how it had
been with Jean Fox. With Mrs. Dunckley, I never felt like I was
supposed to guess at her feelings or look for meanings hidden behind her words.

I don't mean to suggest that Jean Fox had been manipulative or duplicitous. But I'd loved her and felt the responsibilities of love. And sometimes, with my situation, intimacy with Jean had been a burden on my heart. This wasn't the case with Mrs. Dunckley.

At the house, Aric the butler directed me to the salon. Mrs. Dunckley was in her favourite seat, reading. She was dressed in creamy white with a long, silver necklace. When Aric left the room, I tossed down my hat and dipped to kiss her. She raised a hand without lifting her eyes from the book.

"Let me finish this."

I stepped back and waited, feeling a bit foolish as I re-examined the souvenirs she had on display. She had about ten pages left. I understood endings. They always take longer, especially with good stories. You want to draw them out, let the words and images press hard into the memory while the mud's still soft.

At last, she snapped the book shut.

"Good book?"

"Riveting," she said, standing. "Would you like to borrow it?" Without waiting for an answer, she placed the book in my hands.

She continued past me to the phonograph. The Dunckleys owned a large collection, five or six yards of disks housed in cardboard sleeves. A lot of opera. Plus folders of famous philharmonics and symphonies, recorded in London and Vienna.

"Did you enjoy the party?" I asked.

"It was fine."

"I wish we'd been able to dance."

"I don't," she said.

I went to sit.

"Don't."

She selected a recording, set the needle, then returned to me. She wrapped her arms around my neck.

"Is there something you wanted to talk about?" I asked.

"There's nothing I wish to talk about."

The music started, a slow, quiet introduction. She kissed me, then returned to her chair and shouted something in Amharic. Aric appeared in the doorway. Mrs. Dunckley delivered her orders with dry authority. Aric crossed the room until he was standing before me. He removed my jacket and began to unbutton my shirt. I slapped his hands away.

"How dare you?" Mrs. Dunckley said. "He's only following my instructions."

"Well, I don't like being undressed like that. Not by another man."

"This is how it's going to be today."

Aric reached for another button.

My fingernails sliced into my palms. "This isn't something —"

"I ask very little of you, Arthur, don't I? Very little. A few simple rules to follow. And now, I'm asking you this."

"Do I get a choice?"

"Oh, Arthur," she said, as though already exhausted from listening to my protests. "Your choice is to stay or to leave."

My ass cheeks tensed and my toes curled as Aric resumed the disrobing. I focused on his hands, watching for offside moves. He worked steadily. Shirt. Shoes. Trousers. Socks. Underwear with a swift downward swipe. I was naked now, completely exposed while standing in the middle of their living room. If I'd felt foolish before …

Mrs. Dunckley rose from the chair. With practised movements, Aric began to peel away her clothes. He unhooked and untied her complicated underwear and when he finished, we stood naked, facing each other while Aric awaited further instructions. I looked as far away from him as possible without losing eye contact with Mrs. Dunckley.

"Won't he leave now?" I asked.

"Not at all. We need him."

"What for?"

"Well, to change the records, for one thing."

"Mrs. Dunckley …"

"What's wrong, Arthur?" This voice was new to me, almost cooing, and yet also annoyed, even mocking.

"Nothing."

She stepped forward and stood very close to me now, and I smelled that powder she sprinkled between her breasts. She reached below my waist with her open hand.

"Now, you've got it."

Later, with Aric gone, we rested on the sofa, half clothed, limbs tangled, listening to the opera's final act. The room darkened around us. Mrs. Dunckley leaned on my arm. A half smile remained on her lips. We'd gone at it for more than an hour, but I confess that the screwing was less enjoyable than usual. Aric had been a faithful witness throughout. Except to flip or change the records, he had stood statue-like, still and silent. But there had been something mean in his manner. It made me think of a supervisor patrolling the shop floor, making sure the workers didn't slack off. I couldn't know his thoughts, of course, but I didn't like being part of them.

In fact, while I was fond of Mrs. Dunckley and admired her intelligence and free-thinking ways and how she was generally enthusiastic about all the fucking we did, I suddenly found myself disliking many things about our arrangement. I know, I know. I was all for it before. I know! But I'd like to be honest here. The cool impermanence now bothered me. This sham marriage of hers was an open wound. What did that make me? Some kind of disposable compress? If intimacy ever insinuated itself into the relationship, it came in and out, unnoticed, like a cat burglar. Suddenly, this mattered to me. It felt stupid and also confusing and probably hypocritical, too. Definitely hypocritical. As the opera's final side played, I was thinking about these things.

Her body stirred on my arm. She reached for her water glass and said, "Tell me, will you still have to spy on Mr. Julian when you return to America?"

The question snagged me. I shrugged.

"It might be a splendid opportunity for you. It might be a good time for you to resign from the Bureau and strike out on your own."

I'd never told her I wasn't actually a Bureau employee. I had nothing against setting her straight, but the moment was wrong for long and complicated revelations.

"You have a good mind," she said. "I hope someday you'll have the opportunity to use it for your own purposes."

I murmured a response, neither agreeing nor disagreeing.

"Okay, then," she said. "Just don't be like one of those ancient Egyptian servants."

"Which ones?"

"The poor buggers who showed undying loyalty by being buried alive with their dead masters."

It was then that I knew I wouldn't be spending the night. In fact, I was starting to think I'd never see Mrs. Dunckley again.

46

THAT FIRST SOUND
WAS INNOCENT

MEANWHILE, ADDIS ABABA WAS BUILDING ITSELF INTO A
state of near chaos. With the emperor's coronation only weeks away
and preparations well behind schedule, the people in charge were
getting anxious.

Getting anywhere became a real chore. Ten-minute trips
now required half an hour. Even something as simple as
crossing a street could be delayed by some noble from the
countryside parading into town with his riflemen, his lancers on
horseback, and every other servant in his household marching
behind. Other ways were blocked by herds of livestock — cows,
sheep, goats — destined for the slaughterhouse and one of dozens
of planned feasts. Carts overflowing with vegetables and other
foods lined up outside hotel kitchens and banquet halls. Workers
split eucalyptus to construct panel fences that hid the thatch huts
and dung fires from the coronation procession. Electricians wired
light standards while carpenters hoisted arches over the emper-
or's route. The cathedral's new annex was nearly complete, thanks
to a blistering schedule. Policemen decked out in white topees
and polished leather boots tried to impose order. They rousted

beggars from churchyards, waved their arms to direct traffic, formed protective rings around visiting dignitaries. Cavalry and imperial guardsmen drilled constantly, practising their moves under the supervision of Belgian officers brought in for the purpose. Every building had some form of decoration — garlands, ornaments, or bunting hung from below windows and balconies — each unified by the red, gold, and green of Africa's only empire.

Money was everywhere. Restaurants boasted full houses nightly. Tailors and dressmakers worked long hours to keep up with orders while other traders did brisk business with suddenly flush prostitutes searching for new makeup and perfumes, fancier dresses and heels. Others cashed in simply by clearing dung from the streets.

One morning about a week before the ceremony, Malaku Bayen summoned Julian to the gebbi to explain the Black Eagle's part in the celebrations. Back in the hotel, Julian filled me in:

"Ras Tafari commissioned a bronze statue of the former emperor, Menelik II. It will be unveiled the day before the coronation. All the dignitaries will be there. He wants me to do a flyover. A couple of tricks in one of the Fokkers."

But the Fokkers were in bad shape. The strain of so many hours training new pilots had worn on their engines. They flew, but not reliably, and needed several parts swapped out to make them right. A few months back, I'd mailed away to Holland. After Julian received his orders from Bayen, I sent off a cable. Now it was the morning of the unveiling, and they'd yet to arrive.

"The import agent says they're in Djibouti," I told Julian at breakfast. "They should be on the train, probably arriving this afternoon."

"That doesn't help me now, does it."

After breakfast, with Julian off to the airfield, I went to claim a space in the grandstand at Menelik Square. The new statue stood in the square's centre. Three storeys tall from the top to the base of the stone plinth, it was currently hidden by an enormous satin Ethiopian flag. Hundreds of spectators had arrived early and were standing five and six deep behind wooden barriers. Officers in dress uniform and imperial guardsmen with fixed bayonets stood at attention next to veterans of Menelik's army.

A murmur washed over the crowd, signalling the emperor's approach. The Pathé film crew raced with their tripod to get the right angle. They had to wait first, as the emperor was preceded by a long line of dignitaries and nobles, some from Ethiopia's most distant corners. There were princes and dukes, some in decorated velvet cloaks, others with lions' manes draped over their shoulders, walking under umbrellas held aloft by servants.

The orchestra launched into a new tune, and Ras Tafari entered the Square, accompanied by the Duke of Gloucester. The emperor wore a navy cloak decorated with tangled patterns of gold and silver embroidery and a wide white topee that sat low, shielding his eyes and neck. His honoured guest, third son of King George, was a tall, roundish man with a thin moustache. The white feathers on his hat bounced with each step.

After a prayer, Ras Tafari delivered a speech praising Menelik's memory, his military victories, his reforms, and other great works. Mrs. Dunckley had told me about the emperor's political shrewdness and this statue was another example. He'd connected his new regime to the glories of the past, a powerful message to any enemies with coups on their minds. I thought of others who'd done the same: Napoleon, Mussolini, Stalin with Lenin's pickled corpse. Even Marcus Garvey used the same trick, often evoking the ancient Queen of Sheba.

The moment to reveal the statue arrived. Tafari asked the duke to do the honours. The orchestra played a few heralding notes to call for quiet and in that window of silence, I heard the rumble of Julian's approaching plane. Right on time.

Gloucester yanked one end of a long rope and the flag fell away
to a stirring round of applause. The sculptors had put the old king
on a rearing, muscular horse. Menelik looked proud, tough, and
battle ready. A crown burst from his bearded head and medals
covered his chest, shoulder to shoulder, collar to belt. Even his
horse was lavishly decorated, its tail long and thick, its ears high
and alert.

Fading applause gave way to the airplane's buzz. Julian was flying smoothly, perfectly on course. The engine sounded surprisingly
healthy, and I wondered if he'd found some temporary fix for the
Fokker's pistons. But as he flew closer, I realized he wasn't actually
flying a Fokker at all. This plane was smaller, also the wrong colour.
No wonder its engine sounded so sweet: Julian was piloting the
emperor's forbidden Gipsy Moth.

What would ever make him want to do such a thing? I understood that sometimes rewards are great enough to outweigh risks,
but I couldn't fathom what Julian hoped to gain here. No question,
those Fokkers were in bad shape. But that wasn't his fault and with
the right caressing they would fly well enough. Julian knew this!
He'd flown one just yesterday and rehearsed his trick, and while
there was no hiding the state of the Fokker, we had agreed that
nothing could be done. An unfortunate situation, yes, but he'd
simply have to do his best.

What had changed? He hadn't said anything to me. If he had, I
would have seen it as my duty to try to talk him out of it. I looked
to the emperor for a reaction, but my angle didn't allow it, plus his
topee's canopy was too big; all I could see was the tapered end of
his beard.

Back in the sky, Julian had drifted off course, though not so
far that he couldn't correct in time to perform the planned trick.
I waited for it, but he continued on this errant path until, with a
jerk, the plane banked hard to the left. In the next instant, the
lower wing bucked up and he banked in the opposite direction. It
was as though he were flying through an obstacle course, weaving
around invisible pylons. Now the plane was drifting on its side, the

nose angled down, and in this awkward way, Julian flew the Moth over Ras Tafari, his distinguished guests, and the newly unwrapped statue of Menelik.

Tepid applause began and ended as the spectators caught on to the fact that something was going very wrong above them. After clearing the square, the Moth headed toward a clutch of cedars. By then I was certain of the worst and didn't waste my hopes on a miraculous recovery. A hundred yards on, the wing tips clipped a treetop. That first sound was innocent, like a hand slap on bare skin. But the next sounds — the ping of tense wires snapping, the crack of wood splitting — announced the disaster more firmly. The engine cut out. Dust and debris shot from the fuselage and Julian and the Moth were swallowed by the trees.

In the absence of orders to the contrary, the orchestra stuck to their program. From a small platform, the conductor got them going, slicing the air with his baton as the musicians played the lively first bars of the emperor's new national anthem, a tune titled "Ethiopia, Be Happy."

47

YOU MIGHT NOT WAKE UP AT ALL

JULIAN REGAINED CONSCIOUSNESS IN THE ARMS OF SIX IM-
perial guards as they pulled him away from the crash site. Two
other guards shoved at me to follow. As they dragged Julian back
toward the square, he cried out from his broken ribs and sprained
ankle and a hard knock to his head. Still, between grunts and win-
ces and shallow breaths, he managed to claim to anyone listening
that he'd been sabotaged. "I demand ... an investigation!"

The guards marched us past the bank of reporters, all with
pads and pencils out, then through crowded streets to a city jail.
We entered by a rear door that led to a large basement cell, its only
light from a pair of barred windows near the ceiling. After my eyes
adjusted, I saw that we were two of a couple of dozen men inside.
The others regarded us warily. Later, I figured out they weren't real
criminals. These were some of the beggars and lepers the authorities
were stowing away until after the coronation.

I helped Julian limp to a bare patch of floor against a stone wall.
He eased down, using the wall for support until he managed to sit.

"Are you all right, Hubert?"

"I banged up my head. I think I busted a few bones." He
touched his chest and winced. "They sabotaged me."

With the broken ribs, his lungs couldn't gather the needed air, and these last words came out in a violent whisper. Also with a bit more Trinidadian accent than usual. "I'll straighten ... this out," he said.

"What happened up there?"

"The joystick ... stuck. Tried to move it ... Went over too far. Certain it ... was sabotage."

"Who would sabotage a plane you weren't allowed to fly?"

"Am I bleeding?"

"It's too dark. I can't really tell. Wait here."

At the cell door, I pantomimed Julian's need for medical attention by wrapping my hands around my neck and sputtering coughing-croaking noises. The guard found me amusing and beckoned a buddy who also liked my act but offered nothing in the way of actual medical help.

"I should have learned more Amharic," I said.

"Sabotage."

When night came, the stones became harder and wetter. Outside the cell, I heard spitting sounds and laughter. The cell guards were chewing qat, getting high. The coronation had put the whole city in a partying mood, and those men wanted in. I bent my knees to my face and buried my nose in my inner elbows. Somewhere in the near dark, prisoners prayed in quiet murmurs. Others crouched on their haunches, as though readying to pounce. Julian groaned beside me, his breathing shallow and ragged.

It must have been a few hours later that he crawled across the floor to the cell's shitting bucket, bent his head over the foul vessel, and vomited. Two or three voluminous heaves, followed by two or three more with nothing to show. Between each upchuck, he clutched his bruised ribs, gasping from pain. Alarmed, I groped in the gloom and managed to help him back.

"Are you woozy?" I asked. "Are you seeing double?"

"My head hurts is all," Julian said, his speech slow. "A little dizzy, maybe ... Why don't we go now?"

"Hubert, listen to me. We can't leave yet."

"Maybe just a ... nap, then."

I waved my hand, trying to create wind against his face

"I don't think you should, man. You probably have a concussion. You have to stay awake or you might not wake up at all."

"Those French pilots ... sabotaged ... tampered with the cables ..."

"You can't even lie down. It's too dangerous."

"I'd prefer ... sleep."

"Don't. You have to stay awake."

"How?"

"We'll talk. I'll talk to you. You talk to me. Come on now, it'll be morning soon."

In fact, I had no idea what time it was, but I began to ask questions, whatever it took to keep his mouth moving. I tested his memory of Port of Spain, the streets and shops and the cricketing heroes we'd worshipped as kids, plus other landmarks of a youth he thought we'd shared.

"Remember when everyone went to the Savannah to see that first flight?"

"Sure. First-ever flight in Trinidad."

"What was that pilot's name again?"

"Frank ... Boland."

"That's right. Frank Boland. You've got a good memory."

"He crashed and died."

"He did. I remember that, too. Terrible. He could have used some of your luck."

Julian said nothing.

"Are you okay, Hubert? I said 'Frank Boland could have used some of your luck.' Did you hear me?"

"... yes."

"Stay with me, man."

"I'm with you. The way you said ... that word, though."

"Which one?"

"Luck."

"Luck? Luck, luck, luck. I'll say it as many times as you want."

"Reminds me of the woman I ... lost my cherry to."

"Yeah? I didn't know corpses could talk."

"Funny, Tormes. Too bad it hurts ... to laugh."

"Tell me about her. Who was she? Give me details. This should keep you talking. What was her name? How ugly was she? How quick did you blow your load?"

He answered in his druggy voice. "I don't know her name. Or I don't remember it ... if I ever knew it. She was a whore. I'd been having trouble at school, see. Fights. Bad temper. Father determined the time had come."

"Ha! I guess that's one way to take care of too much fighting."

"He sent me to the whore ... not too far from school."

I swallowed, suddenly incredibly thirsty. "Yeah? What'd she look like?"

He sucked in a breath and winced. "I don't remember."

"Try," I insisted.

"Well, she was slender ... a skinny woman."

"What else?"

"I really don't remember. Perky little titties. A nice smell."

"How old?"

"Older than me. She had a little kid, even."

"A boy?"

"Never saw the kid."

"Tell me more about the house. What do you remember? What was on the walls?"

"Too long ago."

"What colour was her hair?"

"Nope."

"Come on. Think!"

"It's just a bit ... a blur."

"Was she a Negro?"

Julian said nothing.

"Come on, Hubert. Keep talking. I asked you if she was Black?"

"No ... white woman. I remember that. But don't remember her name. Perky little titties. She told me ..."

I tried to shift but couldn't with all of Julian's body weight against me. He'd keel over without my support.

"She said losing your cherry … to a white woman meant a lifetime … of good luck. Luckier than a thousand four-leaf clovers. That part … I remember like yesterday."

I wanted to change the subject but couldn't, my mind being stuck in this mud.

Julian continued. "She led me into her place … and took off her dress, slowly, piece by piece and —"

"Okay. I get the picture," I said.

"Thought you wanted … to hear?"

"Well, I don't anymore."

"Just coming to the good part."

"I don't want to hear it. Just shut up, will you?"

48

I COULDN'T QUITE LAUGH

OBVIOUSLY, I'D NEVER BEFORE CONSIDERED THE POSSIBIL-
ity. Though now that Julian had put it out there, why not? Antona
had had wealthy clients; it was how she had paid for my tuition.
Why not their sons, too? That said, she couldn't have been the only
white woman working on the island. There may have been others
in the elder Julian's orbit. What he remembered fit, but his memory
hadn't held on to everything. Despite my insistent interrogation, I
guess I was grateful for the lapses.

As a boy, I had known about Antona's visitors. At certain times
of the day, she had assigned me reading time or picture time, activities that confined me to my tiny bedroom near the kitchen. It
wasn't until later, once she was in the final stages of her illness, that
I put everything together. The doctor told me bluntly that she was
too far gone to keep working and that if she didn't stop, he was
duty bound to inform the authorities. Even today I remember that
man and the hard chill of his tone. As though my mother were a
damaged machine, ruined past repair. He might well have been
telling me to sell her for scrap.

For the first while after she died my emotions wavered, mostly
between shame and anger. But after months and then years sharing

quarters with a crew of misfits and rejects on the *Diego Hurtado*, I gained some perspective. Most of those men could neither read nor write. And forget about any math requiring more than ten fingers. A lot of those guys must have been sons of prostitutes, too.

So maybe it *was* her who had decided that Julian was lucky. Poor Antona. I pictured her with Julian. Not in *that* way, but I imagined her, fully clothed, just *talking* to him. She probably made him believe he was some West Indian Casanova, that when it came to pleasing a woman he had no equal. Crazy to think about, but if it was her, it's even possible that Antona's cooing compliments seeded what eventually grew into Julian's colossal ego. Her promise of infinite luck and put-on admiration immunized him against the kinds of common insecurities and self-doubts that hold other men down.

Being with Antona may have equipped Julian with the very qualities that made him who he was, with worldly ambitions to leave Trinidad and take on New York, the confidence that recommended him to Marcus Garvey, the raw guts to jump into the streets of Harlem, which brought on the attention of Riley Triggs and the Bureau of Investigation and led Triggs to implicate me in his chase.

I couldn't quite laugh at the irony. Not yet, anyway. But I did think for a long time about Antona, wishing I could let my old mum in on the joke.

Something I often wonder to this day: Would it have mattered if, in the end, I'd been able to confirm that Hubert Julian lost his virginity to my mother? Hard to say. Would things have turned out differently between us if I'd never raised the topic in the first place? I'd like to think not. Though I also understand that our thoughts and conclusions are pushed and pulled by many levers, some seen and felt, others invisible.

So? Maybe. It might have changed a few of the things that happened later.

Djibouti, French Somalia, November 5, 1930

TO: BOI Special Agent Riley Triggs

RE: JULIAN, HUBERT (a.k.a. THE BLACK EAGLE
OF HARLEM)

FILE NO: 30-48

Agent, this report will be last from the African
continent. JULIAN and Your Informant have been
expelled from Ethiopia. No trial but Julian certainly
guilty of unauthorized use and subsequent wrecking
of emperor's favourite airplane. Your Informant found
guilty by association. Expulsion order delivered with
efficiency by Malaku BAYEN (see previous reports).
BAYEN, according to Julian, has had it in for him since
the day since he stepped on African continent.

Regarding fiasco with the emperor's plane: your
Informant has read press accounts and can attest to
basic veracity. JULIAN, scheduled to perform aerial
tricks in Fokker at unveiling of the statue (of former
Emperor MENELIK). Instead, in defiance of orders, used
the emperor's Gipsy Moth. Proceeded to crash Moth into
forest of unforgiving cedars. Injured badly (head, ribs,
ankle). Reports that suggest accident occurred at the feet
of emperor are false. At time of accident, emperor safe
distance from crash site and never in danger.

Of probable interest: JULIAN convinced plane was
sabotaged. Instruments altered or mechanisms tampered
with. Reason: To cause disaster and humiliation. JULIAN
suspects involvement of the French flyers MAILLET and
CORRIGER.

JULIAN recovering from injuries, though lingering
symptoms — headache, pain in ribs and ankle — have
kept him unusually quiet for past four days.

Passages on Île de France booked. Due to arrive New
York City November 18.

END OF REPORT

49

YOU CAN PROVE THE LOGICABILITY

I STOOD ON DECK FOR THE LAST FEW HOURS OF THE CROSS-ing, watching New York's skyscrapers rise up into a frozen grey sky. The Empire State Building, its construction barely started when I left, now neared completion. Eight full months had passed since I'd seen the city, but it seemed much longer.

A pair of rubber-nosed tugs coaxed the *Île de France* into her berth. Passengers gathered against the railings near the ship's exit and every few seconds, one or two erupted into a fit of shouts and waves, trying to be seen by a loved one they'd spotted on shore.

"All travel offers some pleasure," Julian observed as we ap-proached the gangplank. "Even if only the pleasure of coming home."

A steward had alerted us to some newsmen waiting on the pier. Julian approached the group slowly, trying to mask his injuries. His head and ribs were healing, but the sprained ankle still caused him trouble and he had to lean on the malacca cane to walk.

The questions began with a man from the *Defender*. "Are you and Haile Selassie on the outs?"

"I don't know where you'd get such an idea," Julian said, his accent regal. "The emperor and I remain the best of friends."

"Is it true you took his personal airplane without permission?"

"Permission? As commander of the Imperial Air Force, I did not need permission."

"Is it true that you crashed it?"

"Flying at that altitude is tricky business. Ask any pilot. Also, the Moth was sabotaged. I can hardly be held responsible."

"What about proof?"

"I don't like to point fingers," he said. "A pair of other flyers were involved, but I won't give up their names. Frenchmen, that's all I will say. My aide here can tell you, if you really need to know. But you won't get anywhere with them. As long as the French government controls Ethiopia's rail route to the sea, the French can act with impunity. My injuries are proof. Look, the emperor and I parted on the best of terms. And you can prove the logicability of this by sending him a cablegram. This is all I have to say."

The newsmen, unsatisfied with Julian's answers, sprayed more questions.

"Were you banished from Abyssinia forever?"

"What happened at the coronation?"

"Can you prove the sabotage?"

"What does this mean for the Abyssinian Air Force?"

"Will you compensate the emperor for damages?"

"Are you worried you'll be charged with treason?"

"Do you think you've failed your race?"

Julian raised his hands. "Forget it. I've given you more than enough without adding to the things you'll get wrong."

50

THIS IS THE WORLD, DO WHAT YOU LIKE

I RETURNED TO MY OLD LODGINGS AT MRS. LIPOMA'S. THE place smelled the same: vinegary foods, cigarettes, six kinds of mould, dodgy plumbing. Mrs. Lipoma beckoned me from the front hall to her room on the ground floor. She was wrapped in green-grey army surplus blankets, one over the shoulders, another at her legs, the letters *U.S.* stamped near her feet. She was thinner and greyer, the darkened half spheres cupping her eyes more death-like than I remembered. She greeted me in her indifferent manner and handed over the key.

"Thank you, Mrs. Lipoma."

The old lady sucked her front teeth. "You remember all the old rules. They're the same anyways. This is the world. Do what you like."

Do what I like? How? I was broke and jobless, though in that respect my situation was hardly unique. That year, 1931, went down as the most miserable of the whole miserable Depression. I spent a lot of time in line with two thousand other guys, waiting to apply for one of two lousy openings. Eventually, I called on my old boss Tommy Kippers. He put a fatherly hand on my shoulder and told me how rough he'd had it. Business was way down, he said. He had had to close two of his five restaurants. The other three? Hanging on by a thread. He'd cut staff and wages. Still, he said, for me, he could find a few shifts at the New Star.

I was grateful and thanked him over and over, even after he told me that I'd be back down in the basement, washing dishes again.

So I worked at the restaurant and got straight back to following Julian around Harlem and other places, and at night I shivered in my room and read library books and typed out my reports. A kind of lazy restlessness took root. I slept a lot but then at the restaurant, I nearly came to blows with a cook who complained about the dishes I sent back to the kitchen. "Your food? A dirty plate improves it," I countered. But before anything became physical, I laid off. Not that I was afraid; he wasn't a tough-looking guy. But why bother?

It was no kind of homecoming, that's for sure. I'd lived in New York for eight years, a full third of my life, but I couldn't bring myself to call the place home. The city had never held that kind of cushioning for me.

Of course, it didn't help that being back also brought up memories of Jean Fox, now Mrs. Jonas Windermere. The city was full of reminders. Flickering movie marquees, little diners, parks, playgrounds, record stores that pumped jazzy music into the street. On chilly nights, when the heat from Mrs. Lipoma's furnace failed to rise to my room, I curled up and thought about how Jean and I once kept each other warm under heavy layers of blankets. I conjured the feeling of her skin and the softness of her nightgown and the way the tips of my fingers felt when they skimmed across her nipples.

And yet, it was more than missing Jean. I had this feeling of everything going wrong all at once, a cascade of unending disaster. On more than one of those sleepless nights I sat up in bed and stared for hours out the window at the same brick wall that had served as my view for eight years. But it wasn't quite the same wall, either. The city had changed. I don't mean the new buildings or shuttered businesses. This was something different. It was as though New York had been melted down and recast, and in the process the original material was stressed and weakened. Weirdly, after eight months in faraway, dusty, impoverished Addis Ababa, the Greatest City in the World now seemed to have taken on provincial qualities. Even with its muscular skyscrapers and subway tunnels, its music, theatre, and movie houses, its banks, factories, and museums, and the rest of those invincible institutions. I know how mad that sounds.

Before Africa, all the money and order of New York had given me terrific respect for the hidden machinery that made the city work. It had felt like someone was standing watch at all hours to make sure everything functioned according to some great design. New York might not have been home to me, but it worked, and I had believed in it.

Not anymore. Yes, the city was still admirable in a thousand ways, but now it was somehow less formidable. A layer had been scraped from its armour, its vulnerabilities exposed. I saw it in the crumbling streets, on chaotic subway platforms, in the garbage-heaped alleys, and in the anxious and worried faces among the customers and my fellow workers at the New Star Restaurant.

The easiest thing to say about the next four years is that they passed more or less uneventfully. Of course, things continued to happen, as they do. I followed Hubert Julian and wrote my regular reports to Riley Triggs. We still met up for debriefs, though not as often. I worked shifts at the New Star and some other restaurants Tommy Kippers owned, emerging from the basement to help him on the main floor again. With more spare time on my hands, I took night classes and finished high school. I stayed in the same beaten-up old room at Mrs. Lipoma's and read books and newspapers at the library and went to movies and ate and drank and slept and shaved and pissed and shat and all of that.

But what strikes me most about those four years is how little actually changed. I turned twenty-five, then twenty-six, then twenty-seven, then twenty-eight. The years ticked by unchallenged. Routine and sameness gradually took over and, as per Jean Fox's old Theory of the Velocity of Time, the years passed quickly and largely unnoticed.

One small new thing: I became one of *The Sun's* most regular readers. I wanted to track Jean Fox by scanning the pages and columns for her husband's byline. Once, I found them in the Soviet Union, reporting on a famine. Then they were in Berlin, covering the election that would eventually put Hitler in the chancery. Somewhere along the way, they'd been in South America, checking in on a war between Paraguay and Bolivia. I read these stories not because I cared so much about the Soviet Union or Germany or the fate of the Chaco, but because I could use named places to feed my imagination. I pictured Jean in these strange lands, standing before Moscow's onion domes or half-hidden in tall South American grasses. I thought about how slowly the time must be passing for her.

And what about Julian? He had a series of air shows and circuses, speeches and appearances. At the Colored Air Circus in Los Angeles, they misspelled Hubert as *Rupert* on the billboard, but the typo didn't prevent Julian from clearing twenty-five hundred dollars by selling kisses at five bucks a smooch. He was back in New York for A'Lelia Walker's funeral and after Langston Hughes read a poem and Paul Bass sang "I'll See You Again," Julian flew over the mourning thousands, dropping gladioli and dahlias, the great lady's favourite flowers.

In 1933, he flew over a parade on Lenox Avenue in a plane painted with slogans. The parade had been organized to protest the trial of the nine Scottsboro Boys in Alabama. The Communists had been all over the case, had even paid for a New York lawyer to defend the falsely accused Negro kids, a connection I emphasized (perhaps overemphasized) in my next report to Triggs.

Mostly, Julian preferred solo performances. He lectured on aviation and on Ethiopia and repeated his charges against the jealous

French pilots. He delivered the keynote at a gala thrown by the powerful Brotherhood of Sleeping Car Porters, who cheered his inspirational words: "From the streets of New York to a brotherhood with a King, that is a path anyone hearing me tonight can pursue. The keys are will-power and personality. They're the alpha and the axis of my success." Sometime around then, he took to wearing a monocle in his right eye.

I grew lazier in my reporting. I still visited him in Harlem but relied more on newspapers for hard information about Julian, especially now that I understood that the first step in any plan he made was always to call the press.

Among these plans were more long-distance flight attempts, the announcements arriving as dependably as spring rains. He would go to Cairo. To Arabia. To Rome. To Paris in half the time Lindbergh had needed. He'd fly six thousand miles to India, where he planned to present Mahatma Gandhi with a bale of cheesecloth. He would go to Ethiopia again, assuring skeptical reporters of the emperor's permission. He even found some planes and posed beside them, their new names painted in white under the cockpit. He called one *Abyssinia*. He called another *Haile Selassie, King of Kings*. He christened a third the *Pittsburgh Courier*. When a calypso singer named Sammy Manning recorded a song praising the Black Eagle of Harlem, I sat in a record store booth for half an hour, listening to the song over and over until I'd transcribed the lyrics for my report.

> At last, at last, it has come to pass
> Alas, alas, Lieutenant Julian will fly at last
> Lindbergh flew over the sea
> Chamberlin flew to Germany
> Hubert saved Paris, all eternity.
>
> Negroes everywhere
> Negroes in this hemisphere
> Come, come in a crowd

Come, let us all be proud
When he conquers the waves and air
In his glory, we are going to share
He saved Paris, all eternity.

How had Hubert Julian saved Paris? No clue. But in my report I made it sound as though solving the mystery remained vital. Same for the announcements for flights I knew would never happen. Even after a half-dozen of these non-adventures, I kept my reports free of cynicism, composing each to give Triggs the impression that this time, truly, Julian stood an excellent chance of smashing whatever record he'd set out to break.

This was all part of the pandering strategy I'd developed to tell Triggs what he wanted to hear and in the way he wanted to hear it. It made the work slightly easier, though those reports were for me what the daily needle is to a diabetic. Odious, painful, inconvenient, but necessary. Still, if Riley Triggs was going to continue to insist that Hubert Julian was a threat to America, what else could I do but agree with him?

DEBRIEF WITH SPECIAL AGENT RILEY TRIGGS
■ **FEBRUARY 15, 1933**

—I never heard of him. What was the name again?

—Father Divine.

—That his real name?

—As far as I know. I figured the Bureau would have a file on him.

—Probably does.

—...

—But who the hell can keep track. You want to sit? I'm going to sit. I'm a bit tired. I have trouble sleeping these days. I'm always waking up with a sore throat. I've put on too many pounds.

—...

—What's this Father Divine about?

—His followers think he's God. I've heard he's connected to the Communists, but I don't know if it's true.

—What's the connection to Julian?

—Hard to say. Julian took him up once when Divine wanted to fly over his followers. But the thing is that he might be a communist.

—So that's all? Julian took him for a plane ride?

—That's it. But did you hear me about the communist angle?

—That doesn't interest me. You want some of this? It's whisky.

—I'm okay, thanks.

—I went fourteen years without a drop.

—Then you've probably earned it.

—Damn right, I did. You got anything else?

—He's suing the Hearst papers.

—For what?"

—Libel. The *American* said Haile Selassie fired him.

—That's old news.

—Sure, but the *American* did get it wrong. Technically. Plus the story referred to him as "Kunnel Julian." *K-u-n-n-e-l.*

—So?

—Well, he doesn't talk that way. He found it insulting. He wants half a million.

—Good fucking luck with that.

—…

—…

—If this Father Divine is in with the Reds —

—This suit is pinching me everywhere. My underarms are all raw. Fucking pants are squeezing my balls. I haven't been sleeping all that well lately.

—…

— I called my half-sister, the doctor, and she told me to drink warm milk.

—I didn't know you had a sister.

—Half-sister. My mother married up. A real cocksucker. I asked my half-sister for some pills. That's when she told me to drink warm milk. That's what you get from a lady doctor. Warm milk. I want Julian, Tormes. I need you to find something on him.

—I'm trying. I really am.

—I like looking out over this river. Even if all you see is dirty ice and dirty factories and leaky boats taking shit one way or the other. Let me ask you a question, Tormes.

—Are you okay, Agent Triggs?

—What would you rather do? Work in one of those dirty factories or on one of those leaky boats?

—…

—I'm asking you a question.

—I don't know. I don't really think about things like that.

—Like what?

—Like choosing between things that don't stand a chance of happening. Given my situation.

—There's an old expression among jailbirds. You only serve two days. The day you go in and the day you get out.

—I don't know if it's so necessary to keep reminding me of that.

—Truth, Tormes? I didn't expect you to last this long. Nine years.

—Ten, actually.

—Ten, then.

—That should count for something, shouldn't it?

—...

—...

—Maybe it should, Tormes. Maybe.

51

SHE DIDN'T GET MY ATTACHMENT TO HER HUSBAND

FATHER DIVINE FADED INTO THE BACKGROUND. OR AT least I never heard anything more about him. In September of 1934, after a few months without a visit, I dragged myself up to Harlem and knocked on Julian's apartment door, only to be greeted by a new tenant.

The Julians had moved out a couple of months back, the woman told me. A directory led me their new place on 119th Street.

"He's not here," Essie said at the door.

"When do you expect him back?"

"If I'm lucky? Never. But I'm not a lucky woman."

I followed her inside. Her brown slippers made a sandpapery sound on the bare floors. From the empty loops, I guessed her dress had been designed to include a belt. It hung like a loose tube over her body.

"What happened? Where is he?"

"England. I'm surprised you aren't with him, the way you follow him around. Well, maybe he found a new secretary or aide-de-whatever-the-fuck-it-is-you-do-for-him."

Essie hadn't trusted me for a long time. Like Jean Fox, she didn't get my attachment to her husband. It didn't fit her notion of friendship. It was only natural for her to wonder what else might be going on.

"I'm going to make tea," she said. "You want some?"

The new apartment was smaller, the same furniture squeezed into a more confined space. On the wall between the two chairs hung the framed issues of the *New Yorker* with the two-part profile about The Black Eagle they had run back in 1931. I remembered when it came out, how angry Julian had been at all the facts they got wrong.

Essie returned from the kitchen. "I can't find the tea. Or we're out. I don't know." She moved a ball of wool and needles from an armchair and sat.

"Whatever is Hubert doing in England?"

"Who knows? He had some idea about entering some race to Australia. He went over there with Amy Garvey. She wants him to raise money for the UNIA. That's what he told me. Or maybe it was something to do with Ethiopia. Who can say how she's paying him."

"I'm sure it's an innocent thing, Essie."

"Oh, I don't care about that. I used to. I used to get all kinds of jealous. He's a man, what can he do? When he went to Africa I was out of my head because those Ethiopian girls are so pretty." She examined her hands, flipping between front and back.

"I can tell you honestly, Essie. All he did in Ethiopia was miss you every day."

"We had some good years."

"And many more to come, I'm sure of it," I said. "Did Hubert mention when he might be coming home?"

"Maybe it'd be different if we'd had children." She stood up. For a moment, she looked like she didn't know where she was. "I need some things at the store. What's the weather like?"

"A little cool. You'll want a jacket. Do you expect him back before Thanksgiving?"

"But I tell you what — you can't be that way forever. It gets to be a burden. At some point you either know or you don't know, and you have to decide what amount of knowing and not knowing you can live with. Why aren't you married, Arthur?"

"I guess I haven't found the right girl."

"Is that it?" she said, sliding her coat's belt into its buckle. "Just a question of finding the right girl?"

"Sure. Why else?"

"You're over thirty years old now. Seems to me like you've had plenty of time to find one."

52

FEWER WERE WILLING TO JOIN THE PARADE

THE AGE ANNOUNCED JULIAN'S RETURN FROM ENGLAND IN early December. Two days later, I went to collect more detailed information about his trip. Essie served tea from a china pot and we sat in our usual configuration in the living room. She was back to her pretty self, hair styled, shoes and outfit freshened.

It had been a successful trip and to prove it, Julian showed me a folder thick with news clippings. The English press were quite taken by him, he said. He told me about London, the receptions and parties, and touring the campus at Oxford. He told me about a close call over the English Channel when, against advice, he'd taken off from France in threatening weather. Sure enough, a violent storm swept down on him mid-flight. Lightning, heavy rain, "a fusillade of hailstones as big as pigeons' eggs." I listened with the kind of selective attentiveness I'd redeveloped since we were in Ethiopia. It allowed me to hear what I needed for my reports while the rest dissolved somewhere between my ear and the place in my brain that retained information.

"What's next, then?"

"I'm not finished, Tormes. I haven't told you about Nana Sir Ofori Atta. I took him up for his first-ever flight."

"Who's Nana Sir Ofori Atta?"

"You don't know? It was a hell of an honour for me. Ofori Atta is Paramount Chief of the Gold Coast. A great man. In 1900, he led his people against the British in the War of the Golden Stool."

"The War of the Golden Stool?" I repeated.

"That's right."

"I guess that shows you — those Brits will fight over any old shit."

In my next report to Triggs, I scribbled some words about the dangerous channel crossing and the flight with the Gold Coast chief. By then, I was communicating with Triggs exclusively via written report. A few years had passed since our last face-to-face meeting. If you'd asked me at the time, I wouldn't have said so, but there had been something different in that final debrief. Triggs was unfocused, drained of colour and energy, his spirit weak, though these deficiencies only took on meaning the longer I went without a summons. That he no longer responded to my reports with notes of instruction, reprimands, or insults told me only that after so much practice, I'd finally mastered the craft of spying and reporting. Thinking that I'd won his approval gave me a perverse kind of pride.

But in all that time, it never once occurred to me that Triggs wasn't out there, somewhere close, silently hovering, lurking, hoisting his pants and breathing heavily, and making sure I complied rigidly with the terms of our agreement.

So I complied. Rigidly. Automatically, I reported everything I saw, heard, or read about Colonel Hubert F. Julian. This included a lot of negative coverage from leading Negro papers, whose editors had grown weary of giving ink and space to Julian's promises of new flights, only to see them (and him) go nowhere. Yes, he still had many admirers and supporters, but fewer were willing to join the parade, having marched along too many times to the same tiresome tune.

Julian read those papers too. He ranted about the negative coverage, the misquotes and misrepresentations, but must have recognized that by the beginning of 1935, his popularity was on the wane. After all, despite the headlines he still generated, it had been some time since he'd actually *done* something headline worthy.

This must have been why, in January of 1935, he made the decision to return to Ethiopia.

53

THE EMPEROR NEEDS
ALL HANDS ON DECK

MAYBE I'M NOT BEING TOTALLY FAIR. EVEN BEFORE ITALY started to cast a shadow over Haile Selassie's empire, Julian and I often discussed events happening in Ethiopia. Also, I discovered that reminiscing about the parties and the people we'd met became a useful way to start him talking, and it drew less suspicion when I shifted the conversation to look for the information I was actually after.

Some recent political developments had begun to dominate our talks. Even before Mussolini took power in '22, Italy had been moving on Ethiopia, conquering Somalia and Eritrea a generation before. Now the Italians had upped the stakes by building a military post at Walwal, on the Ethiopian side of the border. For this provocation, the League of Nations gave Mussolini a firm scolding, which he, in turn, ignored.

So I shouldn't have been totally surprised when Julian announced his intention one night at his apartment. He told me before I even had the chance to remove my coat.

"The emperor needs all hands on deck," he said. "I'm going to join the fight."

I stepped inside. A flash of Essie appeared in the corner of my eye. I looked in time to see the bedroom door slam shut behind her.

"I'm just looking at the shipping timetables now."

"Is Essie okay?" I asked.

"I just told her I was leaving. She'll be fine."

"Last time you left was hard on her."

"The *Europa* leaves on the twenty-third. That should give me enough time to prepare."

"Does the emperor know you're coming? Does anyone from his government?"

"I don't need permission. I'm an Ethiopian citizen."

"Still and all. The way you left things —"

He moved to the dining room table, where he had a list going. "I need to do some clothes shopping," he said. "My old trunks are worn out. I need a new set. And a haircut. It'll be at least a month before I'll be in the same town as a decent barber. Oh! And gifts. For the emperor and empress. For the children, too. Do you remember how many there were? Seven, right?"

"Six," I said.

He made a note on his list. "I'll buy seven, just in case. I also have to call the papers."

"Can I help?"

I thought he'd be surprised by the offer. Instead, he looked at me like it was late in coming.

"You can call the newspapers. Bad to look like I'm tooting my own horn. Best if I look like a man who finds himself compelled to serve."

"Aren't you?"

"Of course I am, Tormes. I'd let you use our telephone, but the calls should come from somewhere else."

"I'll get right on it," I said. "But there's something else."

"What?"

The decision came quickly and certainly without thought. In some ways, it wasn't a decision at all. In my mind I heard Triggs shouting at me. *You're going.* The words repeated, a kind of rhythm section that kept my thoughts pumping to the same beat. This time, I wouldn't agonize. Nothing tied me to the city now. No woman, no job with any future to it. In fact, given how few reasons I had to stay, I actually wanted to leave New York. And anyway, Julian and I definitely agreed about Mussolini and Ethiopia. Though I never expected to be part of the fight, I knew it wasn't right to let the tyrant have Ethiopia without one.

"I'm busy, Tormes," Julian said. "What is it?"

"I'm going to go with you."

Addis Ababa, Ethiopia, April 15, 1935

TO: BOI Agent Triggs
RE: JULIAN, HUBERT (a.k.a. The BLACK EAGLE OF
          HARLEM)
FILE NO: 35-19

JULIAN and Your Informant have arrived in Addis
Ababa. Total travel time: 51 days. Much delay attributed
to visa problems for JULIAN, as (British) Ambassador
BARTON passed word to all concerned consulates to
deny entrance visa. Barriers forced JULIAN and Your
Informant to city of Port Said for visa and then to Aden.
Djibouti route, though faster, viewed as too risky.

JULIAN and Your Informant installed (at personal
expense) at Addis hostel run by Mrs. WEBENDORFER,
German, who came to Addis from Tanganyika. Hostel not
one Your Informant would recommend. Rundown, small
rooms, no running water. Scarcity of funds means room
must be shared.

JULIAN endeavouring daily to gain audience with
the emperor to offer services. To date, no response. Your
Informant understands Emperor SELASSIE not the same
man JULIAN befriended in 1930. As emperor claiming
divine right to rule, he is more distant from this world
and those who occupy it.

With regard to JULIAN, there are changes since
New York. In general, Your Informant finds him quieter,
more contemplative. Not surprising at all now to find him
sitting alone, seemingly deep in thought, where once he
would be recounting life stories to any willing audience.

Your Informant believes JULIAN preoccupied about
role he is meant to play here in Ethiopia, and for whom?

END OF REPORT

54

WE'RE NOT HITTING
THE RIGHT TONE

I GOT RIGHT DOWN TO WORK. EACH MORNING I PACKED UP
Julian's credentials and a letter addressed to the emperor and jour-
neyed down the congested, dust-clouded main street to the modern, new gebbi built to replace the palace on Entoto. At first, the
new building reminded me of a U.S. post office, but after a few
visits, I noticed Greek accents on the columns and Arab arches
framing the windows. One foot in the past, the other in the future, I thought, which was how Mrs. Dunckley had once described
Haile Selassie's approach to rule.

Yes, I'd been thinking about Mrs. Dunckley, and in the
long hours at sea, I allowed myself to imagine a reunion and
the different satisfying scenarios that might follow. In the end,
it didn't matter. A few days after our arrival, after discreet in-
quiries at the tennis club, the racetrack, and the bar at the
Hotel de France, I spoke to a man who worked at the British
embassy and learned that the Dunckleys had left Ethiopia
for good. The news disappointed me. I had tried to temper my expectations but in the attempt, I'd only encouraged
them.

In the gebbi's reception hall, I sat with other supplicants in a row of wooden chairs set against a high wall decorated with oil portraits of the emperors who'd ruled the country before Haile Selassie. I always selected the same seat, directly below Yohannes IV who, during his run in the late 1800s, became known for patience, tolerance, and forgiveness.

At the long room's eastern end, a bureaucrat sat alone at a small desk next to a pair of closed doors. He tended to paperwork and every quarter-hour or so called on a petitioner. In between, nobody spoke, as though to do so would diminish one's chances of winning the man's favour. When my turn came, I presented Julian's letter, which the bureaucrat examined and then set aside. I showed him Julian's credentials, emphasizing the pilot's licence, his Order of Menelik, and the letter the emperor had written in 1930 naming him a colonel of the Imperial Air Force. The bureaucrat nodded as I turned the pages and recited my pitch while pointing to official seals and signatures. While he made notes, I remained at his desk, waiting to proceed to the next stage which, I presumed, would see me invited through the double doors. But nothing ever happened. The bureaucrat thanked me and called for the next applicant.

Julian blamed the letter. Each afternoon, he reviewed every line, making notes, rethinking how to say what he wanted to say. He paced the floor of our tiny room, spinning that monocle between his fingers. Then, with the new angle decided, he dictated a fresh letter to me in French, which meant having to spell out all but the simplest words and pausing to show me where to put the accents.

The new letters changed nothing and each day the bureaucrat shooed me from his desk and the palace. I pleaded with Julian for a new approach. "I'm telling you, it's not the letter. The emperor doesn't even get them."

"But his men do."

"It doesn't matter, Hubert. It's useless. You need to try something else."

"I'm not hitting the right tone. Let's have a few nice lines praising his father. Some sweet words about his mother, too. Do we know her name?"

"Yishimabet," I said, remembering what Mrs. Dunckley had told me about the woman. "A great beauty who tragically passed when the Negus was only two years old."

"Good," Julian said. "That means she didn't have time to disappoint him."

55

THE BROWN BOMBER FIGHTS
THE MOUNTAIN MAN

SIX WEEKS LATER, STILL NO AUDIENCE WITH THE EMPEROR, and now we had another problem: money. We'd spent everything from our own kitty and most of what we'd borrowed — based on the promise of a coming commission — and now we were down to a few desolate coins. Worse than broke, actually, given what we owed Mrs. Webendorfer. We weren't yet starving, but our meals were less frequent and far less filling. At night, with my empty stomach keeping me awake, I thought back to my dishwashing days, all the scrapings I swept into bins. Slivers of fried pork fat, unwanted nubs of golden roasted potatoes, rich smears of gravy, even the decorative sprigs of parsley and wedges of lemon. What waste! Then I thought about inedible things, remembering the story about Magellan stuck in the middle of the windless Pacific. His starving crew, having trapped and eaten every rat on the ship, turned to cutting up their boots and belts to chew on the leather. I even went so far as to lick the top of my own shoe, as though testing for the proper seasoning.

And yet, the Black Eagle remained unperturbed. "You fret too much," he said.

"If something doesn't turn up soon ..."

"Something will. Something always does."

"But Hubert."

"You forget how lucky I am."

"What about cabling your father?"

"Why would I do that?"

"For a loan. We're close to an emergency here. In fact, I'd say we're right in the middle of one."

"What makes you think my father has money to loan us?"

"He owns a factory. Or is it a plantation?"

A moment of estrangement passed over him as his mind worked to align my reference with his memory. He found it in time to reject my idea.

"My father's money is tied up in investments. Complicated instruments. Treasuries and railway bonds. Besides, sending cables costs money. But my commission is coming. It might not look like it now, but being at the gebbi every day is a good idea. It shows persistence, precisely the kind of thing that wins wars."

"And what'll we do until then?"

He didn't answer.

In the middle of it all, we had boxing.

June 26, 1935. Primo Carnera, Italy's 270-pound Mountain Man versus Detroit's Joe Louis, the twenty-one-year-old Brown Bomber. The Italian legation booked the Hotel de France's ballroom and invited everyone to come and listen to the shortwave broadcast from Yankee Stadium. Hubert and I were among the first to arrive, soon after sunrise. We went straight to the buffet breakfast. There were fresh rolls and iced pastries, butter and fruit preserves, cured meats, hard cheeses, fruit cocktails in little stemmed glasses, and a guy with a pan who made eggs however you wanted as long as you knew how to ask in Italian. I paused at every station, sampling liberally and piling the food high, a true feat of engineering that tested the tolerance of the average ten-inch ceramic dinner plate.

We took seats at a nearby table. On the stage, below portraits of the Negus and his wife, a radio operator in headphones twisted knobs and aerials. An orange glow leaked from the receiver's rear vents. Microphones bowed to the lone speaker, and a wire ran from the back of the unit, out a window, and up to the roof, where it connected to an antenna pointed toward the Red Sea.

Julian bit into a hard-boiled egg and nudged me. "Remember that orchestra?" He was thinking of five years ago when all of Addis had come to his party, and the orchestra who'd played on the same stage. But I was too hungry for nostalgia and merely muttered agreement as I went about strip-mining the mountain of food on my plate. It didn't take long to finish it all and while my hunger pangs subsided, a squirrel-ish instinct led me to go back for more.

By then the ballroom was filled with long lines at both the buffet and the bar. Carnera versus Louis wasn't a championship fight but interest was intense, even in Addis. Mussolini was counting on victory, and Carnera must have felt the pressure when Il Duce had him fitted for a signature black shirt to show off to photographers. Meanwhile, Black America, Africa, and anyone else who didn't care for Mussolini put their hopes on Louis, a younger, smaller, lighter man but also crafty, controlled, and efficient. There hadn't been a custom shirt or photo op with FDR, but in Harlem, twenty thousand crowded into the Savoy to listen to the live broadcast.

The Italian embassy had reserved the tables nearest the stage. The ambassador, an old count named Luigi Vinci-Gigliucci, sat at ease among his compatriots, some in military uniform, others in suits so rigid and formal that they might have been uniforms, too. Hosting the event meant that the men at his table were saved the indignity of lining up for food. Instead, waiters in waistcoats and white gloves circled the chairs, serving from silver trays.

One of them looked familiar to me. He was one of the few civilians in the bunch but sat next to the ambassador and bent from time to time to share some private counsel with his excellency. His tan suit was made from a light fabric, too stylish for a military man, but I couldn't think of where I would have met him.

Back at the table, I wanted to ask Julian, but he was already involved in conversation with another guest about an incident from earlier that week when some zoo staffer at the palace had left a lions' cage unlocked. Five big cats escaped into the streets, killed one person, and mauled several others before the police managed to bring them down.

Julian introduced me to Gavin Treddleman, a large man in an ill-fitting light blue suit and a wide, bright-green tie. Big flat forehead. Pencil-thin moustache. He was drinking whisky with his fruit cup and buttered toast.

"Mr. Treddleman is with Coward and Sons," Julian said. "The coffee traders."

I chewed and swallowed, marking the first time since the buffet opened that my mouth was empty. This Gavin Treddleman must have replaced Russell Dunckley, I thought. But before I could confirm, the Italians at the front shouted for quiet. "*Sta iniziando!*"

56

FROM WHAT I HEAR, HE GAVE IT TO HER PRETTY GOOD

THE OPERATOR FIDDLED WITH A KNOB AND LOUDSPEAKERS crackled. Then we heard a voice from New York: *Folks, this crowd of sixty-five thousand is absolutely buzzing ... James J. Braddock, fresh off his upset win over Max Baer is here, and there's Bojangles Robinson a few seats over ... Now the referee calls the two combatants to the centre of the ring ... There's the bell to start the first round.*

When Carnera landed an early inside left, half the room erupted. Then Louis connected with a right hook, and the other half roared. The back-and-forth in that ballroom continued, louder and angrier with each blow. When the bell rang, the whole room rose, each side cheering with equal lust, convinced their man had taken the first round.

Once the noise subsided, I leaned across Julian to ask Treddleman about Russell Dunckley.

"Did you know him, too?"

I nodded, unsure how I would explain my connection to his predecessor.

Then Julian explained. "We were here for the coronation," he said. "Happier times for Ethiopia."

"For Dunckley, too," Treddleman said.

"What do you mean?" I asked.

"Just some gossip."

"What kind of gossip?"

But before Treddleman could answer, the operator cranked the volume for the second round.... *Louis lands three quick rights to Carnera's head. Now he's got the big Italian tied up against the ropes. Carnera misses with the left. Oh! And there's a hard right to the face and Carnera is cut! He's bleeding from the mouth! ... But he's still on his feet ...*

Up front, the Italians furiously puffed at cigars, refusing to believe it. "*Vai Primo!*" they cried. "*Ammazzalo! Ammazzare il negro!*"

Julian jumped from his seat and assumed a Louis-like crouch, punching and ducking according to the play-by-play. He looked down at me, urging me to share the spirit of the moment.

A sharp bell signalled the end of the second. I turned back to Treddleman.

"What kind of gossip?"

"Yes. Well. I don't know much," he said, finally. "But from what I hear, the wife ran around when Dunckley was on the road. Had a little something on the side. Dunckley discovered it and straightened her out. From what I hear, he gave it to her pretty good. More than once, from what I hear. But he went too far. The missus spent some nights in the hospital. Touch and go for a while. The ambassador was forced to intervene."

"I've met Ambassador Barton," Julian interjected. "He was good for England once. But not anymore. The man should really retire."

Treddleman didn't answer and the third round began. I don't remember anything except wanting it to be over so that I could quiz the man more about Mrs. Dunckley. From what he'd said, the rest of the story wouldn't make for easy listening. When the chance came, I asked Treddleman how Barton had intervened.

"Well, you know Sir Sidney. He wanted to have Dunckley arrested. Couldn't though 'cause Dunckley disappeared. Nobody knows where. Perhaps in search of a more resilient wife."

"And Mrs. Dunckley?"

"Back to England. Barton arranged it."

"Makes you wonder if Barton was the other man," Julian said.

"It's sort of funny," Treddleman said. "I only met the fellow a few times, but in all honesty, I'd have pegged Dunckley as a homosexual."

The fight proceeded into the fourth and then the fifth rounds. I chewed on chunks of cheese and slices of fruit, half listening to the action: *Louis smashes Primo in the face ... Carnera counters with a weak jab ... Oh! And Louis throws a terrific right to the big man's chin. Carnera's down! He's down! The referee is counting out ... no, now Carnera is up. He's reeling, folks. I don't know if he's got much more ... There's a crushing left hook to the jaw. Carnera is down again! He's not getting up this time! ... It's over! It's over! A fifth round knockout! Joe Louis has defeated Primo Carnera!*

Julian raised his arms high, then yanked me to my feet and pulled me into a bear hug.

"Incredible. The next heavyweight champion of the world!"

Sure, I was happy for Louis and also for Julian. But I was far too occupied with thoughts of Mrs. Dunckley to celebrate with him. Julian turned to Treddleman instead.

"What I wouldn't give to see Benito's face right about now!" Treddleman said.

"Tomato-sauce red and tear-soaked!"

"Like he was squeezing out a hard shit!"

57

ACCELERANTS OF AN INEVITABLE
CONFLAGRATION (THE SECOND)

EVEN AS THE CELEBRATION CONTINUED, I EXITED THE hotel and started down an unnamed street leading in the general direction of Webendorfer's Haus. My pace was slow. In less than an hour, I had shovelled so much food inside — more than I'd eaten over the last two weeks — that I felt drunk and dizzy. My centre of gravity had shifted, and I walked with an uneasy wobble through the shallow dust, past shops opening for business and a group of young would-be soldiers with their rifles. I turned down the wrong street. Twenty minutes passed before I realized the mistake.

Back in the room, I collapsed on the bed and with my body's energy so devoted to digestion, I fell into a sweaty, coma-like sleep.

Hours later, I woke in the dark to the pounding of rain on the iron roof and with a piercing ache in my gut. That night and into the next day, I was more or less tied to the toilet. My suffering, coupled with pounding rain, kept Julian awake and annoyed. Dressing the next morning, he complained.

"I think there might have been something at the buffet," I explained. "Some bug."

"You ate too much."

"The ham tasted old."

"I ate the ham. I'm fine."

"Something else, then."

"Like a hog, snout first at a trough. That's what Mr. Treddleman said after you left."

"I feel like I've got a fever."

"I'm telling you, you ate too much."

"And I'm telling you I've been poisoned!"

Turns out Julian was right. By the end of that same day, my symptoms had disappeared. Except I kept thinking about Mrs. Dunckley and that final afternoon in her living room, listening to opera music. I'd played things wrong with her. I'd been careless with her husband around and she couldn't have it. It made more sense now, why she'd ended things, why she'd been so abrupt with me. I'd become too much of a risk for her.

A cart rattled past our window, the rusty rhythm of squeaking wheels broken by thwacks from the muleteer's whip. The air felt like rain again; we were entering the season of daily downpours. Julian stirred in the other bed. My mind went back and back, to the early days in New York and my job as a divorce raider and that shrugging expression Cleaves used whenever a raid turned into a quagmire of anger and heartbreak, leaving the crew with a heavy sense of shame.

Accelerants of an inevitable conflagration, he'd called it.

That prick liked to believe that clever phrase excused him, that it gave him permission to make a living from the misery other people inflicted on each other. That it absolved him of any responsibility for what came after. For a few years now, I'd taken on that kind of thinking as a convenience. And yet, I didn't feel in the least absolved.

58

DON'T TELL ME YOU'RE BREAKING UP ETHIOPIAN MARRIAGES NOW

WHAT ELSE COULD I DO BUT WORK HARDER? MORNINGS, I was at the gebbi early, before they opened the outer gates. I pleaded Julian's case more forcefully with the bureaucrats and when this new strategy yielded the same old results, we worked together to redraft the approach. We made lists of men of influence who might be willing to advocate on his behalf, and I stayed up late to type out the letters, finishing by candlelight. We tried some lesser officials too, but those who didn't ignore us wanted bribes and we didn't have that kind of money. We tried to connect with Julian's old students. I managed to track down Dawit and Abel, but they were career officers in the emperor's army and with Julian's history, couldn't risk lending us a hand.

To preserve our dwindling cash, I searched beyond our neighbourhood for cheaper sources of food. I found a woman named Marjani, who sold me loaves of injera, and if I brought my own cans, she'd fill them with warm stews made from lentils, peas, and potatoes. These were tasty, hearty dishes, and I came to enjoy the way Marjani combined her spices. She made chicken, too, grilled on sticks and brushed with sauces. But with so many men coming to Addis, answering the emperor's call to train as soldiers, prices for everything soared, and soon we could no longer afford meat.

And yet, somehow, Julian remained confident, sure that his own luck would see us through. "My commission is coming," he said.

His argument now hinged on some recent developments. "The League of Nations is doing nothing. The French don't care. The dagos haven't budged from Walwal. Mussolini is shipping arms though the Suez. Italian troops are gathered on the Eritrean border. Tanks lined up like new cars at a dealer's lot." He sat down in the desk chair. The speech had winded him and for the first time, I noticed the gap between his collar and his neck.

"And just look at all the newsmen in town," he said.

This much I knew to be true. With diplomatic efforts failing, reporters had been trickling into the city. The largest contingent came from Italy. *Il Popolo*, the fascist daily, sent six men, including two photographers. The *Herald Tribune* dispatched Linton Wells. Margarita Herrera came from Madrid for *El País*. Evelyn Waugh was back, this time for the *Daily Mail*. He arrived soon after the *Morning Post's* Bill Deedes. *The Age* didn't have anyone, but the *Pittsburgh Courier* sent J.A. Rogers. Claude McKay came as a freelancer. He arrived on the same train as George Steer of *The Times*.

These newsmen filled up hotel rooms and bars and restaurants and though their information was the same as ours, their swelling numbers made the war seem all the more inevitable.

The next day, when I returned to the hostel, old Webendorfer was at her usual place behind a short desk. With her hard, curved back and that thick neck holding up her stooped head, she reminded me of an oversized beetle. I couldn't help but think that Mrs. Webendorfer should have been making more money like everyone else, but I guess not so many were so desperate that they needed to stay in her hostel.

Because of this, I was surprised when I stepped into the hall and saw Count Luigi's well-dressed confidant from the morning of the fight. He stopped when he saw me and squinted hard. Then his face relaxed and brightened with recognition. It was only after he spoke —"Arthur Tormes. You. Here?" — that I recognized my old roommate from New York.

"Sergio! Is it really you?" I said.

"It really is. Strange! My God!"

We gave each other a good look. His sharp dress (a different suit, dark and made from fine wool) and pomade-stiffened hair suggested vanities I didn't recall from our days at Mrs. Lipoma's, but otherwise he was pretty much the same. Maybe a little heavier, not as fresh faced. But really, this was Sergio Pratti.

"Man," I said. "It's good to see a friendly face."

"Good to see you, too, old friend. I think you grew an inch or two. And look at that stubble! But were you always this skinny? What are you doing here? Don't tell me you're breaking up Ethiopian marriages now."

I rubbed the back of my head where my fingers brushed against the frayed threads of my shirt collar. "Nothing like that. I'm working for Colonel Julian."

Sergio shrugged. "You say it like I should know the name."

"Hubert Julian. The Black Eagle of Harlem? I told you about him. I must have."

"You told me a lot of things in that room."

"Doesn't matter. It's a long story. But what about you? Why don't we go somewhere and catch up? I'll even let you buy."

Sergio's smile faded. "I'd like that. But not now. I'm a busy boy. And besides, it's probably best if we aren't seen together in certain parts of the city."

"Why not?"

He pointed to a small lapel pin I hadn't before noticed, a gold eagle, wings spread, talons clutching a bundle of sticks, an axe blade protruding below.

I laughed and probably too loudly. "I don't believe it. You? A fascist?"

"Yes, well ... another long story." He stretched his arms to show me the great length of the story and I remembered how hard it was for him to keep still. "I'll tell you all about it when we have time."

"Do you use it with women or something? To show them how disciplined you can be?"

"We'll talk about it soon. It's a promise," he said, placing his hand on my shoulder. "But really, I have to go now. I'll be in touch and we'll get that drink."

He left me alone in the hall. Sergio Pratti a Fascist? It had to be a joke, I thought. Just the sort of thing I remembered him for. Though a joke like that in Ethiopia? It could be dangerous, too.

59

HERE, I'M A MASTER

SERGIO'S INVITATION CAME WITH A HAND-DRAWN MAP OF the route to his house, about four miles from Webendorfer's. With no money for a cab, I walked the distance. By the time I arrived, just after the clouds opened up for the daily downpour, I was soaked. At the front entrance, a woman looked me over. Tall, very pretty, her indifferent expression carried a self-assurance that suggested she wasn't part of the household staff. As the rainwater pooled on the tiles around my feet, I apologized with a few of the Amharic words I'd committed to memory.

"*Yik'irita,*" I said, then pointed to the sky. "*Zinabi.*"

Sergio appeared from another room. "Your apologies aren't necessary, man. Nothing you can do about the weather, though next time you might as well take a taxi." Sergio's dark hair hung in loose curls. His shirt was open at the collar and untucked and he had rolled his pant cuffs a quarter of the way up his calves. His bare feet left little sweat spots on the tiles. This was more like the man I remembered from Mrs. Lipoma's.

"And anyway, Bilan's from Somalia. She doesn't understand your shitty Amharic." He said something to her in Italian. On her way out, she passed the tips of her fingers across Sergio's lips.

He covered his heart with his hands, winked, and made a kissing sound.

"Come to the kitchen," he said. "I'll get you a towel."

The kitchen was bright and modern, with waxed linoleum and electrical appliances from Germany. Sergio opened two chilled bottles of Italian beer and used a silver pocket knife to cut slices of salami and cheese. The cheese had a wonderful tang; the salami was spiced with fennel and pepper and rich with fat.

"You're a hungry boy!" Sergio said.

"I'm a bit low on cash."

"Doesn't Colonel Julian pay you?"

"He's a bit low, too. Maybe even lower."

"That's interesting. Though unfortunate, of course. Here, try this." He unwrapped a long loaf of crusty bread and ripped a hunk from the end.

I brought it to my nose. Morning fresh. The first good bread I'd tasted in months. "Where did you get this?"

"The embassy. The ambassador can't do without his *filone*. It's supposed to be for his family only but I've made friends with the baker." He pointed to his temple. "Remember how crafty I was in New York? Here, I'm a master. Ready for another beer? Have more cheese and tell me everything. What in the world are you doing in this place?"

With a new hunk of bread half-chewed in my mouth, I gave him a brief summary, leaving out the key bits about Triggs and the Bureau. As far as Sergio was concerned, I had chosen freely to be Colonel Julian's employee.

"Not much of an employee if he doesn't pay you. Why stay?"

A natural question. "Because I believe in what he's doing here," I said.

"It must be for real. If you're willing to share a room in that dump."

"To save money until he gets his commission. And it's not so bad. At least he doesn't read me shitty anarchist poetry or anything."

Sergio reclined in his seat, then shot forward and said, "Does he introduce you to beautiful women?"

"Neither did you."

"No? Well, only because I was afraid you would steal them from me."

I laughed and chugged the beer, enjoying the relaxed feeling that comes with having plenty of food in front of you. I went in for another slice of salami and chewed slowly.

"And what about you?" I asked. "I don't see your Fascist pin today."

Sergio poured his new beer, waited for the foam to settle, then drained the bottle. He told me his story, beginning with his deportation in 1924.

"They put me on a ship with a bunch of other poor slobs. A government agent, too. To make sure we didn't try to swim back, I guess." He pantomimed the breaststroke.

"Of course I was lost from the start. I ended up in Rome like everybody else. Things were really happening in Rome."

"I wasn't paying so much attention to politics back then."

"Let me tell you, in Italy you had no choice but to pay attention. Mussolini and his blackshirts marched on Rome and soon enough, he's ringmaster of the whole circus. I couldn't believe it, how everyone rolled over for him and his goons. Me, I was still calling myself an anarchist. Or anyway, I was definitely anti-Fascist. So I started looking around for the resistance and soon I linked up with Matteotti's people. Now there was an upright man, honest, incorruptible. But he spoke out once too often and the Ceka fucking murdered him. It was awful, I'm telling you. They put him in a bag and stabbed him a hundred times. With a carpenter's file. Can you believe that?" He swallowed his beer like he was chasing down a bug. "They killed him with a working man's tool. That's how I knew Sergio Pratti had no future in Italy if he kept complaining about the Fascists."

I shook my head. Sergio's tone was working on me; the injustice grated.

He continued. "So I kept a low profile. Little jobs here and there. In '29, I was desperate for work and joined up with the national railway. A lot of American suppliers made my English useful to them. But because the company is controlled by the government, I have to wear the pin out in public. I don't even notice it, really. They sent me here about three months ago."

"Just in time for the war."

He shook his head. "Nah. It won't happen."

"On the walk over here I passed the bank. People were lined up around the block, waiting to change thalers to silver."

"A few panicky types doesn't mean war is inevitable."

"I saw women collecting blankets for soldiers."

"All I can say is this: as I see it, war will be averted."

"Is that what your bosses are thinking?"

"I wish I knew what they were thinking, but I'm just a lowly railway official."

"Nice house for someone so lowly."

"A lucky find," he said.

"And a front row seat at the fight. Right next to Count Luigi."

He drank.

I hadn't meant to embarrass him. "Who cares. You do what you have to do to survive, right?"

"Cheers to that," he said. "But seriously, I don't hear much of anything. Half the time I'm in Mogadishu. That's where I met the girl. Her name's Bilan. BEE-Lahn. I just love the name! What do you think of her? A real beauty, eh?"

"Isn't the Ethiopian railway owned by the French?"

Sergio pinched the necks of our four empty bottles and carried the lot to the sink. "That's true. But my bosses are thinking about investing in a new line. To connect Addis with Somalia. Improve trade, good for everyone. That's how you know there won't be a war. How about one more beer? Do I even need to ask?"

Again, I was confused. "Why Somalia? Doesn't it make more sense to go north? Up to Eritrea? Plus all those mountains south of Addis. It can't be easy terrain for building railways."

"Yeah, sure. You're probably right." He ran a damp cloth over the table, sweeping bread crumbs and bottle sweat away. "But I just do what the bosses tell me, you know? Don't ask too many questions in case they start asking them back." He flicked his hand to pry the caps from the new beers.

"But I know you haven't told me everything. What about women? Tell me more about this Colonel Julian. Seems like quite a character. What brings him to Addis Ababa?" He handed me the cold bottle.

I began to talk and, for the next hour, as we went through half a fridge of beer and another pound or two of salami and cheese, I answered all his questions, never stopping to wonder why, like Riley Triggs before him, Sergio Pratti was so interested in Hubert Julian.

Addis Ababa, Ethiopia, September 12, 1935

TO: BOI Agent Triggs

RE: JULIAN, HUBERT (a.k.a. THE BLACK EAGLE
         OF HARLEM)

FILE NO: 35-33

Rains finally stopped and after months of waiting,
JULIAN received orders. Not from the emperor, as
hoped, but from mid-ranking minister. Government
wants him to train new recruits for Ras GETACHA, in
Ambo, seventy-five miles from Addis Ababa. Leaving
tomorrow. Must travel by horse and cart as no paved
roads. Also no cars offered for transit needs.

JULIAN particularly perturbed to learn John
ROBINSON, pilot, also American, will lead SELASSIE's air
defence. JULIAN's view of ROBINSON naturally negative.
The two met at Imperial Hotel and, after argument, fist
fight ensued. Knife brandished. Chair smashed. Orders
to march for Ambo received next day.

Something interesting with respect to assignment:
town of Ambo situated due east of capital. Meantime,
theatre of coming war surely to be located to north and
west.

END OF REPORT

Ambo, Ethiopia,
September 25, 1935

TO: BOI Agent Triggs

RE: JULIAN, HUBERT (a.k.a. THE BLACK EAGLE
           OF HARLEM)

FILE NO: 35-35

Into second week in Ambo now, and JULIAN carries out
orders with earnest commitment. Each day he drills
young recruits with spirit and enthusiasm.

Continued arms embargo against Ethiopia means
cadets have no real weapons for practice and nothing
like Italian arsenal. Many do not yet have boots.

JULIAN focused on improving physical fitness. Long
marches. Crawling across fields. Trench digging. Hand-
to-hand combat. Ras GETACHA impressed with progress,
as is Your Informant. Recruits enthusiastic and willing,
eager to defend country for emperor. With luck, proper
weaponry, Your Informant believes they might surprise
the Italians.

JULIAN remains steadfast and loyal to the emperor
and to Ethiopia's cause. Also bent on proving his worth
in coming conflict. While Your Informant understands
U.S.A. not at war with Fascist Italy, he believes that
values JULIAN demonstrating in support of Ethiopia are
true American democratic values.

Bottom line: Your Informant cannot conclude
that JULIAN currently represents threat to security
of U.S.A. This may have been case in early years
of this investigation, but world is much changed. In
fact, JULIAN could be asset for U.S. government as it
struggles to contain global Fascist threats. Would be
pleased to explain further, should you wish to hear
more.

END OF REPORT

60

SHE DIDN'T NEED TO REMIND ME WHICH ONE OF US HAD LANDED UPRIGHT

THE ITALIAN ARMY MADE ITS MOVE IN EARLY OCTOBER. ONE hundred thousand well-equipped soldiers marched across the Mareb River into Northern Ethiopia, opening a sixty-mile front. General De Bono took Adigrat and then, after two days of heavy bombing, Adwa surrendered.

On Mount Entoto, Menelik's war drum sounded a slow beat and Haile Selassie called on his citizens to be cunning and savage in the face of the enemy. "Hide, strike suddenly, fight the nomad war, snipe and kill singly!"

We knew it was coming, had been thinking of little else for months. And yet somehow, the news came as a shock. Ambo seemed paralyzed. Despite all the preparations, nobody knew what to do next.

The next day, Julian ordered his trunks packed for the return ride to Addis. I wondered if we shouldn't hang back and continue to train until further instructions arrived. But Julian said no. His recruits wouldn't be ready for real fighting for months. He'd be more useful in the capital or at the front.

Back in Addis, I handed over a few hundred thalers to Mrs. Webendorfer to be reinstalled in the same room we'd left less than a month before. The money covered only a portion of what we owed, but she was in no shape to argue. Most of her guests had fled the city when the Italians had crossed the border.

In fact, the city we returned to appeared to be almost empty. Soldiers whose training exercises had clogged the streets a week ago were on their way to the front. Wives, mothers, and sisters disappeared, too, following in the troops' path to cook meals and wash clothes.

Italians not attached to the government were among the first Europeans to get out. Then, after a group of young men mistook a pair of Germans for the enemy, pelting them with stones, more white residents hedged their bets and fled, too. Rumours that Italian bombers would target rail lines laid on another layer of panic. The rail company added a special train that exited Addis at three in the morning. Its seats sold out every day.

Me? As never before, I sensed purpose in the moment. For the first time in our long and involuntary association, Hubert Julian and I were seeing the world through the same lens. At night, too charged up to sleep, we talked in the dark with a mixture of excitement, urgency, and fear about the war and how it might play out. Fascist Italy had to be stopped, we agreed. Too much was at stake. For Africa, for the world. I even considered buying a uniform, but we only had enough money for necessities.

Julian left word at the gebbi, letting them know he was willing to join the fight. A day passed without response and then another, and after a third day wasted waiting around, Julian sent me down to the Imperial to gather information. He had an idea that the reporters would know more than we did.

Around dusk, I entered the lobby. I nodded to John Robinson. Obviously, after his fight with Julian, the two of us couldn't be friendly, but I wanted Robinson to know that as far as I was concerned, we were on the same side. I spotted George Steer, the correspondent from *The Times*. Steer was a solid source. He knew the country well, was respected at the palace and with all the legations. At that moment, he was in the middle of an animated chat with a man and woman with their backs turned. As I approached, two porters lifted the first trunk from a small stack, then disappeared down a hallway.

The woman bent for the purse she'd left on another trunk. With a flip of my heart, I recognized that little tendon-lined cave at the back of her knees. I knew immediately. Jean Fox had come to Addis Ababa.

Steer, uninformed for once, spotted me and beckoned as Jean wrapped up a story. "Amazing no one was killed," she said.

I hadn't heard her voice in five years and yet it was so familiar. That steady thrilling tone. She turned to see who had drawn Steer's attention. Before she could say anything, George introduced us.

"Mr. and Mrs. Jonas Windermere. Of New York City. Windermere's from *The Sun*," he added.

"Welcome to Ethiopia," I said, meekly. I shook her husband's hand. Moist. The gnarls of poorly healed broken bones. In fact, all of Jonas Windermere had a gnarled quality, like he'd been thrown down a few staircases over the years. He was skinny like me, but not from lack of food. He just had a wiry build. I admired his fresh haircut, probably from the ship's barber only a few days before. For the last few months, Julian had been cutting my hair and I generally looked like my scalp had sprouted a shrub.

"My wife, Jeannette," Windermere said.

My arm was almost too heavy to lift. "How do you do, Mrs. Windermere?" I tried to read her face but what I saw was Jean trying to do the same to me. She scanned quickly. I was wearing yesterday's clothes. Buttons missing, holes in elbows.

Seeing her produced a rush of confused feelings that, all added up, made me want nothing more than to be back in New York, locked up in that hateful little room at Mrs. Lipoma's, flattened out on that lousy narrow bed while other tenants screamed obscenities through the walls.

"Arthur Tormes. My goodness." She jerked her hand into her purse, rooted until she found cigarettes.

Her husband pulled out a lighter and offered its flame. "You know each other?" He didn't appear to enjoy the mystery.

"We've met," I explained. "Several years ago. In New York."

"You don't need to pretend," Jean said. "My husband and I don't hide things from each other."

She really hadn't changed all that much. Her hair was shorter, more purposefully styled. The corners of her eyes had gained some lines but they were minuscule and faded to nothing when she wasn't smiling. Sure, she looked a little tired. But that three-day train from Djibouti would knock anybody out. And yet, her clothes were crisp and fresh: a cream-coloured dress, a velvet hat that dipped a little in front. Jean Fox had a terrific sense of style, always did, though I don't think I'd ever seen her look so grown up. Not true. The night of the Pulitzers, in that oxblood dress. But this was different. This kind of grown up wasn't about the clothes.

"Arthur and I were once an item," she explained. "A couple of kids, new in the big city. Well, Arthur Tormes had bigger things in his life so he followed a pal of his over here. That was five years ago, wasn't it? Have you really been in Ethiopia all these years?"

She read the papers so she knew I hadn't been, and her insincerity bothered me more than the question itself.

"We got back a few months ago."

Her face sank a little. "Don't tell me you're still working for Lieutenant Julian? Did he ever make it across the Atlantic? I don't think so, unless I missed it. It's so hard to keep up with everything."

She didn't need to remind me which one of us had landed upright. I didn't care for the spite.

"But now that I think of it. I did read somewhere that Lieutenant Julian landed here again. Not by airplane, alas. By boat and train. Like everyone else."

"It's Colonel Julian," I said. I was sure she knew this. "And yes. I'm still working for him." I was also sure she knew what I meant by *still working for him*. It was time to leave now. "Say, I'd like to stick around. But I'm in a bit of a rush. I'll talk to you another time, George. Great to know you, Mr. Windermere."

But Jean wanted the last word. "We'll have to catch up, Arthur. I'm keen to hear everything. Are you married yet? Wait, don't tell me. Save it. How about lunch? Any day is fine with me. Just leave a note with the desk here. Remember, it's no longer Fox. It's Windermere. Like the Lady's Fan, if you know the play."

61

WHEN THE WOMEN
RETURN TO THE GEBBI

I HAD NO NEW INFORMATION ABOUT THE WAR OR ANYthing else when I got back to Webendorfer's. It didn't matter. Sometime during my encounter with Jean/Jeannette and her husband at the Imperial, Colonel Julian had received a summons from the gebbi.

"We need to be there first thing tomorrow," he said, "to receive my new orders."

"Super." I sat on the edge of the bed, unlaced my shoes, then stretched out on the mattress.

Julian remained standing, rubbing his chin, scratching an ear, oblivious to my preoccupations. The royal summons had energized him. Stuck here with me, he had no other outlet. "We have to be ready for anything. Are you ready for anything?"

"Uh-huh." I folded my hands atop my ribs. But I was wondering if Jean was really still angry? It had been five years. Her life had played out pretty nicely. She lived a fantasy, globetrotting from exotic hot spot to exotic hot spot, meeting world leaders, all kinds of fascinating people. All in all, she had it pretty good.

"In a few days, we might be in combat," Julian said. He went to the desk that served as our dining table and selected a pear from a basket I'd purchased that morning from Marjani. They were delicious pears, sweet and crisp, but her prices had doubled since the invasion.

"Toss me one," I said, opening my palms.

I sunk my teeth into the fruit and wondered if I would ever write that note to Jean. The one *she'd* requested. What would come of it? Coffee? Lunch? Dinner? The two of us in a restaurant, ripping apart the same loaf of injera? I wondered if she wanted to let loose with some resentments. Resentments were like those lions who'd escaped a few months back. Once uncaged, there's no telling what damage would result.

Julian woke me at dawn. We washed, dressed, and waited in Webendorfer's lobby for the siren blast to signal the end of curfew. Julian stood at the door like a greyhound at his starting gate, watching for the rabbit to bolt.

At the gebbi, a guard examined the summons and led us into the grounds, up the same stone pathway I'd used each day to present Julian's credentials, and I wondered if that persistence and all that failure had actually been useful for something. We did not end up in the great hall with the oil portraits of old emperors but were instead taken to a side entrance and a small, windowless room with no furniture. There, we were left with another guard, this one wearing a ceremonial uniform and standing at stiff attention before a heavy door. A spear with a polished point rested on his shoulder. We waited more than an hour. I suggested we ask for chairs but Julian didn't like the idea.

"Who are we to complain? Think of the pressure on the emperor."

I didn't disagree. History would be tough on the guy if he ended up losing a three-thousand-year-old empire. At the same time, a couple of chairs for us wasn't going to do much to change that.

"Did you notice anything different about the palace grounds?" Julian asked. He had switched to a low voice, as though the guard were listening in.

"It's quiet. But so is everywhere else."

"The women are gone. Nowhere to be seen. I could use that with the newsmen. Make it part of my mission: *To fight the enemy until the women can return to the gebbi.* What do you think?"

"Very solid."

"You'll have to set up interviews. See what they'll pay for an exclusive. Once we find out where we're going, that is."

But first, more waiting. My stomach twitched at the smell of coffee brewing beyond the walls. Maybe I'd invite Jean for coffee instead of lunch. One of those nice places not many foreigners know about. I could show her something she'd never seen. If Julian got a little money out of this appointment, I might be able to treat her.

In the middle of that thought, the heavy door opened and Colonel Tessema entered. Julian's sharp salute was not returned. Without a word, the officer produced a blue envelope, passed it to Julian, turned, and exited. From its particular shade of blue, I recognized the emperor's official stationery.

Julian ripped open the envelope and unfolded the single sheet of paper. As his eyes zigzagged down the page, his hands, then his lips, began to tremble. He read the note a second time and on the third pass, traced the words with a vibrating finger. Then he crumpled the page and stuffed it into his front pocket.

"Well?"

He didn't hear me. His breathing turned heavy. With a lurch, he went after the departed Tessema, yanking at the brass door handle and pounding the panels with the flats of his hands.

"What the hell is this, Tessema!" he shouted. "What's the damn meaning of this?"

"What, Hubert? What is it?"

The guard shifted the spear from his shoulder to a more ready position. Julian kicked at the door, first with the toe tip, then with the side, like a soccer player. The solid thumps resonated off the stone floors and plaster walls. The guard stepped up uncertainly.

"Open up, Tessema! Open this door, you son of a bitch. Face me like a man!"

"Hubert. Jesus. Stop it. You're going to break your hand," I said. But he continued his assault on the thick wood. The disturbance brought more guards into the little room, each armed like the first with a ceremonial spear. They didn't look like weapons you'd use to draw blood, and none of them were sure what to do next. Julian turned to them, hands raised and poised to fight all four.

I tried again. "What is this, Hubert? What's going on here?"

He clawed at his loose collar. Sweat flowed from his hairline, down each temple. The fight with the unmoving door had taken a toll. With each breath, spit misted from between his lips.

"Why don't we get out of here, Hubert? Don't you think that's best?"

He tried to speak but the words came out garbled and marbly. His face turned greyish and his eyes rolled to the ceiling. He threw out an arm, flailing at the air for something to hold. Finding only empty space, he crumpled to his knees with a bony crack. I winced at the painful landing. His arms and hands hung limp at his sides like weighted sounding lines and he began to sway back and to the side and then forward and when I realized that he had no more control over his body than a tree in a hurricane, I reached out to steady him. But I'd waited too long. My fingers brushed his shoulder just as he collapsed.

The guards backed away. I dropped to the floor and struggled to turn him onto his back, one hand under his belt, the other clutching the material of his jacket sleeve. Leaning with all my weight, I managed to flip him to his side and then over and was still clawing his jacket when he made the turn so that I fell backward and opened the seam at his shoulder.

I gave his cheeks a few light slaps.

"Hubert! Can you hear me?"

His eyes opened. Sweat diverted from his brow to the floor.

"Are you okay?"

He tried to rise to his elbows and as he reoriented himself, his eyes shifted to a wet stain spreading down his trouser front.

"Don't worry about that," I said. "Let's just get you out of here."

I helped him to his feet and gave him my shoulder to lean on. The guards gave us plenty of room. By the time we reached the street, Julian no longer needed me as a crutch. Still, during the whole walk to Webendorfer's, with his trousers soaked and his jacket torn, he said nothing. It wasn't until we were back in our room and he'd removed the suit, his shirt, tie, socks, and underpants and thrown the bundle out the window into the street that I remembered the note.

Whatever it actually said no longer mattered. This much was clear to me: the Black Eagle of Harlem was done in Ethiopia.

62

IT'S WHAT I GET FOR BEING
TOO DAMN CLEVER

AFTER A BATH, JULIAN SLEPT THE REST OF THAT DAY AND all through the night to the next morning. When I woke him, offering something to eat, he told me to leave him alone and rolled back to the wall. For the first time, I noticed grey among the black in his hair.

I left the hotel to search for a cheap breakfast. A block on, a dark-red car pulled up beside me. It was a Fiat 508, a car I'd never liked. Those thin bars on the front grille had all the elegance of a bread slicer. The back door opened, releasing Sergio Pratti. He was wearing the same tan suit I'd seen at the Haus, absent the Fascist lapel pin. Also, he'd loosened his tie and unbuttoned his collar. He kicked the car door shut and shoved his hands into his front pockets. I resented a man who could be so relaxed in a city at war.

"I'm surprised you're still in town. Isn't it too dangerous for you here?"

"I wasn't going to leave with all the excitement, was I?"

"There can't be much railway building happening now."

"My bosses won't let me leave." He shrugged, lifting his shoulders to an exaggerated height. "God only knows why."

"What are you doing, then? Helping to decide who to gas next?"

"You don't really believe that, do you?"

"Why not?"

He placed a flattened hand over his heart and his eyes turned sad. "Hey, it's me you're talking to. I don't like Mussolini either, and even less his generals, but if they used gas? Unconscionable. I would resign in protest if it were true, even if it meant going to prison."

"I heard about the gassing from George Steer."

"I don't know the name."

"Yes you do. Everybody knows Steer. He doesn't make things up."

A man with a rough *shemma* over his shoulder approached us. We were blocking the front of his spice shop. He waved his arms and spoke in a non-threatening way.

"He wants us to move," I said. "He's worried the Fiat is bad for business."

"He didn't say anything about the car," Sergio said, which might have been true. But we moved anyway, the Fiat crawling behind.

"Look, Sergio. I know we were friends once and I know you're in a tough spot, but we're on opposite sides of this fence now." We stopped in front of another shop, this one with boards covering the windows.

"It's unfortunate."

"Yeah, so I'm not sure what you want with me, but I'm leaving town soon, and I've got plenty to worry about until then."

"And your boss?"

"Julian's leaving, too."

"Leaving Addis?"

"That's right."

"Or Ethiopia altogether?"

"We're leaving the country, Sergio. I don't see why you'd care about it."

"I thought he was in this. 'Going to beat up the dagos,' he said. What happened?"

"It's not important. But it's time for us to go."

"What's he going to do?"

"I don't know."

"Where's he going to go?"

"I don't know. I haven't asked. Djibouti, for starters."

"Who do you know in Djibouti?"

"Nobody. Why are you asking so many questions? Why does this matter to you?"

"I guess it doesn't." And yet he looked like he had more questions. Instead, he opened the Fiat's back door. "Good luck, Arthur. And God bless you."

"Aren't you an atheist anymore, either?"

Sergio shrugged. The driver started the engine.

"Hopefully next time I see you, you'll have a different employer," I said.

"Hey, you too!"

63

I KNEW WHAT IT WAS
TO BE UPROOTED

JULIAN FINALLY ACCEPTED AND ATE A PEELED BANANA BUT still refused to leave the Haus, passing two full days in bed huddled under a tangle of unwashed sheet and blanket. If he wasn't sleeping the whole time, he faked it well. He didn't even stir as I typed out my report telling Triggs about the incident at the gebbi and the mysterious, devastating note from the emperor.

By the third morning, a film of stale sweat covered Julian's skin, the dull sheen broken by thickening whiskers. I opened the curtains and window for light and fresh air.

"What about a bath, Hubert? Even a quick soak in cold water might make you feel better. How about it?"

"Later."

"Or I could bring in a sponge and basin if you want to wash in here. I don't mean to be rude but —"

"Not now."

"There's word that the emperor is in Dessye," I informed him, leaving out the fact that John Robinson had flown Haile Selassie to that northern city in the air force's new Beechcraft. "They're saying he manned an anti-aircraft gun during an air raid. He's really putting up a fight."

"Just let me sleep, would you?"

Julian's funk hardened my determination to get us out of Addis. As far as I could tell, we hadn't been officially banished, but moods were variable and could change fast and I didn't want to risk the wait. I remembered that night five years ago in the emperor's prison. The dampness and dark, the hard floors and walls. At least this time there'd be more room. All over the country the jails had been emptied. Yesterday's inmate was today's soldier.

Trouble was we didn't have enough money for train tickets to Djibouti, much less passage on a ship once we got there. Since returning from Ambo, I'd managed to land some piecework with the newsmen. Excited by the war, their editors in London, New York, and everywhere else hiked expense accounts but now demanded more copy in return. Harassed by deadlines, they found me useful as someone who knew the city and spoke a little Amharic, and so I hustled for Gallagher of the *Daily Express* and for the Australian freelancer Neil Monks. For Steer, Bill Deedes, and László Faragó. Never for Jonas Windermere, but for anyone else who asked. Even Waugh. I sent cables, waited for replies, made deliveries, researched, and checked facts. I may have been the oldest copy boy in the history of newspapers.

The best money came from leads I could pass along, and I earned a few thalers here and there from things I heard. I let George Steer know about a shipment of new Mausers from Germany. He ran down the story and paid me well. That same afternoon, he sent me down to the train station to gather quotes from people fleeing the city.

When I arrived, the platform was packed. I sifted through goodbyes and arguments with railway employees over luggage limits. I managed to speak with an Armenian music teacher who'd lost all his pupils to the army and also with Vassily, the Greek tailor, whose family had lived in Ethiopia for three generations. I spoke to them as a man who knew what it was to be uprooted. The music teacher hoped to return one day. Vassily couldn't see it. He feared Ethiopia was lost forever. He turned his moistening eyes past the statue of the Lion of Judah and up to Mount Entoto, then quietly excused himself to claim his seat on the train.

Unfortunately, those golden assignments were rare. Too often, the newsmen already knew what I'd spent a day or two trying to learn. It was part of the work I didn't like, but every miner has to blast through tons of rock to unearth a few nuggets of gold.

With Julian's shaky condition, our situation became more critical, and a few days later I made a drastic decision: I started to make things up. I invented, knitting truth and fact from lengths of vague rumour. I claimed total fluency in Amharic and the man from the *South China Morning Post* sent me off to interview workers digging bomb shelters near the British legation. A phony tale of a mutiny among De Bono's Somali fighters touched J.A. Rogers' interest and netted me a small fee. Margarita Herrera, who had always been kind with me, asked what I'd heard lately and I conjured a story about a defection from the Italian delegation.

My fibs were aided by the difficulty of verifying any claims. Ethiopian officials issued blanket denials as a matter of policy, while the Italians lied according to what worked best for them. That Herrera and Rogers and the others accepted my stories as truth spoke to a trust between us. Breaking it was painful, but necessary.

It's strange to think about those days now. Over the years, I had fought a few times against my own wishes to see Julian dead. Now I was willing to lie and deceive and ruin my reputation and friendships to help him get out of Addis safely. What had changed to make me care? I don't know that I can ever really answer the question except to say that by the fall of 1935, I had been attached to Hubert Julian for over twelve years. A false friendship, yes, not a friendship at all, but still. *Twelve years*. Whether I liked it or not, time had imposed an obligation. Whether I wanted them or not, I had responsibilities.

I thought of it like this: people are like bricks in a wall. Years pass and the mortar between them hardens. After more than a decade, anyone wanting to break them apart better bring something heavy.

At the time, I felt pretty smug about that clever analogy. What I didn't know, as I peddled lies and poisoned friendships, was that someone was handing Hubert Julian a wrecking ball and showing him how to wield it.

64

BEEN INSULTED LATELY?

WHEN I RETURNED TO WEBENDORFER'S, JEAN FOX WAS IN the lobby, waiting in one of the worn-out chairs. She stomped her cigarette on the floor, blew smoke from her round cheeks, and rose to greet me.

"Hello, honey. How's business?" she said. "Been insulted lately?" She saw my confusion. "I guess you don't see many pictures here. Mae West?"

"Movies? No. Not too many, no."

"So you're really staying in this dump? I thought Steer was putting me on. Just look at this place."

At her desk, Mrs. Webendorfer snorted. Hard to understand her offence. The holes above her head were patched with scraps of sheet metal weighed down with chunks of busted brick.

"I'd been meaning to write that note," I said.

"I'd been meaning to read it."

"But I'm glad to see you now."

We fell into an embrace. Tentative, but friendly. I remembered the slope of her middle back and the exact spot where her nose landed on my collarbone. And the familiar smell that rose from her curls. Over the past five years, I had thought often of Jean's face and hair and her body. But the scent only came back to me in the moment of re-smelling.

"I suppose you'll gloat," she said. "Me coming here like this."

"I wouldn't do that."

"No?"

I shrugged. "Nobody to gloat to."

She laughed.

"You look well," I said.

"I worried a dress like this comes off as too cheery for the city. With everyone so on edge, waiting for Mr. Mussolini to arrive."

"If they arrive."

"I admire your optimism."

"It's fading, to be honest."

"Then I admire your realism," she said. "I still can't believe this. That you're here."

"I could say the same."

"I meant with Julian."

"Right. Well, that's something else, isn't it."

"I didn't mean it *that* way," she said and then attempted a restart. "How about we go for a drink?"

"Curfew soon."

Jean reached into her bag and pulled out two cards with stamps and signatures. "Passes."

"Oh," I said. "But another thing is that I'm a bit short. We're having trouble here, you see. Julian, he's —"

"Oh, Arthur, please. Let's just go."

The curfew meant that restaurants and bars closed after dark, but I knew a place. I led Jean down a series of tensely quiet streets, our way lit mostly by a bright yellow moon. Along the way, we passed several wary men leaning in doorways, rifles strapped to their shoulders. This was Addis Ababa now, a city of wary watchers, mistrustful of foreigners. Around the next corner, a tied-up mule we didn't see until we were practically mounting it made us both

jump with its sudden snort. Jean's hand went for my arm, squeezed
hard, then released.

The bar I knew was no bar at all but a window with a hinged
shutter and a few boards laid down in front of a tej-maker's home.
Two dusty kerosene lanterns provided the only light. My knock received a quick answer. Jean showed her passes and the man agreed
to sell us a bottle. He brought out a full flask with glasses and a
small round table and two three-legged stools.

"We're lucky," I said. "Six months ago we'd have had to stand
at the bar. By which I mean that window."

"Popular place?"

"Only one table." I uncorked and poured. "It's called tej."

"Will it make me blind?"

"If you like."

We touched glasses. The lantern lights bounced off the yellow
liquor and the white parts of Jean's dress. She removed her hat.
Her new short hair formed a dark frame around her face. On the
empty table between us, I searched for something to fidget with,
an ashtray or salt shaker. I wondered if this was a mistake. It's true
that something about the moment felt perfect and familiar. We
were polite, civil with each other. But it's also true that I didn't
trust the feeling. It had been five years. And I couldn't ignore how
it had ended between us. Then again, it had been five years. In that
time, she'd found a husband and had travelled the world. I may
have overestimated the durability of my influence.

Jean held out her glass for a top-up. "I like it."

"It's good like this when it's chilled."

"It reminds me of something they serve in the Philippines."

"Is that where you were before here?"

She shook her head. "Berlin. Before that we were in Paraguay for a
few months. Before that was the Philippines. That came after Bombay,
Madrid, Manchuria, and Moscow. I might have the order wrong."

"Which did you like best?"

"Madrid. Nice weather. Friendly people. The Prado's a terrific
museum."

"And worst?"

"Moscow. Freezing all the time and no heat in our hotel," she said, affecting a shiver from the memory. "But mostly I hated it because I lost a baby there."

"I'm sorry."

She shrugged. "Third time unlucky."

"That's really rotten luck."

"Who knows. Could have been a blessing. Imagine having a baby in Moscow in the middle of winter? Your water breaks and icicles drop to the floor."

The dimmed lights of a taxi appeared. The car slowed as it passed then accelerated down the blacked-out street, and except for a few slivers of firelight glowing behind window blinds, the moonlit quiet returned. I picked up my glass, put it down again, and said, "Your hair looks nice. Short."

"Not as short as it used to be," she said. "After you left, I cut it all off. Did the job myself in the bathroom. It took two solid hours at the salon to make me look like I hadn't been caught sleeping with the enemy."

"Must not have bothered your husband."

Jean drank and lit a cigarette and tossed the match into the empty street. She blew a spear of smoke into the black sky.

"I don't want us to be hostile, Arthur."

"No," I said, contrite. "Me neither."

"Good. I didn't come here to be hostile."

She emptied her glass and picked up the bottle.

"Why *did* you come?"

She shrugged. "Good question. Jonas likes wars. It's a perversion. You know how some fellows have a thing for young boys? Jonas has something similar. Only for wars. He's lucky. Not too many people can make a living off their perversions."

"No, I mean to the hotel. Why did you come to the hotel today?"

With a flick of her thumb, ash tumbled from her cigarette. I hadn't meant to doubt her motives, only to satisfy my curiosity.

"I don't know. To talk to someone who I've known for more than a week for a change. To get an insider's view on the hot spots in town. Best places for dancing, both slow and fast. Best places for watching an Italian invasion. I was hoping you'd provide me with some reliable lists. Also, I suppose I wanted to see how you were doing." She sipped more tej and then regarded the glass, as though to analyze the ingredients.

"And, Arthur Tormes, I wanted tell you a few things. Specifically, about something that happened to me that maybe explains how we were. About how I was with you."

"All of that was my fault."

"Oh, I know," she said. "Believe me, I know. And I'm not here to absolve you. But by some force of fate or by some extraordinary coincidence, we find ourselves in the same city in Africa at the same time. It feels like one of those knocks on the door you're not supposed to ignore, if you catch my meaning."

"Sure, I do." And I did.

"I'm glad." She reached into her purse for a few coins. "Do you think your friend would bring us another flask? I'm growing very fond of this stuff."

"I'll ask."

"Do that. Then I'll tell you what happened to me in Paraguay."

I tapped lightly on the shuttered window and handed over the coins. Back at our table, I poured a glass for Jean but paused over my glass. Then, feeling silly and ashamed, I tipped the bottle over my cup.

"The only problem is the hangovers."

"Wish you'd told me that sooner," she said. "Hey, that sounds familiar."

"I thought you didn't want to be hostile."

"Ah hell, Arthur."

We touched glasses.

"I'm listening."

65

I WAS SUCKED IN

THIS IS WHAT JEAN TOLD ME:

"*The Sun* sent Jonas to Paraguay to cover the war with Bolivia. You wouldn't think anything happening way down there would matter a lick to American readers, but someone discovered that Shell and Standard Oil had put up all the money — like boxing promoters, I guess — and all of a sudden, the war was newsworthy.

"In Asunción — that's the capital city — Jonas hired a driver to take him closer to the front. Normally, I'd have travelled with him, but I was sick of places in the middle of nowhere so this time, I stayed behind. I settled in and searched out the little things one always needs for a new home, even one that's temporary. After a few pleasant days wandering (it's a small city, not very modern, the river is nice), I introduced myself to my neighbour, Luisa. She was probably twenty or thirty years older than me, close to sixty I'd say. Widow, no children. Frankly, I was looking for a friend but when she answered her door, she told me in English that she was too sick for visitors. She didn't suggest I return another day, but with nothing to lose, I thought, why not? Two days later, I went by with a pound of coffee. I could tell just by looking that her condition had deteriorated. She was paler, thinner, weaker, a very sick woman. But she invited me to come in anyway.

"Apparently, she had no one to care for her. I never saw or heard anyone go in or out and she never mentioned anyone, either. We got along in a cautious way and she didn't object when I brought over little meat pies and cakes. Over the next few weeks I kind of insinuated myself into her life. I tidied up and watered her plants and sent her laundry out and bought fresh fruits and vegetables to replace what needed replacing in her pantry. Did I say 'insinuated'? No, that isn't the right word. What happened is that I was sucked in. Not by Luisa, but by the situation. Yes, *sucked in*. Like a Hoover. I didn't resist, though. In fact, strangely, I couldn't help myself and soon we were spending most of our days and parts of our evenings together. You know, we didn't have much in common but I really liked her. I guess I felt less lonely, too. Her husband had been an engineer. She'd studied painting in Chicago. I don't think it was a happy marriage. Her house was decorated with watercolours. Of birds, mostly. She told me she'd been planning an illustrated guide to the birds of Paraguay. Over five hundred species. She told me that finding the birds had been the easy part, but capturing them with paint was incredibly difficult. All the luminous feathers.

"That last week, Luisa had zero energy. She couldn't get out of bed and she could barely speak. I made porridge and fed her by spoon and each day, she ate less and less before waving me away. Then one evening, after I'd changed her sheets, she rallied. Not a miraculous cure but she ate a full bowl of fresh papaya and a slice of buttered bread and asked for more. She told me where she kept the wine and while she was still in bed, we shared a bottle. Actually, two. Now that I think about it, we shared two bottles of wine.

"We exchanged stories about our travels. She'd explored every corner of her country several times over and though I'd been to many more places on the world map, her experiences had been so much more intimate. More meaningful. She could actually remember the names of people she'd met. Me? I was lucky if I could remember the names of the cities.

"Then, at one point, she stopped and said, 'This isn't the way I expected to go. I don't know what I expected, but not this. I've been too damn angry about it all.'

"What do I say to that? I asked her if I should call someone. I meant family or friends. She said, 'Thanks, but I don't need the distraction.' What about a priest? I asked. 'Why would I want a priest?' she said. I see the crucifix above your bed, I said.

"'Oh that,' she said — I can't help but laugh; every time I think of it, I laugh — 'Oh that,' she said. 'I put that up after a few years of marriage. I wanted something to look at while he was fucking me.'

"Arthur, I laughed so hard. And yes, I was drunk, but I really must have laughed for half an hour. Luisa, that beautiful dying woman, and there I was, showing all my wine-stained teeth, cackling, tears covering my face. I think I popped a couple of ribs. Imagine: she wanted something to look at while he was fucking her.

"I found her the next day. In her room. On the bed. Her blankets were tossed to the floor and her nightgown had ridden up her pale legs. Her mouth was wide open and there were lines of dried spittle running from her mouth. I stood in her bedroom's doorway. All I could do was stare at her and that's what I did, alone in that doorway, gazing for the longest time at Luisa's half-naked corpse.

"Somewhere in that private little vigil of mine, before I finally got around to calling an ambulance, I finally understood everything I'd needed to."

66

I CHANGED THE CIRCUMSTANCES

"ABOUT WHAT?" I ASKED.

"About my parents. Their deaths."

A stray dog trotted past our seats at the tej bar. He gave us a quick glance and sniff before moving on.

"And?" I said.

"And nothing," Jean said.

"I'm sorry," I said. "But I don't get it."

"But that's the point. There's nothing *to* get. I wasn't meant to understand. You can't imagine the relief I've felt ever since. Like someone took a scrub brush to my head and swept away all the gunk." She shook her head and smiled.

"I'm glad for your relief. But your parents, the way they died. Falling off a skyscraper. It was so unnatural. So out of the ordinary. How could anyone be expected to put meaning to it?"

"Actually, that's not quite how it happened." Her eyes met mine. They suggested apology. "My parents didn't fall off the observation deck at the Woolworth Building. They died of tuberculosis. And not on the same day, either, though it was only a few days apart."

"I don't understand."

"Exactly!" she said. "Neither did I. Their dying, even from something so natural and everyday as TB, made no sense. I couldn't accept that something that felt so damn strange and awful could also be so absolutely *common*. Do you know how many people TB killed in 1921? The same number of people who earned new driver's licences. The same number of people who graduated from college. I'm serious. I've checked those numbers. So to hell with it. I didn't accept it. I refused and I changed the circumstances. I made their deaths absurdly *un*common. I made up the whole story, exaggerating the stranger bits with each telling. The version you heard was pretty much the final draft, all the little details filled in. I even took some artistic licence, lowering the barrier on the observation deck to make their 'accident' possible. It worked pretty well, you know. After a few months on my own in New York, I'd convinced myself of this new cause of death so thoroughly that I even cried once when I walked past the Woolworth Building. Kind of funny, actually."

I still didn't understand. "But why?"

"Because! It fit better. It suited the way I felt and the way I felt also made me behave in some ways … well, you know. With those men, especially. You were there for the last of it. That night with the banker and his wife, Annie Oakley. Pow! Pow! The gunplay was enough to get me to tone things down, but I still didn't understand what happened to my mother and father. I still don't! And I never will! But it's okay now, thanks to Luisa. I hope that makes sense because I really don't have it in me to explain it again."

Jean placed her hand atop mine in the centre of the little table, her fingers cool from holding the glass.

We returned the stools and the table and walked together in the dark back to her hotel. We were half-drunk, maybe a little more than half. She put her hand in my elbow and I felt all kinds of yearnings.

A block before the Imperial's front doors, we had to step aside for an approaching truck. Two guards rode on the running boards with rifles strapped to their shoulders. When they passed, Jean squeezed my arm and in a suddenly sober voice said, "You should get a lawyer. When you get back, it's the first thing you should do."

"What for?"

"Get one of those civil liberties attorneys. Tell him everything. What the Bureau is doing to you isn't legal. They're not allowed to do that to innocent people."

"How do you know?"

"I asked someone about it a few years ago."

"Who?"

"Doesn't matter," she said. "Someone who knows."

I didn't know if she was serious. "I'll think about it."

"What's there to think about? You want to be free, don't you? Am I talking too loud? I need a bed. Just talk to a lawyer, would you? Goodnight, Arthur. And thank you. Thank you for listening, and thank you for introducing me to that delicious booze."

I walked back to the Haus slowly, forgetting about the curfew and the fact that I no longer had Jean's pass to keep me out of trouble. The air was warmer than usual, not so thin. At least it felt that way in my lungs.

Jean was different. She had watched this Luisa die in Asunción and now she was getting on with things. It gave her enough authority to tell me what was what. I still loved her. Or maybe I loved her in a whole other, new way. And she had feelings for me, too. I could tell that much.

So much had changed. So much had stayed the same. Years ago, we had perched for hours on either end of an idle see-saw, hovering and hanging in perfect balance above the cinders. Now we were misaligned. One up, one down.

67

I TOLD THEM THEY ARE
FOOLING THEMSELVES

THE NEXT MORNING I DID MY ROUNDS WITH THE NEWSMEN, but only Gallagher had anything and all he wanted was for me to hold his place in line at the cable office. With my work done, I returned to the Haus and found the room empty. Julian's hat and malacca cane were also missing. A damp towel hung on the back of the chair. I took his absence as a good thing, since it meant that he'd managed to get to his feet at least.

I missed him the next morning, too, but saw from his crumpled sheets that he'd slept in his bed. He'd also left a note on the typewriter ordering me to meet him back in the room that afternoon at three o'clock. "VERY IMPORTANT," it concluded. Underscored three times.

I couldn't imagine what had happened in the half day he'd been out of bed that would provoke the urgency but at half past two, when Margarita Herrera offered hard cash to retrieve a dispatch for her, I had to decline.

Julian beat me back to the room. He'd pulled his trunks from storage and had already filled one with his clothes. He had been shaved; his hair was freshly trimmed. The old moustache had returned, two sharp wedges hovering across his upper lip.

"We leave tomorrow morning." He dropped a stack of newly cleaned undershirts into the trunk. His open luggage occupied both beds, the desk, and chair.

"How's that?"

"I have tickets for Djibouti. The train leaves tomorrow morning. Now pack up. I know you don't have much but I'll need your help later."

I wondered if I was witnessing another breakdown, though obviously quite different from his collapse at the gebbi.

"Only to Djibouti? Then what? I'm making okay coin from these reporters here. Give me a week or two more and I can maybe get us steerage to France."

"No need to wait. I've booked passage on the *Aceldama*. To Liverpool."

Unconvinced, I closed a trunk to use as a seat. "It's good to have bookings. We need money to pay for them, too."

"Already done." He produced an envelope.

I examined the two tickets issued by the French liner company. I knew enough to understand the words *première classe*.

"How can we afford this?"

"What you mean to ask is how can *I* afford this. Don't concern yourself with that. Just help me pack. Then order me a bath. Then you need to go to the Imperial to tell everyone I'm leaving. I have plenty to say before we board that train."

Since the invasion, the Imperial Hotel's dining room had been transformed into a news bureau. Dining tables converted to desks with typewriters and pencil holders. Wastebaskets overflowed with crumpled pages, spent ink spools, pencil shavings. A bank of telephones connected to places in Ethiopia, but if someone needed to talk to London or New York or anywhere else, they had to send a cable. The reporters didn't let the hotel maids in to clean the room and even with the windows open the atmosphere pressed down with cigarette smoke and the ripe smells of men under deadline stress. The room was three-quarters full when I delivered my promise that the Black Eagle would come soon with actual news for them. Not for the front page, maybe, but definitely something solid, I said.

By the time Julian arrived, the corps had dwindled to half a dozen. He had changed outfits since I left him at the Haus and now wore a morning suit and cravat. He looked like he'd come to sign a treaty or cut a ribbon. In my head I whispered the hope that he would leave the monocle tucked in his pocket because by then I was tired of the Mr. Peanut jokes.

He searched for the stage but they'd dismantled it to make room for more desks. Instead, he dragged a chair mid-room and mounted. The six men remaining came closer, notebooks and pencils drawn. Julian raised both hands for quiet.

"Gentlemen!" he began. "I've come to inform you that I will be resigning my commission from the Ethiopian Armed Forces. I will be leaving Addis Ababa tomorrow to return to the United States." His accent that day was a muddle, an Oxbridge shell on a Trini nut.

Pads opened. Various versions of the quote were recorded. Julian gave them time to finish.

"I was assigned to train recruits for the emperor's army. I taught them modern methods and I taught them guerrilla warfare. I asked to train them with modern weaponry. The emperor ordered his underlings to supply the proper arms. But they were lazy and inefficient and the arms were not forthcoming. This is why I am forced to resign. Are there questions?"

Linton Wells went first. "Did you speak with the emperor?"

"The emperor is in Dessye. I spoke with a number of high officials in his government but unfortunately, they did not respect my authority."

Then Gallagher asked, "What did you tell the officials?"

"I told them that they are fooling themselves if they think their tactics will work against the Italian army. They believe in mass attack and standing up to tanks with nothing more sophisticated than knives and spears. It worked for Menelik in 1896, but it won't work in 1935. The Italians will annihilate them."

Again, I wondered about a breakdown. The reporters didn't care. Those who had waited weren't sorry for it.

The final question came from Bill Deedes: "When will you be back, Colonel?"

Julian removed the monocle from his vest pocket. He polished it with a handkerchief, thumb and forefinger working in tiny circles on opposite sides of the lens. After setting it in the left eye socket, he cleared his throat of phlegm and answered. "Never. I am through with Ethiopia. Thank you, gentlemen. No more questions. I must return to my suite now to prepare for my departure."

I watched Julian descend from chair to floor and had started after him when Deedes and Claude McKay intercepted me.

Deedes asked, "What does this mean, Arthur?"

"It means we're leaving, I guess."

"But what he said. About the Italians annihilating Ethiopia."

I had no answer.

"Is the Colonel mad?"

"Of course not," I said.

"Then how do you explain it? How do you explain what he just said?"

Again, I had no answer, but Claude McKay did. "Whatever the reason, it's not good news, Bill. Hubert Julian is not the type of man who deserts a good ship unless it's in danger of sinking."

68

I APPEAL TO THE WORLD

I WILL CONFESS THAT I DID NOT PROTEST THE AMPLE COM-
forts of first-class travel. On the train, I sat in upholstered seats,
drank iced tea, snacked on olives and dates. At the end of each day's
journey, they gave us hot towels to wipe away the travel grime. In
both Awash and Dire Dawa, I enjoyed a clean room, all to myself.

In Djibouti we jumped the queue and were among the first to
board the *Aceldama*, where tip-hungry cabin boys stretched fresh
sheets over my bunk each morning and polished my shoes at night.
At dinner, the waiters poured wine from crystal decanters and refilled
without having to ask. Each rich and filling meal concluded with snif-
ters of brandy to aid digestion. Yes, I took advantage and it felt terrific.
After so many months of discomfort and privation, I felt entitled.

But I didn't understand where Julian had found the money and
soon, the question started to nag.

One evening we were out on deck at dusk. The sun's fiery light
broke on the ridges of the sea chop. A steward approached with a
basket of fresh fruit. Julian selected an orange.

I took a green apple, bit in, and said, "I was wondering about
the money, Hubert. Did you manage to wrangle some funds from
Tessema?"

Julian shook his head. "I haven't spoken with that son-of-a-bitch since that last time at the palace. I won't even say his name."

"Was it Bayen, then? Did you get him to pony up?"

"Certainly not." He squinted into the sun and the cresting coastal sands.

"Well, then, who? I find this whole thing very unusual."

He turned the orange over in his hand, as though trying to figure out the grip for the right spin. He looked down at his feet, brought his toes together, then split them again. "Do you think salt air is bad for my new shoes?"

"Why are you holding out on me?"

Julian dug into the orange, removing the peel with four dry rips.

"Maybe I should keep them packed until we get to London. They cost me twenty dollars in the ship's haberdashery."

We docked in Liverpool and while I tended to the luggage, Julian disappeared to shop for new clothes. I met him later that day in his room. He was at the desk, writing notes on hotel stationery. Boxes wrapped in brown paper were stacked against the wall next to a new suitcase.

"I've got an interview with Pathé News tomorrow. I need to put down a few thoughts."

"That's a real opportunity," I said. "To tell the world what's really happening in Ethiopia."

"Interview's set for tomorrow morning. Ask them downstairs for a wake-up call. Seven should give me plenty of time. Better make it six-thirty. And have my breakfast delivered to the room, too."

At the Pathé studio, a producer showed Julian to a chair behind a desk lit by two powerful spots. A makeup girl took the shine off his face with fine brown powder.

"Let's have those books on the desk with me," Julian said.

I passed over a pair of hardcovers, a directory of British military officers and *Dre* to *Hou*, volume two of an encyclopedia. Julian

opened the latter and set his notes on the right side. The producer
called for quiet.

"Whenever you're ready, Colonel Julian."

Julian swallowed and raised his head, blinked a few times in the
bright light, then turned back to his notes.

"Could I have a moment, please?"

"Of course."

He read the notes, then turned the page over and read the back.
Something on the page dissatisfied him. His gaze lifted back up
to the director, who stood beside the camera between the two big
lights. Julian looked as though he was trying to decide whether or
not to trust the man.

"Colonel Julian?"

"Just a minute more."

But two, then three minutes passed. Not a lot of time, but I
sensed the crew's impatience.

"Anything I can get you, Hubert?"

He thought about the question, then shook his head without looking at me. Nerves, I thought. He was a man accustomed to attention.
Something inside him converted attention to energy, the way plants
make food from light. Pathé was something else, of course. At the time
it was one of the biggest newsreel producers. Millions of people would
see this in hundreds of thousands of movie houses around the world.

"Okay," he said. "Let's go.

The producer called for quiet a second time, then asked, "What
can you tell us about the situation in Ethiopia?"

Julian stroked the monocle's edges with thumb and forefinger.
He blinked against the lighting.

"I have just returned from Ethiopia, where I was chief instruct-
or in the emperor's army." He used that near-British accent to tell
the half lie, but his voice had the unsteadiness of an actor who
hadn't quite memorized his lines. "Because of my knowledge of the
conditions there, I appeal to the world to assist in the settlement
of this conflict between Italy and Ethiopia, without causing a war
between the great nations of the world."

He stopped. The producer waited for more. *Go on*, I thought. Tell them about the gas attacks, the broken promises, how the emperor's army was hopelessly underequipped, how much they needed help.

But Julian remained mum and when the producer asked if he wanted to add anything, he pushed his chair back, slid the monocle into his vest pocket, and asked the makeup girl for a cloth to wipe his face.

Liverpool, UK, December 10, 1935

TO: BOI Agent Triggs

RE: JULIAN, HUBERT (a.k.a. THE BLACK EAGLE
             OF HARLEM)

FILE NO: 35-49

JULIAN and Your Informant booked on RMS Aquitania,
due to arrive in New York City on the 22nd of current
month.

Your Informant wishes to discuss matter of urgent
importance as soon as possible. Please set appointment
for any day that suits after the 22nd. I am receiving
mails at Mrs. LIPOMA's boarding house. You have the
address.

Given the urgency of the matter, this must be my
final dispatch until we meet.

END OF REPORT

PART THREE

Perhaps I was rather brash, too, and very full of myself.

—COL. HUBERT F. JULIAN, *Autobiography*

69

THERE IS NO WAR! THERE IS NO INVASION!

OUR CROSSING WAS MARKED BY ROUGH SEAS AND FRIGID winds, but twelve days later, the *Aquitania* steamed into New York's harbour. I followed Julian ashore, though what I actually followed was not so much Julian but the furry bulk of the full-length beaver coat he'd purchased in London. Word of his resignation from the Imperial Army had preceded us across the Atlantic and a group of reporters swarmed him as soon as he stepped off the gangplank.

"The war isn't over," the first said. "Why did you leave Addis Ababa?"

"Because Ethiopians do not care for the American Negro and do not want his help. American Negroes should face their own problems at home and keep out of international affairs."

"But Colonel, the invasion has been denounced by —"

"There is no war! There is no invasion! Think of some other term and I shall probably answer your question. What Italy is doing in Ethiopia is an act of God in answer to the cry of suffering."

"What about the rumours that you're romantically involved with the emperor's daughter? Are they true?"

"On that matter, you'll have to wait and see."

Bourne of *The Age* stepped forward.

"What happens to you if Italy takes over?"

"When Italy takes over, it will be a good thing. I hope they will permit the emperor to rule and continue civilizing Ethiopians."

"Aren't you an Ethiopian citizen?"

"Not for long. I will renounce my Ethiopian citizenship and apply for American citizenship."

"But why, Colonel? Do you have something against our country, too?"

I waited until the newsmen cleared out.

"What was that?"

"I'll never catch a break from those bastards."

"Have you lost your mind?"

"Certainly not."

"Then what the hell —?"

"I offered an assessment of a difficult international crisis to a group of imbeciles incapable of understanding what's really happening in Ethiopia."

"But you can't —"

"I provided a cogent analysis as someone who is more qualified to speak about the issue than anyone on this side of the Atlantic."

"Then you should have spoken about the issue truthfully."

"You're home now, Tormes. Thanks to me."

"Thanks to you? If not for you I never would have had to leave."

"You didn't have to come to Ethiopia."

"And you didn't have to quit on the emperor."

This stung him in ways I wouldn't have expected. His face slackened and his eyes drifted over my shoulder, pausing for a long thought before he returned to me.

"I got you home, didn't I?" he said. "I don't like the way you show your gratitude."

70

MAYBE I COULD CALL IT A HABIT

JULIAN DIDN'T TAKE LONG TO SETTLE IN BEFORE HE launched his lecture tour. Meanwhile, I tried to restart life in New York. First priority? A place to sleep. I considered returning to Mrs. Lipoma's — she always had a free room or two — but the idea brought me down. Those splintered floors and thin walls and the toilet I had to share with so many other men. I wanted a clean break from all that. I wanted to get on with things.

I found a place on the second floor of a house in Brooklyn, close enough to the college that the landlady, Mrs. Levine, asked me what I was studying. My room overlooked a quiet street and a big yard and came furnished with a good bed, a desk, even a radio. That first night, I listened to a terrific big band performance, Cab Calloway, live from Carnegie Hall.

Eventually, I would have to inform Triggs about my new address, though he still hadn't responded to my request to meet. The silence wouldn't normally concern me. In fact, when it came to Triggs, I generally preferred not to hear from him. But I had been considering Jean's suggestions about civil liberties lawyers and hoped to talk with Triggs before I decided anything, to see where he stood and if anything had changed since we last met.

Incredibly, it had been four years since I'd seen him. It was nearly as long since he had relayed any instructions. A reasonable person in my position might conclude that something had happened. Retirement or dismissal or demotion. Or even that Riley Triggs was dead. That same reasonable person would have seen the cell door neglectfully left ajar and simply walked out. And yet, I am ashamed to admit, none of these possibilities — these totally rational explanations — ever occurred to me. I could no more imagine Triggs dying than the resurrection of my own mother.

So what was the problem? I don't know if I have a satisfactory answer except to say that I had been spying for Triggs since I was seventeen years old, and by now I was accustomed to my circumstances. Probably too accustomed. Jean Fox didn't get that part. She knew the facts, but she couldn't understand how reporting to Triggs and playing the part of Hubert Julian's false disciple had come to define me. Maybe I could even call it a habit, like smoking opium. I guess what I'm saying is this: I didn't know what my life would look like without Triggs or Julian being a part of it. I didn't know what would fill the void or *who* I'd be or *how* to be, and — I'll just say one more thing: Jean Fox, who used to love me, couldn't know that, either.

I picked up a job pretty quickly, selling restaurant supplies for Heron & Sons. From working for Tommy Kippers, I knew their products well and could talk up the virtues to potential customers. I also dropped by Brooklyn College and enrolled in a couple of courses they offered at night. Freshman political science. Freshman English comp. Why the hell not? The classes began in January, after the Christmas break.

I didn't join Julian on his lecture tour but surrendered to old impulses and checked the papers for accounts of his speeches. At every stop he decried Ethiopia's war effort as futile, stopping just short of praise for Mussolini and the Italian army. He claimed to have witnessed the massacre of three Italian drivers at the hands of

Ethiopian soldiers. Ethiopian officials, who were in New York to drum up support, denied his claims and called Julian a liar and an unworthy representative of the race.

After that, several groups cancelled planned appearances. The Boston paper refused to run advertisements for his lecture in that city, labelling him a jackdaw. Later, delegates at the National Negro Congress in Chicago forced Julian from the auditorium to chants of "Traitor!" Death threats mounted and spooked Julian enough that he made arrangements with an undertaker. "Talk of death is unpleasant, but death overtakes us all," he said. "Presidents have been assassinated. Kings and emperors murdered. Why not Julian?"

For a day or so, I entertained the theory that he'd become derailed. But that wasn't right. He wasn't crazy. He continued to speak and dress well. He was still arrogant and short-tempered and self-serving and a whole list of other things he'd always been. But no, Hubert Julian was not crazy.

I tried to impose some distance between my emotions and Julian's bullshit, but found it impossible when the same papers that quoted his critical remarks also reported the war's progress. The Italians had destroyed villages and continued to defy international law and human decency with repeated gas attacks. Their troops were nearing Harar. Addis Ababa was next.

71

IF THERE WAS ONE
THING I HAD RIGHT

AT COLLEGE, I DISCOVERED MY EXPERIENCES IN ETHIOPIA granted me a certain status among the more politically aware, most of whom favoured continued U.S. neutrality. I stood up and warned about Fascist aggression. Where would Italy go after Ethiopia? In Germany, Nazi shipyards were busy building submarines. How long should the world wait to do something? I liked that they listened to me, and I shared some more abstract perspectives. On power and who holds it. On how it gets exercised. On how it's maintained. I was surprised to learn I had some things of value to tell them.

Of course all of that is easy to say now. After all, I have landed on the right side of history. If things had gone the other way, if I'd taken Julian's position, if the other side had won in the end, I might not be sitting so prettily or boasting about my prescience.

At the end of most days, I visited the college's new library, a red-brick building with a pointed, glassed-in cupola. After browsing the Negro press looking for Julian, I pulled the day's edition of *The*

Sun, scanning each seven-column page for Jonas Windermere's by-line. Two or three times a week, I would find him, still in Ethiopia. Which meant that Jean was still there, too. I closed the paper and imagined her smoking in the bar at the Imperial, indulging her new fondness for tej. Or maybe she played bridge now, that game one picks up with age, when sitting down to cards becomes more appealing than a night of music or dancing.

One evening in late February, I left the library and started my usual route home across the empty playing field. Four inches of snow had fallen on Brooklyn the night before. In the half dark, I followed a path of trampled snow, part of a pattern of thread-like lines stomped by various campus migrations. Ethiopia remained on my mind. And not just because of my classmates or because of Jean Fox or even because Julian had just announced that in anticipation of new Italian citizenship, he wished to be known as Humberto Juliano.

Though, of course, I *did* think about those things and also about American neutrality and those who hated Mussolini and the twenty-five thousand in Harlem who marched in the streets against him. Not so long ago, the Black Eagle would have joined the march. Or circled above in a rented airplane and dropped flyers urging action. Now? His appearance might well cause a riot.

I still didn't understand it. Okay, he'd always been a mystery, but if I'd had one thing right about him, it was surely his endless craving for public approval and adoration. Now, with every speech and appearance, he invited fury and scorn. He was quickly becoming the most famous pariah in Black America. And for what? What could he gain from infamy?

It was then, on that snow-trampled campus path on that half-dark February night, that I figured it out. The force of the revelation halted me on the spot and for a moment I felt like a movie detective, standing alone with his conclusions in the middle of that empty, unlit playing field. Beyond the white goalposts, car lights glided past and turned up Avenue H. The snow on my boots began to melt. The cold and wet penetrated my boots and socks to my feet. I ran over the evidence from those last days in Addis Ababa, an exercise I would repeat many, many times over the next few days. It came down to this:

First: Julian was broke and on Ethiopia's side.

Then: Julian had money, was speaking against Ethiopia, and calling himself Humberto Juliano.

And this: Sergio Pratti had visited the Haus and made contact. Sergio knew things about Julian and the emperor. Things I'd told him. He knew we were broke. I remembered all the questions he'd asked, his unusual interest. I remembered how little he seemed to know about railway building.

All of those facts, put into order on the same page, now made perfect sense and could only mean one thing: Colonel Hubert Julian, the Black Eagle of Harlem, had sold out to Italy.

72

THE SOONER, THE BETTER

NOW WHAT?

Not a question I was prepared to answer right then.

I stayed in bed past noon, trying to figure things out. Selling out to a foreign power, especially one with territorial ambitions, was surely a serious offence. This had to be just the thing Triggs needed, the *coup de grâce* that would finally end Hubert Julian's threat to America and release me for good.

Except, what proof did I have? The evidence had convinced me, but was it actual proof? There were no cancelled cheques or secret contracts. No paper trail or signed confessions. And, to be honest, the notion that Julian would betray the emperor and Ethiopia resisted reason. Maybe those speeches supporting Italy's campaign were a ruse of some kind, part of a subversive strategy to undermine Mussolini? It's true that since we'd returned to New York in December, I hadn't seen Julian at all. If I had, he might have let me in on his plan. Now I was hesitating. Until I knew something for certain, it seemed wrong to go blabbing to Triggs.

I contemplated the possibilities from my bed all morning, cancelling a couple of scheduled sales calls. Sometime in there, Mrs. Levine slid the morning mail under my door. I let it sit until I got up. The top envelope had been addressed first to Mrs. Lipoma's and then forwarded. Under all the purple stampings and postal pen scratches, I recognized Jean Fox's script.

Her sloppy lefty handwriting, the backward slant and uneven spacing, slowed me down but I didn't mind spending extra time to read through the first paragraphs, the news about the war I already knew and the gossip from the Imperial: who'd fled the country, who was sticking it out, and the mood in the city with the Italians creeping ever closer.

> Some are trying the train and some are clogging
> the roads making for Kenya, and every morning I go
> outside and feel like the city has shrunk. Well, it
> has, I guess. What remains is so strange and hard
> to imagine: all these people fated to wait it out
> because they have no other place to go.

The next paragraph began with news about Jonas. He'd been reporting from the front and had concluded Mussolini's troops would storm Addis soon. When that happened, the Italians would take over the cable offices, and the reporters from newspapers not friendly to their mission would have to quit the city.

> Jonas is already looking at Spain and Germany, though
> he might convince his editor to send him back to
> China. But I'm no longer so concerned where he goes
> because I won't be going with him.

Here the script turned neater, more deliberate, as though Jean had started the letter with a few drinks in her but now wrote with a measured and sober hand. She said she was sick of war zones, of hotel rooms, of food that disagreed with her.

> It's what I signed up for, I know. I know! But I want
> to go home now.

And so, Arthur Tormes, you are only the third
person to learn the news that my marriage is over.

Three days have passed since we had that
finalizing talk and I'm over the shock more easily
than I would have guessed. A bit of sadness. A bit
of relief. (Maybe you understand those conflicting
feelings?) Jonas is fine, too … I think he's thinking
about children and about finding a wife whose body
won't reject them. I think he believes I'm doing him
a favour.

Truth is, the thing was a hot mess from the start.
We barely dated before he asked me to marry him.
Three months! And I swear, I was going to turn him
down but then I didn't. Well, that's what you get,
isn't it? I think I always knew I wasn't with him for
the right reasons. And don't flatter yourself, Arthur.
It wasn't just because I thought it'd be a quick
way to get over you. I was chasing after something,
something I'd been chasing after ever since my
parents died. He promised to show me the world
(promise fulfilled). Maybe I thought the accelerated
life of a war correspondent's wife would help me
catch whatever I was chasing, and faster.

It didn't. And that's okay. It's been okay for a
while. Certainly ever since Asunción. I know you know
the story.

But now, five years older, I'm coming back to New
York. Which brings me to the whole damn purpose of
this letter: to see if you weren't free for lunch one
of these days?

That same night after I finished work, I re-read the letter twice,
then wrote my reply. Yes, lunch sounded like an excellent idea. The
sooner, the better, I said. In fact, I put a lot of stock into that open

lunch invitation, whether it meant tomato soup and corned beef sandwiches or something more. That second option excited me. Being in love, being loved back. And doing things right this time.

I licked a stamp, sealed the envelope, then went out to post the letter. It had been a warm day and a thick layer of slush covered unshovelled sidewalks. I dropped the letter in the box and let the door snap close and by the time I returned to my room, I had made a decision with a clarity of mind I found both refreshing and a little frightening.

I needed to see Hubert Julian as soon as possible.

73

HE ONCE OWNED THE SKY ABOVE THIS PLACE

THE NEXT AFTERNOON I RODE UP TO HARLEM ON A SUBWAY so packed I couldn't exit at my stop and had to wait for the next. I retreated south, face first into a March wind that stung my eyes. A trickle of cars sped up and down Seventh Avenue. Men formed a long line outside a door, sallow faced and weary. Might have been a soup kitchen, might have been a chance at a job. Half the stores were closed, with sheets of plywood nailed in tight to protect their windows.

In Julian's building I climbed up three flights to their floor. Essie answered my first knock.

"Good God in heaven, I thought we'd seen the last of you."

"Hello, Essie."

She slammed the door shut, leaving me in the hall. Essie was never so hot on me; I think she saw me as an accomplice. Or maybe she had an instinct that told her I wasn't who I seemed. Unlikely that Julian ever tried to change her mind, either. I heard raised voices inside and a minute later, the door re-opened. Julian leaned on the jamb, his hand high. His white shirt glowed. Gold cufflinks decorated the starchy cuff.

"Did you come to apologize?"

"To talk," I said. "Can we do that?"

"I don't have to be anywhere." He stepped aside.

"Not here."

"You afraid of my wife now?"

"How about tea? Downstairs."

Another unit's door opened behind me and I jumped a little. A kid, maybe eight, came to attention before Julian and saluted.

"What's the report, Private?" Julian asked.

"All quiet, Colonel."

"Carry on, then."

The kid scurried down the hall.

"Not much of a family man, are you, Arthur?"

I led the way into a small diner half a block away and went for an empty booth near the back, thinking about privacy. The crowd was bigger than I'd hoped for on a weekday afternoon, but maybe it was better to have the noise of other conversations to muffle our own.

I had my coat off and hung on a hook when I saw that Julian had hung back. "Here's better," he said, indicating the booth closest to the door.

The waitress came over right away. She wore a sky-blue uniform that matched the colour of the walls. I asked for a pot of tea, then tacked on a couple of doughnuts to the order.

"So? What's this about?" Julian asked. He was sitting with his back to the wall, allowing him to scan the other tables. I remembered the death threats and wondered if this also explained why, despite the fresh clothes, he looked a little run down.

"Hubert, there's something you need to know. The Bureau of Investigation has been watching you."

A half smile formed slowly across his face. Despite our spat, he still considered me an ally and on first hearing it, he took this information as a personal favour. He shrugged. "So?"

"It's been going on for years. Back to when you were working for Marcus Garvey. They thought you were a Red."

"A Red?"

"Or something. Some other seditious threat."

"Well, I'm not. Clearly. Though I can see why they'd think so. Good of you to tell me."

I was about to get into the rest of it but the waitress interrupted us with a pot of hot water, a pair of tea bags, and two sugar doughnuts on a white plate.

Julian broadened his smile. "You can take these back, Gracie. Let's make it coffee instead."

"Can't you see how busy I am?"

"I do. And I wouldn't ask. But this poor fool doesn't know how good your coffee is. How's your Milton doing?"

At the sound of her son's name, the woman rested her hand on her chest.

"Out in Detroit now," she said. "Got a job at Ford's, one of those big factories they have. Big as a whole city. I get scared he's going to get lost in there but he says to me, 'Don't worry, Mom, I know my way around already.' But I still worry. I'm his mother, I can't help myself."

"I've met Edsel Ford," Julian said. "Let's get some of that delicious lemon cake instead of these doughnuts. If it's fresh."

"Always fresh for you, Colonel."

Back behind the counter, Gracie laid out saucers and cups and retrieved the pot currently warming on the element. After pouring one cup she changed her mind and sent the rest of it down the sink, deciding instead to make a fresh pot. Why not? Julian had once owned the sky here, above this diner and everywhere else in Harlem. In some places, they still treated him like a hero.

"You were saying?"

"Yes. About the other thing you should know."

"Well? Get on with it."

"The things is that I'm the spy. I'm the one who's been watching you for the Bureau."

"You? A federal agent?" There was hesitation in his chuckle. "You're making this up."

"I'm not. But I'm not an actual agent. I just work for them. Except I don't get paid. Spying on you wasn't my choice, you see. They forced me into it."

"What does that mean?"

"Doesn't matter."

"I think it does."

"They forced me into it. It was a particular agent who saw you as a threat, and he's been making me watch you."

"Since when?"

"Since your first Harlem jump. April, 1923."

"Only since then? Didn't they care about me before? In Montreal? In Trinidad? At the Eastern? Think of all those years they missed!"

"That's something else," I said. "You and I didn't go to the Eastern together."

"You were in my year. I remember you. We watched cricket."

"I'm afraid not. I'm actually ten years younger than you."

"Really?"

"Really."

"Ten years?"

"Ten years."

"Essie always said there was something phony about you."

"She wasn't wrong. She's a smart woman."

But Julian didn't want to hear me compliment his wife. I watched his hands tense, his fingers halfway to forming a fist. He was thinking of violence. Or maybe violence is simply what I expected. Earlier, before I'd even boarded the subway, I'd figured to let him slug me if he thought it would make us even.

Gracie arrived back at the table with the coffee and cake. It smelled strong and bitterly fresh.

"I haven't seen that Essie of yours in some time," Gracie said.

"You know my girl. Always busy with one thing or another."

"You give her my best?"

"I certainly will. I'll say you asked for her."

Gracie went off to tend to another table, a man in a corduroy cap reading the *Racing Form* across from two sisters in the midst of an animated conversation.

"Why are you telling me this?" Julian asked.

"Because I want to give you a chance to come clean with me."

"About what? I have nothing to say to you."

"I want to know why you've been touring the country lying to people. Lying about the war and about Ethiopia being better off in Italian hands."

"Facts are facts. I don't make them up."

"So it isn't part of some big plan? Because if this is some act with a higher hidden purpose, you should tell me now."

"There's nothing to tell. Nothing at all."

I tasted the lemony sweet cake, chewing slowly, nudging the poppy seeds to the front of my mouth, trapping them in my incisors then biting down for that little pop. My fork sliced another bite. I wanted to give Julian time to change his mind. But he said nothing. He hadn't moved, either, not even to swirl sugar into his fresh coffee.

"If you've got nothing to say, then I have to tell you something else."

"I bet you do."

"I'm going to meet this Bureau agent. Tomorrow. And I'm going to tell him what I know. Everything. The agent's name is Riley Triggs."

"What is it you think you know that the Bureau of Investigation would care to hear?"

"I know you've been taking money from the Italians."

"That's a damn lie."

"For the first-class tickets home. For the luxury hotels. For these lectures."

"Wrong and wrong and wrong again," he said. "Boy, I might have taken you for a lot of things, but I never took you for a fool or a liar."

"I'm neither."

"What about a two-faced backstabber?"

"Where did the money come from?"

"I'm not saying anything to you."

"For all the sharp new suits and the beaver coat you bought in London. Those cufflinks are new, too."

"How the hell would you know?"

"Haven't you been listening? I've been spying on you for thirteen years. It was my job to notice things like that."

"I've done nothing wrong," he said. "Where in the hell do you get your balls?"

"For all the speeches you're making. The Italians are paying you, aren't they?"

"I don't know why you keep insisting."

"Because. I know you. I know you pretty damn well. I've been watching you for thirteen years. It was never my choice. I didn't want to go to prison. Riley Triggs ordered me to find something to pin to you so he could put you away, like the Bureau did with Marcus Garvey. I tried. I really did. I looked everywhere. But not once in all those years did you do anything the Bureau should have cared about. But now? Working for a foreign power? With Mussolini? With what he's doing to Ethiopia? Nothing I ever reported to Triggs was ever so … damning. And I have to say, I think it could be bad for you, Hubert."

"You love this. You're having a ball right now."

"I'm not enjoying this in the least."

"These lies reflect more on your character than mine. It shows you for what you are: you are petty and envious. You're a child."

"I wanted to give you a chance to arrange things. Maybe talk to a lawyer. It'd be better for Essie to hear it from you than the papers. I thought I owed you that."

He folded his arms across his chest. "Owe me? You owe me plenty more than that. You're a damn parasite."

"I just figured that after everything …" I peered out the window into the empty street. A cab passed slowly in the curb lane, saving gas as he watched for fares. I turned back to Julian, thinking something in his expression might reveal his thoughts. What was I looking for? Regret? Fear? Part of me wanted to believe that after so many years, I could provoke him. That hearing these things — from me — would hurt. But no. He was angry, but definitely not hurt.

Of course he was angry; I'd accused him of collaboration. Even so, while the charge clearly riled him, his conscience seemed untouched. It occurred to me that Julian probably saw nothing wrong with taking Fascist money to speak against Ethiopia. To him, he was behaving no differently from a press agent. Or a ballplayer who shills for some brand of cigarettes.

And as for the fact that everything between us had been a complete lie? Honestly? I'm not sure it even occurred to him to be bothered.

"Well?" he said.

"I don't know."

"You think you can put me in jail with your lies?"

"You won't believe me, but I hope you find a way to wrangle out of this. And I don't expect you to forgive me, but I have to tell the Bureau what I know."

"Fuck you."

"I'd better go." I pulled some coins from a front pocket. The quarter bounced and swivelled before Hubert stopped it with the flat of his hand. He swept it to the floor with the others. "Next time I see you, it'd better be to apologize. You've shovelled yourself into a hole here, man. It's going to take all my grace and mercy to let you climb back out."

"Goodbye, Hubert." I began to walk away.

"Don't you use that name. My father gave me that name. Don't you dare say it, you son of a whore."

I stopped and spun around. Quickly enough that Julian slid out of his seat and stood up, fists balled. The words stung, but the insult was common enough, something anyone might expect to hear given the situation. I knew Julian enough to know he had chosen his words randomly. After all, he didn't even know Antona's name.

I turned back and walked out the door, buttoned my coat, and turned south to the subway station.

74

A STRANGE FEELING, A CLEAN FEELING

IN THE BUREAU'S MAIN NEW YORK OFFICE THE NEXT DAY, A receptionist led me to a bright room on the thirteenth floor with a window overlooking the unmoving treetops of Foley Square and the stone columns fronting the federal courthouse. Buses and cars crowded the streets, but so far up, I was insulated from all the noise and confusion.

I sat in one of four padded chairs surrounding an oak table. A framed photo of the president hung on the opposite wall. The dark bags dipping from FDR's eyes reminded me of Mrs. Lipoma. I guess the old Finn and the president each had their reasons for losing sleep. I wondered if Triggs had ever sat in this same chair. I wondered if he liked to believe the White House knew about the work he was doing on behalf of all America.

I waited another twenty minutes before the door opened. I pushed back and stood to greet him, but the man who came in was not Triggs. He was younger, with an erect posture, square shoulders, and the veiny neck of a very fit man. The Bureau might have scooped him up straight from a college football field.

He said his name was Agent Donald Springer. He shook my hand, invited me to sit again, apologized for keeping me waiting. He laid a brown file on the desk, *Hubert Julian* printed across the top tab.

"First question, Mr. Tormes. Are you certain about the name of the agent you dealt with? Triggs?"

"Oh yes. Riley Triggs. Absolutely certain."

"And did this Agent Triggs … did he pay you for the information?"

"No."

"When was your last contact?"

"About four years ago. Well, closer to five, actually. But I've been sending reports regularly since then. More or less regularly."

"These reports. They were all concerning Hubert Julian?"

"Correct. Until very recently it was every week. Right on schedule."

"Did he have you looking into anything else?"

"No. Just Hubert Julian. That was my assignment."

"This is the man?" he asked, producing a file photo, a shot of Julian posing next to the *Ethiopia I*.

"That photo is over ten years old," I said. "But yes, that's him."

"Where did you send the reports?"

I recited the address from memory. "P.O. Box 44, Station D, New York, New York."

"Why not directly to Triggs here at the Bureau? Or to one of our safe addresses?"

"Because Triggs told me to send them to P.O. Box 44, Station D, New York, New York."

"Yes, well, that's interesting. Because the Bureau doesn't use P.O. boxes. They're not secure. Every agent knows the policy."

"Maybe Triggs broke the rules? Why don't we ask him? Shouldn't he be here for this?"

"Well, that's another sort of small thing," Springer said. He was treating me with a delicacy I found a little insulting. "We don't have any agents named Riley Triggs here."

"No?"

"No."

"Are you sure?"

"Quite sure."

"Then who was I sending reports to? Who was I meeting with?"

He closed the file, leaned back in his chair, and released a long sigh. "Good question. Could be a lot of different things. Perhaps someone impersonating a federal agent."

"I don't think so."

"Why not?"

"Triggs knew things. He had resources. He had connections with the state police. He knew when I got a job in security. He knew everything, always."

"Can I get you a glass of water? A coffee?"

"Do you think I'm making all of this up?"

"I don't."

"Then?"

He shrugged. An ambiguous shrug.

"You don't have any idea?" I asked.

"I do, unfortunately. But before I say anything, what I'm about to say is strictly off the record. If anyone asks, I will deny it. Do you understand?"

"Funny, Triggs used to remind me of that all the time. I understand what you're saying pretty well by now."

"You see, this Agent Triggs. He may have been working … off the books."

"What does that mean?"

"It happened sometimes, especially back in the old days. An agent would pursue a case on his own, without having to follow Bureau rules. The P.O. box. The blackmail. It wasn't encouraged, but it was tolerated. Not anymore, though. Mr. Hoover put an end to it. A lot of guys from that generation lost their jobs."

"Then Riley Triggs was fired?"

"Could be. Sounds probable, actually."

"Isn't there some way to confirm it?"

He laughed a little. "Not officially. The Bureau doesn't like to talk about those days. Also, Riley Triggs wasn't his real name. We'd have no idea who he really was."

"What if I described him to you? Or to one of the older men who are still around?"

Now he looked at me like I was simple. "You could try. But it's doubtful any of the men who knew him would co-operate. There's a kind of code, you see."

"Because they've got their own secrets to hide?"

Springer said nothing, which, to my mind, confirmed that everyone in the Bureau had something to hide.

"So what have I been doing all these years? I can tell you everything about Hubert Julian. That whole file could be based on my information. Except it should be thicker. Many inches thicker."

Springer shifted. He glanced toward the door.

"I don't know what to tell you, Mr. Tormes. There's nothing in this file that mentions an Agent Triggs or you or an informant of any kind. I don't know about any attempted murder charges against you from 1923, either."

My throat tightened and I asked again. "Then tell me: What have I been doing for the last thirteen years?"

"I know it's a long time," Springer said.

"Not just here but all the way over in Africa. Twice, I went to Africa. Half my life. The good half, too. How could the Bureau let Triggs do this to me?"

"Oh, the Bureau knew nothing about it. I can guarantee that. This man calling himself Triggs acted alone. You were just a kid."

"But then he was fired —"

"Probably fired. I don't know for certain."

"And he kept me going … Why?"

"I have no way of knowing, Mr. Tormes. Did he have something against Hubert Julian personally? A grudge of some kind?"

"They never even met," I said. "I can't believe that fat fuck is going to get away with this."

Then neither of us said anything. Springer wanted to leave the room. But I couldn't move. Not just yet. The lunch hour had arrived. Foot traffic picked up in the hall. Still, I remained mute and as Springer sat waiting, I was struck by a premonition: as with Triggs, Hubert Julian's deal with the Italians was going to go unpunished. Soon enough, he'd capture the public's attention with another stunt or crazy plan and the newspapers would be all over him again and all of this would be forgotten. Of course it would. Julian, that eternally lucky bastard, knew it too.

Finally, Springer spoke. "I don't know what else to tell you, Mr. Tormes. If you don't have any other questions, you're free to go."

There it was. In this tiny government room, my life as I had known it unravelled. And all in the space of half an hour.

Outside, the weather had shifted. Sun squeaked through the clouds and the snow clustered into sharp banks of pre-melt crystals. A warmish wind rubbed across my skin. The street was quiet and calm. A scarlet cardinal flew from the lower branches of a young sycamore. No leaves yet, but buds. Little tender green tubes poised to unfurl.

I turned south and then west, striding slowly, but not casually. I took deep, easy breaths, feeling like a man who knew where he was going, even if I didn't. Not exactly, anyway. It was a strange feeling, a clean feeling, like emerging into a cool night from the steam of a scalding shower. My empty stomach rumbled and I stepped into a lunch counter and ordered pastrami on rye and a box of chocolate-covered peanuts.

Three blocks later I was standing on the slats of the 32nd Street pier next to a long, vacant berth. Creosote-stained pilings waited in their upright rows for the next ship to arrive. Might be the *Normandie*, or the *Europa*, or the *Empress of India*. Might be from Liverpool, Le Havre, or Lisbon.

The terminal building was empty, except for a young couple standing close to each other at the Cunard ticket counter.

Newlyweds, I could tell. Their smart new clothes were a sign and
so was the boundlessly hopeful way the woman gazed at the man as
he conferred with the agent. And also the little restrained bounce
in his step that showed his eagerness to embark and get on with
their lives, together.

At the pier's end, I sat on a wood and iron bench and opened
the paper sandwich bag. It occurred to me that I should have been
angrier, that the years spent chasing Julian had been lost. Stolen,
really. A crime like that. Someone should pay. Yes, I should have
been angry, I should have been thinking about revenge or at least
contacting those lawyers Jean Fox had suggested.

Maybe I would, eventually. But not now. Not yet.

The sandwich was delicious, the meat tender, the bread fresh.
And just the right amount of zip in the brown mustard. I popped a
few peanuts into my mouth, crunching and chewing slowly, letting
the chocolate melt across my tongue. The sun emerged in full now,
warm enough to unbutton my coat. The newlyweds swept past me
and stopped at the pier's end. The man wrapped his cloaked arm
around his bride's padded shoulder. A light pink scarf floated from
her neck.

"Tell me again, what time?" the woman said.

"We sail at noon. Boarding starts at nine."

"Let's try to be the first to board."

"I'd like that."

"And let's get a spot on deck. I want to see the whole city."

"If that's what you'd like."

"I wish it were here now. I wish we could see it."

"It'll be here soon. It's due any time."

"Really? What if it comes early?"

"It might."

"From where?"

"Down there."

He pointed south. The light green tickets flapped in his hands,
as though animated by their own eagerness. I imagined myself
as a guest at their recent wedding, watching from a round table

as they danced alone under a spotlight. I imagined the dreamy, half-drunk smile pasted to my face. Happy for them. Happy for happiness itself.

They held each other and stared down the East River, at the barges and tugs and smoking freighters, none nearly so impressive as the towering black-and-white liner they hoped to see. I pocketed the rest of the chocolate peanuts and nudged my hat back on my head. My English composition class started at four. Leave now and I'd arrive on time. In a minute, I thought. In a minute or two. I continued to share the view with the young couple. Together we searched beyond the length of that long river, past the barges and tugs and smoking freighters, out to the ocean and to everywhere else. Just in case.

Port Huron, Michigan, 1955

AFTERWORD

WHILE I RESEARCHED THE LIFE AND TIMES OF HUBERT Julian extensively, in the end the pull of fiction always outweighed the pull of historical truth.

In short, I made quite a few things up. Then again, so did Hubert Julian.

Some examples: he never served in the Canadian army; he never attended McGill University; it's unlikely his father was a wealthy man. His claims to have commanded the Ethiopian Air Force are dubious. He never ... well, you get the idea. He, too, made a lot up.

However, both our stories contain an incredible amount of truth. Go to the U.S. Patent Office website, search US1379264A, and you will find an *Airplane Safety Device*, Julian's parachutta-gravepreresista. Several newspaper accounts tell us that in 1923, Julian really did parachute into the streets of Harlem at least twice, once while playing the saxophone. These stunts made him a celebrity across America. He also did, in fact, attempt the trans-Atlantic crossing in 1924 and was harassed at that time by an agent of the Department of Treasury named James Amos. (However, there are many, including contemporaries, who contend Julian had no intention of actually completing the trip.)

Julian did travel to Ethiopia in 1930 (recruited by Malaku Bayen, a U.S.-trained physician and key member of Selassie's inner circle throughout the 1930s) and really did successfully jump for the emperor and gain fame in Africa. And he really did fall out of favour in Ethiopia when he crashed one of Haile Selassie's personal planes.

Later, Julian returned to Ethiopia and had a role training troops during the Second Italo-Abyssinian War. A letter from the emperor was reported to have caused a breakdown of some sort and Julian was indeed broke and owing when he left Addis at the end of 1935. Contemporary journalists talk of his efforts to sell his story to foreign correspondents. However, when he returned to America, it was in one of the *Aquitania*'s first-class berths.

Sometimes it was hard to glean Hubert Julian's intent. On a number of occasions, he tried to raise funds to attempt one record flight or another. None of those flights ever happened. Did he know they would never happen? Was it all a con?

Some of the most interesting lies went toward explaining his sudden wealth after months of poverty in the lead up to the Italo-Abyssinian War. At the time, he claimed the money came from an admiring woman. Years later, in his autobiography, the story went that he had befriended Italians in order to get close to Mussolini and assassinate him. According to Julian, the plot failed when Italian agents sniffed him out in Rome.

That he received money from the Italians was never proved and, as far as I know, he was never formally accused, either. Several articles in the *New York Age* and other papers strongly insinuated a deal, but I did not find any specific allegations. This much appears to be true: Hubert Julian was an unpopular man in much of Black America in early 1936.

Part of the challenge of uncovering the facts of Julian's life was in the mercurial relationship he had with a Black press eager for positive race stories. After initial curiosity and then admiration for his jumps and trans-Atlantic attempt, the press gradually began to view Hubert Julian more skeptically. The white papers were amused, the Black papers often contemptuous.

That said, Julian still had many sincere supporters. Undeterred and unconvinced to scale back the bullshit, he attracted media attention for many years. He produced movies, advocated for Father Divine, planned all those record-breaking flights. In 1940 he challenged Hermann Göring to an air duel (Göring did not respond). In that same year he travelled to Finland to help fight the Soviets in the Winter War, arriving in Helsinki with impeccable timing: the Finns had just surrendered.

After Pearl Harbor, though already in his mid-forties, Julian joined the U.S. Army and served as a private. After the war he got into the arms business, where he remained for many years and grew wealthy by completing deals with Jacobo Árbenz, in Guatemala; Fulgencio Batista, in Cuba; António Salazar, in Portugal; and others.

It wasn't just the papers who noticed Julian. During the years it took to write this book, I encountered him in a variety of histories of the Harlem Renaissance, in biographies of Marcus Garvey and Bessie Coleman, in accounts of early Black aviation, and in chronicles of the Italo-Abyssinian War. Even if only in footnotes, these authors found him irresistible.

But I also found him in some unexpected places. Like this small passage from Saul Bellow's *The Adventures of Augie March*, published in 1953.

I'm only trying to gather together what a city-bred
man knew of eagles altogether, and it's curious: the
eagle of money, the high flying eagles of Bombay, the
NRA eagle, with its gear and lightnings, the bird of
Jupiter and of nations, of republics as well as of
Caesar, of legions and soothsayers, Colonel Julian,
the Black Eagle of Harlem.

And, less directly, from Toni Morrison, who referred to Julian's famous parachuting in *Jazz* (1992), with this brief passage.

A colored man floats down out of the sky blowing a
saxophone, and below him, in the space between two
buildings, a girl talks earnestly to a man in a straw
hat.

It was an attempt at a big score with Moïse Tshombe, president of the then-breakaway Katanga province, that landed Hubert Julian in prison in Kinshasa (then called Leopoldville). That was 1962. His jailer, the United Nations, wanted to contain Moïse Tshombe and prevent a civil war in the newly independent Republic of the Congo. At his arrest, Julian protested and claimed he had come to the country for public relations work. The UN didn't buy it, and with good reason. Prior to flying to Africa, Julian had been in Brussels, where he visited the offices of E.J. Binet & Fils, Armes et Munitions, located at Rue Royale, 17. There, he ordered 5,000 pistols, 200,000 rounds of 120 mm shells, 100,000 rounds of 60 mm shells, and 3,500 machine guns.

While he claimed to M. Binet that the guns were bound for Angola, he also bragged that this was a clever smokescreen: "After the munitions get to Angola, I will see my friend Tshombe and sell them to him," he said. All of this we know in such detail today because M. Binet, prominent Belgian arms merchant, also informed for the American government. The day after Julian's visit, M. Binet reported everything in detail to his contacts at the U.S. Embassy.

Essie Julian passed away in 1974. Hubert Julian remarried and died in 1983.

Kingston, Ontario, 2023

NOTES

CHAPTER 4

"Try and be good and may God guide you. I raised you well and now I've put you with a good master. Be well." *Lazarillo de Tormes*, trans. W.S. Merwin (New York: NYRB Classics, 2005, 1554).

CHAPTER 16

Diagram of parachuttagravepreresista. Hubert Julian, Airplane Safety Appliance, United States Patent 1379264, May 1921, patents.google.com/patent/US1379264A/en.

CHAPTER 28

Some of Agent Amos' dialogue is taken from a profile of Julian by Morris Markey, "The Black Eagle," *New Yorker*, July 11, 1931.

CHAPTER 38

Details of the train journey from Jean D'Esme, "Journey to Abyssinia," *The Living Age (1897-1941)*; September 11, 1926.

Some of Julian's quotes are from his autobiography (as told to John Bulloch), *Black Eagle* (London: Adventurer's Club, 1964).

CHAPTER 50

"Brother, once I got there it was just will power and personality —
that's the Alpha and Axis." Robert G. Weisbord, "Black America
and the Italian-Ethiopian Crisis: An Episode in Pan-Negroism,"
The Historian 34, no. 2 (1972).

CHAPTER 52

"Lieutenant Julian," Sam Manning and the Caribbean Serenaders,
OKeh 8567, recorded April 3, 1928.

CHAPTER 69

"Whatever the reason, it's not good news, Bill. Hubert Julian is
not the type to desert a good ship unless it's in danger of sinking."
Paraphrased from Claude McKay, *Amiable with Big Teeth* (New
York: Penguin, 2013). The novel, written in 1941 but not pub-
lished until 2013, deals with Harlem before and during the Italo-
Abyssinian War, though McKay was not in Ethiopia at the time.

ACKNOWLEDGEMENTS
AND SOURCES

SPECIAL THANKS TO CHRIS CASUCCIO AT WESTWOOD Creative for his faith and perseverance. Also to Kwame Scott Fraser, Erin Pinksen, Jenny McWha, Robyn So, Vicky Bell, Laura Boyle, Alyssa Boyden, Maria Zuppardi, and everyone at Dundurn.

Thanks to: Nobu Adilman, Chidiogo Akunyili-Parr, Tim Alamenciak, Willow Bacon, Christian Baird, Tanaz Bhathena, Nic Billon, Renee Bridgemohan, Dennis Bock, Spencer Gordon, Sam Hiyate, Michael Malouf, Alejandro Mangiola, Stephen Nickson, David Morgan O'Connor, Sofi Papamarko, Shannon Parr, Anne Perdue, Costas Piliotis, Gena Piliotis, Robert Plowman, Jacqueline Ramlogan, Geoff Rector, Jon Shanahan, Scott Syms, Sonja Taylor, Damian Tarnopolsky, Abel Tsighe, Morgan Wade, and Drew Yamada. And to researchers Simon Fowler, at the British Archives, and Richard Foster, at the New York Public Library, and to the staffs at the Toronto Reference Library and the National Archives in Washington, D.C. Thanks also to the Toronto Writers' Centre and the Toronto Arts Council.

While this novel is largely a work of imagination, in digging into the life and times of Hubert Julian and trying to figure him out, I consulted a number of sources. Colin Grant provided many of the notes on Marcus Garvey and the UNIA with *Negro with a Hat: The Rise and Fall of Marcus Garvey* (New York: Oxford University Press, 2008). Details about the Harlem Renaissance came mostly from David Levering Lewis, *When Harlem Was in Vogue* (New York: Oxford University Press, 1979), and W. Fitzhugh Brundage, ed., *Beyond Blackface: African-Americans and the Creation of American Popular Culture, 1890–1930* (Chapel Hill: University of North Carolina Press, 2011). H. Allen Smith, who is credited (by some) for coining the nickname "Black Eagle of Harlem," also wrote about Julian in *Low Man on a Totem Pole* (New York: Doubleday, Doran, 1941). Pioneering pilot William Powell's *Black Wings*, originally published by I. Deach in 1934 (reissued in 1994 as *Black Aviator*, by Smithsonian Institution Press), provided anecdotes about Julian's flying career.

Evelyn Waugh's *Waugh in Abyssinia* (Louisiana State, 2007) and *When the Going Was Good* (Penguin, 1946), together with George Steer's *Caesar in Abyssinia* (Hodder and Staughton, 1936) and Jeff Pearce's *Prevail: The Inspiring Story of Ethiopia's Victory over Mussolini's Invasion, 1935–1941* (Skyhorse, 2014) delivered the facts and opinions about the Italo-Abyssinian War. Bill Deedes' *At War with Waugh* (Pan Macmillan, 2013) and Nicolas Rankin's bio of George Steer, *Telegram from Guernica*, 2nd ed. (Allan and Unwin, 2013), were helpful in understanding those figures.

Fan Dunckley's *Eight Years in Abyssinia* (Hutchison, 1935) was useful for its portrayal of Ethiopia from the European perspective in the 1930s. For certain details, I also relied on a series of articles written in the mid-1920s by French journalist Jean d'Esme and published in English in *The Living Age*. Historian Harold Marcus wrote *Haile Selassie I: The Formative Years, 1892–1936* (Red Sea Press, 1987), the best of the books I read about the emperor. Angelo del Boca's *The Negus: The Life and Death of the Last King of Kings*, translated by Antony Shugaar, (Arada, 2012) and Ryszard Kapuscinski's *The Emperor: Downfall of an Autocrat* (Vintage, 1989) were also helpful.

There are three full-length books dedicated to Hubert Julian. The first, *The Black Eagle*, is an autobiography ghostwritten by John Bulloch and published in 1964 by The Adventurers' Club. The second, released in 1972, was written by John Peer Nugent (Bantam) and carries the same title. More recently, in 2013, aviation historian Guy E. Franklin published *Hubert Julian, The Black Eagle of Harlem: The Rest of the Story* (Amazon Kindle). Franklin's is the most critical of the three biographies and debunks many of the myths resulting from the first two. David Shaftel profiled Julian in "The Black Eagle of Harlem: The Truth Behind the Tall Tales of Hubert Fauntleroy Julian," for *Air and Space Magazine* (December 2008).

I also relied extensively on contemporary newspaper and magazine reports from the *New York Age, New York Herald Tribune, New York Amsterdam News, Chicago Defender, Baltimore Afro-American, Norfolk Journal and Guide, New York Times, Time, New Yorker, Pittsburgh Courier,* and dozens of smaller dailies and weeklies whose editors found Hubert Julian as fascinating a newsmaker as I did.

Kingston, Ontario, 2023

ABOUT THE AUTHOR

 BRUCE GEDDES IS THE AUTHOR OF ONE previous novel, *The Higher the Monkey Climbs* (2018). Recent short fiction has appeared in the *New Quarterly*, *Blank Spaces*, and the *Freshwater Review*. He has contributed book reviews to the *National Post* and written for *Toronto Life*, *Canadian Business*, and *Lonely Planet*. Born in Windsor, Ontario, he now lives in Kingston.